THE CHANCER'S CORPS

JAMES PAGE

A catalogue record for this
book is available from the
National Library of Australia

Copyright © 2021 James Page
Publisher:
Inspiring Publishers
P.O. Box 159, Calwell, ACT
Australia 2905
Email: publishaspg@gmail.com
http://www.inspiringpublishers.com
National Library of Australia Cataloguing-in-Publication entry
Author: Page, James
Title: The Chancer's Corps/James Page
ISBN: 978-1-922618-36-8 (Print)
ISBN: 978-1-922618-37-5 (eBook)

About the Author

James Page was born in Canberra in 1970. He worked in the public and private sectors, including occassional intereactions with, and writing the odd speech for Government Ministers, and projects with corporate Australia. Hoping to rediscover his soul he turned to writing. This is his first book.

Chancer: a person who exploits any opportunity to further their own ends

____

While the following is based on real events and people the depiction is fictional. Aboriginal and Torres Strait Islander readers are advised that the following mentions names of the dead.

March 1804, Sydney

'Wake up. Everyone up now. Parade ground, five minutes, full accoutrements,' Sergeant Major Whittle bellowed. 'Now, that means you two new recruits as well. All of you. Move.'

Oliver Williams tried to shake the sleep out of his eyes. He rolled off his bunk and grabbed his trousers and red coat and quickly put them on, then reached under the bed and pulled out his musket. He had only arrived in Sydney a day ago and had no idea if this was a common occurrence for the New South Wales Corps. 'Does this happen often?'

Corporal Smith stopped and looked at him. 'No never.'

Tom Conner, the other new recruit, was frantically searching for a boot. 'Smith, what does accoutrements mean?'

The older man looked at Conner, wondering what they taught new recruits these days. 'It means full kit, ammo, the lot. The sergeant likes to use big words, you'll get used to it.'

All around the bunkhouse men were dressing, grabbing muskets and kit, trying not to fall over each other. The nervous energy heightened the tension. The soldiers concentration split between getting ready and wondering if this were a drill or something real. And if it was real what was the unknown threat and where was it?

'What bloody time is it anyway?' someone asked.

'After ten,' answered Corporal Smith, before roaring at the troops. 'Come on boys, get it together before Sarge comes back. You don't want an angry Sergeant Major Whittle, do you?'

They fell out on the dimly lit parade ground, the air still holding a strong trace of the day's heat. The only sound was the thumping and scrapping of boots on the gravel ground. No drums beat 'To Arms', summoning soldiers living nearby. No officers shouted orders. In a rush like a wave finally breaking they fell in together.

Lieutenant Robert Davies stood and looked at the troops. 'Right lads this is it. Real action. We are marching to Parramatta to meet the major, then we will get further orders. Make sure your Brown Besses are loaded and you have your bayonets,' Davies said.

The troops reached to the long scabbards hanging from the left side of their belts to check they had the sixteen-inch bayonets. When attached, the Brown Bess musket and bayonet together stood at almost six feet tall and could be used as a pike to break enemy ranks.

'Quiet as you go lads, we don't want to wake the neighbours and draw attention to ourselves,' Davies said.

Smith looked around. Drawing attention to themselves was what soldiers marching into action did. Troops played fifes and sang, with drummers beating time, marching behind officers and flag bearers. There was a psychological battle to win before shots were fired.

Tonight there were only hushed voices and stealthy movement. Something was very wrong. Smith searched the faces barely visible in the dim light, seeing questioning looks betraying fear and uncertainty.

He counted the small number of men; just sixteen. It was barely enough to defend the barracks, let alone deal with something bigger. There were plenty of soldiers nearby who could be summoned in minutes.

If the call 'To Arms' sounded soldiers and officers living with their families in nearby Soldiers Row, Pitt's Row, Durrack, Spring and Camden Row would come running. If all arrived the numbers of those on the parade ground would swell dramatically.

'Real action', Lieutenant Davies had said. What did that mean, Smith wondered? The possibilities were few, local Aborigines, convicts playing up or something unknown? And why the secrecy? Who was not supposed to know?

Before Smith could ruminate any further the order to march came. As one the troops moved quietly past the sentry box at the edge of the barracks. The famous English red coats and black shako hats were lost in the gloom as the small party turned into Church Street and headed westwards.

Soon they veered onto High Street, moving away from the barracks. The pace set by Lieutenant Davies and Quartermaster Laycock was brisk. Sergeant Major Whittle brought up the rear keeping a watchful eye for any stragglers.

The small group of New South Wales Corpsmen quickly cleared Sydney town and turned on the road leading to Parramatta. Tall grey and white ghost gum trees stood sentry on each side of the road. Occasional sounds of animals could be heard amongst the forest. The pace was brisk, some of the men already breathing heavily.

The troops whispered amongst themselves, speculating on all manner of possibilities about what lay ahead. Williams momentarily slowed his pace and allowed two rows of soldiers to pass until he fell in next to Corporal Smith, who was already holding court. As the veteran of the group, Smith's verdict on what may be ahead held great weight for the young soldiers.

'It wouldn't be Bonaparte's Frenchies invading, otherwise we would be headed for the coast. So its got to be either a convict uprising, most likely the Irish, or Aborigines, causing trouble for settlers.'

The word quickly spread amongst the group. They spoke quietly of where the threat may be and their number, without knowing the nature of that threat. Of whether this threat would fizzle out like others before, or result in something more. Smith looked at Williams. 'So, fresh off the boat and already we're up for action. I wonder if you and Conner are good or bad luck?'

Williams looked at Smith. 'If you are putting this on for us you don't need to. And I am not bad luck. Never have been and never will be.'

'Where you from?'

'East Sussex.'

'And what, pray tell, is a fine East Sussex lad doing in His Majesty's army on the arse end of the world?'

Williams looked at the older man, who held his gaze. 'There must be a story in that somewhere. There's always a story as to how a man manages to arrive in New South Wales,' Smith said.

'My father was a clerk, good with numbers,' Williams said. 'In fact he was so good with numbers he embezzled money from the company he worked for. It was a year before anyone worked it out.'

Williams sighed. He hated telling the story. It was a reminder of his past and a future that was not to be. He enjoyed numbers and had quickly taken to the book work his father taught him. Now that was gone, replaced by the army.

He was still trying to work the army out. Understanding things, making them work for him was what made Williams tick. But the army was not something he understood. He had had plenty of time waiting around to learn about army life. Williams had learned one thing quickly, the more time men had on their hands the more they wanted to fill that time with idle chatter. The first thing a new recruit was asked was how they came to be in the army.

There were so many other questions that seemed in need of answering, thought Williams. Like how the army made decisions, for one. After joining up he was assigned to a regiment. Days of training and sitting around followed. Then the regiment was told it was going to the Americas. That brought about a flurry of activity, preparing to march, packing up gear, stand ready, stand down, stand around. Mostly the last, stand around. A day later they were told their destination was Portugal, then someone said it was training near Aldershot, before an about face to Bristol.

The whole time they had marched no further than the parade ground. So back to where they had started a wag had commented. Which seemed to sum the whole thing up. A means to keeping men busy rather than time for second-guessing those in charge. Or realising those in charge had no better idea of what was happening than the enlisted men.

No-one it seemed had any idea of what to do next. Then suddenly orders arrived. Men were divided into groups and marched out. When the whole unmerry circus ended Williams and Tom Connor were told to board a ship for New South Wales.

That was another lesson Williams soon learnt. What was said and what were ordered were often very different. Nothing was ever really certain, until suddenly it was. The more sudden the decision the more likely it was to stick. Those orders that were preceded by rumour turned out to be just that, rumours. And so that was it, the story of how he came to be marching on the road to Parramatta after arriving in Sydney a day ago. But in the army everyone had one of those stories and no-one really cared to hear it.

It took Williams some time to understand that the story of how a man joined was not what he was being asked. What soldiers wanted to know was *why* a man had joined. Those stories helped to pass the time waiting for orders. Stories of the fateful decision to join up told others about a man and who he was.

Williams was not keen on retelling the tale of his father and running out of options. Too often it led to men turning away. There were plenty of petty criminals in the army, many of them still busy with illicit enterprises or thinking up new ones. But the son of a criminal. What did that mean? Should they invite him into their little schemes or shun him?

Usually they chose to shun him. He didn't mind greatly, he thought about things very differently from others. But a man on his own was a man without friends and the army could be a dangerous place without friends. The army had its rules, written and unwritten and one of the few unwritten rules was no story could remain untold if you wanted to befriend a man.

'So that's it,' Williams said.

Williams sighed, in a way that seemed a little too practised to Smith. It was a story that had been told so many times it was more performance than heartfelt, a sigh every now and then aimed at drawing sympathy. This one is smart, Smith thought.

'Don't tell me, he got transported and you came out here to keep an eye on dear old dad?' Smith asked.

'No. He shot himself when he was discovered,' said Williams sighing again.

The two men walked on in silence for a time.

'Well that is hardly your fault young man,' said Smith, satisfied they were now at the heart of the story.

'No it's not. My father taught me bookkeeping and reading before his crime was discovered. I was going to be employed at the same company, but once he was found out no one wanted to employ the son of a criminal. So I left home and enrolled in the army. Me and Conner were supposed to go to the Americas, but when our regiment got orders to break up we got the short straw for New South Wales.'

'Well,' Smith said, 'you just might've got the best of it. The Americas are hard. Most of the time is spent on ships patrolling the coast. And it could have been India. That can be a bad place for soldiering, particularly in the Punjab, or God forbid the Khyber Pass. New South Wales, now that is another story.

'Here we live well, there's plenty of food nowadays. The convicts largely look after themselves and we provide the muscle from time to time. Like tonight. The rest of the time, well we have our mercantile interests and plenty of downtime. A bright young lad like yourself might do very well indeed.'

'I don't understand, I thought we stood in the sun for hours guarding unruly convicts.'

'Told that by the other lads in the regiment, were you?'

Williams nodded.

'That's what everyone thinks. But I can guarantee you that His Majesty's New South Wales Corps do not spend their days watching convicts. We haven't done that since the earliest days of the colony.

'The convicts have a system of overseers, drawn from amongst themselves. The overseers are responsible for ensuring each day's work is done. Nowadays the convicts get enough work for a morning, are done by lunchtime and spend their afternoons hiring out their labour. Or drinking and gambling the fruits of it away.

'Convicts run their own court system and ensure punishments are handed out appropriately. Most have a good life here, far better than anything they could hope for in England.'

Williams was surprised that Smith had said 'in England'. He expected the older man to say 'at home'.

'But what stops the convicts from running away?'

'Look around you. Would you want to run off into that bush? If convicts want to chance it in the bush so be it. A few manage to survive, most who try are back in town in a couple of days. It's dangerous out there.

'And as to getting passage on a ship out of here, that's strictly forbidden. Any convict that tries that is likely to get transported to Coal River to mine coal, or Norfolk Island to, well, die. Ship's captains and owners pay huge cash bonds to the government not to smuggle convicts. If they're found out they lose the cash and possibly their freedom. That's the fast track to becoming a convict yourself.'

Smith looked at Williams. 'So, tell me about your mate Conner?'

Williams shrugged. 'We joined up at the same time. Tom is quiet, keeps his head down. He seems a bit naive about the way of people but he's been a good mate to have.'

'Spent a fair bit of time together on the boat I take it?' Smith said.

'Yeah. Not much of a talker but he will stand his place in the line beside you. And he is popular with the ladies,' Williams said.

'Well that is always handy to have beside you when engaging with the ladies,' Smith said.

'I suppose so,' Williams said.

'Anything else I should know about him?' Smith said.

'Tom tends to see the good in people,' Williams said.

'Well he didn't have your education about people; the one your father dropped you into,' Smith said.

Lieutenant Davies stopped up ahead, and the order for a five-minute break came down the line. The soldiers sat down in a small clearing, beside which stood a staging post and beyond that a small bunkhouse, the midway point between Sydney and Parramatta. Smith and Williams sat and took a drink.

The bush loomed large in the dark, edging onto the clearing. The moon and stars provided a surprising amount of light in the clearing and into the first few metres of trees. The trees appeared almost ordered, with grass underneath them and little if any scrub and undergrowth. Despite this there was something foreboding about the tall trees and tumbled order, evoking both nature and man at the edge of control.

Smith, sitting beside Williams, felt the younger man suddenly sit up. He was about to say something when Williams quietly but urgently whispered to him.

'There are people out there, walking near us.'

Smith peered into the darkness but could see nothing. 'Steady boyo, you're imagining it. The bush can play tricks with the eyes.'

Williams carefully pointed into the bush. 'There, I can see them. Right there.'

Smith looked again. 'Are you sure?'

'Yes.'

Smith stood and grabbed Williams, hauling him to his feet. 'Keep an eye on them and come with me.'

Quartermaster Laycock watched the two soldiers stand and walk towards where he sat with Lieutenant Davies. He stood and marched quickly to meet the two men.

'What is it corporal?' Laycock said, expecting to hear a sob story from the younger of the two men.

'Private Williams here says he can see people in the bush. Point them out to the quartermaster young man.'

Williams pointed into the bush, describing a set of reference points for the two older men to follow. As he described the final copse of trees a human form moved, Laycock and Smith both seeing it.

'There, can you see him?' said Williams. 'There are more out there.'

Laycock immediately turned and marched to where Davies was sitting. 'We have company sir. Aborigines I think.'

'Get the men up quietly. Be ready,' Davies said. 'Point out where these people are. Right, both of you with me,' Davies said to Williams and Smith after Williams had pointed out the Aboriginals. Then he set off into the trees. Smith and Williams followed. The light that came from the moon and stars struggled to penetrate the darkness the further into the trees they went. Cold fell all around. Smith shot Williams a look. 'You better not have dropped us in it boyo.'

As the three advanced, Laycock and Sergeant Major Whittle organised the men into two lines facing the bush. Each man took out gunpowder and readied to load their muskets. Bayonets were fixed. The soldiers in the front row knelt down, muskets pointed towards the trees. Those soldiers in the second line stood ready to step foward and shoot once the front row had fired their muskets.

In the trees Davies walked carefully forwards. There was a strong smell of eucalyptus and the air felt damp and heavy. Smith noticed Davies pull out a pistol, taking care to conceal it by his side. He slung his musket over his shoulder and motioned to Williams to do the same. Then the corporal pulled out his bayonet. Williams swallowed hard and quietly unsheathed the sixteen-inch long bayonet.

The three soldiers entered a clearing, and before them stood a small party of Aboriginal men holding spears. Before Davies could do anything more natives materialised from the trees as though they were the ghosts of the surrounding gums. The three soldiers stood outnumbered ten to one. The two groups looked at each other from a short distance, waiting for the other to make a move.

'Good evening,' Davies said, uncertain what else to say.

A tall Aboriginal man replied with a hello.

Smith whispered to Williams. 'I think they're a war party. Pray that this isn't who we're out here to stop boyo.'

'Quiet,' Davies said. Then he spoke to the tall Aboriginal. 'Where are you headed?'

The man pointed northwards with his spear.

Davies pointed westwards. 'We are headed that way.'

The Aboriginal man nodded.

'My men are having a break, a drink.' Davies gestured as though drinking, keen to reassure the Aboriginal leader that the three soldiers were not alone. Again the Aboriginal man nodded. Then he turned and began walking on a track that led north. The other Aboriginal men followed, disappearing quietly into the bush. Davies breathed out and relaxed.

'Were they a war party?' Williams asked.

'Yes.'

'Shouldn't we stop them?' Williams said. He immediately realised it was a mistake to question an officer. 'Smith, I said shouldn't we stop them,' Williams said again, hoping that Davies would let the mistake pass.

'Well Corporal,' Davies said, smiling. 'Answer the lad or else I'll have to deal with his insubordination.'

'Sir, I suspect that the dealings of the natives are not our concern. War parties travelling at night are most likely not our concern,' Smith said, unsure what else to say.

Davies nodded. 'We have a bigger fish to catch tonight. If that group are going to make trouble for settlers then we'll deal with them. But we have no reports that that is the case. Most likely they are off to have a mock battle with another tribe.'

The three retraced their steps back to the small group of soldiers still standing in ranks. When they emerged from the trees there was an audible sigh amongst the men. Davies gave the order for the men to stand down, then spoke to Laycock.

A minute later the quartermaster ordered the march to resume. The soldiers quickly formed two columns and began moving westwards towards Parramatta. For the first time that night the men felt a chill in the air, most glad for the quick pace that the lieutenant set.

As the soldiers started out Laycock waited until Smith and Williams marched past. 'You two up front with me.'

Smith shot Williams another look. 'Don't say it,' said Williams. 'I had better not've dropped us in it.' Smith smirked at the younger man and nodded.

Laycock walked up behind the two soldiers. 'Since you have such keen eyes Private Williams, you can walk at the head of the column and keep an eye out.' The three men walked past the other soldiers and slipped into the first row of troops.

The column marched quickly on in silence for another two hours before the settlement at Parramatta came into view. They had just completed a march that could take between four and six hours in a little over three hours. Many of the men were exhausted, running on adrenaline and fear, all the while knowing that somewhere ahead an enemy lay waiting.

Davies called the column to a halt. 'Private Williams, Corporal Smith, scout ahead until you are sure our men are in charge of the settlement. Then report back to me,' Davies said. 'Make sure you are not seen and make it quick.'

The two soldiers carefully moved ahead, keeping low and walking as quickly as they dared. 'Next time you see something in the bush keep your mouth shut,' Smith told Williams.

'I was already thinking that myself,' Williams replied.

The two soldiers approached the outskirts of the town. It was eerily quiet and many of the houses appeared deserted. Unusually, there were no light spilling out from the houses, nor any noise or revelry coming from the taverns and gaming houses that dotted the streets.

The pair emerged from the trees and ran in a crouching style for the cover of the first buildings. Williams ran hard towards the nearest building. He half-turned sideways to use the building to stop his momentum and hit the wooden structure far harder than he had wanted to and was surprised when the building creaked and cracked loudly. Smith shot him a look, then put his finger to his lips to indicate silence.

He signalled Williams to wait while he peered around a corner. Then using the buildings as cover Smith started to walk carefully down the street, never straying far from the sides of the nearest buildings. At each break between buildings he carefully peered down the narrow side streets before ducking across the exposed space. Satsified that there where no threats he signalled Williams to cross the road and work his way along the buildings opposite. They repeated the process down a series of roads, inching their way towards the barracks.

Williams began to feel uneasy and worked hard to try to steady his breathing, which was becoming more ragged and breathless the closer they moved towards the barracks. No matter how hard he tried he could not dismiss the fear that the barracks may be overrun by convicts or Irish rebels or Aboriginals. He desperately wanted to cross the road and stand next to Smith.

Williams looked ahead and saw Smith stop at the corner and peer carefully around it. Smith turned and motioned to Williams to come forward. The younger soldier cautiously crept up the opposite side of the road to the corner, seeing the barracks ahead. There was light spilling from windows and no signs of violence. It took several moments before Williams could make out the shako hats and redcoats on a handful of the men at the Parramatta barracks. He gave Smith a thumbs up sign and Smith crossed the road to where Williams crouched.

'Looks good,' Williams said.

Smith breathed out heavily, the only sign that he too was felling the tension. 'Alright, let's get back and tell the Lieutenant the news,' Smith said. As quickly as they dared, keeping close to the side of the road, the two soldiers moved back to the column.

"Good news Lieutenant, the barracks is ours,' Smith said. 'The whole town is dead quiet.' Smith immediately regretted using that term.

'Right, move out carefully,' Davies said. 'Smith, Williams on point and lead us in.'

The column quickly approached the town, heading to the barracks. As they neared the barracks Captain Abbott, head of the garrison, and several soldiers came forward to meet the column and escort them through the gate. There was a small parade ground and to the left of that a line of trees. A group of people dressed in civilian clothes stood and sat under the trees. Whether the civilians were there for protection or some other reason was unclear. The bunkhouses behind the mess hall that stood adjacent to the parade ground were a hive of activity as soldiers prepared for action.

'Lieutenant, how was your evening stroll?' Captain Abbott asked.

'Uneventful. So I assume we have you to thank for our evening's exertion?'

'Apologies dear boy, however, our Irish problem has come to a head. I have it on very reliable authority that the Irish at Castle Hill are revolting, in both senses of the word, if you will pardon a poor pun.'

Davies smiled and looked at Abbott. 'The good Reverend Marsden sent word earlier this evening. He has not been wrong on the past occasions the Irish have planned an uprising,' Abbott said. 'The major is on his way from Annandale along with reinforcements. Governor King is also speeding his way here, which is meant to reassure us, but fills me with dread.'

'How is the Governor coming?' Davies said.

'By river.'

'Nice of him to offer us a ride. He could have had fresh troops for battle rather than have us marching through the night,' Davies said. 'Besides the Governor will likely only delay things and knowing the major he'll want to head to Castle Hill and cut the head off the snake. Given our limited numbers speed and surprise are our best allies.'

'That they will be," Abbott said.

'Where's Marsden? It would be helpful to hear what he knows.'

'The Reverend took a boat downriver. He doesn't want to be here if the Irish come at us in force.'

'How many are we up against?' Davies said.

'Perhaps a thousand men or more. Reverend Marsden indicated that there are three groups of Irish involved. The main group are at Castle Hill, right where Governor King put them. You need to head to Government House as quickly as possible to rendezvous with the major and another contingent of the Corps. These fine patriots gathered here will accompany you,' Abbott said, indicating the civilians standing under the trees by the parade ground. 'They may come in useful should things not go as planned.'

Davies looked to the large number of civilians, many armed, though few with muskets. Most had farm implements, fewer swords and some clubs hewn from wood. He estimated perhaps eighty men gathered in the gloom. He was relieved to see familiar faces amongst those gathered, mainly former Corps men. These men held the majority of the firearms. Davies ordered his own men to sit and take a break. He continued to talk with Captain Abbott for several minutes. A small group of soldiers, including Quartermaster Laycock, Smith, Williams and Conner sat nearby. Lieutenant Davies soon joined them.

'Excuse me sir,' Williams asked, 'but how do we know that this is not another false report?'

'Young man, you're starting to make a habit of questioning me,' Davies said. 'It's not a good habit to get into, even if you have a good question.' Davies smiled at Laycock. 'Perhaps, quartermaster, you may wish to council Private Williams on this issue, lest I have to deal with more questions.'

'This is not the first time the Irish have planned a rebellion,' Laycock said. 'Their plots always have a flaw. They rely on escaped convicts living rough in the bush to convey messages between their different groups working on farms. Some of those runners come to town and talk too much, and some of Reverend Marsden's small network of informants hear things. The dumb Irish still haven't figured that out yet.

'Now the Irish usually have the idea of marching on Parramatta, where their strength of numbers would likely overwhelm us. If they did that they would put to death any soldiers, and others they plain don't like, such as Reverend Marsden. They brag about this and our informers hear it too.

'So the informers have been able to tell the Reverend, who has told us of each planned uprising,' Laycock said. 'The leaders have been quickly arrested before any action begins. Weapons have been hunted down.

'And the wonderful irony of the whole thing is that the leaders of the planned uprisings have got exactly what they hoped for, passage out of Sydney on a ship. Of course the fact that the ships have been sailing for Norfolk Island is a bitter irony for those leaders. Others would call it just dessert.'

Williams started to say something but stopped and looked at Lieutenant Davies. The lieutenant smiled at the young soldier then turned to Laycock and Smith. 'I do think he is beginning to learn his place. No insubordinate questions. Just the blissful sound of silence from the ranks. Well that should be rewarded. Quartermaster, perhaps you could answer the private's first question. Why is this time different?'

'After the last uprising Governor King had what he considered an epiphany of sorts,' Laycock said. 'The governor ordered all the Irish be sent to Castle Hill to work clearing land there. King locked them all up in one place separated from their leaders.

'The problem with his so-called epiphany was putting most of the rotten eggs in one basket. And since Governor King has allowed Catholics to attend mass, he has created another network for Irish bastards to stir up trouble. It would be funny were it not so serious,' Laycock said.

Davies looked at the troops gathered nearby. 'Tonight that foolish idea has reaped a particularly nasty harvest. According to Marsden's intelligence, Irish convicts have seized control of the farm at Castle Hill. They intend to meet up with another group here at Parramatta, the signal being a hut set on fire. We think they are waiting near Constitution Hill for that signal before raiding Parramatta. Then they intend to send a message to the Hawkesbury for other Irish to rise up and together they will march on Sydney. They want to commandeer ships and sail to freedom.

'Fortunately, the small group of Irish here at Parramatta have been persuaded by a show of force not to light any fires. The messenger sent from Castle Hill has been intercepted. If a fire is not lit soon odds are good that the main group will turn and march for Windsor and then Hawkesbury.

'Alright check your weapons and be ready to march,' Davies said. Quartermaster Laycock and Sergeant Major Whittle began spreading out amongst the groups of men, repeating the order. Williams turned to Smith. 'How did they get so many civilians together so quickly?'

'Weren't you listening to the quartermaster. The Irish plan was to raid Parramatta. A lot of good people would've been killed. Here it's just like England, no one particularly likes the Irish, and doubly so given what they have promised to bring tonight. I suspect we may have more men than is useful, such is the current hatred of the Irish.'

'So we're going to see real action then, shooting and killing?' Williams asked.

'I don't doubt it.'

It was after 3 am when the small column readied to march out of the barracks for the governor's residence at Parramatta. Before the column could leave several horses and riders came trotting in through the front gates. Davies was relieved when he saw Major George Johnston at the head of the riders' party. He also recognised Trooper Anlezark and several soldiers who lived in and around Parramatta.

The major and his group dismounted, tying their horses to a nearby tree. Davies ordered water be brought for the horses.

Johnston walked up to Davies and Laycock. 'Good to see you gentlemen. I suggest a quick round of water and food and then on to Government House.'

Johnston stood and ate with the men, then after drinking some water headed back to his horse. 'Right let us go and see what the governor thinks a suitable course of action, if any.' Johnston winked at Davies as he said it. Davies tried hard to suppress a smile.

A large column of troops and civilians departed and quickly marched to Government House. Johnston, Davies and Laycock entered the gates and walked up the driveway to the two-storey whitewashed house. At any other time the house, its surrounds and views would have been a sight. Instead, Major Johnston was irritated, annoyed that the trip to Government House was delaying the chance to chase down the rebels.

As they entered the house the men took off their hats and wiped their boots. An aide to the governor came up to the trio, looking sleepy and distracted. He held a bundle of papers and grunted to the soldiers to distribute them quickly.

Johnston looked at the bundle of papers and then the aide. 'I suggest you inform the governor that Major Johnston and the troops from Sydney are here.'

Davies grabbed one of the papers and read it quickly. 'At least the governor is being of some use,' he muttered under his breath. He handed the paper to Johnston who read it, noting the key lines.

I do therefore proclaim the Districts of Parramatta, Castle Hill, Toongabbie, Prospect, Seven and Baulkham Hills, Hawkesbury and Nepean to be in a STATE of REBELLION; and to establish Martial Law throughout those Districts...

'So the governor had declared martial law,' Johnston said. That was all he needed to know. Johsnton turned to the aide.

'Let the governor know that the New South Wales Corps are pursuing the rebels and will offer amnesty or break this rebellion,' Johnston said. At any other time Johnston would have waited for a formal order from the governor, but that meant delaying sending soldiers to confront the rebels.

Johston turned and marched out the door, followed by Davies and Laycock. The three walked back to the waiting column. Johnston outlined his plans. The redcoats would divide into two groups. Lieutenant Davies would lead the larger contingent from Parramatta barracks north to the farm at Castle Hill to quell any rebels still holed up there. Johnston along with Laycock and a smaller group were to march west towards Toongabbie, along the road where a large group of rebels had last been seen.

Two soldiers were sent to retrieve Father James Dixon, the Roman Catholic priest at Parramatta. While the officers and men waited the aide emerged from the governor's house with instructions from Governor King.

Johnston read them quickly, then in a sarcastic voice said, 'Well fancy that, the governor thinks it a good idea for we soldiers to pursue the Irish rebels and offer them mercy, and failing that death.'

Davies and Laycock smirked. 'Now why didn't we think of such a clever plan,' Laycock said.

'Thank goodness itself the governor came down the river to provide such insight,' Davies agreed.

The aide took the hint and disappeared quickly.

Johnston looked at Davies and smiled broadly. 'Good hunting Lieutenant.'

'You too Major.'

The two columns formed up and soon after 4 am marched out heading north and west into the new day.

Within minutes of leaving the barracks the two soldiers sent to retrieve Father Dixon caught up to the column. They escorted Father Dixon to the head of the marching soldiers. Major Johnston wheeled his horse and went to talk with the priest.

Smith and Williams marched near the head of Johnston's column, with Tom Conner and George Newbank following. Conner - along with Williams the other new member of the Corps - asked permission to speak.

'So Oliver, sorry Private Williams here, says that we may see action,' Conner said.

Smith, as the oldest of the four, nodded.

The column walked in silence for a time. Smith could feel the anxiety amongst the men.

'You shouldn't worry, we have the major on our side. He's seen more than his share of action. The rumour is he was at Bunker Hill.'

'Is that near here?' Newbank asked.

'Oh to be young and naive,' Smith said. 'Bunker Hill is in the Americas. The battle there was the first battle of the American Revolutionary War. The major was probably little more than a boy. Our lads charged up the hill into the American lines. The Americans were ordered not to fire until they could see the whites of our lads' eyes, so the English were almost on top of their positions when they opened fire. The rebels gunned down our standard bearer and the colours fell to the ground. The major grabbed the colours from the dead hands of the standard bearer and helped lead the charge into the American guns.

'You know we won that battle at Bunker Hill, with the major at the front. He has had quite a career in the military. He was wounded during action against the French in the East Indies while serving on HMS *Sultan*. That was another victory. When the major is in the thick of battle his boys always win. Mark my words it will be the same result this morning should the Irish have the stomach for it.'

Smith slapped Williams on the shoulder and gave him a wink. 'I don't mind being dropped in it with the major.'

The road towards Windsor was similar to that from Sydney to Parramatta. Low grass bordered the verge and trees stood grouped in lines and copses. There was very little undergrowth, with clear views in amongst the trees. Williams took a few moments to take in the view as the sky gradually lightened. It helped distract him from what lay ahead. As soon as he thought about the prospect of fighting, of standing in the line while men shot at him, he felt a queasiness inside. Could he do it, could he stand and hold his place while shots whistled by?

Williams looked around and saw the tiny column of soldiers then tried to remember Smith's words about the major. He had yet to meet the acting commander of the New South Wales Corp. Johnston was older than most of the men but still looked fit. He carried himself almost ramrod straight and radiated something intangible that drew men to him.

'It looks like they are headed to Toongabbie station,' Laycock said.

'Good,' Johnston replied. 'We should be able to intercept them on the road ensuring they have no cover. We will invite the leaders to parlay with us and use that to our advantage. I have no intention of acting honourably with these bastards. They would gladly slaughter us in our beds given half the chance.

'Mr Laycock, you will command the troops, while Trooper Anlezark and I will lead the negotiations. I want two groups fourteen men apiece with two ranks of seven in each. We will draw the leaders out and then act accordingly. No shooting unless ordered or deemed necessary.'

'Yes sir,' Laycock replied.

They marched on until the first smattering of light appeared in the eastern sky. Already the heat of the day was warming the soldiers and civilians, who were beginning to fall behind. As the light increased Williams got his first real look at the land. There were fields under cultivation, some farm animals, and up ahead to the left a few odd-looking animals Smith named as kangaroos. All around grasslands opened onto picturesque views of sweeping hills and plains. It reminded Williams of some of the finer estates and gardens that dotted those parts of Sussex he had roamed as a youth.

'Smith, this bushland is not at all what I imagined. It looks in places like Sussex.'

'The locals, the natives, keep this area under control through fire and land clearing. Most of the undergrowth is limited or cleared. It is surprising how many people say it reminds them of gardens and estates back in England,' Smith said.

There it was again, back in England, rather than back home.

'You can say what you will about the Aborigines, but some of them are experts at clearing and managing the land. Of course far too many of them now hang around the settlements at Sydney, Parramatta and Hawkesbury, doing odd jobs in return for scraps of food and rum. But those that haven't got lost in the worst of English ways still live in the bush,' Smith said.

'So all this is planned?'

'I suppose you could call it that,' said Smith. 'I had never really thought of it that way. Where we grow crops and tend cattle, the Aborigines hunt and gather, so in their fashion they do manage the land to keep it clear and easy to find food.'

The column was nearing the last place the Irish had been seen. Two riders were sent ahead. It was another hour of hard marching before the riders returned, reporting the Irish gathered on and around a hill around two miles ahead.

Johnston immediately halted the column. 'Laycock we have arrived.' Johnston glanced back the way he had just ridden. The civilian column had fallen far behind. 'You will continue to march hard to cover as much of the distance as possible. I will press ahead and see if any sense can be talked into this rabble. Trooper Anlezark you are with me.'

Johnston and Anlezark rode on ahead while Laycock led the column. The two mounted soldiers looked smaller and smaller as they rode away.

Johnston and Anlezark rode some way, before coming over a small rise and into a shallow valley. On the other side gathered on a hill were between two hundred and fifty to three hundred Irishmen. The two soldiers reached the bottom of the hill and then slowly paced their way up. When they were within pistol shot of the Irish masses Johnston spoke.

'Governor King has declared martial law and an amnesty for any man who stands down now. This does not have to end in blood,' Johnston said. He let that idea linger on the gentle breeze for many seconds. Not one of the Irish made to lay down their arms.

Johnston looked at the men, armed with muskets, pistols, swords and almost every manner of pike and farm implement imaginable. Combined he estimated that a good twenty per cent of the colony's weapons may well be held by the rebels.

'Death or liberty' shouted one of the Irish leaders. For good measure someone added 'and a ship to take us home.'

Johnston stared at the group, knowing that surrender was now off the table.

'Send forth two representatives to tell us what you want and we can negotiate a settlement.'

There was a rush of activity in the Irish ranks with furious conversations taking place. Two men were at the centre of the talking, with much pointing and gesturing taking place. Johnston looked at Anlezark who glared at the Irish.

'We want to talk to you, negotiate a settlement,' Johnston yelled again, eager to quell any stupidity. 'Send out two representatives and we can negotiate. It is not too late to parlay.'

The activity in the Irish ranks reached a crescendo and for a moment Johnston feared they would fire en masse. From such a close distance, any massed firing of weaponry would likely strike its target. Anlezark glanced at Johnston who steadied his horse.

Johnston counted the seconds in his head. The moment to end the rebellion peacefully was slipping away. There was no where to run, nor would he. English officers did not retreat.

For a brief moment his thoughts turned to his Esther and their seven children, a picture forming in his mind of his family on the farm at Annandale. Johnston closed his eyes then opened them. He saw the Irish ranks on the hill above and used them to ground his senses. He knew from bitter experience that too many men let thoughts of home and loved ones and what they stood to lose cloud their judgement in battle.

He took a few moments to take in the Irish rebels. They were spread across the top and sides of the hill, without any coherent order. Those holding muskets were not grouped closely together to increase their likelihood of hitting the same target. Many with muskets were closer to the rear than nearer the front where their shot could do real damage. Most likely these were the bully boys who ensured they had the best weapons but were also furthest from the action.

For the first time he hoped that there was a chance to avoid any fire. Johnston knew that he and Anlezark were the only targets and would be unlikely to escape harm. The conflicting ideas and emotions began to fill him with dread once again.

Still the Irish leaders talked amongst themselves. 'Father Dixon is travelling with us, will you talk with him?' Johnston said.

A new round of debating began. The two men Johnston had seen earlier at the centre of discussions featured prominently. Johnston braced for the call of death or liberty and readied himself for the volley of fire to come. He glanced at Anlezark and was proud to see the trooper set his shoulders squarely at the Irish. In battle it helped to have good men beside you.

'Alright, bring the priest up,' one of the rebel leaders yelled.

Johnston and Anlezark swung their horses around and headed back down the hill. Johnston's troops were not yet visible, concealed until the two riders crossed the smaller rise opposite the hill. They rode on to the column of troops. 'This will give the column more time to catch up. The plan still stands, we lure the ringleaders out,' Johnston said.

'Yes Major,' Anlezark said.

The two riders covered the ground to the remainder of the soldiers as quickly as possible. 'Get Father Dixon on a horse, he has an appointment with his brethren,' Johnston said. He watched while two soldiers walked Father Dixon to a horse, out of earshot.

'Quartermaster, I will delay them in negotiations as long as possible. Once you come over that rise ahead you will see the Irish on the far side of the hill. There is a shallow drop to a small valley. Cross it as quickly as you can, then get the men into shooting range as rapidly as is possible. Form up immediately and be ready to open fire. Anlezark and I will try to take the leaders. If we do, fire continuously.'

'With pleasure major.'

'Father, are you ready?' Johnston shouted.

Father Dixon nodded from some distance away and rode over. Together the two soldiers and the priest rode towards the hill. They rode over the small rise and the hill came into view. The Irish had begun to form two ranks running along the side of the hill. As they neared, Johnston noted that some of the musket bearers had been grouped together. Somebody up there knew what they were doing.

'Father, let me know if you recognise any of the leaders,' Johnston said. Father Dixon looked at the major.

'Why do you need to know that?'

'So I can address them by name, of course.'

As they neared the Irish lines the two leaders who had led the earlier parlay stepped in front of the lines.

'Major, the one on the left is William Johnston, the other Philip Cunningham. He is a veteran of the 1798 Irish uprising in Ireland.'

The three riders closed in on the Irish positions, again moving to within pistol shot. Major Johnston turned to Father Dixon. 'Let me speak first and then I will give you your chance. It would be wise to invite the leaders forward so we can converse on civil terms.'

Johnston dismounted from his horse. 'As promised I have brought Father Dixon. Let me again say that any man who steps forwards now and throws down his weapons will receive amnesty. I do not want to see bloodshed, nor do you Father.'

'The major is right,' Father Dixon said. 'Come forward and let us talk about your demands and a way out from this. I beg of you in Christ's name.'

Cunningham looked at his fellow Irishman Johnston. The two spoke quickly for several moments.

'Alright Father, we're coming over.' The two Irishmen began to walk towards the English soldiers and Father Dixon. Anlezark dismounted from his horse and lent down to check its foreleg. Major Johnston pretended to glance towards Anlezark, instead sneaking a look back towards the rise they had ridden over. His troops should be clearing that rise within moments.

The two Irishmen continued to walk forwards, away from their own ranks. Father Dixon added encouragement as the two stopped a metre shy of the English soldiers.

'If we work together then we have a chance to end this peacefully,' the priest said.

Johnston moved a step forward. 'As I said earlier, Governor King has declared martial law, and under such arrangements he has allowed amnesty for any who peacefully surrender.'

Anlezark slowly edged forwards, following Dixon as he held out his arms to his fellow Irishmen. 'Listen to what the major is saying, and end this peacefully,' Dixon said.

Quartermaster Laycock had marched the troops as quickly as he dared. They had been marching on and off since 10 pm the previous night. The best part of twelve hours had passed and now they faced a battle, outnumbered by as much as ten to one.

The heat was building as the morning slipped away. Laycock had pushed the soldiers as hard as he dared. By the time the troops came to the bottom of the small rise it was 10.30 am. The quartermaster turned and addressed his troops.

'Right lads, over this hill is the real thing. When we go over the rise we will march rapidly into position on the far side of the valley floor. Each group will not fire until I give the order. Then we will fire until we break them so make as many as possible count. We will be firing from a distance so go for the largest groups of men. For God's sake don't hit the major or Anlezark. Once the firing is done I will give the order to advance. Are we clear?.'

A resounding 'yes quartermaster' rang out.

With that Laycock turned and began to march up the rise. The small column of troops reached the top and saw for the first time the full extent of the rebel mob. They were spread over a wide area of the hill in two loosely formed lines. The lines began to break up when the Irish saw the approaching redcoats. Some started backing or walking away. Others continued to face the approaching English soldiers. More than a few headed towards a copse of trees on the side of the hill.

The column of twenty eight redcoats moved quickly down the road, their discipline in sharp contrast to the group of Irishmen, disaffected convicts and rabble-rousers on the hill. Behind the red coats the civilian militia were still some way distant. They would be of no help in the battle ahead.

Laycock saw the major and Anlezark standing with Father Dixon and two Irish rebels, easily within pistol shot of the nearby Irish front rank. The quartermaster judged the distance to be close enough to do real damage to the Irish ranks and bellowed out the order to form ranks.

Two groups of redcoats formed into ranks, each consisting of fourteen soldiers in two ranks of seven. The troops appeared ridiculously outnumbered.

Laycock waited a moment and saw the major move, followed in quick succession by Anlezark. With that he gave the order and the redcoats opened fire, a massed volley heading into the centre of the front line of Irish rebels. Laycock yelled to reload. The Irish returned fire, but it was sporadic and uncoordinated. A round whistled by near Laycock, the quartermaster unsure if it was real or imagined.

Johnston and Anlezark were stalling for time when they saw the redcoats come over the rise and rush to take up position. The Irish leaders, Cunningham and Johnston, saw the redcoats come over the rise too.

'English bastard,' Cunningham yelled. He turned to see if his rebels were reacting and in that moment Johnston pulled a loaded pistol from the sash around his waist and rammed it into Cunningham's temple. Anlezark moved just as quickly, a pistol appearing in his hand as he grabbed the Irishman Johnston and rammed the weapon into his neck.

Johnston heard Laycock bellow out the order to fire. He smiled grimly, pleased that the quartermaster had not hesitated. The Irish rebels returned fire on the redcoats, abandoning their leaders to their fate.

The two soldiers grabbed a rein of their horses and manhandling the shocked Irishmen started to move diagonally away from the Irish lines, providing a clear field of fire for Laycock and their troops. Their horses provided a small amount of cover, as did the presence of the two Irish prisoners.

In the heat of the moment Johnston had forgotten Father Dixon. He turned and glanced back, seeing the priest a few yards behind, mouthing something in his direction. From the few words Johnston heard it was clear that Dixon's words were not very Christian.

Soon they were clear of the space between the two opposing forces. Johnston and Anlezark, still holding their prisoners, made a direct line for the civilian militia who were beginning to come over the rise. The redcoats continued to fire towards the Irish positions. Father Dixon followed, his words drowned out in the booming noise and echoes of battle.

Round after round crashed out in the mid-morning heat. Gun smoke began to form clouds around the redcoats. Many had faces turning the colour their famous coats from the heat and exertion.

Williams worked furiously to reload his Brown Bess, repeating in his head the instructions he had first received a world away. Powder the barrel, drop the ball, drive it home. Powder the pan, cover the pan, cock the rifle. Aim. Fire. Over and over again he repeated the process, pouring a small amount of powder into the barrel, followed by the lead ball, driving it home with the ramrod. Then he would pour a small amount of powder into the pan, cover the pan with the frizzen and cock the flint piece. Aim and fire.

Smoke irritated Williams' eyes. It clawed at his throat and filled his nose. The smell was acrid, reminding him of bonfires as a child. Together with his fellow soldiers they fired two to three rounds a minute, each man vaguely aware of the others, trying hard to keep pace with their fellows in loading and firing. Occassionally a round whistled past nearby or kicked up dirt in front of the line of redcoats.

They fired volley after volley into the Irish lines. Soon there were few groups of more than one or two Irishmen to fire at. Most of the rebels were running up and over the hill or scattering into the nearby trees as fast as they could. A handful continued to try to fight, but were unable to reload their muskets and pistols with any speed. Outmatched and outgunned the last of the Irish broke.

Laycock gave the order to advance, drawing his sword. The New South Wales Corpsmen lowered their muskets from their shoulders, holding them at hip height, pointed towards the Irish. At least a dozen lay dead, with more injured.

Johnston had by now turned the two Irish leaders over to the civilian militia, with clear instructions neither were to be harmed. He moved to follow his troops as they advanced on the Irish positions. As the troops reached the Irish lines their discipline cracked out of hatred, tiredness, fear and anger. The soldiers broke from the lines and began slashing with bayonets at the Irishmen laying injured on the ground. Two or three were run through by bayonet.

Johnston ran towards his troops. He saw Cunningham, the Irish leader, run across in front of him, heading towards Laycock. How the Irishman had escaped he did not know, yet there he was in the thick of battle rather than in the hands of the civilian militia.

Laycock saw him coming and waited until he was close enough. He slashed down across the Irishman's face with his sword. Half of Cunningham's face fell away, his head partially collapsing inwards. Johnston swore under his breath. His men had given themselves up to blood lust and were now determined to kill as many Irishmen as possible. Johnston had seen this after battle: the victors' relief at being alive; intense emotions experienced so quickly and deeply, pouring out into violence.

The major drew his pistol from his sash. He reached the bulk of his men and grabbed one of them, yelling 'I swear I will shoot you if you continue to kill in cold blood. The battle is won.'

He pointed the pistol at another and then another soldier until they stopped, like men coming out of a drunken stupor and looking around to see where they were. Quartermaster Laycock sensed the men stopping and turned, ready to rouse them forward. He stopped as he saw the major.

Johnston yelled to the men to form ranks. Gradually, many stumbling with exhaustion and the realisation of what they had done, the men joined into ranks. None looked at another. They hung their heads or looked at the carnage left after the broken promise of rebellion.

The Irish rebels were broken completely, none willing to fight on now that the rebellion was over. Those still holding weapons threw them to the ground, screaming for mercy. Groups of the civilian militia, emboldened by the fear now displayed by the Irish, were coming forward, eagerly taunting the wounded Irishmen. Johnston was afraid they too may make cold-blooded war on a defeated enemy.

Johnston yelled at Laycock. 'Get the militia to get these men water, then the civvies can start rounding up the wounded. Make sure things do not get out of hand quartermaster'.

Johnston turned and headed towards where he had seen Cunningham cut down by Laycock. As he approached he looked for a sign of the fallen leader, yet could not see him. A small group of militia milled around.

'Where is that Irish Cunningham?' Johnston said.

'They took him, dragged him off that way. Said they were gunna hang him,' one of the militia men said.

Johnston looked the way the man pointed, where the road to the Hawkesbury ran. There was no sign of Cunningham. He remembered his own namesake, the Irish leader William Johnston and turned and made his way down the hill towards the largest group of civilians. The Irishman was no where to be seen.

'Where is the Irish prisoner?'

Several men pointed towards some nearby trees. Johnston looked and saw a man hanging from the tree, although he did not recognise the dead man as his Irish namesake. Johnston sighed. This was how rebellion too often ended; the victors abandoning the rule of law for vengeance. Sowing the seeds of the next rebellion as they did so.

George Johnston looked around. The killing had mercifully ended with the hanging of an unnamed Irishman. His own men were now sitting in the midst of the battlefield, many fighting the waves of exhaustion breaking upon them.

The wounded were soon rounded up and forced to form a line. A number of Irishmen were coming forwards gingerly, hands held high. They too were rounded up and shoved and manhandled into the column of prisoners. Members of the civilian militia agreed to escort them back to Parramatta. The militia leaders spied Johnston and headed his way. Father Dixon was amongst them, Johnston noticed.

'Major,' one of the leaders asked, 'who will bury the dead?'

Johnston looked around, counting at least fifteen dead Irishmen nearby and spying more on the hill above. 'Leave them where they lie and let them rot. Father Dixon, you may provide whatever benediction or blessing you deem necessary, but they stay on this hill as a reminder to all of the consequences of rebellion. Any man that moves them will be considered a rebel sympathiser and treated as such.'

Father Dixon looked at the major. 'First you bring me here telling me you wish my help in the negotiations, only to use me to lure out the leaders. Now they are to be denied a Christian burial. Is this English compassion?'

'Father, these men were preparing to kill settlers, convicts, whomever stood in their way. Then they intended to sail back to Ireland to wage war. They are not soldiers, they are criminals and traitors. They are being treated as such. If you have a problem with that take it up with Governor King. And perhaps at that time you may wish to explain why messages in relation to this rebellion were being passed at your church services.'

Johnston stared at the priest for a long time, happy to let the threat hang in the air. He turned away, then smiling turned back to the priest. 'Thank you for your help today Father. It may provide you just enough redemption in the eyes of the authorities here.'

Johnston turned and walked towards the growing number of Irish and convict prisoners. He slowly looked along the line of men, finally recognising the Irishman William Johnston. Then he wearily headed towards his men.

'Lads, I am immensely proud of you. Your spirit and willingness to do what needed to be done has secured the future of this colony. This land many of us now call home. We will rest here awhile,' Johnston said, 'before heading back to Parramatta. The militia can begin the cleanup work. We'll let the escaped rebels live rough in the bush for a few days. After that most will be willing to surrender or be rounded up by the militia.'

The soldiers sat in a group, under the shade of a eucalypt. For twenty minutes no man spoke. Each was lost in his thoughts, trying to make sense of battle. The shooting and killing and surviving. Of life and death compacted so closely together into a few brutal minutes. Several embraced the waves of exhaustion and fell asleep to escape their thoughts.

After a long silence Corporal Smith looked around the group, seeking any man willing to talk. Eventually Tom Conner returned his look. 'I am looking forward to a strong drink and good meal, I tell you.'

Conner smiled a quick smile. 'That sounds good.'

'So are you cooking then Corporal?' Private Robertson asked. 'Get your orders in lads. Mine is the roast beef swimming in gravy, lashings of vegetables done just so with several pints.'

The men laughed and began shouting out orders. 'Roast lamb,' said John Bowes.

'I'll have the kangaroo and oysters Corporal,' Robert Jones shouted. 'With two pints on the side. For each dish.'

Within a matter of moments the competition to better the last order was on, the men glad for the distraction from what had taken place before.

'I would not get too excited,' Laycock said. 'The only time I have ever known Corporal Smith to cook is when there is a bonfire on Christmas or Easter and the result is always the same. Everything is burnt. We would be better to let the Corporal pour drinks when we return. After all his pints are the most generous in the Corps.'

'Only when he is pouring for himself Quartermaster,' Private Robertson offered.

'That is true Private,' Laycock said laughing. 'And no different to you either.'

'That's not fair. You are only saying that because I can't argue with a higher rank.'

'Permission to argue granted Private. Before you do, I call as my witnesses the whole Corps.'

'In that case I concede, and will have to excuse myself from pouring drinks for anyone but me.'

'I agree,' Laycock said laughing.

The soldiers continued the banter and lighthearted insults for a few more minutes until the mood had shifted and smiles were again on faces. Johnston, watching from nearby, waited a little longer until he walked over and gave the order to march.

'Right lads, let's begin the journey back to Parramatta. Easy as we go, and a rest stop each half hour to begin with. Except for Corporal Smith and Private Robertson who can march ahead and start pouring the rum.'

There was a general round of laughter. 'On second thoughts that's not such a good idea, as we want some left for the rest of us,' the major said.

The group set off laughing and in good spirits, marching at an easy pace. Once they had cleared the area the militia set about marching the Irish prisoners and wounded in a long column. The body of the unknown Irishman was left hanging as a reminder to those thinking of rebellion.

It was late in the day when Lieutenant Davies and his party of troops caught up with Major Johnston's column.

'Major, I heard that you broke the rebellion, congratulations,' the Lieutenant said.

'That we did Lieutenant. What's the mood up Windsor way?'

'There's no appetite amongst the locals to join any rebellion, quite the opposite. The locals have taken it as their patriotic duty to put the Irish into line. Up at Hawkesbury a handful of rebels identified as leaders were hung. One of the rebel leaders from your battle was dragged the whole way bleeding profusely and hung from the staircase at the new Windsor stores. I doubt he would have lived much longer anyway, someone had hacked half his face away.'

'That was Quartermaster Laycock, who distinguished himself admirably. As did all of our men. Their spirit was exemplary. The only fault I could find in them was being too fond of blood once they broke the Irish lines. So you are confident that the rebellion is over in Windsor and Hawkesbury before it has even begun?'

'I am Major.'

'Good, Governor King will be pleased.'

Johnston then described the battle to Davies, downplaying his own role while celebrating his men.

'This day will give long pause to any thinking of rebelling. We have shown our worth to the governor, more than paid our dues and have earned the right to conduct our business in peace.'

It was well after nightfall when Johnston and Davies were ushered in to Government House at Parramatta. Johnston wondered if it was only that morning that he had last been here. The opulence of the setting, the furniture and rugs and aides buzzing around made Johnston squirm. He hated ceremony at the best of times. Standing in his grimy, sweat-stained uniform with the smell of burnt gunpowder still fresh only exagerated that feeling.

This time Governor King met the two New South Wales Corps officers himself. He was a small but heavy man, slightly hunched with the disdainful look of a bureaucrat, dismissive and haughty all at once.

'Major, well done, well done indeed. The rebellion is over and the colony safe again.'

Johnston noted that the governor did not say thank you. Nor did he offer a hand. That would be a step too far given King's past criticism of the Corps. Most of that criticism was directed either at the trade in liquor by the Corps or the taking up of land by it's officers. King had changed the rules around land management, creating a series of commons on which private settlers could freely graze animals. This was, Johnston suspected, more about quarantining good farm land from the Corps than any effort to make life easier for the common man. That decision, along with attempts to stop liquor trading, had created a sharp enmity between the governor and his soldiers.

Johnston would be prepared to forget the past in return for a thank you from the governor. He waited in vain. Those words did not come.

'Now we need to round up the rest of the rebels,' King said. 'Given that martial law is still in place I propose that the leaders be hung. How many do we have as prisoners?'

Johnston ignored the use of 'we' in the governor's comments. Of course King had no intent to be involved in any of the hard yards rounding up convicts.

'Governor, the ring leaders of this rebellion are already dead or in custody. A handful more who were their lieutenants, are also dead or held prisoner. The rest that have been caught are now under militia guard.'

'We'll need to make an example of a few more. It will give the settlers peace seeing a few more hangings.'

'I doubt anyone finds peace watching a hanging. We have left the bodies of the fallen Irish rebels on the hillside where they were shot. One of the Irish leaders hangs from the store house at Windsor. I think that is a sufficient message that order has been restored.'

'Nevertheless Major, a few more examples will help calm nerves. I would suggest around a dozen more rebels should swing. Identify the leaders. You can talk to Marsden for help and interrogate any prisoner you need to. There will be a court martial tomorrow for these rebels, and then hangings. I want this done.'

'Yes Governor.' With that Johnston turned and walked out of Government House, followed by Davies.

'The last thing we need now is a witch hunt,' Johnston said. 'All it will do is create a whole new set of resentments that will fester down the years. King thinks he is being smart - hang a few and let the remainder off free.'

'So as to ensure his precious convict workforce is still available to him?' Davies said.

"That's correct Lieutenant. I suggest we bunk the lads down here tonight and have search parties out at first light tomorrow. You will lead one, and I the other. That way when the sentences are delivered we are far enough away so as not to be involved."

The two soldiers mounted their horses and rode slowly back to the barracks. Johnston looked around at the settlement, seeing a number of flags and pictures hanging in windows celebrating the victory over the Irish. He longed to ride home to the farm at Annandale, to hold Esther and sleep in his own bed, but that would have to wait.

Johnston and Davies rode through the barracks gate slowly. Captain Abbott came out to join them. The parade ground was quiet, the bunkhouses dark. Two privates from the barracks took their horses.

'Congratulations Major, a wonderful victory for you and the Corps,' Abbott said.

'Thank you Captain. Unfortunately it's not over yet. We will head out at first light to check the neighbouring settlements and search for any parties of rebels still in the bush. Your men will patrol the town and surrounds.'

'Pardon my asking but is that necessary?'

'Governor King has it in mind to hang the ringleaders and is convening a court martial. He would like to drag us into it, which is why we will not be here tomorrow.'

'There is little harm in hanging a few rebellious Irishmen,' Abbott said.

'The English Crown has been doing that for a few hundred years and all it has done is feed the fire of rebellion. They are broken here and know it. All we will do now is breed more hatred of authority amongst the Irish. And anyone else who resents authority. Which is rich pickings around here.'

'I understand.'

'Good,' Johnston said. 'Now I need a rum and a bed for the night, as does Lieutenant Davies.'

The first patrols began marching out with the sunrise. Williams and Conner were in a ten man patrol led by Quartermaster Laycock, with Corporal Smith as second-in-command. Williams had a notepad provided him by Captain Abbott and orders to note down any lost or stolen items. The patrol's first stop was the government farm at Parramatta, established to provide produce for the colony. The farm supervisor, Thomas Rose, greeted them.

'Good morning lads and a hearty thank you to you all,' Rose said.

'Happy to help out,' Laycock said. 'Have you seen any men about this morning, any rebels?'

'No. But we did have a few things stolen the night before last: farm tools and two muskets along with some grain.'

'Private Williams, make a note of that,' Laycock said. 'We have a group of civilian militia escorted by a few of our brave lads heading up to the battle site today to collect any remaining weapons and farm tools. Once they are back here we will let you know.'

'And tell me Mr Rose, how is your missus? In good health?'

Rose blushed a little. 'She is fine thank you.' There was a chuckle from a few of the older soldiers. Williams looked at Smith who quietly muttered 'later' under his breath.

'We will take a look around. Can you show us where the weapons and tools were stolen from? Then we will check the buildings,' Laycock said.

The patrol spent the next hour searching the buildings on the farm. Laycock took the task at a leisurely pace, remembering Johnston's order to stay outside Parramatta until close to sunset.

Once the search was completed the patrol began to move through the outlying farms. During their second stop Williams asked Smith about the exchange between Laycock and Rose.

'Smith, what was the quartermaster up to asking after Rose's missus. Clearly something is up.'

'Mr Rose is one of the original free settlers who came out here in 1793. The Mrs Rose that sailed with him is not the same Mrs Rose now. Seems the original Mrs Rose got replaced by a younger lady,' Smith said. 'It's one of those minor scandals that happen a bit around here. But given Mr Rose is the supervisor of the government farm, well he is a bit more well known.

'The free settlers and others like to think themselves above such things. They would have us all believe that only convicts get up to such shenanigans, but well, people are funny. Rich of poor, free or convict there is a lot that is the same in all of us.'

The morning passed by as the soldiers visited outlying farms and checked sheds and copses of trees for any rebels. None were found. The only excitement was the reports of stolen farm equipment.

'So Private Williams, tell me how much farm equipment was stolen?' Laycock said, as the patrol ambled down the road towards Prospect.

'Twenty-three muskets, forty-one hoes, forty-three scythes, and nine horses, so far.'

'There isn't that much farm equipment this side of Bristol. And nine horses. Nine. I didn't see any horses yesterday. Did you?'

'No Quartermaster.'

'You have to hand it to these farmers, they never waste an opportunity to get the government to pay for things.'

'Should I keep taking notes then Quartermaster?'

'Absolutely son. If we don't let these whingers have a whinge we'll likely be facing another group of rebels. So record it all son, record it all. We'll give it to the governor's men and they can decide what to do about it.'

Soon after noon the patrol stopped for a long lunch, the soldiers grateful for the slow pace set. After lunch the patrol stopped by another farm near Prospect and were tipped off about some rebels seen nearby. The three Irish men were believed to be hiding in an abandoned hut near the road that ran through farms just outside Prospect. A second farmer confirmed the rebels were last seen hiding in the same hut and were unarmed.

'Right lads, the road ahead has a couple of abandoned huts. Some of the locals think the first hut is being used by some Irish rebels. They are likely unarmed according to our inteligence. Corporal Smith you will drop back with Conner, Newbold and Jones.

'When my group see the first hut we will march past it. Private Williams, since you are always the first to speak up consider yourself our volunteer. When we pass the hut you will loudly announce that you have to take a shit, urgently. I will mock you and you will beg me to take relief. I will then send you off to take your dump. You will head for the hut. Corporal Smith, you will take your men and skirt around behind the hut, and using Williams as a decoy close in on the hut from the rear."

'Begging you pardon Quartermaster but I thought Williams was going to bring up the rear?' Smith said.

'Are you finished Corporal or would you like to provide your arse as the decoy? Right, so once Smith and his lads move in we move in quickly too. Williams you will help out Smith if needed until we arrive.'

The patrol headed up the road. Smith along with Newbold, Conner and Jones waited before heading into the bush. Smith led the three soldiers using a line of trees to move towards the broken-down hut.

Laycock marched on past the hut.

'Ohh, Quartermaster! Quartermaster, that meat you told me not to eat, it has got me.'

'What on God's earth do you mean Williams?'

'I gotta go now. Ohh, ohh.'

'You expect me to stop the column because you need to take a shit. Sorry Private, we have places to be. You shit on your own time in the Corps son.'

'Ohh, please!'

'Alright, go here.'

'I can't do it here, the other men sir...'

'Dear Lord, should we all turn around? Over there, go over there,' Laycock said pointing towards the hut.

Williams did his best impersonation of a desperate man in search of relief, waddling over to the hut. Laycock yelled to the remaining men to take a break. Then he motioned a handful of the men to start edging towards the hut.

Williams rounded the corner of the hut out of the eyeline of his soldiers. He pretended to unbuckle his breeches, placing his musket against the half-collapsed wall of the hut. Suddenly from inside he heard a noise of a body shifting.

He counted the seconds. Where was Smith? This was taking too long. He dared not peak around the broken wall and alert the men inside. Again he heard a noise that sounded like a snort. Startled and unsure what to do he unbuckled his breeches and let then fall down and then squatted. He began to make grunting noises, praying that Smith and his small party would arrive.

The snort that he heard before echoed out again. It sounded like snoring. He looked around and saw Smith, Newbold, Conner and Jones standing at the edge of the hut, smirking. Laycock and the remainder of the troops made their way over.

Williams swore at them and pulled his breeches up. 'You took your bloody time,' he said.

'Quiet now Private, you may wake our sleeping Irish rebels,' he said, and pointed to the three Irish rebels snoring away in the corner of the hut. 'It's good to know that when you follow a plan you really follow a plan. Exactly how you intended to help us take these bastards down with your britches around your ankles I have no idea.'

'Well if you hadn't taken so long,' Williams said.

'We saw them asleep and decided to see what you would do. You may have a career in the theatre ahead of you with such commitment Private Williams. Although maybe that should be Wee Willy Williams,' Smith said. 'I didn't see much to inspire the ladies.'

'Being a decoy with my britches down doesn't exactly get me excited.'

One of the Irish men slowly rolled over and opened his eyes. 'Jesus, Mary and Joseph,' he said.

'Not quite sonny,' said Laycock. 'Not quite.'

With that Laycock kicked the feet of the other two Irishmen. Each woke and stared dumbfounded at the redcoats before them.

'Up you get, and slowly. Now are any of your fellow rebels nearby?'

The three shook their heads. Each man was searched and no weapons were found. Laycock ordered each man to have his hands bound, then the patrol made its way back to the road.

Laycock continued the leisurely pace throughout the afternoon, taking regular breaks. As the soldiers were finishing a mid-afternoon break Laycock spied a kangaroo grazing about fifty yards away. Bored by the prospect of further marching, the quartermaster couldn't resist a little fun.

'A barrel of rum to the man who shoots that roo down,' Laycock said.

All the men began hustling to get their Brown Besses and working feverishly to load them.

'Hold on a moment, we aren't just going to shoot. Private Williams and Private Conner, as our newest recruits you may have the first two shots. Let's see how well you do.'

Williams stepped up and finished loading his Brown Bess. Then carefully he raised the long musket and sighted down the barrel towards the kangaroo. At that distance the shot would fly straight and true, the result being deadly. Williams squeezed the trigger. The recoil sent the butt of the musket back into his shoulder and kicked the barrel upwards. A small cloud of smoke wafted around in front of him.

The kangaroo looked up at the sound of the shot then bounded a few yards away, adding another ten yards to the distance between it and the soldiers.

'Dear God how can someone who can see so well be such a bad shot?' Smith said.

'Did you see the shot hit that tree? It must be five yards to the left of the target,' Laycock said.

'I would say more like eight yards,' Smith said.

'Private Williams reload your musket and take that roo down. Now!' Laycock said.

Williams dutifully reloaded his Bess and then repeated the process of raising the barrel, aiming and shooting. This time he managed to raise a puff of dust almost ten yards to the right of the kangaroo. Having had two lives, the roo wasn't waiting around any longer and bounded off into the bush.

'Did he miss right this time Corporal Smith?' Laycock said.

'That he did Quartermaster. I don't think I have ever seen anything like it. I have known soldiers to miss but … And then they at least get near it. By God boyo we have our work cut out getting your shooting up to scratch.'

'I think we should all give thanks that the private here didn't accidentally hit the major during our skirmish with the Irish. The major and Anlezark would have been safer had you actually aimed for them son,' Laycock said.

"I wonder if he actually hit any of the Irish rebels at all,' Smith said. 'Well don't worry boyo, I'll teach you how to shoot.'

Laycock turned around and looked at a barn seventy yards away. 'Corporal do you think that the private could hit that barn?'

'From here?'

'Yes from here. Well what do you think?'

'Er, no. Maybe if we took him a bit closer.

'How close?'

'I was thinking inside the barn.'

'Even then Corporal, I would not rate him a certainty.'

'That is being a bit harsh Quartermaster. Then again, I suppose it's not that big a barn.'

'In the meantime I suggest we keep Private Williams here in the front rank of any future action. If we keep him in the second row he may well shoot some of our own lads,' Laycock said.

'What about the barrel Quartermaster?' Conner said.

'I suggest you take it up with Private Williams son,' Laycock said.

In the late afternoon sun the patrol wearily made the trek back to Parramatta. The three Irish prisoners were all of the day's takings. Most of the farms that the patrol had visited reported thefts of farm implements and tools, and a handful of muskets. Williams had dutifully recorded all the details in the notebook he carried. The list of farm implements almost numbered the times he had been called Wee Willy since the capture of the Irish rebels.

Smith walked up beside him. 'Sorry mate, but I was only obeying orders. Don't take it too much to heart, and some good will come from it, I promise.'

Williams glared at Smith. 'I don't care what you were doing, it wasn't very nice.'

'I know,' Smith said. 'Trust me, don't let it get to you. Good things are in store for you.'

With that Smith walked ahead and left Tom Conner marching next to Williams.

'What do you suppose the Corporal meant?'

'I really don't care right now,' said Williams.

'And whose orders do you think it was? The quartermaster's?'

Williams looked at Conner. It had to have been Laycock.

Parramatta was alive with activity when the soldiers marched down its main street. Groups of people milled about shops. Animated discussions were taking place on street corners.

Taverns were bustling and the air of promise for something to explode was palpable.

Most of those talking ignored the red-coated soldiers marching past. Instead they pointed at the three Irishmen. Some shouted abuse. One woman ran up and spat on the first Irish prisoner. Several people threw whatever they could find. The occupants of one tavern started spilling out into the street. Bottles were quickly emptied. Some started to reverse their holds on those bottles, gripping them by the neck, turning them into potential weapons.

'Double-time march, now,' Laycock ordered.

The soldiers accelerated to a quick walking pace, not quite breaking out into a run. The three Irish prisoners were glad to be moving quickly and easily matched the pace of the soldiers, eagerly moving in amongst the soldiers. Abuse continued to fill the air. A crowd started to gather behind the patrol, swelling in numbers.

The patrol turned a corner and Parramatta barracks came into view. Laycock urged the patrol forward. A small group of soldiers on sentry duty marched out to meet the patrol then formed up as the soldiers passed them. They formed a line between the patrol and barracks. For several moments the crowd yelled and swore at the soldiers. The patrol finally marched through the gate before slowing to a stop. The sentries carefully backed away from the crowd and entered the barracks. Soldiers ran to the gates and closed it. Gradually the crowd lost momentum and broke apart.

'What in God's name is going on?' Laycock said.

Johnston and Abbott stepped through the soldiers gathering around. 'Quartermaster, glad to have you back,' Johnston said.

'Governor King has followed through on his promise of hangings. Nine ringleaders of the rebellion have been found guilty and are to be hung.'

'Guilty of what?' Laycock said.

'Rebellion, treason, being Irish, take your pick. The court martial didn't actually specify that. Instead the Governor has had notices placed around the town announcing the hangings. The whole town has gone into a frenzy. The prospect of hangings has brought out the worst in the people. All it has done is fuel the hatred of the Irish, when we should be making peace,' Johnston said.

Johnston handed a copy of the notice to Laycock.

PROCLAMATION

Governor King hereby lets it be known that the Irish rebellion has ended, and its leaders have been tried by court martial today at Parramatta.

Nine of the leaders of the doomed rebellion will be hung

Philip Cunningham - hung at Windsor 5 March

William Johnston - hanging in a public place with his body then hung in chains at Johnston Bridge at Toongabbie and left to rot

Samual Humes - hanging in a public place with his body then hung in chains on the road to Prospect and left to rot

Charles Hill - hanging at Parramatta on 8 March

Jonathon Place - hanging at Parramatta on 8 March

John Neale - hanging at Castle Hill on 9 March

George Harrington - hanging at Castle Hill on 9 March

John Brannon - hanging at Sydney on 10 March

Timothy Hogan - hanging at Sydney on 10 March

Other leaders will be given 500 or 200 hundred lashes and then be sent to Coal River Penal Settlement or Norfolk Island

The bodies of those killed in the insurrection on the road to Toongabbie are to stay where they lay for all time.

Martial law will end after the final hangings on 10 March.

'Well that has calmed things down a treat,' Laycock said. 'Who led the court martial?'

'At this stage we don't know that Quartermaster. Right now my concern is that we keep these prisoners safe. The last thing we need is a mob at the gates baying for Irish blood. I want at least four soldiers on guard each shift tonight. Tomorrow we will head out again on patrols and see if we can round up any more rebels.'

'Alright lads, bunk down for the night and tomorrow we set out on patrol again,' Laycock said.

The officers turned and walked away. Johnston motioned for Laycock to walk with him and soon the two were deep in conversation. Watching the officers walk away Williams saw the major stop, grip Laycock on the shoulder, then throw his head back and laugh. The major then turned and spotted Williams and smiled a knowing smile.

'By God, what does it take for a man to rebel. To think that he knows better than the powers that be and want to overthrow them?' Smith said. The patrol had finished their second day searching for any remaining rebels. Most of the farmers the soldiers had met had little to report. The day's takings were five Irish rebels, all of whom surrendered to the patrol without incident. They walked, roped together, in the middle of the small column.

'Are you expecting an answer to your philosophising Corporal?' Lieutenant Davies said.

'Sorry Lieutenant, it's just it does make one wonder what the rebels were thinking?' Smith said. 'Why now? Life here is not that bad?'

'Perhaps they lack a certain discipline,' Davies said. 'Perhaps you should consult with the troops. Ask them why discipline is so important and why the army shoots deserters if you wish an answer?"

'I think the Corporal is wondering what led them to rebel all at once,' Williams said. 'Isn't that right Corporal?'"

'Couldn't have said it better myself lad,' Smith said. 'I understand why deserters run away but that's a personal thing right? This is hundreds of men working together to overthrow the Government and to return to Ireland and overthrow British rule there. I mean don't you wonder what causes that? Is it one man working others into a frenzy or do they all arrive at that point separately and then start talking? And do you ever wonder if that could be, well, us one day?'

'No Corporal, I do not wonder about such things and perhaps you should not burden yourself with that either,' Davies said.

'Oli you know what I am talking about don't you?' Smith said.

'I think you are wondering what it would take to make us rebel?' Williams said.

'Yes, in a way. Do you think we would ever be so bold?' Smith said.

'I don't think so. But then who knows what it would take to push us that far?' Williams said.

'For God's sake lads, enough,' Davies said. 'Or someone is going to think we're willing to rebel.'

At 5.30 pm on Thursday evening a large contingent of soldiers led by Major Johnston marched out of Parramatta barracks in full uniform. The fifty soldiers headed to the hanging ground and gallows that had been erected near the river.

The New South Wales Corps soldiers formed an orderly group near the centre of the crowd, which stood at more than a thousand people. Groups sang, others danced, and many talked loudly, enjoying the festive atmosphere. Food and drink were plentiful. Parramatta had not seen a public hanging in many months.

At 5.45 pm the prisoners Charles Hill and Jonathon Place were marched forward by a contingent of police. Both men had their hands bound tightly behind their back. It took several minutes for the two condemned men to be led through the crowd to the gallows. A show was made for the sizeable audience of testing the ropes and trapdoors. Delighted, the crowd shouted and roared as each trapdoor sprung open.

Just before 6 pm Hill and Place were pushed forward up the stairs to the gallows. Place tried to maintain his dignity; Hill looked terrified.

Father Dixon quickly offered each man a short prayer, and then the two were hauled forward and placed over a trapdoor. The charges of treason and rebellion were read out by a small man in black. Johnston recognised him as one of Governor King's many aides.

'Charles Hill, you are charged with treason and rebellion against the Crown and the authorities of New South Wales and have been found guilty. Do you acknowledge the justice of this verdict?'

Hill mouthed something. One of the convict police officers prodded Hill in the back with a wooden truncheon.

'I acknowledge that justice is served,' Hill said. A hood was placed over his head, and the noose dropped over his head and then tightened.

'Jonathon Place, you are charged with treason and rebellion against the Crown and the authorities of New South Wales and have been found guilty. Do you acknowledge the justice of this verdict?'

'Justice is served. I acknowledge that English justice is served.'

The crowd booed loudly.

Place had a hood roughly shoved over his head, followed by the noose. The hangman made an elaborate display of tightening the noose before whispering into Place's ear.

A wave of sound slowly washed back through the crowd.

'What did he say?' A hundred different voices asked.

The answer coming flowing backwards. 'He said "You asked for death or liberty, all we can offer is death. Enjoy it."'

A raucous laugh followed the sweep of sound back through the crowd.

'Let the sentences be delivered,' said Governor King's aide.

The crowd fell silent. There was nothing to fill the void of silence until the first trapdoor dropped open, followed a moment later by the second.

A roar came up from the crowd. All the fear, anger and hatred that the rebellion had unleashed echoed out. Hill went limp straight away. Place struggled, his legs kicking out. Johnston watched as it took the best part of a minute for Place to stop struggling. So that is why the hangman took so much care with tightening the noose for Place, thought Johnston. Those efforts ensured that the Irish rebel did not have his neck broken immediately, unlike his compatriot Hill who would have died almost instantly. Poor bastard.

The bodies were left to hang for a half hour. The crowd began to ebb away, the thrill of the execution souring after all the pent up emotion had rushed out.

Johnston waited until most of the crowd had left and the bodies were taken down. He felt the glare of Father Dixon looking at him but did not let it affect him, instead nodding an acknowledgement and wry smile to the priest.

After the bodies had been taken away for burial Johnston led his troops back to the barracks. An extra ration of wine was served to each man. The officers drank Cape red, wine imported from Cape Town at the southern tip of Africa.

'Major, will we head out to Castle Hill for tomorrow's hangings?' Lieutenant Davies said.

'I've already had my fill of hangings. No, we'll march back to Sydney tomorrow, get these soldiers back to their own barracks and give them some much-needed rest. They have excelled themselves, as have all of you. I am immensely proud of all of you.

'Gentlemen, a toast. To the New South Wales Corps, defenders of liberty here in this great land.'

'To the Corps,' the officers said.

The march from Parramatta to Sydney was undertaken at a leisurely pace. Major Johnston's detachment were cheered whenever they came across a group of people. 'Johnston's brave boys', 'Hoorah for the Corps', 'God bless you all', these and a dozen other kind phrases rang in the ears of the soldiers all the way to Sydney.

Upon entering Sydney the cheering intensified. English flags flew in windows besides pictures imagining the battle. Most of the etchings and paintings showed the Irish fleeing before the red-coated English soldiers. Children marched beside the soldiers, using sticks as rifles and trying their best to imitate the marching soldiers.

'This is quite something,' Williams said.

'Lap it up boys, it makes a nice change,' Smith said.

'Change from what?' Conner said.

'Well we're not always the most popular people in town, given our mercantile interests and the like. A lot of people think we get the first pick of the best land and goods for sale. And they would be right,' Smith said, between laughs. It was hard to do much else given the excitement of the crowd.

Once the detachment turned into High Street the cheering went into overdrive. Bunting in red, white and blue hung from shops and houses. A band played an impromptu jig with the people dancing merrily. As the detachment approached Church Street and turned towards the barracks a drummer from the Corps stepped forward and played the opening bars of the 'The British Grenadiers'. On the fourth beat more drummers and fife players joined in.

The detachment marched through the gates with Johnston at its head like a Roman general and his army at a triumph, revered, loved and adored by the large crowd that began to clap in time to the music.

Johnston led the troops in through the gates and onto the parade ground. The large crowd swelled towards the gates. Those soldiers who lived near the barracks and had not been woken to join Davies's small group several nights before waited on the parade ground. Sentry John Gray looked at Lieutenant Minchin, looking resplendent in full uniform, who simply nodded.

Johnston's detachment stopped on the parade ground.

'Attention,' Minchin shouted.

The members of the Corps gathered before Johnston's detachment stood ramrod straight, in perfect formation. They beamed with delight, though each of them held a kernel of regret that they too had not been a part of the action. At Minchin's command they saluted Johnston's small band of soldiers before them.

'On behalf of the New South Wales Corps, we humbly offer our congratulations, appreciation and respect for your fine victory. Your deeds shall live forever in the history of this colony. Hip ...'

'Hoorah,' the soldiers shouted.

'Hip ...'

'Hoorah.'

'Hip ...'

"Hoorah." This final shout rumbled across Sydney as the crowd joined in.

'Thank you,' Johnston said.

The Corps musicians struck up another song and Johnston ordered Davies and Laycock to dismiss the detachment.

'Lads, tonight is going to be one hell of a party,' Smith said. 'Now remember, don't do anything I wouldn't do, or more to the point, don't do anyone I wouldn't do.'

The officers retired to the mess hall. The mess was comfortably appointed with whitewashed walls and wooden floor. Near the only door was a ragtag bunch of chairs and cushions grouped around a few old and tattered rugs. To one side stood a bar bench, and tables and more chairs were stacked in the far corner. The remainder of the large space was empty. An old regimental flag was mounted on one wall, along with a few pictures of Sydney. The mess was the heart of the barracks, a place of retreat and comraderie from the world beyond.

Johnston walked in followed by the officers. A few of the old timers also followed. Most of the enlisted men were already drifting off into the crowd, to find a party at which they would be guests of honour. Inside the mess hall Minchin had already ensured that half a dozen bottles of fine Cape red were opened on the bar.

'Major, my apologies Colonel Patterson wasn't here,' Minchin said.

'Not a problem. Besides, this means far more coming from you and the men.'

'Thank you sir. I have assumed you will be staying tonight, before the governor arrives tomorrow.'

'Yes, it would be poor form not to be there when the conquering hero arrives,' Johnston said. 'And have we heard from the Colonel, or is he still sick?'

Colonel Patterson was the head of the Corps, but had been unseen in public for many months after complaining of illness. His illness was the result of a duel with John Macarthur, a Lieutenant in the Corps. The original insult that resulted in the duel was never made clear, nor which man called out the other.

On the day of the duel Patterson shot first, wide of his adversary. Custom dictated Macathur discharge his weapon wide too. That was supposed to be the end of it. Yet Macarthur chose to hit Patterson. Those men of the Corps who witnessed the duel spoke of the look of incredulity on Patterson's face after the shot slammed into his shoulder.

Patterson had sent Macarthur to England for courtmartial, sure that that would be the end of it. He had not, however, anticipated the impact of the duel on his health and standing. The shot had caused significant damage and infection followed. Patterson had barely survived. His judgement, in fighting a duel against one of his officers, in shooting wide and in altogether misjudging Macarthur's mettle had come into question. Rumours and gossip followed, something Sydney excelled in. For Patterson it all became too much and he withdrew from public life rather than face his men.

'No word yet from the Colonel. You know him too well Major. There is talk that he intends to take leave and travel to Van Diemen's Land to recover.'

'His dignity or his wounds?' Davies said, prompting laughter.

'Now now lads. We should have greater respect for our commanding officer. Having said that, I have no doubt that he will manage to rise from his sick bed tomorrow. Now who wants a drink?'

The arrival of Governor King was more subdued than the previous afternoon's revelry. King stepped off a boat, having travelled down the river from Parramatta, to a band playing. There was a small crowd and sporadic cheering, but none of the spontaneity that marked the Corps' arrival.

His progress from the wharf to the barracks was rapid. As the governor entered the gates the Corps band struck up 'Rule, Britannia'. A small crowd gathered nearby with a few mumbling the words.

Paterson fulfilled Johnston's prophesy, rising from his sick bed to greet the governor.

'Governor, on behalf of the New South Wales Corps and the people of New South Wales. I congratulate you on your fine victory and on re-establishing control over the interior.' It took Paterson a moment to realise he had suggested the governor had lost control of the colony. He whinced and rubbed his wounded shoulder. That damned Macarthur. He wondered how to undo the damage of his words without drawing attention to it while he continued to massage his shoulder, his mind drifting back to Macarthur and the duel between the two men. It took him several moments to realise the governor had been talking and he had no idea what had been said.

'The Corps has commended your actions and they are formally noted in dispatches. Again congratulations Governor,' Paterson said.

King looked at Paterson with pity on his face. 'As I was saying, the Corps did a good job of recovering the situation, although perhaps they would be more effective acting prior to such events.'

'Steady gentlemen,' Johnston said to his officers.

'I humbly accept your congratulations. Now I have a task for you. We are going to build a fort on Flagstaff Hill to control the road to Parramatta and the view over Sydney. It would be appropriate under the circumstances for your soldiers to have some say on its design. I will send over some drafts in the next few days. Now Colonel, are my guards at Government House or have you a contingent here to escort me home?' King said.

Paterson looked around, unsure of the answer. His shoulder still bothered him. He rubbed the scar and again silently cursed Macarthur. 'Major, do we have the governor's guards here?'

'Governor, half of the duty roster for your guard house are on duty at Government House, the remainder are ready to escort you there at your convenience."

'Excellent, I wish to return now.'

With that King strode off towards the gates of the barracks. Johnston motioned to Ensign Bell of the Governor's Guard. Bell's men jumped to attention and formed two rows. King strode past them without an acknowledgement, climbed into the waiting carriage and began his progress to Government House.

Paterson walked slowly off the parade ground, still rubbing his shoulder while muttering to himself. He left for his home.

'Lieutenant Minchin, if it would please you perhaps you may lead a small contingent of the Corps out to the hanging today. I do not expect any trouble, however it would be worth a few of us being seen. Once that business is done I suggest we keep a low profile. And the lads should have the freedom of a couple of days off. I suggest we meet here again next Tuesday and then we can discuss how business is going.'

'Yes Major. Do you wish an escort to Annandale?'

'I will be fine, thank you Lieutenant. I don't think we need to put any more miles into the legs of these men on my account.'

Johnston rode out a short time later, welcoming the anonymity that came from riding alone.

'Right you new lads, you need to get to know the town. Let's get to it,' Smith said. The soldiers had spent much of Saturday recovering from the week and the party that ended it. Many had very sore heads on Saturday morning and few the energy or appetite for anything more than lazing around.

Tiredness had not stopped them the night before. A contingent of soldiers from the Corps, led by Smith, had set up shop drinking in a pub near the barracks.

'So tell me again about Conner,' Smith said to Williams, once the two were onto their second round of drinks.

'Not much to say really,' Williams said. 'We spent a bit of time together on the boat. He's the only boy in the family of seven children. Or was it seven sisters and him?'

'Sounds like a target-rich environment to me,' Smith said.

'Target rich?' Williams said.

'Women, boyo, plenty of women,' Smith said, pointing to where Conner was talking to two young ladies in a dark corner of the pub. 'And judging by how young Conner is faring right now, it seems having a wealth of sisters has given him a knack with the ladies.'

'Lucky bastard,' Williams said.

'Ain't nothing lucky about it,' Smith said. 'Some lads just have it and I suspect he has it in spades.'

At that moment Conner was trading kisses with both young women. Then he said something and turned and walked towards Smith and Williams.

'Bloody hell Oli, I'm on to something here,' Conner said. 'They are looking for another soldier to join the party, assuming you don't mind Corporal?'

'I suggest lad that you get yourself over there now,' Smith said

'I don't know...' Williams said.

'Well if you're just going to sit there so be it,' Conner said. 'Don't say later I didn't offer.'

Conner was half way back across the crowded pub when he suddenly turned and headed back to Smith and Williams.

'Begging your pardon Corporal but er, where exactly do I take the young ladies?' Conner said. 'I mean the barracks ain't an option, is it?'

Smith smiled widely. 'No, the barracks ain't an option. Hold here a moment.'

With that Smith disappeared and came back a few moments later. 'Out the back is a shack. You go down the path, past the head and at the trees you will see the shack. Here is a key. Leave it clean when you're done.'

'Thank you Corporal,' Conner said before wading into the crowd. Then moments later he shepherded the plumper of the two young ladies out the back door of the pub.

'Lucky Tom I think we'll call him,' Smith said. 'He has the makings of a good soldier, knows when to step up, knows when to keep quiet and knows how to make the most of an opportunity. You don't want to get left behind when fortune knocks young Oli, best remember that.'

'Any other sage words of advice?' Williams said.

'Yep, your round son.'

Later that night Williams had found himself next to Robert Jones, a long-time Corps member. 'So then, first battle out of the way, first night out with the lads, how you finding it?' Jones said.

'It's different to what they told me it would be,' Williams said.

Jones laughed. 'Yep, they all say that. Thing is we have it pretty good out here, as does anyone smart enough to keep his head down and get on with things. You remember that and you'll do well.'

'Tell me about Smith?' Williams said.

'What's to tell. Nate is Nate.'

'That's it?' Williams said laughing. 'There's gotta be more than that.'

'Nate came out here when the colony was still in its early days. He joined the army 'cause he got into trouble at home - something about a woman and a duel - and well, that's why he joined. Thing is he found somewhere he belonged when he joined. Best thing that ever happened to him. He'll look after you, show you the ropes, if you treat him right.'

'Okay. So is he the longest serving person here, I mean in the Corps?'

'Nah, there's still a few from the First Fleet. Thing is with Nate, it just suits him. The army life I mean. See the British army ain't built on the officers, the toffs who issue the orders. Nor is it built on the soldiers. It's men like Nate, the corporal's and sergeants that hold it together. They're the ones that make it like a family. Nate is kinda like all our big brother, the one who takes you under his wing and shows you things no one else tells you and defends you and the like. He know's he's on a good thing here and is smart enough not to put that in peril.

'So thing is, with Nate, well he has the brains to go further but that also means he knows that this suits him. So he doesn't push for advancement. He knows the officers value him, he knows the men well enough to ensure things get done without driving them too far. He's a curious type too, he likes figuring things out. He's a good man.'

'What about the quartermaster?' Williams said.

'Ah now that's another story. Thing is he is a stickler for tradition, from an army family. His loyalty is to the Major first and last. The two have been through more than a few battles and scrapes together. He is tough and as good a soldier as you'll find. If you stay on Laycock's good side you won't have a problem.'

'And if I fall foul of him?'

'Oliver, I wouldn't recommend that. The quartermaster is ruthless as they come when someone crosses him or the Corps.'

'What about the officers?'

'The two we have here at the barracks, Minchin and Davies are both good enough. A few years here has taken the toff out. They know how to be aloof and all that carry on, and they don't like to be spoken to by the men, but they will still talk to us. It's just got to be on their terms. Let em lead and think they are in charge and things are good.

'The others, like Abbot and Kemp at Parramatta, well they aren't worth much. There are a few more who live off barracks with their missus' and we don't see much of them. It's Minchin and Davies you'll deal with most of the time.'

'And the major?' Williams said.

'Ah the major. He is a good man, has our best interests at heart. I think he has seen enough soldiers live and die to know that soldiers need a bit of looking after. And he is keen on Sydney. His Esther, his lady, is an ex-convict.'

'Really. Is that normal?'

'Well I tell you what young Oliver, you ain't going to find too many non-convict ladies hereabouts. Just 'cause a woman has been a convict, doesn't mean she's bad. Probably means that she stole some bread to feed herself and got sent out here. So don't hold a position against the convict women. Accept that they're like the rest of us, keen to make a go of it here.'

Jones had spent the next half hour waxing lyrical about Sydney, its possibilities and rewards, before slipping off into the night. At the end of the evening Smith had rounded up the troops.

'Come on Oli, don't want to be here as the lone Corps man. Time we be going,' Smith had said as he stood beside Williams. Conner and a few Corps men were standing near the door waiting on Smith and Williams.

'Why not?'

'I'll tell you tomorrow, or maybe Sunday. For now trust me, it's time we left.'

'Right you are then Nate,' Williams said as he stood and walked to the door. Then the group left and marched in very irregular time back to the barracks before turning in for what little remained of the night.

They were allowed to sleep late on the Saturday morning, the final reward for subduing the Irish. Once the soldiers had fulfilled their duties and fixed up their equipment most had turned in early.

The sun was shining and Sunday morning was pleasantly warm when Smith, Williams and Conner slipped quietly out of the barracks. The two younger men had taken in little of the town since arriving just eight days ago. They had marched from the wharfs to the barracks, spent a day meeting the men, and then marched into the night to help quell the Irish rebellion.

'Righto lads, our first stop is Flagstaff Hill. It is the highest point in the colony of Sydney, has views out to the ocean through the heads and up river towards Parramatta. We use the flagstaff to signal boat arrivals, threats and the like.'

The three walked through streets of sandstone and wooden dwellings, heading northwest past The Rocks. 'This area is the oldest part of Sydney, where the First Fleeters settled. You can see across to Sydney Cove over the tops of those storehouses.'

They walked for a few minutes up the increasing incline until they reached the hill. People sat in the sun, there was a cricket game underway and wagering on the side. A few informal clothes lines had been erected and a number of children ran between picnic groups.

The three soldiers climbed to the windmill on the top of the hill, the view opening up over the harbour to the north shore. Small houses dotted the hillsides rising up from Port Jackson. An array of boats, in all shapes and sizes danced on the harbour, with a number bobbing along two lines, one headed upriver, the other down, as though on an imaginary maritime road.

Williams looked around towards the town. The first thing that struck him was the number of windmills and weathervanes that filled the skyline. Everywhere his eye took in buildings there were windmills, most turning slowly in the fluky breeze. The ridges of raised ground running east to the ocean and west to the interior featured lines of windmills.

'Okay lads, so you see the mouth of the Tank Stream over there? That is the heart of the town, where the wharves and store houses are. You'll get to know that well. Now if you follow the Tank Stream from the Cove into the town you'll see our barracks to the south. That whole area around the barracks and parade ground on the western side of the Tank is military turf. We own it, we police it, we decide who comes in and out. In the main, convicts found on our side of the stream get what is coming.

'To the east of the Tank is public land, for housing and the civil administration. You can see the governor's mansion and some of the administration buildings. On that side of the Tank we tread slowly and deliberately. The civilians don't necessarily like us, so don't wander off on your own.'

'Why don't they like us? God they loved us the other night. Isn't that right Tom? You were well loved by that comely young lass!'

'Oli, shut up,' Tom Conner said.

'Now lads what happens outside the barracks stays outside the barracks,' Smith said. 'Did you get her name though Tom?' Smith winked at Williams.

'You didn't answer me. Why don't they like us?' Williams said.

'Because of our monopoly on rum. Since the early days of the colony the Corps have taken first choice in buying any imports, expecially rum,' Smith said, mispronouncing especially. 'In the last few years a group of new traders, Simeon Lord, Robert Campbell and others have taken a fair share of the trade, but we still do well enough.

'We buy most of the liquor that is imported. We then on-sell it to the taverns and shop keepers around town. They know we have the muscle to ensure that we get what we want.'

Oliver Williams and Tom Conner looked at Nathaniel Smith in shock.

'The Corps came out here when there was nothing. We helped build this town you see before you. We have made lives out here. We have taken the chance to make ourselves rich too. Every other bastard that comes out here starts thinking the same. This is not like England where your station in life comes from what class you were born in. They sent us all out here to get rid of the riff raff, the criminal and lower classes.

Which means we are all thrown in together. And together we can make better lives for all.

'Look around. This is now a thriving port. Whalers and sealers come here on a regular basis. There are shopkeepers from India opening up, boats from America arriving, traders heading to and from China, all trying to import all sorts of things. Emancipated convicts are doing well for themselves. We decided a long time ago not to stand idly by while that happened.

'Sure we may be a bunch of chancers, but why walk away from opportunity when it falls in your lap. So what do you both intend to do: your time and then go on to some other regiment or war, or make a life here and get some good land and settle down?'

'I'm in,' Tom Conner said.

Williams spun around and looked at Conner. He thought about the choice he faced: becoming an outcast within the Corps or a participant in its scheming. Williams looked at the people sitting and lying in the sun, closed his eyes and felt the warmth reach within him in a way that never happened in England. At that moment he realised that he had not seen it rain since he arrived. Eight days without rain in England in autumn was a rarity. He remembered how it was so dark and damp and cold so often. And here, he thought, the sun shone all day, he enjoyed the warmth and loved the brightness of the days. The activity. If he went home to England he knew he would have few choices: stay in the army or leave it and get a job in some dull yard or on a farm. Scrounge for food in a city. Feel the cold seep into his bones and bring the creak of age with it long before time.

'Count me in too,' Williams said.

December 1804

Construction of the fort on top of Flagstaff Hill was almost completed when the summer came around again. Built from stone, the octagonal shape helped support gun placements, lending the top of the hill a squat, imposing crown.

Oliver Williams looked at the view from the fort. He had spent a good deal of time up here on Flagstaff Hill since throwing his lot in as a chancer, and already the dividends were paying off. There was the little bit of money that he had been able to put aside, he carried extra weight around his middle thanks to the food Corps members ate. He held the confidence of Major Johnston and the officers now that he was doing the books for their rum trade.

It had all happened so quickly after his first visit to Flagstaff Hill. Along with Smith and Conner he had enjoyed seeing the sights before returning to the barracks. Two days after that Major Johnston had returned and asked to see Williams.

'So young man you have been here less than two weeks and already distinguished yourself. Lieutenant Davies and Corporal Smith have both commended your actions during the rebellion, and Quartermaster Laycock still gets a smile on his face whenever anyone mentions Wee Willy.'

Williams flushed and looked down.

'Don't worry, that is the last time I will use that name for you, and the men have been told to leave off. Quartermaster Laycock may use it from time to time however, although he thinks very highly of you.'

'Thank you Major.'

'Now to business. Corporal Smith reports that your father taught you bookkeeping. Is that correct?'

'Yes sir. Did he tell you anything else about my father?'

'He did but you have no more control over that than I do over the winds here. Corporal Smith also said that you are keen to get involved in our mercantile interests.'

'Yes sir.'

'I want you to start doing bookkeeping for our rum trade. It has all been a bit haphazard of late, and I am very keen to get a tighter rein on it. Corporal Smith will fill you in on the details. As you will be keeping the books you will receive a small stipend that you may do with as you please. Is that alright with you?'

'Absolutely sir!'

'Good. I will talk with a couple of the officers and smooth the way. Corporal Smith will be your liaison. Well done young man and keep up the good work.'

Williams still smiled at the memory of his induction into the chancers. He walked over to the western side of the fort, looking out over the growing town. He saw the ramshackle dwellings mixing beside the grand governor's mansion and gardens, and the rings of houses radiating out from Sydney Cove. Each ripple, like those emanating from a stone dropped in a pond, was a little less impressive, losing its form as the dwellings became smaller and more broken down. Those on the fringes of Sydney town were the worst, some barely looking like they would survive the next summer storm.

There was a flurry of activity at the flagstaff. A series of pennants and flags were quickly run up the mast. A ship had entered the heads and would soon be docking. Williams walked over to the eastern side of the fort and strained his eyes, seeking out the flagstaff and tower on the top of South Head. He could barely make out the flags flying.

'Here comes the race,' Tom Conner said. He, Smith and George Newbank all moved quickly to the north-eastern corner of the fort. The first boats were already heading out, with several on the water turning and making a beeline for the heads.

'They're off. That little dinghy with the red sail is my bet,' Smith said.

'I think you have missed the two boats out on the far side of the port. See em? They'll win,' Newbank said.

Within minutes the handful of boats had swollen to a mini regatta, the prize being the first out to the large ship now clear of the heads and safely inside the harbour. Every size boat from canoes to small dinghies and sailing vessels were all converging on the large ship.

'It's anyone's race now,' Conner said. At least a hundred small vessels were converging on the large ship, which was spilling the wind from its sails lest it overrun part of the flotilla. Several small boats raced forwards, waiting until the last moment to tack and slip alongside the ship. Men could be seen scrambling up the sides of ship, seeking to be the first aboard and discover where this new arrival was from and what news she brought.

As the ship neared Sydney Cove half a dozen sleek nowie canoes rowed by naked Aboriginal warriors sped out to the ship. One of the canoes pulled alongside and an older warrior climbed aboard.

'There goes Bungaree to welcome them to the country,' Conner said. 'No doubt half the ship is staring at his nakedness and the other half don't know where to look.'

'She'll be in soon lads, we best get down and see what she's carrying for us,' Smith said.

The four soldiers grabbed their redcoats and hats and began the walk down the hill and through The Rocks to the wharves of Sydney Cove. There was little need to hurry. Before the ship could dock the Naval office would send a small dinghy to assess the cargo. That could take up to an hour. Then the ship would be directed to an anchorage or to dock. If she was to dock, the last few hundred metres to the cove were always the slowest. Many of the smaller vessels that hung like floating barnacles near the larger ship would race to get back ahead of the new arrival, impeding its progress. By the time the ship was docked and ready to unload the soldiers could have walked to the barracks had a rum or two and then ambled back to the dock.

Strolling through The Rocks, Smith turned to Newbank. 'George, you can take the lead on this. She looks American by the flag. Have you dealt with them before?'

'No. Don't they dislike us English 'cause of the war?'

'When it comes to trade it pays not to let things like history get in the way. You will find that they are offering a fair price. If they even know what that is here,' Smith said chuckling.

They turned a corner and ran into Lieutenant Minchin. 'How are we doing lads?' Minchin asked.

'On our way to see what the new arrival has in stores. Do you want to tag along sir?' Smith said.

'You know that an officer of the Corps can't be seen boarding a ship. Besides Governor King seems to have it in for us. If only we had a governer prepared to leave the rum trade alone. Lord knows little gets done around here without the convicts having a good dose of rum to lift their spirits,' Minchin said.

'Leave it to us. We are just going to carry out our usual inspection of the ship. And a touch of commerce on the side to keep the colony well lubricated,' Smith said.

'No harm in that then, is there?' Minchin said.

'Perhaps you should tell that to the governor,' Smith said laughing. 'We best be heading down and seeing what this ship has for us Lieutenant, if you will excuse us?'

'Never let it be said I am one to stand in the way of commerce lads. Good hunting,' Minchin said.

The four soldiers walked the short distance to the wharves and settled down to watch the ship dock. A large crowd was gathering, buzzing with anticipation. Every ship meant that the colonists were not alone in the world, that somewhere people remembered them.

The ship was named *Atlas*. She was one of the largest traders that had docked all year and would have an array of trade goods. American traders favoured the long voyage across the Pacific to the tiny colony, knowing that their goods, particularly liquor, would sell easily. The *Atlas* finished docking and began to drop her gangplank. The soldiers stood, pulling their redcoats on and shaking the dust off their shako hats.

'Trouble gents,' said Conner, spying a small party of constables walking towards the ship with a member of the governor's staff.

The soldiers watched as the constables cleared the crowd from the edge of the wharf and proceeded up the gangplank. After a brief exchange the captain of the *Atlas* made his way forward. Williams saw the governor's man hand an envelope over to the captain who opened it, read it and then began remonstrating with the small party of constables and the governor's man.

'By God,' Smith said.

'What's happening?' Newbank said.

'I think the Governor has just issued an order refusing permission for the ship to offload. Chances are it's a no to selling any spirits. Knowing the way the American's see us they will have a cargo mostly made up of spirits. This is a disaster,' Smith said. 'Tom, George, get back to the barracks and tell one of the officers what just happened.'

'What do we do Nate?' Williams asked.

'We wait and see what happens.'

The crowd, sensing something was not right, began murmuring and pointing at the constables. Rumours started running, speculating that no grog would be allowed off the ship. The constables turned and marched down the gangplank followed by the governor's man. Together they walked to the side of one of the store houses adjacent to the wharf and hammered a small note to the wall.

Once they had moved away the crowd began to edge forward towards the store house. A hush fell as one of the crowd read the note. 'The Governor has ordered that no rum be allowed off the ship,' a male voice shouted.

A series of boos rose from the crowd. Most turned and looked for the small party of constables. The constables and the governor's man were clear of the crowd and heading up the hill towards the governor's mansion. Hearing the booing they quickened their pace dramatically.

'Take your coat and hat off Nate,' Williams said. As he spoke he unbuttoned his coat and took it off, turning it inside out so the distinctive red colour was less obvious. Smith copied him and then as Williams took off towards the *Atlas* followed.

'What are you doing Oli?'

'I'm dropping us in it of course Nate, now hurry up.'

Behind them the two soldiers could hear the loudmouths in the crowd taunting the constables. 'You had better get out of here quick,' and 'Why don't you come and tell us what this says.' Both taunts rang out loudly followed by cheering.

The constables turned a corner and disappeared from view and from the vitriol being shouted behind them.

Williams raced across the wharf and up the gangplank with Smith hot on his heels. They reached the deck and moved quickly towards a small party gathered around the captain. The Americans, seeing two unknown men, formed a protective barrier around their captain. Smith saw a couple of sailors disappear below decks only to reappear moments later with swords and pistols.

'Captain, we mean you no harm. We are with the military here. We are the ones that usually buy up large quantities of spirits,' Williams said.

'Stand down gentlemen,' the captain said in a hard Yankee accent. 'I have been told not to offload any spirits or other alcohol, however there is little other to trade.'

'Perhaps we can help you sir,' Williams said. 'It's best we not be seen talking to you here. In town there is a tavern, the King's Arms. Look for us there tonight after seven. Corporal Smith and I will be there together with a few of our soldiers. Look for the group wearing the redcoats. We can talk about other arrangements to buy and offload your merchandise,' Williams said.

'Thank you, and agreed. The King's Arms after seven it is,' said the captain. 'Now can we shield you amongst our sailors so you remain unseen?'

Williams looked around, unsure of the best way to get off the ship. Smith smiled. 'No need sir. Come on Oliver, let's take the maritime route,' Smith said. Smith and Williams walked to the far side of boat and looked around. There were a handful of water craft. Smith spied out Will Worrell's dinghy and called to him. Worrell quickly rowed over.

'Will we need a trip to Cockle Bay please. We can pay in spirits on arrival' Smith said.

'Happy to oblige you,' Worrel said.

With that the two soldiers scrambled over the side and into the dinghy. Worrell pulled quickly away from the *Atlas* before settling into a more gentle pace as his dinghy bobbed nearer the other maritime traffic.

'What time did you agree to meet the captain?' Lieutenant Minchin said.

'Seven o'clock Lieutenant. I told him to look for Smith and me, and a couple of redcoats.'

'Well done, that was good thinking. And you are sure you weren't seen?'

'As sure as can be under the circumstances. Besides which, if someone did recognise us, I doubt they would inform on members of the Corps. Not even the governor's reward would be enough incentive. And they would all but ensure that the American liquor sails away, and no-one really wants that do they,' Williams said. 'Nor would they want to make an enemy of us.'

Smith watched the exchange with a growing sense of affection of Williams. The corporal had a strong place in the Corps; the old hand who loved military life but was still one of the boys. Smith knew his fortunes had never been better since befriending Williams. He found himself again impressed by William's intelligence.

'Well then lads,' Minchin said, 'you had best go pretty yourselves up. You have an appointment tonight.'

'It is early afternoon, we don't need to rush,' Smith said.

'You are going to need all afternoon to do something with that ugly mug of yours Smith.' Minchin said.

'This ugly mug is what comes from working with you Lieutenant, but I will do the best I can.'

Minchin grinned at the Corporal. 'Careful,' he said in a good-natured tone. He waited until the two soldiers had left and then looked at Johnston and Davies. 'Young Williams is a quick one. Thanks to him we may be able to get our hands on that rum after all.'

'Yes, he did very well. He is quickly becoming a genuine asset to us,' Johnston said. 'Now are you both comfortable letting him and Smith take the lead on this, or should one of you be there tonight too?'

Davies and Minchin looked at each other. 'There is no harm in being there. After all, even officers of the Corps get thirsty. I will take a few the men with me, just to be on the safe side,' Minchin said. 'Besides, my presence may help convince this American that we are serious about taking his load off his hands.'

'Good. Let's aim for ten shillings a gallon as our ceiling. We can turn that around for twenty shillings a gallon, the standard shares applying,' Johnston said. 'In the meantime I will write the usual letters to King, asking that we be able to offload some of the spirits. Better that he thinks he is in control.'

'It would be far easier for everyone if the governor just took a position and maintained it,' Minchin said. 'One day he bans whole ship loads. Then the next he allows us to buy overs on what he had previously set as our annual limit. Each time he confuses more people and gives everyone a reason to hate him. I wager that this ban will well and truly have the people against him.'

'Should we encourage that sentiment?' Davies said. 'If he loses the support of the people he is finished as governor. We did Governor Hunter in, maybe this is our chance to do King in too.'

Johnston looked out the window towards the parade ground. The two lieutenants exchanged a knowing look while they waited. If a charge up a hill towards an armed enemy were needed both men knew Johnston would not hesitate, but on matters of politics the major was likely to take a cautious approach.

'We wait and see what the public reaction is. I do not think it wise to push something that is not there. I would rather stoke the fire than try to start it,' Johnston said.

'We'll keep our ears open for any dissent,' Davies said. He shot a glance at Minchin who shrugged his shoulders to say what else were you expecting from the major.

Williams and Smith were already inside the tavern with Conner and Newbank when Lieutenant Minchin and a small party of red-coated New South Wales Corps soldiers entered. The noise subsided for a few moments and most of the eyes in the tavern followed the soldiers as they moved near to where Williams and his friends sat.

Several groups of convicts, settlers and emancipated freemen moved. Two of the redcoats pulled newly abandoned chairs over and sat. Two more soldiers went over to a table where four convicts were seated on a bench. The convicts stood up and walked away, the soldiers carrying the bench over to their comrades and the two then sitting on it. Most of the people in the tavern went back to drinking but kept a wary eye on the redcoats.

Corps soldiers were known to drink at the tavern but not often. Most stayed and drank in the barracks once tattoo had sounded on the bugle at the end of the day, recalling the soldiers to barracks. Some socialised in nearby soldiers' houses dotted around the barracks. Despite the fact that the Corps did not drink at the King's Arms often, most knew to stay out of the way of thirsty soldiers.

Shortly after seven a group of men entered the tavern. They looked around and then two disappeared out the door. A few moments later the two returned with a third man.

'Here he is,' Smith said. He got up and wandered over to the newcomers. 'Haven't seen you around these parts. Where are you men from?'

'We arrived today on the ship,' one of them said.

'So you are Americans are you? How about you share a round with us and we make our peace about the war,' Smith said, pointing to the soldiers.

'We don't want any trouble,' one of the Americans said.

'Nor do we, but it is always nice to hear news from elsewhere in the world. Come join us,' Smith said. He glanced around the room and saw that no one was paying any attention. Had someone been listening the little charade would be enough to convince them that the soldiers were simply being friendly.

'We would be most obliged,' said one of the men who Smith recognised as the captain of the *Atlas*. 'John Miller of Conneticut. 'Pleasure to meet y'all.'

Smith quickly provided the introductions for himself, Williams and the other soldiers and then shepherded Miller and his compatriots towards the bar.

Both sides made a good show of getting to know one another and buying a round. The captain told the soldiers the news from the Americas and what they knew of the situation in Europe with Bonaparte and the French.

The large group were well into the third round of drinks when Smith sensed that most in the tavern had lost any interest in the Americans. He nodded to Williams and the two casually moved to sit either side of the American captain.

'So shall we get down to business?' Williams said.

'We had heard that this port was the place to sell spirits and wine. It was a terrible disappointment to find out otherwise,' the American said.

'On behalf of the Corps first let me apologise for that. What you had heard is correct - this is the place to sell and we are the ones who can do you a fine deal. However, from time to time the governor here changes his mind about the sale of spirits. Unfortunately you ran into port when he is down on drinking. Having said that there are ways that we can help lighten your load for your return trip.'

The American smiled. 'That would be most agreeable. We have spirits aboard, and a smaller consignment of Californian wine,' Miller said.

'Good. I think we can manage most if not all of that. The usual price here is six shillings a gallon for the wine and seven shillings for the spirits,' Williams said.

'I would be happy to offload this cargo to you, however I do not want to sail away feeling I have been robbed blind. Ten shillings for the wine and twelve for the spirits and you have a deal.'

Williams saw Lieutenant Minchin, listening nearby, shake his head. Williams knew those prices were unacceptable and for a moment resented the Lieutenant's presence.

'We couldn't stretch that far with our finances. Besides, there is no-one else in the colony who could possibly take even a tenth of your cargo. The governor has placed you in an awkward position.'

Williams let that hang in the air while he picked up his mug and slowly drank a swig of wine. He swirled the last of the wine in the bottom of the mug then slowly placed it down, looking around the room. A poor negotiator would have cracked by now, yet the American held his tongue. Williams could see Minchin looking at him and urging him to talk. Sometimes the best trick to these things is silence Williams reminded himself.

'Nine for the wine and eleven for the spirits,' Miller said. It was a fair deal and a good one but it didn't manage the ten shilling per gallon ceiling. Williams still had an ace up his sleeve and chose to play it.

'What are you intending to buy for the return trip?' Williams asked.

The American turned and looked at Williams, thrown by the change in tack. Before he could answer Williams jumped in.

'We can provide a letter of introduction to a seal trader in Hobart, which is not too far down the coast. With that letter I am sure you could get a good price. There may be some whale oil in it too.'

'I thought that this colony was under the auspices of the East India Company?'

'It is, but given we enforce that ruling I think that problem can go away. So my offer with the letter is eight shillings for the wine and nine for the spirits.'

There was a long silence. Miller mulled over his options which were few. He had it on good authority that Port Jackson was the place to sell large quantities of spirits and wine, yet had arrived to find that option forbidden. He could sail away and try another port in Asia but his odds of a profit lowered the longer he went without a sale. And all the traders knew that Sydney was the place to sell liquor. If he couldn't offload it here, where else Miller wondered. The letter of introduction, while no guarantee was tempting. He had not intended to buy goods here, but even a small consignment of seal furs or whale oil could make this a tidy voyage.

'How do we get the cargo off the ship?'

'Stay in port a few days, write to the governor begging he change his mind. He won't and then you sail off having sold anything else of value. You leave the governor a letter asking that he inform the American consulate in London of this new arrangement and saying you will pass this new policy on to your fellow captains.

'You then sail down the coast and stop at Botany Bay - it is only a few miles south once you pass out of the heads. We will organise to meet you there and take the cargo off your ship.'

Again the American paused. He ran through the same arguments in his head as before and saw no other option.

'You have a deal sir,' he said.

Williams smiled. He saw Minchin smile too. It was the first time anyone has called him sir. Williams liked the sound of it.

Over the next few days a flurry of letters were dispatched to and from Government House. Captain Miller of the *Atlas* wrote begging leave to offload his cargo of wine and spirits. Major Johnston wrote asking that the Corps be allowed to handle the *Atlas's* cargo of alcohol.

Governor King wrote back to each man refusing their requests. 'The good moral health of the colony demands that less rum be consumed,' he wrote. King cited the Irish rebellion and the mood of the people as reasons for his decision.

The *Atlas* crew sold a small cargo of trade goods, then after a week slipped her mooring and headed out of the harbour. Within an hour of the *Atlas* clearing the harbour the first poem appeared, next to King's original note on the storehouse banning the importation of liquor.

Why oh why cruel Governor King
The thirsty people did sing
Can we not have a tot
Of fine American rum
To fill our parched tum
That is not asking a lot

If Governor King had assumed that the mood of the people justified banning the importation of rum from the *Atlas*, he could not have been more wrong. The main thing affecting the mood of the people was seeing the *Atlas* sail away with a full hold of liquor.

That night the taverns were full when the a series of poems started to circulate. There were at least half a dozen, all smearing the governor. In trying to maintain the moral health of the colony King had instead unleashed a wave of defamatory and morally dubious sentiment, all aimed at himself.

Lieutenants Davies and Minchin sat in the mess hall of the barracks drinking a Cape red wine when reports of the poems came to them.

'Gentlemen, if I may interrupt, I thought you should see this,' Sergeant Major James Cox said. Cox handled over a small bundle of papers. Minchin and Davies read them, the smiles on their faces spreading wider with each new page.

'Where did you get these Sergeant Major?' Davies said.

'A few were posted around the town, the rest one of the lads brought back from one of the taverns. Evidently all the taverns are circulating the papers,' Cox said.

'Thank you for bringing these to our attention,' Davies said. As he spoke Minchin got up and fetched a cup and poured a full glass. 'Have a drink before you go.'

'Thank you,' Cox said, before he drained the glass in one long go. The two officers watched him walk out.

'Seems like on this occasion the major got it right; it was best to wait and see what happened,' said Minchin.

'I suspect that we will not have to do anything such is the mood of the people. A toast, to the sound judgment of the people of New South Wales,' Davies said.

Minchin touched his mug to Davies's and drank, before looking out the window. 'I wonder how the lads are going over at Botany?'

Over the previous few days groups of two and three soldiers had quietly slipped out of the barracks, each carrying a small bundle of gear. None of the soldiers wore uniforms. Williams, Smith, Conner and Newbank left the barracks separately before meeting up down at the wharves.

They waited a few minutes before Will Worrell shuffled over. 'Will how are you travelling?' Smith asked.

'"Well enough Corporal Smith, and yourselves?' Worrell said. Before giving the troops time to reply he continued on, 'I have two good boats ready, neither too large, both sea worthy. So where are we heading?'

'Need to know Will, and best that you don't know till we are on the water. Who is captaining the boats?' Smith said.

'Me one and my brother-in-law Dick the other. He can be trusted.'

'Good. Then let's go. We have a bit of the trip in front of us.'

Smith and Williams boarded the larger of the two boats under Worrell's captaincy, Conner and Newbank the other under Dick Brace's command. 'Out the heads please captain,' Smith said.

The boats headed out of the harbour, reaching the heads in good time. The gentle swell of the harbour met the rolling pitch of the ocean and soon the two ships were bobbing up and down.

'Where to now Corporal?' Worrell said.

'We want to go to Botany Bay, but let's head north and then out to sea away from prying eyes if you may Ca'pn.'

The two small boats looked tiny against the stunning cliff-tops of the harbour heads. The boats turned and started sailing north. Williams felt the familiar feeling of seasickness come on, the inside of his head pitching out of time with the ocean waves. He closed his eyes and tried to sleep, but soon felt his insides stop churning and start running up his throat. He barely made the side of the boat before throwing up.

'Better to get it out early, you'll feel better now,' Worrell said. Williams turned and looked at him, smiled, then threw up again.

The two boats sailed up the coast for a short distance and then headed out to sea before turning south and sailing the short distance to Botany Bay.

As more men slipped out of the barracks, the officers of the Corps encouraged those men left to head into town of an evening, when the drinking began, and be sure to be seen at a number of taverns, but not to get drunk. 'The idea,' said Lieutenant Minchin,'is to be seen, so it looks like business as usual. This will give the lads heading out to organise things at Botany Bay some cover.'

Next came a messenger with urgent news. A surveying party, bribed by the Corps to provide some juicy information, reported finding a large distilling operation south of Sydney near Botany Bay. Governor King had spent much of his time in charge sending out exploration parties large and small, by foot and by boat, to map the area around Sydney. What better story to provide the governor than matching two of his favourite themes, mapping the local area and stamping out the trade in rum, Johnston said.

The major sent an urgent note to the governor, outlining the finding of the still, expressing concerns about the mood of the people and suggesting that he send out a patrol to investigate. Johnston pointed to the mood in Sydney and suggested that rather than reduce the number of constables in Sydney, the Corps go and burn down the still. The governor agreed and a patrol under the command of Sargent Major Whittle with a dozen troops was sent to investigate.

The patrol marched out of the barracks and wound its way through the streets of Sydney, crossing the Tank Stream and heading east before turning south. The equipment they carried, including tents, did not attract much attention. The patrol would need to locate the surveying party and then carry out surveillance of the still until those responsible showed up. That could take several days.

As soon as the patrol cleared Sydney and were out of sight Whittle stopped the patrol. 'Right lads, enough of the subterfuge. We are now bound for Botany Bay.' The group laughed and burst into a rendition of 'Bound for Botany Bay'. The march took the best part of two days. Once they arrived at Botany Bay they found the campsite set up by the non-uniformed soldiers who had already left the barracks. The camp was beneath the large sand dunes, out of the sight of any passing ships and well away from any known roads and settlements.

'Right lads, I want a good perimeter, half a mile. No-one comes near here. Once the ships are in and the cargo transferred we will head off again,' Whittle said.

The two boats captained by Worrell and Dick Brace made the trip down the coast line without incident. Once at Botany

Bay they anchored just inside the sheltered waters and began the wait for the *Atlas*. After several hours the *Atlas* bobbed up on the horizon, then dropped beneath it again. This pattern was repeated for several minutes before the American trader became clearly visible. An hour later the small boat captained by Worrell sailed out and pulled up alongside the *Atlas*.

'Lovely to see you gentlemen here,' Captain Miller said.

'Good to see you too,' Williams said. He swallowed hard, trying not to throw up again in the deeper water. 'If you follow us, we will lead you in. The waters in the bay are deep so if you steer our course you will find a safe anchorage.'

They entered the bay and made for the large sand dunes to the southern end of the sheltered waters. Worrell sailed the smaller boat through the middle of the channel and around to an anchorage just off the shore from the camp. The *Atlas* followed closely behind. Waiting on the beach were the soldiers who had walked out of the barracks along with Whittle's patrol. Once the anchors were down Williams and Smith rowed across to the *Atlas* and half the payment was made.

Offloading of the cargo using the small dinghies on all three boats took many hours. A quarter of the cargo was transferred to each of the smaller boats, with half going ashore. A temporary depot was established to house this cargo, where it would stay for some time. Smith and Williams stayed aboard the *Atlas* while the transfer was completed, chatting with Miller.

'Could you not get enough boats?' the American said, pointing to the boats going ashore.

'We decided it best to hold some of the supply back,' Williams said. 'If we flood Sydney with grog over the next couple of weeks it will be obvious where we got it from. That won't be a problem for you, but it could be for us.'

'Besides, when the supply is low the price goes up and that can only be a good thing if you know where to get more. We will transfer this back to Sydney gradually, and let a few of the local merchants sell it too.'

'It sounds as though you gentlemen have done this before?'

'Buying after a ship has had its cargo banned is a first for us. Usually we buy once ships have docked in Sydney,' Williams said. 'As a favour please don't go talking about this. We would rather this arrangement stay discreet, for your benefit and ours.'

'Of course.'

The final transfers were completed, the remainder of the payment made and the letter of introduction to one of Hobart's leading seal and whale traders delivered. Worrell, Smith and Williams led the *Atlas* out of Botany Bay and turned north while the large American ship turned south.

Conner and Newbank waited two days in Botany Bay before heading back to Sydney. Like Worrell, Brace would sail out to sea then north, skirting the heads before sailing towards shore and approaching the harbour from the north.

The boat carrying Smith and Williams bypassed Sydney Cove and anchored in Cockle Bay. Over the next few nights a number of soldiers from the barracks rowed out in small tenders and took consignments of rum and wine ashore. Some were delivered to local taverns, with most of the con-signments stored in nearby warehouses. All the men kept a small amount for themselves. Two nights after that boat first anchored at Cockle Bay the second boat arrived, with Conner and Newbold aboard. The whole process of offloading was repeated.

Williams and Smith had disembarked once back in Cockle Bay. They did not walk back to the barracks, instead heading down towards Sydney Cove. They stopped at the Londoner, a tavern run by Henry Adams. Like many tavern owners Adams held a public licence to serve liquor. The number of licences issued each year varied enormously, from around sixty to over one hundred.

Most public houses were little more than shacks where convicts and freemen could buy liquor of all descriptions. A number of taverns were run out of homes. Some of the liquor sold was imported, some distilled illegally and some bought via local suppliers. The Londoner was at the upper end of the menu of taverns and public houses, being run from a building made of sandstone and wood.

Williams and Smith walked to the bar counter, spying Adams standing and talking to one of his labourers behind the bar. Smith recognised him as a convict whose sentence was due to expire in March 1805. He was clearly out to make a go of it, working with an industrious energy growing more common amongst the convict class.

Adams walked over to the two soldiers. 'What can I get you two fine gentlemen of the Corps?'

'I think the real question is what can we two fine gentlemen get you,' Smith said. Adams took the hint and directed the three to a quiet backroom that doubled as a cellar. Williams was pleased to see it closer to empty than full.

'Nathaniel, Oliver, pleased to see you. So you are selling?'

'That we are. We have barrels of rum and wine for twenty shillings, take it or leave it.'

'Twenty shillings is a bit steep. Can you lower it to fifteen shillings for each?'

Williams looked at Smith. 'Is the King's Arms our next stop, and then the Malting Shovel at Kissing Point? That's James Squire's establishment. He knows a good deal when he see it.'

Williams began walking out, but stopped at the door and leant with his back against it. Smith moved with a speed that came from years of training. Within a moment he had Adams shoved against the wall, his throat being squeezed in a head-lock, constricting his breathing.

'When the Corps offers you manna from heaven you fucking well get on your knees and say thank you, that price is more than fair. What you do not do is seek a better price. Do we understand each other? Well? Answer me.'

'Nate, you may want to let him breathe, that will help him answer,' Williams said. Smith released the pressure a little.

'I understand,' Adams said between gulps of air.

'Good. Have your man come around to the warehouses at Cockle Bay tomorrow evening, we will have someone waiting,' Smith said.

'Looking at your supplies I think it safe to put you down for a hundred gallons of rum and wine. And when that is gone let us know and we can arrange more. But make sure you let us know,' Williams said. 'We wouldn't want to show up and find out you are short of supplies when we have enough to go around. Besides this is quality wine and rum and given that we are offering it to only five taverns to start with you stand to make a tidy profit yourself.'

The two soldiers walked out of the room, closing the door behind them. Adams breathed heavily for a number of minutes, gradually regaining his composure. Then he forced a smile and walked out to see how the evening's trade was going. He hoped it was good, he needed the money.

Smith and Williams visited four more taverns over the next two nights, with negotiations being far more congenial. They organised sales of five hundred gallons of wine and rum at twenty shillings a gallon to each of the five taverns they visited.

At a purchase price of eight shillings a gallon for the wine and nine shillings for the rum they were making twelve shillings profit on the wine and eleven on the rum, totalling 11,500 shillings.

Deliveries were made via convict labour hired on the afternoon, once the convicts had finished their government duties. The convicts travelled to the warehouses in groups and then back to the taverns to deliver the liquor. Word quickly passed around that liquor was available.

Sargent Major Whittle's patrol arrived back in Sydney to find the colony alive with energy and enthusiasm. 'Lads, I dare say that the grog is flowing. We will head to the barracks and report to the officers of our find.'

Whittle's report to Lieutenant Minchin did not need stating. Minchin knew what was going to be said. The letter from Johnston to Governor King had been drafted even before Whittle's patrol had left the barracks more than a week before. Now that Whittle had returned it could be dispatched to the governor. Despite that Whittle, always a stickler for proper procedure outlined the patrol's activities.

'So Lieutenant, we found the remains of a large distilling operation, hidden in a small valley southeast of the colony. They were using the water supply that flows into Botany Bay, however, as is well known, that is a less than reliable source.

'The patrol clandestinely watched the area for a number of days in the hope that the distillers may return seeking to recover some equipment. After a week the patrol concluded that there was no longer point in waiting. The patrol entered the distilling camp and broke up the equipment that remained, burned it and then marched back to Sydney,' Whittle concluded.

'Thank you Sargent Major, a good job by all. Just one little thing. If anyone else asks you about this please don't repeat verbatim the major's report to the governor. It may raise suspicions,' Minchin said.

Whittle smiled. 'Apologies Lieutenant, I memorised the report before we left. I hadn't realised that what I said was what you had written. It sounds very good though.' Whittle spun around and left the room laughing. Minchin watched him go before he too burst out laughing.

Governor King hardly even glanced at Major Johnston's report on the illegal still. He was more concerned with the growing backlash from his decision to deny the *Atlas* permission to land its cargo of rum and wine. The poems that were circulating were continuing to grow in number and defamatory sentiment. King was many things, but a man of the people he was not.

He had decided to ban the Atlas from importing liquor after he proposed the idea to his aides. People were, he said, growing tired of public drunkeness. The fact that most of that drunkeness took place on the outskirts of town was conveniently ignored. So too overlooked was the fact that a person living in England was likely to drink more liquor than one living in New South Wales.

Instead one of the defining traits of government led King's decision; consensus for promotion. All the governor's aides were seeking to advance their careers and one did not advance by telling the most powerful man in the colony that he was a fool and out of touch with the people. Most of King's aides had enthusiastically seconded the proposal and the rest had offered tacit support. It wasn't until one of those aides ran into Government House fresh from banning the Atlas unloading its cargo, that King first got an inkling as to how badly he had misjudged the mood.

King had gone pale and quiet as the aide recounted the terrifying flight up the hill from the cove to Government House. It mattered not that the aide exagerated the pursuit by the crowd. The message was loud and clear, the people were deeply opposed to King's decision.

As letter after letter arrived at Government House begging the governor to have a change of heart King prevaricated. He could back down but then he would look a fool. If he confirmed the ban that would show him to be strong and unwavering. But would that further anger the people? A paralysis took hold of King as he weighed up the options. Finally he resolved that he would hold the course and reaffirm his announcement, but by then the poems were circulating. Each day idlers were milling about outside the gates to Government House. King watched them from his bedroom window. They were worming their way into his thinking. And a thought grew and grew in his head, that he had lost the people and they had begun to turn on him.

On one thing King was right. The people, who relied on alcohol to keep their spirits up, were no longer content to be lectured. Rum was a part of the life of the colony, fuelling work, numbing pains, washing away the frustrations caused by the colony having four men for every one woman. King's war on alcohol was seen by many as a continuation of the class wars that defined English life and its assault on the lower and criminal classes. One of the enduring freedoms of the colony was that class mattered a great deal less than in England.

A man who worked hard could better himself in New South Wales, even if only by having more than he would in England. Relationships may be fleeting. A man and woman sleeping together was enough to define them as husband and wife. That often only lasted until the merest excuse presented to leave one another. Women were left with little choice but to find a man to sleep with for protection. Some of these relationships worked, most did not. For women, the one difference from life in England was that they had the right to leave the relationship and to keep what they owned.

Rum was the glue that stuck the colony together, and instead of trying to ensure enough of it, Governor King wanted to end its consumption. In the minds of the people he wanted the colony to come unstuck from its present form and be remade to resemble a feudal England.

All of these sentiments poured forth in the poems circulating freely. One of the most popular captured the mood of many.

Stuck in New South Wales
With the rum not flowing
Because the Governor fails
To keep the liquor going

My woman up and left
I'm all out of luck
Sober and bereft
Unsure of my next fuck

We don't want a guvnor
To undo what we have made
Another toff and bore
To make our freedom fade

All around is malign
My head I need to dunk
In a gallon full of wine
And get forgetful drunk

February 1805

Oliver Williams was sprawled out on his bed watching some of his mates playing cards. He had learnt early on that the surest way to part with his money was through gambling. Whether it was the horse racing at the track at Hawkesbury or any of the games of chance at a hundred different venues the theme was constant; drinking, losing and fighting, usually in that order. The only time any of it surprised him these days was when the order changed, which it did occasionally.

Nate Smith looked carefully at his cards, longingly at the pot of money in the middle and then wistfully back to his cards. He has not got a winning hand, Williams thought.

Sure enough, Smith threw his cards down in disgust and muttered a string of obscenities under his breath as he walked away. The other men knew enough to let him go before they resumed. Williams waited a good ten minutes before he headed outside after Smith.

'Damn it Oli, I need something to happen. All this hanging around the barracks, waiting for who knows what. Each day just seems to be repeating over and over,' Smith said. He kicked at an imaginary resentment and then kicked again. 'This damn summer heat has it in for me, and there is still two months to go before things start to cool.'

Williams too felt the monotony. He kept busy with the Corps' bookkeeping. What must it be like for Smith and the others, he wondered, when everyday was the same. The trade in rum continued unabated, with the Corps sharing first option to buy liquor and trade goods with a handful of entreprenuers. Williams had proposed the arrangement to Minchin who had then relayed the idea to Johnston.

Together the three had met with Simeon Lord and Robert Campbell, along with a small group of traders. They had agreed upon a roster system, whereby each trader would get first pickings from the next arriving ship. Where there were long periods of no ships arriving, or large disparities in the size of cargoes, negotiations took place to ensure a degree of fairness. The alternative was a fight for each cargo, groups competing to outbid the others and things getting out of hand. As Williams put it to Minchin, 'We all get richer or a few of us get very rich and the rest don't'. So an agreement was entered into and everyone profited.

The Corps continued the trade in rum, their profits growing. They sold to a range of taverns and establishments. The governor had gone quiet, evidently in extremely poor health having just managed to survive the winter. Major Johnston was mostly on his farm in Annandale. The soldier's had little to do other than train. Some called it a routine, Smith called it hell.

'Nate, I know the days are dragging along.'

'I'm an old soldier and sometimes I need action. Something, anything.'

'Lets do the rounds. At least that will get us out and about for a time.'

Nathaniel Smith glared at Williams a long time. Then he smiled and agreed.

The two soldiers walked out of the barracks and headed towards the wharves. Their first stop was a market shop. More and more small traders were popping up all over Sydney, offering small goods, clothes and hardware and a range of finer merchandise. Several of the new arrivals were from India, Ravi Chandra being the first to set up shop. He had quickly fallen under the influence of the Corps as had most of his newly arrived countrymen.

'Good morning Ravi, how is business this fine morning?' Smith said. Ravi Chandra looked up. He stood before a shelf with bags of flour and boxes of tea that he had been tidying up. Chandra looked at Williams and Smith and swallowed hard.

'It is fine,' the Indian said in his subcontinental accent. 'I was not expecting you for another week. I have not yet sold all the rum so do not have the full payment for you.'

'Relax Ravi, we know you'll come good. We're simply enquiring as to how our investment is going,' Williams said.

Many of the Indian merchants that had arrived since the turn of the century traded in Indian wine, one of the staples of the colony. Williams had proposed to Johnston expanding the number of merchants selling rum. He had singled out the newly arrived Indian merchants as the best avenue.

'Either we get them selling rum or allow them to import Indian wine and sell it and become our competition. That cannot be a good thing for us. The number of people here in Sydney grows all the time, so let's increase the number of places our rum can be bought from,' Williams had said to Johnston.

Johnston had agreed. 'Do it, but quietly, we do not want to raise too much attention.' From there it had been simple. Smith, Conner, Newbank and Williams had visited Ravi Chandra and proposed a deal, that he sell rum supplied by the Corps. The usual rate was proposed, Chandra would sell it for twenty shillings a gallon, seventeen shillings would go to the Corps, the remainder to Chandra.

Williams still remembered how the Indian had reacted. 'This is hardly a fair or equitable arrangement, particularly as I can import wine cheaper and sell it for a greater profit.'

'Of course you can import your wine and sell it for a greater profit. But you might find your licence to sell wine revoked. Mr D'Arcy Wentworth, who issues the licences, is a good friend of the Corps. And of course if your licence is revoked your permission to import wine will be refused. Then where will you be?'

'Why Oli I think he would be completely dependent on us to sell any wine,' Tom Conner had chipped in.

'Fancy that. Completely at our mercy. That would be a predicament to be in,' George Newbank had said.

'Look Ravi, the more of our product you sell the more profit you will earn. And once that is sold you can sell your wine. Best of all, we can support your endeavours. We can let it be known in certain places that this is a good shop to buy at, but only if you are willing to be our partner,' Williams said.

From there it was a simple decision and so Ravi Chandra had begun to sell Corps rum. He was given a monthly quota, which he readily accepted. The handful of new Indian merchants that arrived with Chandra had followed his lead and entered into partnership with the Corps.

Williams always worried a little for Chandra. The poor man would sweat every time he and Smith came to visit. As he listened to Chandra talk about sales, Williams watched the beads of sweat form and roll down Chandra's forehead.

'So sales are going very well,' Chandra said, before he wiped the sweat away and smiled a wan smile. He tried not to look at his hand and then carefully tried to see without consciously moving his head, which only drew attention to what he was doing. 'Sorry Mr Williams, what was I saying?'

'You were telling us sales were going well, which is good to hear.'

'Yes, I am confident that all your rum will be sold by the week's end.' Chandra wiped more sweat away and smiled the same smile. Then he looked at his hand and back to Williams. 'Sorry Mr Williams, remind me of what I was saying.'

'The sales Ravi, the sales are going well.'

'Yes, very well.' Chandra self-conscously wiped his brow again.

'That all sounds good Ravi, we'll see you next week,' Williams said as they walked out of the shop. The two soldiers visited the other three Indian merchants and then stopped by a few taverns, including a visit to Henry Adams at the Londoner.

'Henry, how are you?' Smith asked.

'Well Nathaniel. Good to see you too Oliver. Can I get you a drink to refresh you both on this fine afternoon?' Adams swallowed hard and hoped that the cheery tone carried through over his distaste at seeing the two soldiers.

'That would be wonderful,' Williams said. 'Now Henry, what do you know?'

'That business is good. My important suppliers will be paid on time and in full. All in all things could not be much better.'

'That is good to hear. You will join us for a drink?' Smith said.

'Of course. By the way, have you heard about the troubles up the Hawkesbury?'

Smith immediately straightened in his chair. 'What troubles?' he almost shouted.

'Some of the outlying farmers have been complaining of thefts and raids by Aboriginal war parties. It is not the usual pattern of large groups, you know the type that attract attention and demand immediate action. These are evidently small groups. A band of Hawkesbury settlers were here a couple of nights ago. They are hoping to see the governor.'

'I doubt King will do much, he is still recovering from illness,' Williams said with a smile.

'Are the settlers still here?' Smith asked.

'That I do not know. They were staying at the boarding house on Bridge Street just over the Tank,' Adams said.

'Drink up Oli, we have a stop to make.'

The boarding house was dark and smelt of woodsmoke and sweat. The owner sat in a corner on an old rocking chair, newspaper in hand. He did not look up from his reading when Smith and Williams entered, instead he pointed to a small, crudely written sign advertising the going rates for a room. After making their enquiries, Smith and Williams found that the Hawkesbury settlers were still in town. They waited a while until a small group of poorly dressed men entered. The owner looked up from his newspaper and nodded to Smith.

The settlers saw the two redcoats rise up from the bench on which they had been sitting and walk towards them, and uncertain of what that meant they simply stood motionless.

'Are you the gentlemen from the Hawkesbury region?' Smith asked. He noted their reticence. 'I am Corporal Smith of the New South Wales Corps. This is Private Williams. We were told you have been having some problems with the Aborigines up in the Hawkesbury.'

'I am John Cable. I represent these men. And yes, we have been having Aborigines raid the outlying farms. We have been trying to see the guv'nor but he does not seem interested in the problem, beyond issuing orders that we work together against the natives.'

'Let me assure you that we are willing to hear of your problems,' Williams said. 'Are you able to come to the barracks tomorrow morning?'

Cable looked at the other men who all smiled and nodded. 'Good. Then we will see you then,' Williams said. Smith turned to walk out. Williams delayed a moment, looking at the paper being read by the owner of the boarding house. 'Have you spoken to the newspaper, to the *Gazette*? They might be interested in this and could help exert some influence with the governor.'

'Thank you. We will go to see them now.'

Major Johnston rode into the barracks early in the afternoon in a one man buggy that was his only personal indulgence. At his age, Johnston found it far easier than riding a horse and more fun too. He would ride carefully in Annandale or Sydney town but at speed on the empty roads between the two. For Johnston there were few greater thrills in life than to be seated in relative comfort while running at speed in the buggy.

He parked the buggy and one of the soldiers came out with feed and water for his horse. The major grinned at the soldier and offered a heartfelt thanks. Johnston was happy as he strode into the mess hall. He had enjoyed the ride, the summer day was delightfully warm and the governor was deeply unpopular. For George Johnston life was good.

The major spied Lieutenant Minchin. 'A fine afternoon to you on a fine day.'

'And to you too Major.'

'I wanted to come to Sydney to see the mood of the people. In Annandale and surrounds the talk is entirely of the governor and his poor standing. You could make an old soldier very happy by telling me that things are the same here.'

'Oh I assure you Major, the news I have will make you more than happy. Ecstatic might be closer to it. The governor has taken a great deal of the poems and gossip circulating to heart, and has fallen ill as a result. The word is that he wrote to London some time ago seeking a leave of absence,' Minchin said.

'Really. Well that will teach the old fool to take us on,' Johnston said. 'He has spent years trying to break us and at the end of it all what does he have to show for it? The hatred of the people and the scorn of even the lowliest convict.'

'There is more though,' Minchin said.

'Tell me he is not trying to convict people for writing poems? Not again.'

'No, its not like King's attempts to convict Captain Kemp, and Hobby and Bayly for libel over some limericks, just as he did a few years back.'

Johnston smirked. 'Now those were fine days. King really thought he had us, and would end up with Kemp, Bayly and Hobby guilty in court. He genuinely believed that I would sit idly by while he stitched up our men. Imagine what he would have done then. He would have come after the rest of the Corps and cleaned the officers out one by one. Well we showed him. Our lads cleared of charges. His man tried by court-martial and convicted,' Johnston said.

'One of your finest hours Major. You defended the Corps and showed everyone the tyrant that King pretends not to be.'

Johnston waved Minchin on. The lieutenant took a drink of wine and continued.

'At that time a number of letters went to England decrying King's leadership. Well Mac has written to say that King is entirely on the nose in England and has lost the support of the authorities back there. Mac has also been having a quiet word in a number of ears pushing the case against King. Word from Mac is that the governor is to be recalled. Evidently King wanted a leave of absence to return and act as chief witness to an enquiry he suggested, for the purpose of looking into us. Instead the leave of absence has been taken as evidence that he is no longer up to the task of governing.'

'Let that be a lesson to all. When you go to war with the Corps you had best be prepared to see it through.' Johnston sat back a moment, letting what he had heard linger. 'So King is done. What else does Mac say?'

'He is cleared to head back to Sydney and is bringing a number of merinos with him.'

'What on God's earth is a merino?' Johnston said.

'A type of sheep.'

'The only thing Mac loves more than himself and Elizabeth are his damn sheep. Well that should be a sight to see when he gets back,' Johnston said.

'Macarthur and his sheep. I suspect he loves them so much because they don't talk back,' Minchin said. Johnston laughed hard.

'And because he thinks they will make him richer than any man before,' Johnston said.

The conversation was interrupted by Sergeant Major Whittle. 'Begging your pardon sirs, Corporal Smith and Private Williams would like a word.'

'What mischief have those two got into this time?' Johnston said.

Minchin grinned at the Major. 'Well at least it should be entertaining.'

Smith and Williams came into the mess, which was surprisingly cool given the heat of February in Sydney.

'So, let's hear it. Should I fetch the major a wine or do you have good news to report?' Minchin said.

'Go on Oli, tell them,' Smith said.

'This was your idea, you tell them.'

'Someone start talking or I will have you cleaning my buggy,' Johnston said.

Smith nudged Williams who began speaking. 'We were doing the rounds when Henry Adams told us that there has been some trouble up the Hawkesbury way. It appears the natives have been conducting raids. It turns out there is a group of farmers from up Hawkesbury and Windsor way in town. They are seeking to petition the governor to do something about it. The governor has hinted at some action on the matter, involving orders that the locals work together on the problem which is not really any help at all. So we, well we met the farmers and suggested that they come here tomorrow to meet with some of the officers to talk about the matter. You know, give them a hearing. We also suggested that they talk to the *Gazette*.'

A long silence fell over the room. Smith shifted from one foot to the other, Williams remained calm.

'We were thinking that it is not really our place to do something, it is up to the civil authorities, the constables up there. But I thought, we thought, that at least we can hear them out. We could suggest to the governor that he send us up there. I don't think that will happen, but at least as the Hawkesbury men see it, the responsibility, if nothing is done, falls on the Governor,' Williams said.

'That's right, that is what we were thinking. Good thinking Oli,' Smith said.

There was another long silence. Johnston stared at the two men. He was unsure if Smith was nervous or needed to relieve himself, the man was shifting from side to side so rapidly. What he knew with certainty was who the brains of the two was. As usual Williams had got it right. He let them stand in silence for a few more moments.

'Lieutenant I take it from this report that it's best I stay the night here and meet these settlers tomorrow. Well done lads. Sergeant Major see these men get an extra ration of rum tonight. And send a message to the settlers that we will meet them tomorrow at 10 am.'

John Cable and his fellow settlers arrived promptly at 10 o'clock. They were ushered to a small building across the parade ground.

'Gentlemen, Major George Johnston, at your disposal. I understand that you are having some conflicts with the natives up your neck of the woods.'

'That's right Major,' Cable said. 'I should say thank you for meeting with us. There are few here in Sydney who seem interested.'

'So tell me, what is the character of these raids?' Johnston said.

'Well Major, it is small groups mainly. That is what worries us. In the past it was usually a larger party and that brought out the constables and occasionally the soldiers like yourselves which then scared them away. But this is different. They hit farms, take what they can carry away. They seldom hurt anyone yet, but we reckon that might change if they continue to get bolder.'

'How large are these parties of natives?'

'Usually only a handful, sometimes as many as eight to ten, but never more. There are reports that a few people have been attacked or followed by small raiding parties on the roads too. And now we are coming up to the end of the corn season, which is ripening soon. That will probably only increase their activities,' Cable said.

'Is there anything you can do? A patrol of redcoats, begging your pardon if that is not the right term, a patrol would probably be enough to keep things in check.'

Johnston nodded his agreement. 'Unfortunately there is little I alone can do. My orders on such matters must come from the governor, otherwise this is the province of the constables and civil administration. And let me say gentlemen you know the temperament of my men as evidenced in the Irish uprising. We have the stomach for the fight, what we lack is the permission.

'So let me leave you with this assurance, I will personally write to the governor seeking a mandate to operate against any native groups that transgress the law. However, I am afraid that to do so we will need more augmentation of our forces. The governor will baulk at that request, but still we will make the request.'

The group talked for another half and hour, mulling over tactics and operational realities. Johnston offered all he could in this area, but without an armed force able to respond rapidly, things were in grave danger of getting out of hand.

Lieutenant Minchin escorted the group out.

'Gentlemen it was a pleasure to receive you, even if the circumstances are less than felicitous. Rest assured we will do what we can to influence the Governor. As I am sure you are aware he is currently more interested in rum trading. Let us hope that you are able to return to the Hawkesbury in peace and remain in that state with the natives.'

'Thank you again,' John Cable said as the group left. 'We will endeavour to keep you informed of situations up our way.'

Minchin strolled back across the parade ground to where Johnston sat. 'So that is probably the last we shall hear of it, but at least they will go home knowing that we are tied up in bureaucratic knots rather than unwilling to act.'

'Yes. Young Williams read it correctly. I think it time we consider that young man for advancement, don't you?'

'I wholeheartedly agree Major.'

In early April news came from the Hawkesbury that John Llewellyn, a former Corpsman granted eighty acres at Lower Half Moon Bend, had been attacked and killed by an Aboriginal raiding party. His convict servant John Knight, who had also been attacked, survived to tell the story which was reported in the *Gazette*. At the barracks Lieutenant Minchin began outlining what was known.

'Llewelyn and Knight were stopped for lunch when they were approached by Branch Jack, a local native. The native agreed to join them,' Minchin said.

'You mean John Llewelyn who used to be one of us?' Sargent Bremlow asked having only just walked in the room.

'Yes. The *Gazette* has more details. Branch Jack "had scarce ended his meal before he took an opportunity of seizing the settler's musket and powder, and by a yell summoned his companions, who instantly put the unfortunate settler to death, and left his servant, as they thought, in that state."

'It goes on. Listen, this details the attack. "About 20 others that had before concealed themselves…now came forward and discharged several spears at the unfortunate men, two of which entered the master's breast, who fell immediately."'

'My God,' Bremlow said, 'the poor bastard.'

'The report continues,' Minchin said. 'Knight must have been tough to survive this, speared in the chest, struck with a tomahawk. The paper says "each blow occasioning a dreadful wound." God, the native savages then threw him in the river thinking him dead. He was still alive and survived two days before someone passing on a boat found him.'

'Bloody hell,' Private Hutton said.

The room was silent.

Lieutenant Davies came rushing in. 'Lads, have you heard the news?'

'I just finished telling them about Llewelyn. I hope we get the job of hunting these bastards down.'

'I know about Llewelyn, it's in the papers. No about Adlum, Thynne Adlum. You remember Llewelyn and him were always side by side in anything the Corps did. Adlum is dead too, burnt alive in his hut by the same native party that killed Llewelyn. Adlum was on the next farm up the Hawkesbury river.'

'King is going to have to do something now,' Bremlow said.

'I hope you are right Sergeant,' Minchin said. 'King did nothing in February when those natives set their dogs on a flock of sheep. He didn't act when the two salt boilers were robbed of everything at Broken Bay. Surely even King must see that this is escalating.'

'The major wrote to King after those incidents requesting more troops and permission to sort things out. King is content to issue waffling orders and useless suggestions. I swear since he unleashed the fury of the mob on him King has all but given up,' Davies said.

'So what do we do, Lieutenant?' Williams asked.

'Unfortunately at this point there is nothing we can do. It is up to the settlers and constables up the Hawkesbury way to act.'

Only a few days later came reports of two more killings, this time of two stockmen on the Cumberland Plains. Further reports of boats being attacked on the Hawkesbury River arrived a few days after that. Then at the end of April came news that a settler, James Dunlop, had been seriously wounded in his home at Prospect.

'This cannot continue unabated. Something must be done,' Williams said to Smith after reading the *Gazette's* report on the Dunlop attack.

'He must do something. The Governor can't ignore this. Everyone is talking about it. People are on edge not sure of their safety.' Smith said. 'It's time to bring the soldiers into things.'

Two days later reports emerged of an attack on the government stock farm at Seven Hills. 'What does the report say Oli,' Smith said, handing over a copy of the *Gazette*.

'No one was hurt but it says here that "after launching several spears at the hut-keeper, happily none of which took effect" for which the hut-keeper is probably very thankful,' Williams added, 'it says they "contented themselves with stripping the little habitation, with the whole contents of which they made off.'"

'I bet the hut-keeper was less than contented,' Smith said. 'The worry is that many of the settlers are armed with muskets yet that is not a deterrent. It's time that we were the deterrent.'

The mood in the colony was becoming fearful. The *Gazette* pushed the matter relentlessly, with headlines asking for action. Johnston continued to write to the governor, asking for more troops and permission for a detachment to travel to the Hawkesbury.

Finally, as April ended, King could idle no longer. Williams was sitting in the mess hall going over the books with Major Johnston and Lieutenant Minchin when Davies and a handful of soldiers came running in. Davies had a copy of the *Gazette* that he waved about.

'King has finally acted. He has said a detachment will be sent to the outer settlements. The paper says that no natives are to be suffered to approach the grounds of any dwellings of settlers until the murderers of Llewelyn and Adlum are given up. There is more too. Settlers are required, the paper says, to "assist each other in repelling those visits,"' Davies said.

'What does that mean Major?' Private Gillard asked.

'Well it means that the Governor is content to correspond with us via the newspaper, rather than directly. It also means that ordering settlers to assist each other will likely result in expeditions heading out from the Hawkesbury to find those responsible. All of which leaves the settlements undermanned and vulnerable. Every time the governor gets involved in something he makes it worse, not better.

'Lieutenant Davies, I want you to get a detachment together now and get a boat and get up the Hawkesbury as quickly as you can. I don't want any large parties heading out to find the natives responsible without at least a few of the Corps with them. Make sure some of your party stay close to the settlements and try to keep most of the settlers at their homes. At this rate the governor will have half the Hawkesbury wandering the bush with no one left to protect the settlements.'

'Yes sir. What will you do Major?' Davies said.

'I think I need to call on the governor, ensure that he understands that we cannot have the entire Corps heading up there and leaving Sydney and Parramatta defenceless. I will try to get a few small detachments to work with local constables at Cumberland and Windsor to ensure the settlers are protected. Now you best be on your way.'

Davies looked around at the men in the room, who amounted to no more than eight soldiers excluding officers.

'Right you're with me. Fetch me Corporal Smith and three more men. Get your gear together and be ready to march out in half an hour. Private Williams, you and Smith organise a boat for us, something quick. We will march from here to the wharves at Sydney Cove and meet you there.'

'Yes sir,' Williams said.

'Lieutenant Davies, given you will have only one corporal, I suggest we make a temporary promotion of Williams here to corporal. Do you have any objections?' Johnston said

'None at all Major, an excellent idea. Corporal Williams, congratulations. Now let's get moving.'

As Williams stood up and made to leave Johnston gently tugged at his sleeve. 'Don't let this go to your head son. Keep doing what you have been doing and we may make this a more permanent arrangement once you return.'

Williams flushed a little. 'Thank you Major.' Then he grinned widely and turned and raced out.

In the bunk house men were calmly assembling their kit. Most had weapons and a basic field kit ready to go. The mood of the colony was such that even hardened soldiers felt the odd flicker of fear with each new report. Several of the soldiers sat quietly saying a prayer. It was one thing to hear the reports, another to contemplate going out into the bush to fight the natives. That was their territory and most of the soldiers knew it.

Smith stood ready. He had been waiting for this action for a good two months. When he saw Williams enter the bunkhouse he walked over to his friend.

'So it appears I can no longer order you around corporal. I suspect it won't be too long before I have to salute you. You are going places. Just remember me when you get there.'

'Thanks Nate. Couldn't have done it without you and the boys supporting me. Now let's get that boat.'

The two Corporals headed down to the cove. They put the word out for Will Worrell. Within a few minutes Worrell's brother-in-law, Dick Brace came over. 'Will is laid up this morning gents, can I help?'

'We need a boat to transfer a dozen soldiers up to the Hawkesbury settlements today. Can you organise that?' Williams asked.

'Of course, but it would be best to leave sooner rather than later.'

'The lads are only a few minutes behind us, so we can leave within the hour.'

'Good. I must say that there are more than a few sailors who won't head up those waters any more. With you lads aboard though ... well we may even get lucky and find a few of the black bastards responsible.'

Brace disappeared after leaving directions on where to meet him. Williams and Smith waited for the remainder of the detachment.

'Looks like we are getting dropped in it again Nate. Don't look so excited.'

'Is it that obvious? Finally a chance for some action, for something different than the everyday. The soldier's lot boyo, monotony followed by action. I wouldn't have it any other way.'

'Here comes the lieutenant and the lads.'

The Corps detachment made a grand parade of it, letting all and sundry know they had finally been granted permission by the governor to sort things out up Hawkesbury way. Brace met the men by his boat and soon had them underway. It took most of the day to reach the settlements. Unfortunately for Brace his wish to encounter a raiding party went unfulfilled. Once at the settlements Lieutenant Davies and Corporal Williams visited the constable's office but found it empty, so the two soldiers tried the largest of the local taverns.

'Can you tell us where to find the constables?' Davies asked the proprietor, who pointed to a large group of men standing in one corner. Davies led the way over to hear a man addressing the group.

'I am putting together a party to hunt down these natives. We have engaged two Aboriginal guides, both Richmond Hill natives, to lead us,' the constable said. He looked up as Davies and Williams pushed through the gathering. 'Well, not before time the redcoats have arrived. I think you will need more than two of you though to sort this mess out.'

'My apologies for not getting here earlier. We are, unfortunately, in such matters, unable to act until the governor gives us orders. I am Lieutenant Davies, this is Corporal Williams,' Davies said.

'So people have to die before you show up,' the constable said.

'We have been petitioning the governor since February to come up here and help you sort this out,'

'T'is true chief,' said John Cable. 'We met Major Johnston in Sydney back in February and he wanted to help us then. This young lad here,' Cable said pointing to Williams, 'and another soldier found us and asked us to meet the major. Back then they said they needed the governor to issue orders and told us to go to the *Gazette* and seek support.'

'We only got the order from the governor earlier today,' Davies said. 'If you are putting a party together I will send a couple of my soldiers and have the rest remain here to protect the settlements. You will find the presence of the Corps here will deter the natives.'

The constable looked around the room at the gathering of men, sensing their liking for what Davies was saying. 'Alright then Lieutenant, better late than never. We meet at first light here tomorrow. Be armed and have supplies for a few days out.'

Most of the men quietly departed. Cable and two other settlers Williams remembered from the meeting in Sydney came over.

'Private Williams isn't it?' Cable said.

'Corporal Williams now. It's good to see you gentlemen again. This is Lieutenant Davies.'

'It's good to have you soldiers up here. We have been doing all we can writing to the governor. Why did he take so long to act?'

'He is a politician, and politicians only act when the public is overwhelming in their demand. Once settlers were being attacked here and at Cumberland he really had no choice,' Davies said. 'Now, pray tell, who was the Constable?'

'That is the chief constable, Andrew Thompson,' Cable said. 'He's a good man and means well, but he has been subjected to a lot of anger up here. He's the man responsible for ending these attacks. He too has been asking for help from Sydney for a long time. I hope you forgive him as I am sure he will welcome you tomorrow.'

A large group of men gathered at first light near the tavern. Davies and his Corps men marched up, greeting Cable. 'Gentlemen,' Davies said, 'my apologies we were not here weeks ago. From today our job is to protect your settlements, which we will do through regular patrols. I am sending Corporals Smith and Williams with your expedition and I wish you luck in hunting down these murderers. Chief constable, good hunting.'

Andrew Thompson watched as Davies walked to him and stuck out a hand. He hesitated a moment before grabbing Davies's hand and shaking it. 'Thank you Lieutenant. Right then, best we get to it.'

With that Thompson headed out of the settlements, taking up a place behind the two Aboriginal trackers. The task facing the group became clear within an hour. Much of the district was still flooded from heavy autumn rains. Instead of taking a direct route to the suspected hideout of the murderers, near Yarramundi, the expedition was forced to make a number of diversions. Thompson had established a baggage wagon and organised a boat to help with some of the river crossings.

At first most of the land they passed through had been cleared for farming, with settlers' farms nestled against the riverbanks. Most of the houses were situated well back from the river. The land was less open than that around Sydney. Trees surrounded farmland growing corn, offering ample cover for any approaching war parties. No wonder those parties could strike so quickly and then disappear, thought Williams.

As the group moved further from the settlements the bush became denser and the waterways harder to see until the guides warned the expedition of water immediately ahead.

'I think we should've brought our waders Oli,' Smith said.

'I think you're right. How many of these men do you rate?' Williams said.

'There are a few who look like they know what they are doing, but more than half I wouldn't get too near if we have to stand and fight. They are either likely to shoot us by mistake or knock us over in the rush to get away.'

The bush was becoming difficult to pass in many places and flood waters made the task treacherous. At times the going was easier, but much of the march was a slog. As they passed through the Green Hills one of the Aboriginal guides sat down and started to examine the bottom of his foot.

'Anything wrong?' Thompson asked.

'My foot, I think I have something in it. I will catch up,' the guide said.

The party continued on. Williams looked back and saw that the guide was gone. 'Smith, that guide, he's disappeared. We should tell Thompson?'

The two soldiers made their way up the column. 'Constable, the guide, he's gone,' Williams said.

Thompson too had noticed the guide disappear. 'I know. Quietly start letting the lads know that we should be ready for trouble.'

'Do you think he's betrayed us?' Smith said.

'I don't know. I suspect not, but you never know these days,' Thompson said.

There was a commotion in the bush just ahead. Men scattered in all directions. The missing guide and another Aboriginal stepped out of the bush. A number of the men raised their muskets.

'Don't fire, hold your fire,' Thompson yelled. Smith and Williams took up the call too. Soon most of the men either lowered muskets or returned to the column from the places they had run to hide. That didn't bode well if the column met a real war party.

'Thompson, what you doing here?' said the Aboriginal man who was not the guide. He stood with the characteristic stance of the native warrior, on one leg, leaning on a long spear, the other leg bent at the knee and resting on the weight-bearing leg.

'Yaragowby, I would ask the same of you?'

The man named as Yaragowby must have sensed the mood of the column. 'I am here under every friendship. I was hunting a kangaroo. Who you hunting?'

'So you give me every assurance of strict friendship then? You are not working with the natives waging raids and war?'

Yaragowby held up his hands. 'I am a friend to you Thompson. Last year I helped settlers against the Branch natives. I help now if you need.'

The two Aboriginal guides started talking loudly. 'We don't need your help,' one said. 'You should go, we are leading these men,' the other said.

Yaragowby looked at the two guides. Again he held his hands up. 'I will go, I have no need to join you unless you want.'

Thompson looked at Yaragowby. 'You may leave as our friend. Swear your assurances of strict friendship then you may return to your hunt.'

Yaragowby looked slowly up and down the column. A less trustful man than Thompson may have taken the slow searching look as an assessment of the strength of the expedition. Williams and Smith felt Yaragowby's eyes linger on them for a time.

'I don't trust this one Oli,' Smith said. 'He is too cool, too calculating.'

Thompson looked to where the two soldiers stood. 'He has helped us in the past against unruly natives. He is a man we can trust. Now Yaragowby swear your strict friendship.'

'I swear it to you Thompson.' Then he smiled and turned to go. No one stopped him as he disappeared into the bush.

Smith looked at Thompson. 'Do you trust him?'

'As I said, he has helped settlers in the past. Last year he helped against the Branch natives.'

'What do you mean by Branch natives?' Williams asked.

'It refers to the natives who live near the upper branch of the Hawkesbury,' Thompson said. 'Settlement up here takes two forms. There are those towns like at Windsor and those who have taken up land along the rivers for farming.

'The natives are grouped by their tribes, the Dharug and Darkinjung. The Dharug are hunters and woods people, who have moved into the area from the Cumberland Plain. They were forced out from the plain as more settlers took up lands down there.

'The Darkinjung are the Branch natives, they live in the area around the junction of the Lower Hawkesbury and upper branch of the river. The settlers adopted the term branch set-tlers because they have grouped around the upper branch. That title then flowed on to the natives.

'There are also Richmond Hill natives of which Yaragowby is one and there are also mountain natives. Richmond Hill natives are usually friendly and helpful. Our guides are from Richmond Hill. That is why I trust Yaragowby, the man you saw. The mountain natives are likely the ones we are hunting. They come down out of the foothills of the mountains and raid, then retreat back there. This is, as you can see, not easy coun-try to get about in. Up higher it gets even harder, with ridges and valleys of dense forest. For now though we have to negoti-ate the creeks and flood waters to get to that area.'

It took all morning to criss-cross the flooded network of creeks and valleys dragging the wagon and boat. Finally a little after lunch they reached the upper area of the Hawkesbury and prepared to cross the river. Water flowed by quickly in some places yet formed eddies and backed up on itself in others.

'How do we cross this?' Williams said.

'Someone will swim across tied to a rope, if he makes it then he secures it to the other side. If he's in trouble we haul him back and someone else tries,' Thompson said.

One of the settlers stepped forward, stripping down to his britches. He was a large burly figure with the marking of a flogging on his back. Without saying a word he grabbed the loop of rope, pulled it over his head and tightened it around his torso, and waded into the water.

The man was able to wade almost a third of the way across before he reached deeper water which rushed by. Williams expected him to launch himself into it, instead he waded back a few metres towards the shore, then headed upstream. The swimmer picked an area of water near a large eddy and carefully waded out until his feet could no longer touch the bottom. Then he began swimming with an awkward sidestroke for the far bank.

The current was weaker where he was swimming but it still pulled the swimmer downstream. 'I don't think he is going to make it,' Williams said.

'Watch carefully Oli, I think he will. See how the water is pulling him across the river even as it sends him downstream. The man knows what he is doing.'

'He certainly does,' Thompson said. 'We have regular flooding up here and a few people are lost each year. That fellow there, Roberts, grew up in Anglia near a flood plain. He has spent most of his life swimming in floods, when he wasn't in gaol for stealing.'

As they spoke Roberts slowly emerged from the water, standing waist deep on the far side of the main channel. He moved carefully over the last area of water almost falling twice. Then he climbed the far bank and found a strong gum tree to tie the rope around, before he slumped down on the ground. From the other side of the river the men could see his chest heaving and taking in large draughts of air.

The settlers began breaking down the wagon and putting the first lot of supplies in the boat. It took eight trips in total to get the men, weapons, supplies and wagon across the river, by which time the heat had gone from the day. Each trip two men would sit in the boat and use the rope to pull the boat across the river. A third sat in the middle with a long oar, occassionally taking depth soundings, sometimes using the oar to push the boat free of an unseen obstruction or to parry away debris floating downstream. The effort left most of the men drained and with the light fading the party settled in for the night.

Thompson set the men to establishing a camp, collecting firewood and making a large fire. He then organised the men into shifts to stay watch during the night. 'We don't want to be surprised by the men we are hunting,' he said to Smith and Williams.

'Now gentlemen, perhaps we can talk over tea,' Thompson said. The fire was beginning to take hold in the pile of wood, centred within a stone circle. The three men sat down warming themselves.

'I should apologise, I was hard on you and your lieutenant last night,' Thompson said. 'We have had a tough time of it up here. One of the women was set upon and raped by at least half a dozen of the settlers two months ago, and that goes unpunished.'

'Does that happen up here often?' Williams said, interrupting Thompson as he began talking again.

'Occassionally. There are too few women up here and too many men. Usually someone gets drunk, pushes too far and then it's on. There is very little that can be done, other than more women being brought up here. But then there is also a shortage in Sydney, so I hear.

'Anyway after that the raids began and then we had the murders of Llewelyn and Adlum, and now more raids. The people have been at us constabulary to do something. There's little that can be done unless we catch them in the act.' Thompson paused and stared into the fire. 'To tell the truth I'm glad that we did not, for these natives have no fear of us up here. God knows what would have happened had some-one chanced upon them during a raid. I hope that you will change that and that is why I was angry you were not here earlier,' Thompson said.

'We wanted to come up here sooner but our hands have been tied,' Williams said after a long pause.

'Thankfully that has changed,' Thompson said.

'Tell me about the native trackers,' Smith said. 'Can we trust them?'

'They are Richmond Hill men who asked only the chance to seize and retain a wife in exchange for their involvement,' Thompson said. He saw the looks on the faces of Smith and Williams. 'By wife I mean Aboriginal wife from amongst those we are hunting.'

'They bring their women along?' Smith said.

'We are heading towards an encampment at some caves near Yarramundi. It is where we think they are camped. There will be women there.'

'And you're going to allow these trackers to seize one each?'

'It would probably be safer for the women. If the men chance upon the camp and find only the women we may well have a repeat of the rape a couple of months ago.'

Thompson stared into the fire for a time, the three men sitting in silence. 'This is a good place to settle. The land is abundant and provided the floods are not too great, well, there is the chance for a man to make something of himself here. We are pretty much equals, all holding small farms and making a go of life.'

'You sound fond of it,'" Williams said.

'Most of the time we have it good up here. None of us would ever make it rich but together we can set down roots,' Thompson said.

'Don't you want to be rich?' Williams said.

'I would rather have a good life up here, a woman and a small farm, if it stays the same as it is most days. It is only the bad days like the rapes and the raids that upset the balance. It would be good to grow old here with things just being as they are, albeit with some more women,' Thompson said.

'Do you think that things will stay the same up here for ever?' Williams said.

'I hope so. It'll be better when we can end these raids. And it would help us more if the governor did not encourage those men wanting a monopoly on trade. However, I think recent events have shown us that the governor has little interest in us. Hopefully a new governor will work to encourage us and ease up on the monopolists that seek to own everything. Sorry, I shouldn't talk politics with you lads. Not good form really. I think I'll turn in for the night. Good night,' Thompson said. He stood and walked a short distance then collected his bed roll and spread it out.

The next day the party made good time and by early afternoon had cleared the flooded land and were heading towards the foothills of the Blue Mountains. One of the settlers doubled back along the line and called to Thompson.

'Chief, there is a fire up ahead. A ways out but definitely a fire,' Richard Sewell said.

'Are you certain? It could be their camp?' Thompson said.

'That's what we were thinking too,' Sewell said. 'What do we do?'

'Let's establish a camp here quickly. We drop the gear, grab the weapons and sneak up on them,' John Cowcroft said.

'Sounds good John,' Sewell said.

Within minutes the supplies had been dumped and the weapons retrieved from the baggage train. Several of the settlers, those who had disappeared the previous day when Yaragowby had emerged from the bush, set to establishing camp. The most eager of the expedition were already heading out towards the fire.

'This is not how we do things. It is a trap to lure you,' one of the guides said. The settlers, led by Sewell and Cowcraft stopped.

'Are you sure?' Smith said.

'Yes, they want us to come,' the guide said.

'We have them cold,' Cowcroft said. 'The longer we delay the less chance of making it to them by dark.'

'We'll wait a moment and listen to what our guides say,' Thompson said.

'Do you really trust them? They bring us here and we can see their camp fire and now they say wait it's a trap,' Cowcroft said. 'We can have revenge on them by nightfall.'

'Careful with your language John,' Thompson said. 'This isn't about revenge. It's about justice.'

'Whatever it's about we're wasting time,' Cowcroft said.

'Gentlemen, what's your opinion?' Thompson said to Williams and Smith.

'Do you trust the guides Chief Constable?' Smith said.

'Yes I do,' Thompson said. 'Their motives may be rather odd, but they know what they want and delivering the murderers of Llewelyn and Adlum is the way they get it. If they say this fire is a decoy then I believe them.'

'Then I suggest we reconnoitre the area carefully, following the guides,' Smith said. 'If this is a trap they'll find it. If not then they can lead us to that fire by the best route.'

The two Aboriginal guides nodded. 'Follow us.'

The going was slow, but within an hour the guides motioned everyone to stop. Then they pointed at Thompson, Smith and Williams. The three men quietly edged forward. One of the guides whispered in Thompson's ear and pointed ahead, sweeping his hand from left to right.

Following the guide the three men walked quietly for around a hundred metres. Progress was slow in the bush near the base of the mountains. Their route kept them up near the top of the ridge, just below the skyline. Then the guide got down on his stomach and edged his way to the top of the ridge. The two soldiers and constable did the same thing. Just before they reached the top of the ridge they heard voices, though it was impossible to make out any details.

Slowly the four men worked their way the last half metre until they could peer over the ridge. Below in a small clearing was a large group of Aboriginal men sitting around a larger pile of weapons. Williams looked around and saw that the fire was further up the slope above the waiting Aboriginal war party. A narrow valley below the clearing offered the easiest path towards the fire.

All four men carefully retraced their movements down the ridge and back to the settlers. Once they were far enough away Smith answered the question that was in Williams head.

'Their position is perfect to ambush a group of people heading towards that fire. We would have gone through the valley below that ridge and they could have sent spears and other weapons down with little chance we could effectively fire back. It was a trap.'

The party of settlers retreated a short distance. Thompson laid out the plan. The expedition split into two groups, with Thompson and Williams leading one group and Smith and Sewell the other. Each group was to be led by a guide.

'There is a large group of natives up ahead waiting for a party to come through heading towards that fire. They intend to ambush us. We will instead ambush them. The guides will lead each group and position us near the edges of the camp. Once ready we will open fire, trying to hit as many of the warriors as possible,' Thompson said.

'Once we open fire they will scatter," Smith said. 'Let them. Is that clear? Do not chase them into the bush, that's what they want. We will take the camp and then take care of any still alive.'

'Make every effort to be as quiet as possible. Our best hope is to surprise them before they realise we are here,' Thompson said.

The two groups gathered up their muskets and powder and began to move out. Smith walked over to Williams. 'Here we go again, dropped in it,' Smith said with a wicked smile. 'Good hunting Corporal Williams.'

'Good hunting Corporal Smith and try not to enjoy it too much,' Williams said. He watched as Smith's smile grew even wider before his best mate turned and walked away.

It took a good half an hour for the two groups to make their way to the ambush site. Each man was careful not to make any sounds. Once near the site Thompson and Williams each took half the men from their column and established their positions. There was a pause of a minute or more once Williams settled down. He took aim at a native dressed in English clothes, without doubt taken from one of the men who this group had murdered.

Williams passed the time by concentrating on his breathing, imagining the moment between inhaling and exhaling when his hands and body were still and he could take the most accurate shot. Smith had taught him how to do this as part of shooting practice. Not that the practice had helped Williams's aim.

The group would only fire one shot each before rushing into camp. Some of the settlers had swords. Most had been told to reverse their grip on their muskets and use them as clubs if needed.

The moments of quiet grew and Williams could hear faint murmurs of words he did not understand and the sounds of animals in the bush. Then shots rang out. A volley of fire swept over the camp site. Williams breathed in, held the air in his lungs and fired at the native dressed in the English clothing. He peered through the smoke but the man was still standing. Then he heard another shot and saw the man fall.

The Aboriginals in the camp either jumped up or fell down writhing in pain. Those still on their feet ran to the bush on the edges of the camp. Williams noticed that they did not scatter in every direction. Most headed up hill towards the direction of the decoy fire.

'Up and at 'em lads, let's go,' Williams yelled. He stood and started running as best he could through the scrub. Settlers rose up from their positions and followed him. Soon he saw Nate Smith and other settlers emerging from the bush ahead and Thompson and his group coming into the camp too.

At least half a dozen Aboriginal men lay dead. Williams organised his group of settlers to reload their muskets and establish a perimeter around the camp. He turned and watched as Thompson and Smith carefully prodded and kicked each of the bodies. One of the men Thompson kicked jumped to his feet with a tomahawk in his hand. Smith shot him from close range. After that no other natives laying on the ground moved.

Thompson approached the Aboriginal in the English clothes. He was lying face down. The constable gave him several hard kicks. The man did not move. Carefully Thompson and Smith used their legs to roll the man over.

Williams immediately recognised him. 'That's Yaragowby.'

Williams watched as Thompson kicked the dead body again before spitting on it. 'Traitor,' was all Thompson said.

All around the camp were piles of weapons. Thompson quickly ordered all the settlers to ensure their muskets were loaded. Then the chief constable ordered a group of settlers to gather up the spears and clubs. Many of the spears had barbs and jagged edges near their tips. To be hit by one of those spears, Williams thought, would be to have your flesh ripped apart.

Thompson ordered two of the settlers to set fire to the spears. At that moment a group of Aboriginal men appeared on the ridge above and hurled a few spears towards the settlers. They were too far away to do any real damage, yet it did not stop a few of the settlers from firing at the group.

'Corporal Smith, Corporal Williams, can you take a group of settlers after those men. The guides will lead you. Be cautious, this is native territory,' Thompson said.

'You men, with us,' Smith said. He had pointed to the men who had not discharged their rifles, hoping they at least knew how far a ball travelled when fired by a musket. In the bush against a group of natives that sense could be vital.

The two guides quickly disappeared up the ridge before one came down and motioned for the party to follow. As quickly as they could Smith, Williams and the settlers followed. A crude bush path marked the way ahead, offering an easier passage than through the scrub. The party moved quickly along the path, heading upwards and then along the top of a ridge.

A small group of natives appeared on their left. Two threw spears towards the settlers and then the group began retreating down the far side of the ridge. The settlers now had the taste for blood and the means to deliver it. Better yet the trail left by the Aboriginal warriors was easy to follow.

Cowcroft moved after the warriors and several settlers followed. Smith was a few paces behind with one of the guides. Ahead of Cowcraft and his fellow settlers, a group of warriors appeared and launched a few spears that were easily dodged. One of the settlers fired as the first of the warriors disappeared, leaving only a few shaking branches to show where the Aboriginal warriors had been. The smoke from the settler's musket obscured the view ahead.

Smith reached the group but before he could stop them they headed along the trail left by the warriors. Williams reached the group with the last of the settlers who were more nervous in the unfamiliar bush. At that point he had no idea if all the settlers were grouped together or not.

Tendrils of smoke stretched like fingers upward and outwards. Williams looked at Smith. 'We're getting spread out,' he said.

'Some of the settlers really want blood,' Smith said.

From up ahead there were more cries and two shots rang out. Smith, Williams and the guide ran towards the sound. More smoke hung in the air making it impossible to see the track ahead. One of the settlers was squatting over something on the ground.

'I hope that isn't one of ours,' Smith said.

'Wallaby,' the guide said.

'What?' said Williams, running behind Smith and the guide.

'It's a wallaby on ground. They shot it thinking it was a warrior,' the guide said.

Williams tried to do a head count but with men running, smoke floating around and the general confusion he was uncertain of how many men were accounted for. As he started another count the Aboriginal warriors stepped out ahead and threw more spears. None had much hope of hitting targets on the rough path with overhanging branches. The distance between the two groups lessened the chances of hitting the settlers even further. Then as quickly as they appeared the warriors turned and ran.

Again Cowcroft and some of the settlers ran off in pursuit. A shot rang out from up ahead. By the time Smith and Williams reached the traces of smoke from the shot they found no settlers. Smith was beginning to feel uneasy. Every time the warriors appeared and then disappeared into the bush and the settlers followed they would find the natives again.

'Oli, this is another trap,' Smith said. 'Slow up, slow up,' he said to the settlers. A number raced forward past Smith and continued the pursuit, emboldened and not wanting to miss the kill they were certain lay ahead. Smith grabbed one of the guides. 'The natives, are they travelling slower than usual?'

The guide nodded. 'It is a trap.'

At that moment the other guide yelled to the settlers who were racing ahead. A few stopped but several more crossed a ridge and raced down a hill. The guide nearest Smith pointed ahead and upwards. At the top of an escarpment were a group of Aboriginals holding what looked to be large rocks and tree branches. Two of the warriors were wedging a large branch under a rock and beginning to push down on the branch to lift the rock, which threatened to tumble off the escarpment.

The path the settlers were following ran directly under that escarpment.

Smith watched as more of the group started to use the branches to lever under large rocks in readiness to send them crashing down. Others were pushing rocks with their hands and several held projectiles ready to throw. They were standing right above where the settlers were now headed in pursuit of the Aboriginals.

Quickly Smith pulled his musket from his shoulder, checked the powder, and fired it towards the settlers. The two guides raced after the settlers who had stopped at the sound of the shot behind them and turned around. Each guide grabbed the nearest settler and pulled them back, yelling 'Look out, it is a trap.'

Finally the last of the settlers, led by Cowcroft, saw the Aboriginals above them and turned and ran just as the first rocks and boulders started to fall. The settlers scrambled their way up the hill.

'They planned that trap,' Smith said. 'They're using the terrain against us. We'd best get back to Thompson and regroup.'

At the ambush site progress in burning the spears was slow going. Large piles stood beside the fires that refused to take a hold. Some of the settlers were breaking spears, wedging them into the ground at a forty-five degree angle and stomping down hard to break the wood, however this too was slow going.

Williams and Smith led the settlers into the camp.

'Did you get them?' Thompson said.

'No, they tried to lead us into another trap. We saw it before any real damage was done, but we thought it best not to follow any further,' Smith said.

'How long till dark?' Williams said.

'Probably another hour at most, but in half an hour it will be very difficult to see. We either need to leave now or bunk down here for the night,' Thompson said. 'If we leave there is nothing to stop the natives from coming back and retrieving these weapons.'

'Then we stay and secure a perimeter. We will organise watches and set some smaller fires near the edge of the clearing. That way we can continue to burn the spears and at the same time see anyone approaching,' Smith said.

Thompson issued orders to the settlers outlining the plan. A number looked worried about the prospect of camping at the ambush site for the night. 'Shouldn't we get back to the main camp area?' Cowcroft said.

'It's too late for that now. Besides we can't leave these weapons unattended,' Thompson said. 'Now enough stalling, get to work.'

Within the hour a series of small perimeter fires were set. Spears were piled beside each fire for burning. The dead Aboriginals had been moved to a hollow besides the camp. A larger fire had been established in the middle of the clearing for warmth and to continue the task of burning the spears. The guides killed and cooked a wallaby and served it with a few bush berries and edible plants.

'At least we have a decent meal,' Thompson said to Smith and Williams. The constable was silent for a time staring into the fire. 'How many do you think got away from us?'

'It's difficult to tell,'" Smith said, 'but at least a dozen. Not including those on the cliffs above us.'

'What really worries me though is that Yaragowby was working with them,' Thompson said.

'Don't take it to heart. He fooled us too,' Williams said.

'That's only part of it,' Thompson said. 'He's a Richmond Hill native. The others are Dharug and Darkinjung. We identified one of the dead as possibly Talloon, a native leader. It looks as if some of the tribes are coordinating these attacks, working together.'

'Is that unusual?' Williams said.

'Very unusual, and if it's happening then it represents something new and different. The government has always sought to play rival tribes and groups off against each other because it breaks their power. It's based on what worked in the Americas and in India. That policy has been effective here too. But if the Aboriginals have teamed up then this is more like a declaration of war than a few local raiders causing some mischief,' Thompson said.

The three men were quiet while they considered what such an alliance meant. One of the guides came over and offered the three more food, which they gratefully accepted. Smith waited until the man had walked over to some of the other settlers. 'Do you still trust those two?'

Thompson looked at the guides for a few moments. 'Yes I do. But even if I didn't what choice do we have out here? We need them. Tomorrow I will get them to lead us to a nearby farm and we can work out our next steps after that. Now I suggest we eat up, it is going to be a long night.'

Twice during the night spears came sailing out of the darkness into the camp. Each time the settlers on watch fired blindly into the night. During the first attack a number of settlers who were sleeping grabbed their muskets and fired.

'Don't shoot. Stop your shooting, save your powder,' Smith bellowed. 'They are trying to rattle us and your odds of hitting one of them are next to none. Stop firing.'

After the second attack no one slept. By first light most of the men were close to exhaustion. They broke camp once there was enough light to walk by and returned as quickly as they could to the main camp. The settlers still at the main camp prepared a breakfast and after a rest and short sleep Thompson ordered the expedition to move out.

The party headed west towards the farm of Obadiah Aiken, a former Corps man. It took most of the day to make the trip. Often one of the settlers would shout that there were natives in the bush and a number of shots were fired.

'This is getting out of hand,' Thompson said. 'Men are shooting at phantoms and seeing natives where none are.'

'They are getting inside the heads of these men,' Smith agreed. 'It spreads panic and fear. I suspect that this is exactly what the natives want.'

'What do we do about it?' Williams said.

'There's not much to do. We wait till we are at Aiken's farm. More familiar territory might help the men see things clearly,' Smith said.

Night was falling as the tired troops arrived at Aiken's farm. Aiken greeted the soldiers and set to organising food. 'I'm glad to see you lads, especially two of the Corps' finest. With all the hoo-ha it's comforting to have you here,' Aiken said.

'Happy to oblige you Obadiah,' Thompson said. 'We'll put the men in the barn if you don't mind, and the soldiers and I will bunk down in the house.'

'Right you be, though I wouldn't call that old shed back there a barn.'

The settlers made their way to the ramshackle barn and quickly set out bed rolls. Most were asleep soon after dinner. Thompson, Williams and Smith, along with Cowcroft and Sewell sat inside Aiken's simple farmhouse.

'Tell me Obadiah, have you seen many of the natives around?' Thompson said.

'Only Charlie, who shows up regular enough. I did think I saw some dust like a large group would raise, out on the west of the farm yesterday afternoon late, but you never can tell up here. It could just as easily be a wind coming down from the mountains.'

'What about any past trouble with the natives?' Sewell said.

'None of any reckoning. Occasional theft of some maize off the stalk but nothing from the barn or the house. Suppose I have been lucky to date. Mind, some weapons help too.'

'What do you have in the way of weapons?' Smith said.

'A couple of muskets, a pistol, two swords and a hatchet. Not much point having more without someone else to fire them.'

The group chatted for a while longer when one of the settlers knocked at the back window. 'There's an Aboriginal coming,' the settler said before turning and heading back to the barn.

'Let's go wait in the bedroom, see what happens. Obadiah here can take care of himself, and if more arrive then we'll intervene,' Smith said. 'If that suits you Obadiah?'

'Fine by me,' Aiken said. 'It's probably only Charlie on the scrounge again.'

Aiken showed the men into the bedroom and then pulled the door to. He cleared the dishes and left one on the table where he sat back down. Soon there was a call from the yard.

'Are you in Obidi?' the voice said.

'I am Charlie. You're welcome to come in for some leftovers if you like.'

'That is good.'

The door swung open and Charlie stood there. Usually he would push the door open and walk straight in and sit at the kitchen table, but tonight he stood and carefully looked around. Aiken suppressed the urge to look to the bedroom.

Slowly Charlie walked in the room and instead of heading for the table he wandered towards the bedroom.

'Charlie, here is some food, sit and eat,' Aiken said.

Charlie walked back from the bedroom reluctantly and Aiken had the feeling that Charlie was on to the soldiers. At that moment Aiken realised that Charlie was carrying something in his left hand. It could be a club or just a stick, but it occured to Aiken that Charlie never carried anything. An urge to yell to the soldiers swelled up in his chest. He slowly breathed out.

Charlie looked at the food and picked at a scrap or two while still standing. Aiken watched breathing heavily. Usually Charlie sat and ate the food quickly. 'What weapons you have,' Charlie said. The hair on the back of Aiken's neck raised up and he shivered as dread ran down his spine.

'There is raiding parties around,' Charlie said. 'I will let my people know you are my friend. But what weapons you have?'

Aiken looked at Charlie and knew that his former friend was here to betray him. Charlie again asked about the weapons before heading towards to the bedroom door once more. 'Don't go in there, that is my private room,' Aiken said.

'I just look a little, see if there are weapons in there.'

'Charlie, please don't go in there,' Aiken said moving to block the door with his body.

'You fucking don't trust me. You let me fucking in there to see what is in there,' Charlie said, raising his left hand.

'Help me!' Aiken yelled.

The bedroom door flew open and Charlie turned and ran. He reached the main door and ran out of it, pursued by Cowcroft and Smith. Cowcroft fired a shot and Charlie fell to the ground. The settler swiftly reversed his grip on the musket so that he could use it as a club when Smith burst through the door and to his horror Smith saw a dozen armed natives standing near the farmhouse. Smith fired in their direction then grabbed Cowcroft by the belt and hauled him back toward the farmhouse.

As Williams came through the door he saw Smith dragging Cowcroft back toward the house. Williams saw the natives and fired a quick shot in their direction. Thompson and Sewell raced out the door, followed by Aiken. From the corner of his eye Williams saw some of the settlers coming around the side of the house, raising their muskets at the natives. Two more shots rang out before the raiders disappeared.

Charlie lay in the yard. Smith ordered four of the settlers to advance towards the body. Thompson followed and kicked Charlie hard without reaction, then he carefully bent down and turned the Aboriginal man over. Charlie was dead.

'Right, everyone back to the house now. We take it in turns to sleep. Those in the barn break up into three watches, four hours each. We will do the same here in the house. If there is trouble fire one shot only to let the others know,' Smith said. 'At first light we will look at what defences we can mount.'

The night passed very slowly. Most of the men got a few hours fitful sleep. At first light the settlers roused themselves. Smith and Williams were already out in the yard, looking at how best to mount a defence should the group of Aborigines return.

'There's not much cover, so we're probably best to advance in a group and shoot together,' Smith said.

'What about that old wagon and pile of wood? Could we conceal a few men behind that and have them fire first?' Williams said.

'Good idea Oli, you can lead that group,' Smith said, smiling. 'Once you draw them in we can then advance from behind the house and shoot, giving you time to reload. I would suggest Cowcroft and Sewell with you, and Thompson and I can lead the others.'

'What about Aiken, should he be with me too?'

'I would rather he be with my group to help steady them. He's a former Corps man after all. If my group lose their nerve it will be every man for himself. Right, let's lay out the plan to the others.'

Shortly afterwards Williams, Sewell and Cowcroft took up position behind the broken down wagon and wood pile, which had managed to merge into one over the years. 'Remember if they come we fire on my command, aiming for the leaders, then get down. Smith and Thompson will then have the settlers come round and fire a volley. We spend that time reloading,' Williams said.

The three men sat down and each found a comfortable position. Williams made sure he had a line of sight to the house, where two of the settlers were on lookout. The sun gradually warmed the day and Williams fought off a sudden drowsiness. Beside him Cowcroft was asleep.

'Is this your first action, other than yesterday?' Sewell whispered.

'No I was in the group that fought the Irish rebels,' Williams said. Sewell fidgeted, unable to sit still. Williams sensed the wait fraying Sewell's nerves. 'Concentrate on your aim, and your reloading, if the time comes. Pick a target, breathe in, hold that breath and shoot. Then think, powder and ball, powder and ball. We will be behind this cover so we can reload in safety. Then find a target again and repeat the whole thing.'

'But don't you ...getting hit, shot... don't you worry about that?'

'No point in worrying about it. The best thing is to concentrate on your aim and reloading, aim and reloading. How did you end up out here Sewell?'

'I got transported for stealing, food mainly. At first I thought it the end of my life, but once here I learnt to keep my head down, do my work and then to work for myself in the afternoons. I saved enough to get a small holding up Hawkesbury way. It's better than anything I could have hoped for in England. Now I have a future of sorts.'

'And your story?' Sewell said.

'I joined up because...' There was a signal from the house. Williams followed the line along which the lookout pointed carefully peering around the wood pile. 'Cowcroft, wake up. They are here,' Williams said quietly but forcefully.

Cowcroft shook himself awake and made to stand up. Williams held him down until Cowcroft realised where he was. 'Check your powder and have your muskets ready,' Williams said. 'They are coming from our right, at least a dozen of them.'

'Do we shoot now?' Sewell said.

'Wait until my signal.' Williams then turned and glanced at the house. The lookout signalled with one upraised finger, meaning only one raiding party was visible. Smith glanced around from the side of the house.

Williams again peered around the wood pile. They were still seventy yards out rendering any shots at such a range almost useless. Williams looked again at the corner of the house. Smith signalled with his hands, pointing first to himself and then cocking his fingers like a pistol. Then he pointed to Williams.

'Smith will tell us when to shoot,' Williams said to Sewell and Cowcroft. 'Remember aim, take your shot then get down and reload.'"

The native raiders walked forward slowly, trying not to make any noise. They were spread out across an arc of around ten yards, having learnt not to bunch up too closely. Most of the Aborigines held a spear above their head which was extended forwards toward the house. Some held a clutch of spears in their other hand, a few tomahawks. They advanced as would Aboriginal hunters stalking prey in the bush, treading lightly and carefully in a slow-motion, high-stepping dance.

Williams could feel Sewell shift and squirm. 'Steady, aim and reload,' he said to the settler, before reaching out and laying a hand on Sewell's shoulder to calm him. 'Steady, aim and reload. Get ready.'

Smith raised his hand like a starter signalling a race was to begin. Williams watched his mate. 'Steady, aim and reload. Steady aim and reload.' Was he saying that aloud or merely thinking it.

Then Smith dropped his hand. 'Now!' Williams said.

Williams, Sewell and Cowcroft rose together. The native raiding party was far closer than any of them had expected, barely fifteen yards away. 'Fire,' Williams said. Three muskets discharged together, the sound amplifying to be shockingly loud. Two of the natives fell.

Williams ducked down then realised that Sewell had forgotten to take cover and was standing trying to reload his rifle. Williams grabbed him and pulled down with all his weight. Sewell fell beside him as a volley of spears bounced and clattered into the wood pile, several ricocheting and bouncing off the wood and sailing over the heads of the three men.

From the corner of his eye Williams saw Thompson lead his settlers out from the left side of the house. Smith emerged from the right of the house at the front of the second group of settlers. Thompson's men took up position first and began firing before the constable could issue the order. Only one native fell. Thompson's men had fired all their shot leaving the group exposed. The natives rounded on them with many drawing back their arms to full extension to throw spears.

Thompson and the settlers scattered with two of the men falling over each other. As the first natives planted their feet to throw a shout of fire followed by a shattering volley came from Smith's group. At least half the native raiders were hit.

Several whirled to throw at Smith's settlers when Williams, Sewell and Cowcroft stood and fired again. Another native went down.

Thompson had managed to regroup a handful of his settlers, some of who had reloaded their muskets. Thompson shouted fire and four muskets discharged and another two raiders fell. Smith yelled to his men to fire and half the group fired while the rest reloaded.

The natives broke. Those still standing ran into the bush. Most of the men on the ground managed to stand and run off. Two of the natives did not move and were dragged off by the remaining Aborigines.

Shots were fired as the natives retreated but none found their target. A pall of smoke drifted over the ground. The last of the natives disappeared into the bush. Spears and shields and tomahawks on the ground were all there was to show the raiding party had been there.

Williams stood and looked at Sewell. 'You all right?' Williams said. Sewell nodded. 'Cowcroft, are you all right?' Williams said. Cowcroft muttered something that sounded like yes.

All around groups of settlers stood staring at the battlefield. Obadiah Aiken walked out and picked up a spear. He snapped it over his knee. Some of the settlers walked forward and did the same, several pocketing tomahawks.

'Do you think that's it?' Sewell said.

'They have too many wounded to do any damage now,' Williams said.

The two men walked over to where Thompson and Smith were sitting on the ground. Williams and Sewell half sat and half fell to the ground.

'Hit anything this time Oli?' Smith asked.

'I don't think he did,' Sewell said.

'It doesn't matter now. We've broken them,' Thompson said.

The journey back to the Hawkesbury settlement was uneventful. Two of the settlers, both former Corps men, volunteered to stay on with Aiken for a few more days. 'We don't expect you to have any more trouble from the raiders,' Thompson said.

'I think we have put the fear of muskets back into them for a while at least,' Aiken said. 'Safe travels and thank you for the help.'

'Right lads we best be getting back and seeing how things are at home,' Thompson said.

The flood waters had receded further making the going easier. It was late afternoon of the second day when they reached the outskirts of Windsor. Most of the men took their leave and headed to their homes and farms. The remaining few walked wearily into town.

'Welcome home lads. How did you fare?' Lieutenant Davies said.

'I think we have broken the back of them Lieutenant,' Thompson said. 'We managed to ambush a group of them in the bush and seize and destroy a large number of weapons. Then we shot a number more at Obadiah Aiken's farm. That will set them back for now and should return some of their fear of muskets.'

'Congratulations Mr Thompson,' Davies said.

'Lieutenant I must also commend your men. Corporals Smith and Williams were invaluable to us and helped greatly during both battles with the native raiders.'

'That's good to hear, I will pass that on to Major Johnston who will be very pleased.'

'Has it been quiet here?' Thompson said.

'Very quiet. I think the presence of the Corps has done the trick. We have now twenty of us here and have been patrolling the outer farms and making a show of being seen. Are you worried that there are more out there?'

'Yes. I think some of the local tribes have formed some kind of alliance to make war. We encountered both Richmond Hill and Branch natives working together. That's unusual.'

'Rest assured Mr Thompson we will stay up here for another few days. If things quiet down we will return to Sydney. If the raids continue then we will send out a larger hunting party,' Davies said. 'Now I suspect you lads may be thirsty. Let's get you all a drink.'

For the next three days the soldiers patrolled the region making a loop around the farms and back to town twice a day. The air was cooling as autumn fell and the march was leisurely. A number of the farmers closed their doors as the patrols neared. They still remembered the high prices of goods and particularly rum that had been driven up by the Corps for profit. Poor farmers struggled to pay for things at the best of times and seeing red-coated profiteers marching through their district was too much.

'Why are they closing their doors. You would expect that we should be treated better than that Lieutenant,' Williams said.

'While you were out in the bush we had a few run-ins with the locals. Most of them think the price of rum is too high. Actually, they think the price of everything is too high, unless they're selling it. Farmers are the same here or there. Given that we have run an effective monopoly on trade goods for many years the logic up here says that we are the ones pushing prices up.

'Then of course they have been asking us why it took so long to arrive up here. Most of the locals have had to deal with the Aborigines themselves for a couple of months. They don't realise that the governor has sat on his hands all that time. So instead of seeing that we got here as soon as we could they think we have been down in Sydney trading in rum rather than protecting their farms.

'The stories being told about what happened out in the bush don't help either,' Davies said. 'Most of the settlers from the Thompson expedition have figured there are a couple of free drinks at the tavern by talking up their own roles and down-playing what you and Smith did.'

'We saved half of them at least twice,' Williams said. 'Four or five would be dead out there if not for Smith.'

'I know lad. Mr Thompson gave me a very fair report and commended both Smith and yourself. The reality is that we are only ever up here when there is a problem and the rest of the time we get the blame for things that don't concern us. That is the lot of the Corps. We are only popular when we put down an uprising of the Irish or put over-zealous governors on boats back to England.

'On the plus side, Thompson has now established a militia of sorts based on his expedition. There are a number of ex-soldiers now settled up here and Thompson is working with them to create small parties that can move quickly throughout the region. He was also very appreciative of the tactics Smith and you deployed at Aiken's farm. The militia intends to use that type of close fire against any future raiding parties.

'The pity of the whole thing is that some of the murderers are still out there being hidden by the Aborigines. Word from the major is that Reverend Marsden is working to identify those murderers and bring them to justice.

'Don't get too down about the lack of appreciation up here Oliver. Tomorrow we will head back to Sydney. You can find some love there,' Davies said, winking at Williams. 'Now time to get this patrol over with and get home.'

The Corps detachment from Windsor disembarked at Sydney Cove and made the short march up the hill to the barracks. 'It's good to be home again Nate,' Williams said. 'I've missed Sydney more than I thought I would.'

'She does grow on you, our little colony, doesn't she?' Smith said.

'Yes she does.'

The detachment was greeted by Major Johnston and a parade of soldiers. 'Well done indeed lads, well done. It appears that you have broken the resolve of the natives up Windsor way and helped the constabulary create a new force to keep that threat at bay,' Johnston said.

Once the formalities were over, the men put their gear away and drifted into the mess hall. Williams and Smith were summoned to a meeting with Johnston and Davies.

'Right then, the brains of our outfit are back. We can all relax gentlemen,' Johnston said.

'I do think the officer's are getting it Oli," Smith said.

Johnston cleared his throat and Smith went very quiet, straing at the floor. 'I have it on Lieutenant Davies's authority that you both distinguished yourselves up in Windsor,' Johnston said.

'Thank you Major,' Smith said.

'Corporal Williams, I think it safe to say that your promotion is now a permanent one. Well done lad,' Johnston said.

'Thank you Major,' Williams said. Smith slapped his mate on the back. 'Well done Oli,' he said.

'Now before you two go out celebrating and finding a whole new type of mischief to drop us all in, I need to update you on what has been happening here.

'The populace have taken a set against any Aborigines, and the whole of Sydney is on edge. There was an incident near the halfway houses between here and Parramatta a few days back with reports of a raiding party. We sent two detachments, one by road the other by river to come up behind any raiders, however it proved to be a false alarm. We have had more false reports than real problems.

'Nonetheless, the outer districts claim to have seen several raiding parties and we have been running patrols. To date our presence has been enough to stop any raids, but this situation cannot continue.

'The Governor has issued an order banning Aborigines from the settlements and settlers from helping any of the natives. That means many are starting to grow hungry. A large number of natives are milling about on the edges of the Cumberland Plain.

'Reverend Marsden and his missionary fellow William Crook have been working to establish negotiations with those groups to find the ringleaders of this stupidity. The Reverend assures me that he is close to being able to identify the culprits. For now we will leave it in his hands. Our role will be to run sweeping patrols across the outer settlements. You two will each lead a patrol, every second day. If things change I will let you know. That is all for now.'

Smith and Williams walked out of the mess into the fading afternoon light.

'By God Oli, a corporal eh? Congratulations. We are going to go out and celebrate tonight. I don't know about you but Madame Brigitte is calling me,' Smith said.

'That place is all back to front Nate. You pay money to be with a whore and all you get in return is pox. Better we go to one of the taverns and find a couple of women there.'

'These days most of the good women are taken, shacked up with officers or officials or ex convicts. There are too few available women, if you know what I mean. That's why I like to mix my pleasure with their business. But suit yourself, I know you have a couple of ladies that like you and now you are a corporal you will find it easy to get one to settle down.'

'I aint ready for that yet Nate. Nor do I want to pay some whore for the pox either.'

'Well Oli most of the women you want are already running households. For the rest of us we have to content ourselves with enjoying the fairer sex when and how we can.'

'Nate. Look sorry, I'm just not up for whoring tonight.'

'Okay then Wee Willy. Sorry, I know better than that. Once I get this out of my system, or maybe twice or even three times out of my system, I will be able to think clearly again. Last chance to tag along.'

'Good night Nate, and I mean that in every sense.'

The following day Williams led his first patrol, tracking out from Sydney to the Cumberland settlements. One group of Aborigines was spotted near the fringes of the scrub but they turned and walked off quickly once they spotted the redcoats. A number of farmers reported small-scale thefts though nothing more serious. Most were glad to see the New South Wales Corps reasserting order.

Increasingly farm houses and fences dotted the countryside with more and more bush being cleared for farming. The sun was pleasant and the patrol was making good time without pushing too hard.

'So Oli. Apologies, Corporal. How much longer are we out here?' Tom Conner said.

'Well Private Conner,' Williams said, 'that depends on if you can march any faster, doesn't it. So at your speed probably another two days.'

Conner laughed. 'Its already gone to his head. The power and the honour have changed you Corporal.'

Williams laughed in turn. 'We're nearly done. We'll head back to Parramatta, stay the night at the barracks and then retrace this route in reverse tomorrow. Are you happy with that Private?'

'Yes oh grand and high corporal.' Conner turned to George Newbank. 'You know George I knew him back when he was a humble Private, just like us.'

'He was never like us. He's far smarter than you and a bit smarter than me, Tom.'

'Steady on. First the corporal is dishing it out and now you.'

'You get what you deserve Tom.'

'Okay lads, that's enough,'" Williams said. 'We have cows ahead.'

Up ahead several cattle were chewing grass along the side of the road. There were no farmers in attendance. Williams eyed the stand of trees near the side of the road and just metres from where the cows grazed with concern.

'Lads, keep an eye out and be ready,' Williams said.

Nearby, several more cattle were grazing. Williams saw a man coming towards the patrol. He took his musket from his shoulder. 'Lads, be ready.' The patrol pulled their muskets from their shoulders and kept a wary eye on the approaching man.

The figure grew closer and Williams could see it was a white farmer. 'At ease lads, but keep your besses handy.'

'Hello there,' Williams said.

'Hello to you. My name is Isaac Nichols. I have a farm near here. Last night we were raided by a group of natives.'

'Is everyone all right?' Williams said.

'Yes. The farm was plundered of some grains and my stock spread. These are my animals.'

'How far is the farm?'

'Half a mile.'

'We're happy to provide an escort for you and your stock. Righto lads, keep an eye out for any natives.'

'Thank you,' Nichols said.

Nichols began the task of rounding up the cattle, all of which looked small and mangy. After a short time two convict helpers joined in. Forty minutes later the animals were back behind the wooden fence on the small farm.

'So tell me Mr Nichols, how many men were in this raiding party?' Williams said.

'It was hard to say in the dark but probably half a dozen at least. I heard the name Tedbury called twice, he is the leader of these natives according to the *Gazette*.'

'He's one of the ringleaders. There are others too.'

'Yes but Tedbury is the son of Pemulwuy, the ferocious warrior. The rumour is that Tedbury learnt his warrior skills from Pemulwuy,' Nichols said. Williams could almost sense the dread in Nichols everytime he mentioned the name Pemulwuy.

'Rest assured that plans are in place to bring these natives in,' Williams said. 'The orders preventing natives from approaching farms are having an effect. It is only a matter of time. If you like we can stay here for a few minutes and have a look around.'

'Thank you, that would be appreciated.'

After an hour, during which Williams walked around the farm instructing Nichols on the best vantage points for defending the property, the patrol moved on. They walked into Parramatta late in the day.

Williams was surprised to find Major Johnston at the Parramatta barracks.

'Major, I was not expecting to see you here.'

'Corporal Williams, we have taken Tedbury captive thanks to intelligence from Reverend Marsden. The Reverend also has a list of the ringleaders and several have been located. That list will be published in the *Gazette* tomorrow.

'The ringleaders are Talboon, Corriangee and Doollonn, who are all mountain natives. Boon-du-dullock from Richmond Hill is included as are Moonaning and Doongial, branch natives. So it does seem there is an alliance of tribes at work.'

'Who caught Tedbury, Major?' Williams said.

'A group of constables from Parramatta together with some settlers from the northern boundary and Baulkham Hills. They're bringing him here where Marsden and I shall question him. Hopefully we can break these raids tonight.'

'I hope so. Many of the farmers have tales to tell of theft. And all of them are scared. If you don't mind my asking sir but does this really end the raids?'

'Corporal, I really don't know. Some are fond of saying that this was their land before we took it and what should we expect. I suppose there is something in that but such is the world. The reality is there is plenty of land to go around. We are bringing civilisation here and that should be the end of it. Alas we know otherwise. I expect the governor will rescind the current orders once the ringleaders are caught and once the natives know that we can deprive them of the benefits we bring. That should do it for now.'

The gate of the barracks opened and Reverend Samuel Marsden strode in. The Reverend spied Johnston and marched over. 'By the grace of God we have him George. Now I am told you will help me to prevail upon this wretch to give up his secrets.'

'That is so Reverend. May I introduce Corporal Williams, Corporal the Reverend Marsden.'

'Were you involved in Tedbury's capture son?' Marsden said. 'No Reverend. I have been leading patrols across the region.' 'Good for you boy.'

'Samuel, Corporal Williams has only just returned from the Hawkesbury where he helped constable Thompson on his successful expedition,' Johnston said.

'Good on you boy. Now George, the wretch is almost here; time to get to it.' Marsden grabbed Johnston by the elbow and shepherded the major away from Williams. They headed towards a strongly-built bunkhouse. At that moment the gates opened and the Parramatta constables entered with Tedbury.

Williams had imagined that the native would be bigger and wilder looking. Instead he looked like any other native warrior; lean and with markings on his body, which was clothed only by a covering of the loins. Williams looked at the native. How easy it was to imagine more of an enemy than what they turned out to be.

The constables pushed Tedbury to the bunk house and shoved him in. 'All yours Reverend. I hope you will pray for him only after you break him,' one of the constables said. Johnston and Reverend Marsden, along with two troopers, entered the bunk house. Two hours later the four emerged. Williams had little idea what happened in the bunk house nor did he want to know. Whatever happens in there he had brought it on himself, Williams thought.

'I think we have enough to break this rebellion open, George,' Marsden said when they walked out into the cool of the night. Neither man revealed most of what they had done to break Tedbury, but it was clearly very effective. Over the next few days the rebellion was swiftly ended.

Tedbury led a detachment of constables to the Jerusalem Caves where he revealed the main staging post for the native raiders. Clothes belonging to one of the stockmen murdered several months earlier were recovered.

Tedbury was then persuaded to provide even more information. He gave up the names of those leading the rebellion, including Bull Dog and Musquito. Dawn raids were carried out by constables and armed militia across the region rounding up the majority of leaders of the raids. Only Bull Dog, Musquito and Branch Jack remained at large.

Once word of Tedbury's arrest got out Bull Dog and Musquito were soon betrayed by their own people, desperate for food and a return to Sydney and Parramatta.

After attempting to break out of Parramatta gaol and then threatening to burn it down both Aboriginal leaders were sentenced to seven years' hard labour on Norfolk Island. Branch Jack was the only other leader remaining at large and he soon disappeared.

In return for his cooperation Tedbury was released after Bull Dog and Musquito were captured. The release of Tedbury was on strict conditions. Johnston and Marsden only ever spoke publicly about what they had said to Tedbury once. 'Your chances are finished, and if you fail to cooperate all that is left is a musket ball or a noose.' And that was Reverend Marsden, a man of God.

Johnston had pressed harder and promised Tedbury to 'hunt down you and your family if you are implicated in any violence and to have the constables pay back tenfold to your women what has been done to us.'

Aborigines began returning from the Cumberland Plain to Sydney and Parramatta, working whatever jobs they could. The natives learned to approach farms in groups of two or three, and usually with a woman and child in tow. A way of life disappeared, to be replaced by something different, something lesser for the Aboriginal people of Sydney and surrounds. Peace returned to the farm settlements.

The mood in Sydney gradually returned to one of routine and hope. One question still remained to be answered, who would replace King as governor.

June 1805

'Ladies and gentlemen, ladies and gentlemen, the heads of the harbour of Port Jackson should be in view within the hour,' the captain of the *Argo* said as he walked through the small corridors of the whaler.

The captain knocked on one of the doors. 'Mr Macarthur sir, we are approaching Port Jackson.'

There was no answer. The captain turned and walked towards the back of the ship, where the makeshift sheep pens were housed. Knowing Macarthur as he now did it was obvious where the man would be.

He found John Macarthur assessing his prized merino sheep. All of them had made the voyage successfully, in no small part thanks to Macarthur ensuring that they were given the finest of treatment.

'Mr Macarthur sir, we are approaching Port Jackson.'

John Macarthur looked at the captain. 'Wonderful,' he said. The captain turned and left Macarthur with his sheep. As he did he shuddered a little, not from the cold, but from the sense that Macarthur would no doubt choose the sheep over him should it come to it.

He recalled the approach in England of a group of wealthy men, seeking to buy the *Argo*. The tall, curly haired man who stood at the back of the group was introduced as John Macarthur. The men at the front, all rich, were patrons of Macarthur, yet the captain had no doubt that the man at the back was calling the shots.

They wanted to buy the *Argo*, fit her out with sheep pens and sail Macarthur and his sheep to New South Wales. At first the captain thought the idea insane, but the silver tongue of Macarthur had lured him. He talked of his sheep delivering the new golden fleece to the empire, his words more enticing than any Jason had heard from the Siren's song on board the original *Argo*.

And so it was that almost a year later he was now navigating the entry to Port Jackson. Macarthur, part-owner of the *Argo*, walked up beside the captain. 'How I have missed this place,' Macarthur said.

Soon the *Argo* was inside the harbour with a flotilla of small boats approaching. Welcoming back the conquering hero, Macarthur thought to himself. He spied the sleek nowie canoes speeding out, then Bungaree was aboard.

'Macarthur, it is you,' Bungaree said. He performed an elaborate welcome to country dance, then was gone as quickly as he arrived. John Macarthur had that affect on people. They entered his orbit and rapidly sped out of it again. 'People are a means to my plans,' he always told himself. 'Once they have delivered what I need they are best out of my sight.'

He smelled the salt water and fancied the air held a trace of eucalyptus. The vista of the harbour was stunning. The memories flooded in. There was the undoing of Hunter as governor of the colony. The man had the temerity to try to break the power of the New South Wales Corps, and its trade in rum and other goods. Macarthur thought back to the campaign to unseat that odious little man, the social boycott, the unwillingness of

Colonel Patterson to support his own officers. Hunter had been replaced as governor by King, and now King too was done.

Not all the memories were pleasant. There was the unfortunate matter of James Marshall and his assault on Macarthur and Captain Abbott. Predictably, Colonel Patterson had sided with Marshall. So too had the new governor, King. Macarthur had made a blackmail attempt on Patterson, a just reward for siding with King over one of his own men. That had led to King trying to send Macarthur to Norfolk Island as commandant. 'As if I would ever go to that god forsaken hell hole', Macarthur said to himself as he took in the magnificent harbour view. He had refused the post. King had responded with trumped up charges and a court-martial of Macarthur. Macarthur had easily outwitted the governor by having that court-martial held before the officers of the Corps.

Then Colonel Patterson had demanded satisfaction for the way Macarthur had used him and tried to turn him against the governor. The duel was supposed to be one of those affairs where each man discharged a pistol near to the other rather than to wound the opponent. Instead he had aimed to hit Patterson and had done so. The man deserved it having gone against his own men and their interests, Macarthur thought. So what that Macarthur loaded both pistols. 'Why let another do that when it is my life on the line', he had said as justification. 'There is honour only in victory, not in defeat.'

King then made what Macarthur believed to be the only smart move he had ever thought of, sending Macarthur to England for court-martial. The huge dispatch King sent on board that outlined his case against Macarthur had conveniently disappeared when Macarthur had found it and sent it to the bottom of the Timor Strait. There was the providence of stopping at Amboyna after the ship dismasted and meeting

Sir Richard Farquhar, son of Sir Walter, the physician to the Prince of Wales. For what else could it be but divine providence, anointing himself with Royal patronage, Macarthur reminisced.

It had all fallen into place Macarthur remembered. The lack of evidence for the trial, the suggestion that with witnesses in Sydney, New South Wales was the place for a court-martial. The rebuke of King for not handling the matter better himself. Orders to send Macarthur to Norfolk Island were upheld, leaving Macarthur no option but resigning his commission. The realisation that this decision freed him up to finally remake the colony into a mercantile powerhouse was a moment of pure liberation. Sir Walter opening doors that would otherwise have been closed so Macarthur could present that vision of a remade colony. The growing understanding that wool from the colony was the best in the world and the acceptance of his vision to make this happen and break the Spanish monopoly on wool. The patrons who flocked to Macarthur, his ability to shepherd them into his corner.

What could have been more fortuitous, more prophetic, than buying a ship called the *Argo*. If ever there was a case to doubt the divine nature of Macarthur's task in New South Wales it was rebuked by sailing in the new *Argo* with the sheep that would produce a new golden fleece.

Then the coup de gras, Lord Camden had signed off on Macarthur's masterplan to run the colony's emerging industry. There was the coopting of Walter Davidson, Sir Walter Farquhar's nephew into the plan to gain control of the Cowpastures, the finest grazing land in New South Wales. With their joint grants they would control all that land, Macarthur thought.

Macarthur looked out over the harbour, his mind turning to the future that he would write. There can be no stopping me this time, he thought. He had Royal patronage, the approval of Camden and the authorities, grants for the best lands and he knew he could manage Davidson until he could take his land. King was finished as Governor, acting in name only. The Corps were loyal to Macarthur, who controlled the land, the authorities and the military muscle. And now he had returned from England to remake Sydney.

Macarthur looked at the growing settlement coming into view as the *Argo* slid further into the harbour. I am the new Jason, the bringer of the golden fleece that will transform this colony. I am home.

Major George Johnston spurred the horse ahead, thrilling as the buggy flew over the open road. The messenger had arrived barely two hours ago telling him that John Macarthur had returned. He had greeted the news with joy, quickly getting the buggy ready. The outskirts of Sydney, which seemed to encroach further into the bush with each new visit, loomed ahead.

Johnston negotiated the traffic as best he could. Every time a new ship arrived the colony became a little unhinged, sent into raptures from knowing the world had not forgotten it. The major was able to move through the streets reasonably quickly until he reached the military precinct. His progress was rapid from that point. The day was not too cold and the light rain of the morning had long ago cleared.

Once at the barracks Johnston disembarked the buggy and sauntered into the mess hall, expecting to see a large number of officers and soldiers gathered around Mac who would be regaling them with stories of England. Instead it was empty.

Johnston walked outside and looked around. The whole barracks was devoid of life. He walked to the sentry post on the gate.

'Where is everyone, Private?' Johnston asked.

'Mr Macarthur is back Major. The men have gone down to the wharves to see him,' Private Gray answered.

'Thank you Private.'

Johnston thought about taking the buggy but decided to walk. It was not far and the buggy would be impractical once he got closer the hubbub of people and activity near the cove. He strolled down the hill to the cove and saw a sight that made him wonder if he were dreaming. John Macarthur, dressed in civilian clothing, was carefully shepherding a number of large sheep down the gangway from a whaler. All around people milled, watching the spectacle of one of the colony's leading men carefully soothing and cooing to a flock of sheep.

Johnston then realised that a number of soldiers of the Corps were actively forming a perimeter around the remainder of the redcoats, who each tried to hold one of the sheep in place. The whole scene would be comical were it not so serious a breach of discipline and etiquette. Soldiers of the Corps did not engage in manual labour and especially not in front of half the population of Sydney.

At that moment one of the sheep managed to wrangle its way out of the hands of Private Mulligan and began running towards the perimeter.

'Get hold of that sheep man,' Macarthur yelled. 'Hurry man, don't let it escape.' Private Mulligan raced after the sheep. The large animal headed towards the crowd which quickly parted, many laughing at the sight. Privates Wilford, Hutton and Gillard quickly closed on the sheep, and Mulligan came up from behind and managed to grab a large handful of the sheep's wool. 'Grab the bloody thing Thomas,' Johnston heard Wilford say.

The crowd began booing as the sheep was subdued. Macarthur came down the gangway, red in the face and clearly furious. He was about to yell something at Mulligan.

'Hello Mac,' George Johnston said, stepping between Macarthur and Mulligan.

Macarthur looked at Johnston for several seconds before he blinked and came out of his fury. In those moments Johnston searched the face of his friend, reminding himself of the man who had sailed out of Sydney more than four years ago. There was something different that Johnston could not place. He was unsure if his memory had failed him or there was something else that was new, that he was seeing for the first time.

'Major, what a delight to see you. It has been far too long.'

'Welcome home. Now do you think we can get this panto-mime show over and done with quickly so that my soldiers can resume their usual duties. Or do you think we should start charging admission and make a few shillings from the crowd?'

'Tempting though the money is, I think you are right. There is only one more merino left aboard. Once she is disem-barked we can begin the process of moving my flock to the Cowpastures.'

'The Cowpastures are reserved for the government cattle Mac,' Johnston said. Here we go again Johnston thought, Mac is back and already the scheming is underway.

'No, the Cowpastures are mine. Lord Camden has signed them over to me. We have a great deal of catching up to do George, but all in good time.'

Johnston didn't mind the officers calling him George in private, but not here in front of the men and a great deal of the local population.

'I think my officers should use the term Major in public, Captain,' Johnston said.

'Oh, I have resigned my commission and am no longer one of your officers, but again let's talk about that later. Right now these sheep are the priority.' Macarthur turned from Johnston. 'Right lads that is the last of them. To the barracks with the sheep, and then to the Cowpastures.'

Macarthur turned and said something to one of his sons. Macarthur then issued some orders to the captain of the *Argo*, who seemed to respond with great urgency.

Johnston wondered how Macarthur had got the man eating out of his hands. For that matter Mac had the whole Corps under his command within minutes of landing in Sydney, and this despite him no longer being an officer. For a moment Johnston felt envious of Macarthur's ability to bend men to his command with just a few words. Oh to have such a skill, Johnston thought, he would be head of the English army now.

He looked at the spot where Mac had been and realised that the former captain of the Corps was already moving, leading the procession of sheep, soldiers and amused onlookers up the hill towards the barracks. Johnston turned and headed up the hill after his men. He had a foreboding sense that he would be spending a lot of time chasing after John Macarthur. George Johnston shuddered and wondered if it would be his downfall.

The procession finally made it to the barracks. Any semblance of order had long since vanished, to the delight of the crowd. An enterprising vendor was selling bread dipped in wine, which was only making the crowd rowdier. Johnston had a memory of walking a similar route through an even larger crowd after subduing the Irish rebellion. At least on that occasion there was a genuine reason to celebrate. This was only going to go to Macarthur's head, Johnston thought.

Private John Gray heard the noise of the crowd before he saw it. He wondered what on earth was happening, unsure whether to investigate or wait at his post. Gray was still wondering what to do when he saw John Macarthur turn the corner into Church Street.

His eyes widened as he watched Private Richard Mason round the corner, awkwardly shepherding a large sheep. To Gray's amazement more of his fellow soldiers came round the corner, many holding a sheep, others forming a protective ring around the main group of soldier/shepherds and their sheep. Gray blinked a few times, unable to process what he was seeing. Then the crowd spilled onto Church Street from every direction, chanting and screaming and laughing. There was no way he could stop that mob.

'Private Gray, how wonderful to see you,' John Macarthur said as he walked past. Gray stared at Mac for several seconds, his mouth hanging lower and lower as each second passed. Finally he remembered the need to salute and half raised his arm before leaving it hanging in mid-air, as his fellow soldiers walked in, sheep in tow.

Major Johnston walked in with Lieutenant Davies. Gray still had his arm hanging in mid-air. 'Are you saluting us or the sheep Private?' Davies asked as he walked past, grinning at the Private. 'Now make sure the crowd disperses please Private.'

Gray looked at Davies, swallowed hard and looked at the crowd.

'Close the gates Private,' Major Johnston said. 'That should be enough to clear the crowd.'

Gray slowly did as he was asked, and the crowd booed loudly.

John Macarthur strode across to the gates, waved at the crowd and received a rousing cheer. 'I am thrilled to be home.

Can you all do me a favour and go and let the governor know I am back.'

The crowd cheered and sparked by the idea of causing mischief with the unpopular governor, turned and headed down from Church Hill, crossing the Tank Stream as they progressed along Bridge Street. It took quite some time for the crowd to arrive at Government House. The governor's guard had quickly closed the gates of Government House and stood inside the grounds, muskets ready, unsure of what was happening.

Fortunately for the governor the crowd did not transform into a rabble, instead choosing to follow the lead of one wag who yelled, 'Mr Macarthur is back in town and bids you well Governor King, so at least one person still likes you.'

The crowd took up the chant as the light of the day faded fast and the first taverns were opening. There was a pause in proceedings and the wag yelled again, 'I am sure it will not take long for you to piss off your last friend. Now we are off to get on the piss.'

There was a roar. Singing and chanting the crowd disappeared into the night, flooding into dozens of taverns.

The mess hall of the New South Wales Corps was busy too. John Macarthur held centre stage regaling the men with tales of England, Java and Cape Town. Johnston and Davies watched from the sides as the young soldiers all sought to bask in the glow of Macarthur's presence. At that moment Macarthur was talking about Amboyna.

'The heat of the tropics, the blueness of the waters and the placid nature of the locals make it a paradise, one that is not easily forgotten once left. We stayed a number of weeks during which I tasted any and every fruit you can imagine. The flesh of the fruits is so delicious and abundantly ripe, such perfection in your mouth as must be tasted to know it.

'The island itself, in the Maluku Islands, is made of the enmeshing of forests with beaches. You see sand that is so dazzlingly light in the sun, bordered by shaded groves of forests amongst which all delight of creatures roam.'

Davies turned to Johnston. 'Mac hasn't lost that knack of knowing how to deliver the most wonderful visions.'

Johnston took a deep draught of wine. 'No he hasn't. Mind you, if it were me after so many years away I would not be seeking an audience of soldiers but an audience with my Esther. I wonder what Mrs Macarthur will make of this?'

'I suspect Mrs Macarthur will survive one more night apart from her husband. She has thrived to this point, running the farm by herself. One might suspect she actually enjoys the challenge of proving what she is capable of,' Davies said.

'I would advise you not to say that to Mac, nor to suggest to him that you have taken any interest in the affairs of his home while he was away. You know as well as I that Mac changes his tune with the wind if it suits him. And I do think that there are times that if the wind does not change he talks the wind into changing direction to suit him. I swear he could talk all but the most obstinate of men into whatever he wills.'

'You sound concerned Major.'

'Do you think that Mac has changed?'

'I am not sure I understand what you mean, George?'

'I'm not sure I do either. It just seems to me that something is different in Mac, and I do not know what that means for him. Or for us.'

The drinking and stories continued late into the night. 'Well gentlemen... and officers,' Macarthur said to much laughter, 'I must retire for tomorrow I propose to visit the governor, give him my well wishes and expedite the land claims that are mine.'

'Three cheers for Mac,' Sargent Bremlow shouted. 'Hippip … hooray. Hippip…hooray. Hippippp….hoorrrayyy.'

The officers and men gradually left the mess hall, until only Macarthur and Johnston remained.

'George, I would greatly appreciate it if you were to accompany me to see King tomorrow. A united front between the mercantile class and the Corps will break whatever resolve King may still have.'

'Mac, what exactly are your intentions here?'

'While I was in England opportunity presented itself to me in a way I had not thought possible. The authorities there have little understanding of what this land may become. Most think it nothing more than a provincial backwater. But I was able to illuminate their minds with the spark of what we can bring to Sydney. Wealth, a vital place in the Empire and a new model for living, with the merchants running the land. The wealth can flow down to all. But none of that is possible without the assent of the governor and the authorities in England.

'Don't you see, what we have built is just the start. This land can be abundant in producing wool, wheat and beef. Even wine may be grown here in time, I firmly believe that. But to make this happen we have to move beyond the idea of Sydney as a penal colony. It must become a mercantile hub, producing wool that is in demand the world over. And this is so easily possible. All I need are the Cowpastures for my sheep and some convict labour to run them. Then we can start producing real wealth through commerce. We will not need to rely on rum trading, that can be a sideline activity.

'King is broken, and if we can present a united front, let him know that the Corps backs my plans, his resolve will crack like a dropped egg. Stand by me tomorrow and stand with the future of this colony, so we can make it into a grand centre of the world.'

Johnston looked at his friend and knew that he had changed. To stand against Macarthur would be to invite all the fury and vitriol of the obsessed and Johnston knew he was not strong enough for that. This was his home and what harm could come from making it richer?

'Alright Mac, I will come with you. Just remember that in the days ahead, and remember where you have come from. You were a Corps man before you were a mercantilist, and for that I will stand with you. Good night.'

Johnston turned and walked out. His lot was with Mac now and he hoped to hell that it worked out.

Macarthur and Johnston walked up the driveway to Government House at 10. Once inside they were ushered into a small meeting room where they waited for twenty minutes before Governor King entered.

Johnston was shocked to see the governor. While never a big man King had always appeared robust in health, carrying perhaps a little more weight than comfortable. The thin, pale and hunched-over man that now inhabited King's body looked completely broken. The haughty arrogance of King's face was replaced by a vacancy that came from chronic pain.

'Gentlemen, how may I be of assistance? For it is surely assistance you come seeking.' King coughed hard and long, doubling over at the end of the fit. He reached for the back of a chair and nearly fell. Johnston closed the space between them and helped King stumble into the chair. He turned and looked at Mac who had a glimpse of a smile on his face and a gleam in his eyes.

'Governor, I come bearing dispatches from Lord Camden, the Colonial Secretary, and, I should add, my friend, relating to the establishment of a wool industry here in Sydney. To achieve this I am granted five thousand acres of my choosing. Once exports of wool begin to England I am to have another five thousand acres.

'Upon reflection I believe the Cowpastures are the only land that would be suitable for this enterprise considered vital to England's future. I have already brought here fine Merino sheep to breed a new flock. So without delay I intend to move these sheep to the Cowpastures and establish operations.'

King looked at Macarthur. 'Sir, you are back but one day and already up to your scheming again. I cannot simply grant you public land and turf out the cattle grazing at the Cowpastures. You and I well know that this land is the best in the colony. It has been reserved for all to graze.'

'Here, Governor, are the dispatches. There is one in there confirming your recall once a suitable replacement has been found.'

Johnston stared hard at Macarthur. He had read the official dispatches to the Governor. There were limits that should be kept, even for John Macarthur. Before Johnston could say any-thing Macarthur continued.

'I may suggest that a convenient option would be for you Mr King, to approve this grant on an interim basis, and then leave the official approval to the next Governor. This would go a long way to mending the enmity between ourselves, and between yourself and the New South Wales Corps. There is no need to continue to fight us when you could work with us to build a brighter future for this col-ony and side with the mercantile class that is ushering in this bright future. And as a further sign of your support I have deeds for land here in Sydney that will form a base for exports. All you have to do is agree, I will organise the rest. Alternatively you could continue to fight. How is your health by the way?'

King looked aghast. He tried to rise but that only sparked another fit of coughing. It lasted so long that Johnston feared it may be terminal. He opened the door and shouted for the governor's aides to help. Two came running and helped the governor to his feet. Johnston was surprised to feel pity for this man who had been an enemy of the Corps and rum trading for so long. It was clear that King was broken.

His aides helped lift him and carry him out of the room.

'Governor, you have not answered me,' Macarthur said.

'Mac, this is not the time. We should return later,' Johnston said.

'Governor, I will take it that you are in agreement with my plan and begin moving my sheep to the Cowpastures. And you offer no objections to the land in Sydney. Unless of course you say otherwise now.'

King could barely breathe let alone talk as his aides helped carry him out of the room.

'Thank you Governor, and get well,' Macarthur said. 'But not too soon,' he muttered under his breath, a wicked smile on his face.

As they walked out of the governor's mansion Johnston looked at Macarthur. There was no doubt in his mind now that Mac had changed.

'You pushed that very hard Mac.'

'The future direction of this colony is at stake, I will push as long and hard as needed to make that future real.'

Williams stared at the books again, trying to make sense of the numbers. The accounting books were clear, there should be one hundred and twenty pounds in the Corps's money box. The problem was only seventy pounds were in the box. The where-abouts of the missing fifty pounds was a complete mystery to Williams. Worse, he didn't know what to do about it. Worst of all, he didn't know how to tell Minchin, Davies and Johnston.

For two days he had gone over the books until the columns merged into each other and the numbers swam about in his head as he slept fitfully. All the usual taverns distributing liquor had received their normal monthly consignment. They had each paid the usual amounts. The sales profit had come back in as evidenced by the receipts that Corps members had signed to account for monies collected. After the monthly distributions to Corps members there should have been one hundred and twenty pounds left over, kept in the money box. However, there was not one hundred and twenty quid. There was only seventy quid.

Somehow he was fifty quid short. The receipts added up so why not the cash he wondered for the hundredth time.

'What's up?' Smith said as he walked in.

'Nothing,' Williams said too quickly before slamming the books shut.

Smith looked at Williams and went to say something before thinking better of it. Both men knew not to push the other. Smith went over to his bunk and sat down. He watched Williams for a time. The younger man was fidgety, sweating and continuously glancing from the closed book of figures to the money box.

Smith took a moment to place what was wrong. The money box should not be in the sleeping quarters, it was always kept in the mess under lock and key.

'Oli, what is it?'

'I said nothing.'

'It won't be nothing if someone else comes in here and finds you alone with the money box.'

'Nate, I don't know what I did wrong.'

Smith shivered in fear. He had never seen Williams looking so lost, so out of control. There was something almost manic in his eyes.

'So tell me slowly what's wrong.'

'The books add up but the money doesn't.'

'Humour me, what does that mean?'

'It means that according to the books there should be one hundred and twenty quid in here,' Williams said pointing to the money box. 'But there is only seventy quid. I am missing fifty quid sterling.'

'Right...' Smith said drawing the word out.

'Nate, I don't know where the money is. Besides me only the quartermaster and Johnston have a key.'

'Oh shit,' Smith said. 'So one of them is stealing?'

'No, nothing has gone missing before. It isn't one of them. It can't be. Christ there's no use talking to you about it.'

'Oli, sorry I don't understand. What are you saying?'

'I've lost fifty quid sterling. Because of my father who do you think they're going to blame? I'll be accused of stealing. God can they shoot me for that?'

'Shoot? No,' Smith said. 'Hang you, maybe.'

'Oh shit,' Williams said.

'All right, so if it wasn't stolen where is it?'

'If I bloody knew that do you think I would be panicking?'

'All right, first things first. Let's get that money box back before someone notices.'

Williams didn't move. He sat rooted to the spot, looking from the books to the money box and back.

'Oli, we need to get that box back to the mess. Now!'

Williams turned abruptly from looking at the box and slowly focused on Smith. Then he lifted the box and put it and the books under some rags. Smith went to the door and cracked it open before giving the all clear. Then as casually as the two could muster, which looked like two men walking away from a robbery at speed, they crossed the yard.

Smith stopped at the door and checked the mess. Fortunately it appeared empty of soldiers and the two quickly crossed to the locked cupboard before Williams unlocked it and shoved the box and books back in.

'I was wondering who it would be,' Laycock said icily as he stepped out of a shadowy corner.

'Quartermaster Laycock, it's not what it seems,' Smith said.

Laycock looked at Smith and wondered what would happen next. He held the pistol in his left hand, his body hiding the weapon from sight. 'So we are fifty quid short of where we should be and someone has to go down for this.'

'How do you know it's fifty quid? It was you,' Williams said. He recalled the humiliation of Wee Willy and Laycock's relish when he told Johnston the story. He always suspected the quartermaster did not like him. Then fear swept across Williams as he realised just how close Laycock was to Johnston. He recalled how ruthless the quartermaster was at the battle of Castle Hill, the warning Jones had given him, and knew that the man would not hesitate to do what was needed.

'No it wasn't me, you bloody thief,' Laycock said.

'But you know fifty quid is missing,' Smith said.

'I double check the books for the major,' Laycock said.

'Really? You can read the books?' Williams said.

'I know enough to check the bottom line against the money in the money box,' Laycock said. 'And I know when it comes up short. Most of all I know that whoever returned the missing money box is the thief.'

'It wasn't me,' Williams said.

'That's what they all say sonny,' Laycock said, raising the pistol. Smith who had been edging away from Williams froze.

'Do you think I would take the bloody money box out if I was stealing from it,' Williams said.

'Seems like a convenient way to lift some money,' Laycock said. 'What was it, got a whore into trouble or lost too much gambling or what?'

'I didn't do it,' Williams pleaded.

'Well from where I'm standing it makes perfect sense to pin this on you.'

Smith shot a look at Williams, wondering if it was Laycock after all, and he and Williams were being set up to take the fall.

'Anything you want to add Corporal? I always thought you were a decent man,' Laycock said.

'Show him the books Oli,' Smith said.

'What about the books?' Laycock said.

'They add up,' Smith said.

'So what?' Laycock said.

'So the books don't show money missing,' Smith said.

'I think we are all aware of that,' Laycock said.

'So if you do the books why not cover your tracks in the books,' Smith said.

'So sonny, are you cooking the books?' Laycock said. 'Or hadn't you quite got around to that yet?'

'Christ Quartermaster, he's had access to the books for days. Why steal from the money box and not match it up on the books,' Smith said. 'Tell him Oli, Show him.'

Williams stood mute staring at the barrel of the pistol still pointed at him.

'Oli say something,' Smith said.

'Well sonny, last chance before things get really fun,' Laycock said.

'The…the books add up. There should be one hundred and twenty quid in the money box,' Williams said. 'But there is only seventy. Why would I steal and not fix the books up?'

'So you admit you can do that can you?' Laycock said. 'Fix the books up?'

'Yes but…' Williams started.

'So then, show me,' Laycock said, cutting him off.

'Can you at least lower the pistol?' Williams said.

'It doesn't mean I won't use it shortly,' Laycock said.

Carefully Williams unlocked the cupboard and pulled the books out and opened them. Then he moved to the nearest table, followed by Smith.

'You stay back there Corporal,' Laycock said, waving the pistol. Smith retreated back to his previous place beside the cupboard. 'And you sonny, anything funny and I will use this.'

Williams waited until Laycock was near enough to see the books and then showed him the receipts, the columns and the bottom line that all added up. 'So you see it adds up in the books, yet when I went to check the money box it was fifty quid short.'

Laycock watched Williams, whose face flushed and burned with embarrassment and fear. It seemed as if he might cry.

'So say I believe you? Where is the fifty quid then?' Laycock said. 'It don't bear thinking about if it wasn't us that stole the money.'

'I don't think it was stolen,' Williams said. 'Why would someone start now? Do you think any of the officers suddenly has need of it?'

'No I don't,' Laycock said.

'Which leaves only one other option,' Williams said.

There was a pause of several moments.

'Well enlighten us then sonny,' Laycock said.

'It's my fault, I made an error,' Williams said. Then he flushed red and wiped at his eyes, the shame and fear tumbling out.

'So then what do you propose?' Johnston said, sitting in the small living room of his farmhouse.

Laycock, Smith and Williams had gone out to Annandale to see the major. 'Its better this way sonny,' Laycock had said when he first proposed the trip. 'Or would you rather do this in the mess?'

Williams had agreed to go and see Johnston. Smith had said he should go; although whether out of solidarity with Williams or curiosity about what would happen next or some other motivation he couldn't be sure. 'And who could pass up the chance to see the major in his domestic setting,' Smith had whispered to Williams when musing on his reasoning for tagging along.

That domestic setting was a large, neatly kept farmhouse, with children of a variety of ages and sizes and Johnston's Esther providing refreshments. The rooms were cosy and well ordered with a clear feminine touch. Although she was a former convict Esther was well respected amongst the Corps and beyond, despite being known as a homebody. The social circuit was not one that the Johnston's paid much due to, both considering it a necessary evil that they attend the occasional ball.

As Smith and Williams walked in it was immediately clear who ruled the roost. Johnston seemed different in his home environment, less imposing and softer. The children who moved around at a variety of speeds looked at Johnston with affection, something the major returned to his children in spades.

Esther was the one issuing the orders to the children when they took too long to give the visitors some space. Johnston seemed bemused by the whole episode and clearly unwilling to speak too forcefully to his children.

Williams recalled Smith regaling the troops about Johnston's heroics at the battle of Bunker Hill when the major was little more than a boy. Jones' words at the pub after the men returned to Sydney from the battle at Toongabbie also echoed; about the major caring for his men. Perhaps that was why the Major was so lenient on his children, letting them enjoy the full benefits of a childhood that Johnston himself had never had. Seeing Johnston at home amongst his children only increased the affection Williams had for the major.

It took Laycock several minutes to extract Johnston from his family and convince the major to speak in private. Laycock had smoothed the way, mentioning that he believed Williams. 'It takes a real criminal to stare down the barrel of a pistol and keep calm and coldly lie,' Laycock had said. 'And our boy here practically dissolved, hardly the calculating mind of a thief.' How exactly Laycock had reached that conclusion he didn't share, but it certainly sounded good.

'So you are prepared to believe the lad then?' Johnston had said. 'Well that's good enough for me.' At which point the meeting had shifted and Johnston turned to finding a solution.

'Answer the major lad," Laycock said. 'What's your solution to this?'

'I will repay it out of my pocket,' Williams said.

'You misunderstand me,' Johnston said. 'The money is not the issue, it's cleaning up your own mess. You have the brains to figure it out, so work out where we went wrong and fix it so it doesn't happen again. Can you do that?'

'Yes sir,' Williams said.

'And Corporal, next time something goes wrong you tell me immediately. I don't want to have to find out about it later, is that clear?' Johnston said.

'Yes sir.'

'What disappoints me the most is that you didn't place your trust in the Corps,' Johnston said. Then he paused far longer than needed, letting the idea drill deep into Williams's psyche. 'All we have out here is one another and the people we love. If you cannot trust in that then you need to rethink your place in the New South Wales Corps,' Johnston said.

Williams dropped his head and tried not to let the tears well up, then blushed with shame again as tears fell.

'Well Major I suggest we take this as a sign that the lad understands now,' Laycock said.

'Quartermaster truer words have not been spoken,' Johnston said.

Williams, Smith and Laycock had headed back into Sydney late that afternoon. The journey back had been quiet with Laycock and Smith giving Williams time to ruminate on the major's words. Williams heard Johnston's words echo around his mind. 'What disappoints me the most is that you didn't place your trust in the the Corps.' That stung deeply.

Back at the barracks Williams had gone straight to the mess. 'I need to have another look at the books. Maybe something will jump out at me.'

'Oli, rest up, have a look at it tomorrow,' Smith said. 'You look exhausted.'

'I think Corporal Smith is right lad, rest up,' Laycock said.

Williams went to bed early and slept well for the first time in two nights. Then the next morning he set to looking at the books with a fresh eye.

'Nate, whose writing is that?' Williams said.

Smith looked at the receipt that Williams was holding. 'I don't know. Who's the receipt from?'

'I think it's for the liquor sold by John Evans at the Red Sea.'

'You think?'

'Well it's bloody hard to read. It's more scribble than proper writing.'

Williams looked at the receipt for a few moments longer, twisting and turning it as though in doing so the mystery of the scribbled writing would reveal itself.

'Why that receipt Oli?'

'What?'

'Why that one? Why not any of the others?'

'The date. It should be the fifteenth of the month, only it's not. Well I think it's not. The writing is so hard to read. There are a few others here too all the same.'

'So who collects from the Red Sea?'

'Tom does,' Williams said. He quickly organised the receipts that had the same scribbled, illegible writing, then stared at them for a few moments. Then he ordered the other receipts into groups and compared each group to the books. 'All these receipts that are scribbled on, they add up to fifty pounds. Every other group of receipts matches up to a soldier and the pubs they collect from and have all been signed. But not this group. And you know what they have in common? They are all on Tom's round. I'd better go see him.'

'Mind if I tag along?'

'I would rather do this alone.'

'And I think you'd be better not to do this alone. We don't want anyone going off on a wild goose chase, or worse.'

'If you must Nate.'

Conner was at his small house in Pitt's Row when Williams and Smith knocked. His wife, Jess, who was considered one of the most beautiful women in the colony, opened the door.

'Well here's trouble,' Jess said.

'We were hoping Tom was in,' Williams said.

'He's out back. I'll get him,' Jess said.

Smith watched Jess walk through the house, admiring her almost perfect shape. 'Lucky Tom indeed,' he said.

'What?

'I was just admiring the view and thinking how lucky Tom is to have a girl like that.'

'This is serious. Do you think you can keep your head out of your pants for a few moments?'

'If you're telling me you are seeing that heavenly vision and not getting distracted, even a little, I'm worried for you boyo.'

Tom Conner walked into the room. 'Oli, Nate, can I help you?'

'Tell me why you are fifty quid short on your collections last month Tom?' Williams said, moving threateningly towards Conner.

'What the hell are you talking about Oli?' Conner said.

'Christ Oli, slow down. I thought we're just asking a few questions,' Smith said.

'Well the money that is missing was his responsibility. Put two and two together Nate and what do you get?' Williams said.

'Overwrought I think,' Smith said. 'Just steady on a moment and think. If Tom didn't put his money in why are the books up to date.'

Williams stopped and looked at Smith. 'It doesn't work like that Nate, and it was his receipts that were scribbled on.'

'What are you talking about Oli?' Conner said.

'There's fifty quid missing from the collections last month, and I checked all your receipts and they're all just scribbled on. Like someone thought that they could not sign their name and get away with things. And your receipts all added together total fifty quid. So what are you playing at? Did you pocket the money yourself?'

'Last month. Last month I was sick, don't you remember. You said you would do the collecting for me?' Conner said. 'Nate you were there too. Oh God don't you rembember. You both came here with some food and Oli said don't worry about the collections, he would do it. I gave you the receipts so you could do it.'

'Oh Christ Oli, we did. It wasn't Tom, it was us. We came here and then we stopped at the Londoner, at Henry's and got drunk,' Smith said.

Somewhere in the recesses of Williams's mind a hazy series of images played out; of standing in the room they were in now and talking to a very sick looking Tom, of running into a few of the Corps lads and then a series of broken pictures. Nate laughing, someone spewing, a person falling off a table, more falling over, laughter, spewing. And then signing some receipts while drunk. No wonder he couldn't match the writing to Tom's script or any other. It was his own when drunk.

'Oh bloody hell," William said. The shame of the previous day flushed back into his face.

'Well if there's one group who would understand getting drunk and forgetting something important it's the Corps,' Smith said weakly.

'Tom... Tom, I am so sorry. I accused you and it was me,' Williams said. There was quiet for many seconds.

'Do you know why I like you Oli?' Conner said. 'Its not because you're smart. God knows you're smarter than the rest of us common soldiers put together. Or because you are going places and some of us may benefit from it. Its because you're decent. You don't make my life harder. You make it better.

I always feel better when I see you. That's why I like you. And I know that we have our own lives now and maybe we aren't as close as what we thought we would be sailing out here, but that's all right too. At the end of the day I know you have my back and will do what is right by me. So I will go out today and collect the money for you, and you will have it before sundown.'

'That sounds fair Oli,' Smith said.

'I accused you with no evidence. You don't have to do that. I can,' Williams said.

'Oli, you did me a favour. Let me do one for you, to show there are no hard feelings. Please,' Conner said.

'Cmon Oli. Let's go and tell the major what happened,' Smith said. 'We owe him that.'

Johnston tried to suppress a smile and when he couldn't the smile triggered the laughter. Laycock burst out laughing and then Smith started too. It took several moments before the major and quartermaster finally regained some control.

'Well at least you are honest,' Johnston said. He looked at Laycock who smirked and started laughing again. Before long the three men, Johnston, Laycock and Smith were laughing. Only Williams stayed quiet, staring at the floor.

'Don't...' Johnston said, then laughed. 'Don't let it happen again. I am proud of the fact that you got to the bottom of this and had the courage to front up and tell me. And if there is one place that such behaviour is an excuse it's probably the Corps.'

'That's what I said,' Smith said proudly.

'Well Corporal, I wouldn't be too proud. Knowing you, you were most likely the ringleader of the drinking and central to this little debacle,' Johnston said. 'So you are tasked with making sure it doesn't happen again.'

Johnston looked at Williams, who now sat looking at the floor. He knew it would take Williams a bit of time to recover his confidence. 'And Corporal Smith,' Johnston said quietly, 'you had better get him back to being his old self soon. We have had a good run with young Williams looking after the books and I want that to continue. Is that clear?"

There was a tone of command in Johnston's words that an old army man like Smith could not fail to recognise. He swallowed hard. 'Yes Major.'

'There is something unpleasant that I must do before we sign off on this,' Johnston said. 'You are demoted to Private again Williams.'

Johnston watched and waited for Williams to drop his head. Instead he was surprised as Williams held his gaze. 'Good. You earned that stripe once, work hard and you just may do so again. Now best you two be out of my sight.'

'Yes sir,' Williams and Smith said. Then the two left quickly.

'Was I too hard on him?' Johnston said to Laycock.

'No.'

'Let's see if the boy has the fight in him to come back from this.'

August 1805

'Its Bligh,' Minchin said as he burst into the mess hall of the Corps.

'William Bligh has been announced as the new governor,' Minchin repeated.

'You mean Bligh of the *Bounty* mutiny? Bloody hell,' Davies said.

'Sounds like London is sending a hard nut that will not be so easy to crack,' Minchin said.

There was silence for a few moments.

'Are you going to enlighten us with your theory Lieutenant Minchin, or should we just sit here in the warm glow of your smugness,' Major Johnston said.

'Well, you send a hard nut to break another hard nut; like for like,' Minchin said.

'Do you mean us?' Davies said.

'Why not? After all the man is renowned for being a disciplinarian and for going hard on those who fail to comply. Perhaps this appointment is as much about us? We have, after all, broken the last two governors. This may be a warning to us to tread carefully.'

Again there was silence.

Johnston smiled.

'What is so amusing, pray tell Major?' Davies said.

'Who's going to tell Mac? And can you see Mac and Bligh meeting? Now there is a picture.'

'This isn't going to end well, is it Major,' Davies said jokingly. He had no idea how prophetic that statement would be.

'What do you mean Bligh?' Macarthur said. 'That useless idiot from the *Bounty* that lost his crew to women in Tahiti. What the hell is Banks thinking?'

John Macarthur stared at George Johnston. 'Banks told me the next governor would be manageable. Not some stupid bloody sailor who likes to whip his crew into mutinies. I met with Banks. Don't you see George, I met him and told him of my grand plan to establish the world's best wool industry here and he heard me. He heard me. And now he sends William bloody Bligh. This is a betrayal. He wants to end me.'

'Who wants to end you Mac? Do you mean Bligh?' Johnston said.

'Not Bligh, Sir Joseph bloody Banks, that's who. Probably thinks some of his precious plants will be eaten by my sheep.' Macarthur suddenly burst out laughing. 'Nothing will stop me setting up the wool industry here George, nothing. Do you want a drink?'

Johnston looked at his old friend and was surprised at how quickly Macarthur's mood could shift. He pondered what that meant; was it a sign of Macarthur's genius or of some darker madness.

'Thank you, a drink would be lovely.'

'You know George, once we get the wool going and export it I think we could grow wonderful wine grapes here and start producing wine here in New South Wales.'

'Really, that would be something,' Johnston said. 'So your sheep, these merinos, they are doing well?'

'Extraordinarily well dear George,' Macarthur said. 'They are such a robust and adaptable sheep. Do you know they come from southern Spain, around Extremadura and are considered one of the main reasons for Spain's commercial fortunes in the fifteenth and sixteenth centuries? Their wool is fine and soft. The rams that I have bought in England will breed with my flock here and start to pass their traits over.

'The first man to bring merino sheep to England was Joseph Banks.' There was a long pause and Johnston wondered if Macarthur would once again rail against Banks. 'Of course, the wars with Bonaparte have all but destroyed the Spanish industry, which is why we are so well placed to fill that gap.'

Macarthur spent the next ten minutes lecturing on the topic of merino sheep. By the time Johnston stood to excuse himself he felt he knew more about sheep, and merinos in particular, than he could ever have hoped to. Or wanted to for that matter.

'John thank you for that. I do believe that you will make a great success of this. By the way is Elizabeth at home?'

'She is out helping with the manageemnt of the flock. It seems while I was in England Elizabeth took to the task very well. Shall I say hello when she returns?'

'Please give her my regards, and those of Esther too.' Johnston gathered his hat and walked out to his buggy. Macarthur stood on the verandah and watched Johnston climb into the buggy and drive off. So it is Bligh, Macarthur thought to himself. 'Well it will take more than Bligh to stop me,' Macarthur muttered as he turned and walked inside.

'Come on Nate, the warehouse is full and you are dillydallying. They won't be able to hold off the colonists all day,' Williams said. He and Smith were on their way to the port warehouses to meet Lieutenant Minchin and pick over the latest trading goods that had arrived the day before.

'Steady on Oli, I was just saying hello to Madame Brigitte. It is considered polite to doff one's hat to the ladies and make a little small talk,' Smith replied.

'I'm not sure how the two of you can talk with your tongues halfway down each other's throats. Come on.'

'Well you seem to have your confidence back Private,' Smith said. 'Don't forget you are talking to a superior.'

'Superior what Nate?' Williams said.

'Careful you cheeky bugger or I will have you up on charges.'

'And drop me in it. Where would you be without me Corporal?'

'Clearly my efforts to rebuild your confidence have not been in vain.'

Williams blushed a little. The shame of his recent mistake still carried a sting. Laycock had enjoyed calling Williams Wee Willy again. 'Don't worry lad, I am not referring to your manhood, rather another deficiency. Wee Willy short a fifty I should say. But nothing to cry over then,' Laycock had said. Even now Laycock would occasionally drop that line and Williams felt the sting as his cheeks flushed.

There was the first time he had faced the troops again as a private, unsure how they would react. Unsure of just about everything, he recalled.

'Don't worry too much Oli,' Tom Conner said. 'You'll get back to Corporal soon enough.' George Newbank and a number of the other younger men had said much the same, almost willing one of their own to rise again from the ranks. That provided a little reassurance to Williams.

For Williams it was the older men that were the hardest to face. Many took the chance to bump into him in the barracks, or to insult him directly. Williams expected it to last for a day or two but after a week he was still the victim of insults and seemingly accidental collisions.

'Nate, how much longer will this go on?' Williams had asked at the end of the first week.

'Oli, they just don't know how to handle you. A week ago most of 'em were convinced you were going to be the next lieutenant. Now you are one of them again and a few want to remind you of that. A couple of the wiser heads - and bearing in mind that wisdom in that lot is in short supply - they're just getting their shots in while they still can,' Smith said. 'Best I can say is to hold fast for a few days longer, then it'll go away.'

'There's something else too Nate,' Williams said. 'Did I get promoted because I am a good soldier or because…well because I am good at running the rum trade?'

'What does it matter Oli. You got promoted and that's what matters.'

'So it was because of the rum side of it then?'

'Oli, soldiers get promoted for all types of reasons. Because they're good soldiers, because they are ruthless and don't care about ordering others to their deaths, or because they know to make officers look good or because they can do things others can't. If you stop to think about it too long you can find any number of reasons for your promotion. So the major values the rum trade, so what? If it gets you a promotion then accept it.'

Williams ran that conversation through his head each night as he tried to fall asleep, contemplating his fall from grace and his change in circumstances. In fretting over the idea he nurtured it and allowed it, like a weed, to find a place to seed. It only added to his misery, seeing malice in the looks of soldiers when none were there, retreating inside himself with only his thoughts.

Williams had cared little for anything during that time. It took another two weeks until the insults and pushes and shoves stopped, until Laycock stopped with the Wee Willys every time he saw Williams. Yet Williams still did not feel part of the group.

He endured the shame of knowing that the others knew he had made a mistake. However it was late one night that things had taken a turn for the worse.

'Well then Isaac here he is,' Robert Hall said.

'And yet what is missing is our money, Robert,' Isaac Champion said.

Several of the younger soldiers cleared the room upon seeing Hall and Champion. Both were sergeants in the Corps and both had a reputation for being men not to be crossed.

Williams stood up.

'Not you bright boy, not you,' Hall said. 'You stay. The rest of you out now.'

'So we were counting our share of the profits and it's short,' Champion said. 'And that is unacceptable Corporal. Or is it Private? I can't keep up with these changes.'

'What you need to do, young Wee Willy, is find the five pounds we are each owed, and pay it now,' Hall said.

'You got paid your share,' Williams said.

'I don't think you get it, our shares are going up five quid a go and you are going to cover that,' Hall said.

'I can't do that,' Williams said.

'Sorry Sergeant Major Champion, did you hear the correct use of my title by this private?' Hall said.

'Sergeant Major Hall, I did not, so perhaps we teach the young man a lesson,' Champion said.

With that Hall moved quickly and backhanded Williams across the cheek, sending him sprawling across the bed.

Champion then flipped the bed over and kicked Williams hard in the stomach.

'Anything you want to say now bright boy?' Hall said.

'What we are looking for is "Here is your money sargeant's" and with an appropriate tone of respect too,' Champion said.

'I can't do that Sergeant Major,' Williams said.

Champion and Hall left the barracks ten miutes later. 'He ain't gunna give in is he?' Champion said to Hall.

'We've been here too long, enough of the men saw us. Best we be off,' said Hall.

'Now listen bright boy, you tell anyone and by God this will be the least of it, understand?' Champion said. 'Understand?'

Williams nodded slowly. The two sergeants turned and left. Williams crawled to his bed and slowly turned it over and rearranged the mattress.

Smith found Williams later that evening, nursing his wounds in his bed.

'Jesus Oli, what happened?'

'I tripped over Nate.'

'Just tell me who did it and by God I will give them a going over like they won't ever forget.'

'Leave it Nate, it's done.'

'I won't leave it, just tell me.'

'I can't Nate, trust in that.'

'Oli, whoever it was …'

'Nate I can't say. Leave it.'

Smith looked at William's beaten face, his left eye already closed over from swelling. 'Oh shit, it was some of us wasn't it?'

'Leave it Nate, please.'

Williams was excused from duty for several days by D'Arcy Wentworth when the surgeon examined him the next morning.

'Care to mention any names to me and things will happen,' Wentworth had said. 'The major will not stand for this.'

'Please Mr Wentworth, I'll recover. There's no need to tell anyone, please.'

'Last chance. It will all happen quietly,' Wentworth said.

Williams looked away through the window and tried to focus on a branch of a tree moving in the wind. He watched the branch for as long as he could, fighting the temptation to name Hall and Champion. Time seemed to stop.

'Alright then,' Wentworth finally said. 'The major will be disappointed in the fact you have kept silent. He is quite fond of you after all. However it is the right thing to do.'

Williams recovered slowly. He took a small comfort from knowing Johnston had a fondness for him. It still hurt that Johnston seemed unwilling to acknowledge that fondness. The major had simply nodded at Williams on the next few occasions the two had seen each other.

'Nate, all he does is nod at me,' Williams had said to Smith. 'I should have told Wentworth who did it.'

'Trust me Oli, you did the right thing. The major rarely talks to the enlisted men so don't get upset. Just bide your time.'

For Williams, not having the recognition of Johnston and his fellow officers was the hardest part to bear. Each time he saw an officer he felt the shame rise. He missed the sense of belonging to the inner circle of the Corps. His dealings with the officers relating to the books and rum trade were confined to Lieutenant Minchin or Quartermaster Laycock. The other officers kept their distance, an aloofness that stung Williams harder and longer than any blow Hall or Champion had landed.

Williams hated that his exile was still going on months later, hated the blush that flushed his cheeks when he was reminded of that exile. The worst of it was it was his own fault. He had made a choice to go easier on the liquor following his demotion. It helped that each drink brought back the memory of his foolishness and its consequences. And in the back of his mind the thought nagged away; his promotion had more to do with his book keeping and running the rum trade than with his abilities as a soldier. He tried to ignore the thought but it never truly went away.

The whole time Nate Smith had dutifully worked to get Williams on the up, talking to him about what was happening in the mess, offering tidbits about the officers. It helped lessen the sense of remoteness from the officers.

'Don't worry Oli, the major is very happy with how the rum side of things is running and he complements you to the other officers,' Smith had said. 'He is impressed with how you haven't buckled under and dare I say it is fond of you. It may take time but I think the major will promote you back to Corporal. You did a good job before so he knows you can do it again.'

For Williams that was the turning point, the moment that he started to find a way out of the maze of negative thoughts and doubts. Smith had got him more involved in the day to day business of soldiering and general shenanigans, ensuring Williams went out with his mates drinking and did not miss out on the fun.

It had taken a few months but eventually Williams was back to his old self and Smith was both relieved and grateful. He had not realised how much Williams had come to mean to him, how close the two were.

As he walked to the docks Williams in turn was glad Smith chose to study the street ahead rather than look at him.

The two soldiers eventually made it to the warehouses alongside the wharves of Sydney Cove. Lieutenant Minchin was already inside, along with Newbank, Conner, Gillard and Mason.

'Nice of you two to join us. Next time we shall send word when a ship departs England and you might just make it on time,' Minchin said. 'We have the inventory here. Oliver if you will please work your magic with the numbers and tell us what we can and cannot buy.'

Williams always found it amusing that Minchin used their names and not their ranks to address the soldiers when they were buying up trade goods. At any other time a senior officer would use rank and surname to address his men, but in the half-way world of mercantile commerce those rules no longer applied, even if the hierarchy still stood.

Williams read the inventory quickly. The Corps would buy the rum and wine by the barrel, and of course sell as bottles to maximise profit. Williams quickly noted down all the wine and rum. The coal was of little value due to the plentiful supply in the public store and winter almost at an end, so Williams put a line through that. There was cedar and oak, both in demand for building. Wheat was plentiful at the minute but stored well and his experience up in the Hawkesbury had shown Williams that a large flood could wipe out much of the wheat supply. There were a range of foodstuffs from the exotic to the mundane, including relishes, sugar and dried peas. We best get those and use the smaller traders to sell them off, he thought, noting down names next to each item.

The smaller traders that the Corps preferred were mainly ex-convicts, who could be easily leant on and who understood how these deals worked. Williams knew them all by name. Most of the smaller wholesalers supplemented their incomes selling from their houses, taking a small profit off the top. None were so stupid as to not make good on their debts to the Corps.

They all knew the stories of those ex-convicts who had failed to make a payment or tried to cheat the Corps out of their share. Most of the stories were variations on the same theme. The courts were not used, rather a more direct approach involving several soldiers 'having a quiet word' with the offending ex-convict. Those quiet words were heavily punctuated with violence, both to the person and any property of value. In one extreme case threats were also made to the ex-convict's woman with suggestions that she could pay off the debt by entertaining the soldiers. The truth of the stories was never fully known but the Corps were in the habit of reminding their ex-convict business-partners of some of the stories as a condition of good working partnerships.

Williams had only ever been involved in one such visit and found the whole thing unsavoury in the extreme. Afterwards he had vowed not to be involved in any future "quiet words" with suppliers. He preferred the figures, the handling of currency and books, contributing through his skills. Thanks to those skills the Corps were better organised in their mercantile ventures than ever before.

Williams had heard some of the old timers, the original Corps members talk about the good ol' days, when hard currency was in short supply in the colony. The officers and soldiers were paid in sterling and had the only disposal income in Sydney. That had made trading easy. When supplies were short the Corps simply imported trade goods or otherwise bought the best from arriving traders. Several months earlier, before Williams was demoted, Johnston had got to talking of the old days over a couple of glasses of strong Cape wine.

'Before your coup with the *Atlas* we hired Captain Raven of the *Brittania* to bring in a whole ship load of trade goods. That was a fun day when he arrived back, we hoisted him on a chair and paraded him around.

'Quartermaster Laycock,' Johnston said, turning to Laycock, 'what was the song we sang the day we paraded Captain Raven around the town, when he arrived back with a full ship of goods in 1792?'

'It was 'He Comes, the Hero Comes'. Though it ought of been, he has eaten the profits. To this day I think that fat bastard ate a good quarter of the foodstuffs we paid him to import,' Laycock said.

Williams smiled at the memory. He continued to look down the inventory. Tea. That, along with cotton, was always in demand. Most of what remained was worthless.

Campbell could have the rest to pick over, Williams thought. Robert Campbell was increasingly becoming the commercial enemy of the Corps. Despite the arrangement between traders to share purchasing of imports Campbell always managed to get more than his share. The man had arrived via India and began to establish a trading business. Campbell lived with his family at Campbell's Cove in an Indian style house. As a trader he was formidable, willing to lobby the governor for support and use his money and influence to repay favours.

It was getting harder and harder to beat Campbell to the punch and have first go at the inventory of arriving ships. Campbell would argue that he should have first go, and buy up the best goods while leaving the lion's share of what remained to the government to sell through the public stores. That only underminned the Corps' position, with the government subsidising sales at lower prices. Not this time, thought Williams. Today it was the Corps' turn to get first go.

Williams took a few more minutes before he finalised the list. He walked over to Minchin and whispered a sum in the lieutenant's ear. Minchin sauntered over to the ship's captain and a lively conversation took place. I must learn to saunter like that, Williams thought. The officer's swagger the men called it.

Minchin returning, smiling. 'Write him a promissory note Oliver, he agreed to your price.'

Williams wrote out the note. As he did the captain walked over with a distinct lack of swagger. Instead he had the seaman's rolling gait from weeks at sea combined with a distinct sense of deflation from accepting a lower price than he imagined. Williams handed him the note and told him where he could cash it.

'Righto lads, let's get the goods and distribute them,' Minchin said.

For the rest of the day soldiers of the Corps came and went from the warehouse, supervising a hired labour force of convicts and ex-convicts. Deliveries were organised and carted and carried to the houses of wholesaler-sellers. The rum and wine was delivered to the taverns and drinking houses, with a large component taken to the barracks.

By the end of the day the goods had all been moved. Williams took a barrel of wine, a bottle of perfume he had paid for himself, two cotton sheets and a bag of sugar.

'And where are we heading with this load young man?' Smith asked.

'You know full well. I am going to deliver this to a young lady I know and you are going to deliver yourself as far away from me as possible, is that clear Nate?'

'As you wish Oli.' Smith made to walk off but then stopped and stood still.

'What are you still doing here Nate?' Williams said.

'So you don't need a hand carrying all that yourself then? If that is the case I will be buggering off.'

Williams pocketed the perfume and half the sugar, grabbed the sheets and then unsuccessfully attempted to pick up the barrel. He tried again and nearly dropped the sheets. Then he put the sheets down carefully and picked up the barrel but almost dropped the remaining sugar. Smith walked slowly to the small door on the side of the warehouse and opened it.

'Alright Nate, give me a hand, but you are not to stay once we make this delivery,' Williams said.

'Don't worry, I will be long gone before you try to make the delivery you really want.'

Williams blushed. 'Why I do believe that Wee Willy intends to rise to the occasion tonight,' Smith said. Before Williams could say anything Smith scooped up the barrel of wine and shot out the side door.

Mary Groves watched Oliver Williams and his friend Nate Smith walk up the small hill towards her house. The overwhelming feeling of happiness that burst forth upon seeing Oliver Williams surprised her. They had only recently met and had spent a few evenings together. He had promised to call on her and was doing so with an arm full of goods.

Mary watched as the two grew nearer. They were arguing in that playful manner that good friends did, at once serious and frivolous at the same time. At first Mary had been unsure of Oliver Williams's intentions. Many a young lady had freely given herself over to a Corps soldier in the hope that it would lead to a relationship, perhaps even marriage, if in name only. Most of those same women had found themselves used and discarded after just a few nights, in some cases after just one night.

Yet the hope of capturing the heart of a soldier with all the protections that offered was more than enough incentive for many of the women Mary knew. She had seen some of her friends find a man and then seen the relationship disappear in acrimony as quickly as the hope that had borne it had risen.

Being the fairer sex in New South Wales was a series of tricky negotiations. Outnumbered five to one and with many women willing to trade sex for security, finding a loving husband or defacto partner was not easy. Then there was the probability that a good number of the men in the colony were prepared to take sexual gratification in any way they could. Mostly that meant plying women full of drink until they either gave up their virtue or became so drunk they didn't know it was being taken. Or worse they were stone cold sober when it was taken.

There was an infamous incident when two Corps men had demanded of a tavern owner that they be allowed to "fuck your wife cause she is a sort and has given us the eye". The inn keeper had watched as the two raised their pistols and dragged his wife out the back. The threat of rape was one that was a constant for many women. A good number had been subjected to it. Some made a kind of cruel accommodation with it, others never recovered.

Mary had been fortunate not to have had to endure that deprivation and degradation. Yet, Mary, she told herself. She had to keep her guard, be smart and stay away from those places - the well known taverns, country roads, the mean-edge of town - where such things happened too often to be bad luck.

'Good evening Miss Mary, I was hoping I could stop by for a time,' Oliver Williams said.

'Its been a long time since anyone called me Miss Mary, Oliver Williams. You had best get any fantasies about my purity out of your head if you want to be calling.'

Williams looked at the ground. Nate Smith shoved his mate with his arm. 'Well aren't you going to introduce me?'

'Nate Smith we have met, although I am not surprised you cannot remember, you were so drunk. Last weekend at the King's Arms. You don't remember do you?'

Smith swallowed hard and looked at the ground, finding the same interesting rock that appeared to have consumed all of Williams's attention.

'Lord have mercy on you both. Will one of you say something?' Mary Groves said.

'I … I brought you a couple of gifts Miss, sorry Mary,' said Williams.

'Oh for goodness sake stop moping in the street and get in here will you. Nate, are you staying?'

'I had best be off, I have clear orders to follow, Miss Groves. Good evening to you.'

'Nate, you said you would stay a little while.' Williams said.

'You bloody well told me you would cut parts of me off if I stayed. Sorry Oli, I am off.'

Smith turned and headed down the road at speed. He didn't move that quickly when the Irish were rebelling, thought Williams.

'Well are you coming in or not Oliver?' Mary said.

'Um, in, yes, I would like to be in.'

'I bet you would,' Mary said slyly.

'That is not what I meant Mary.'

'Really. Is there something wrong with me that you don't me find attractive?'

Oliver Williams stood in the doorway paralysed and wondering what to say, what to do. What!

'I am only teasing you Oli, relax,' Mary said as she reached out and took Williams's hand. At that moment Williams knew he loved her. Mary was the only one who could put him in his place, she was beautiful and smart. And here he was, a puddle in her hands.

'What have you got there?' Mary said.

'This is for you, some wine, and cotton sheets.'

'Does one follow the other then? Is that your intention?'

'My intention? Mary … I just want to make you happy.'

'Let's get something clear Oli, and I will make this easy for you. I like you a lot. You are going places Oli and I want to go there with you, but drop this make you happy silliness please. I have been married, I have been a convict and I know that you are very new at this courting, while I am not. So if you want things to happen don't try to make me happy. Be yourself and let's be real about this and take things as they come.'

'Okay Mary. Are you always this straightforward?'

'I am these days. I have to be. We all do, we women. There are so few of us and you men all come romancing and promising the world and then take the only thing in it you seem interested in, which is for your pleasure and not ours. I have done that here twice already. The next time will be the last.'

'The next time?'

'I mean this time Oli, this time. If you want that?'

'I do Mary, I do.'

'Then come over here and pour me a drink.'

Now we find out, Mary thought to herself as the two lay in bed the following morning. He was a serviceable lover, and there was plenty of potential. She got out of bed and walked across to the table. The house was like most in Sydney, one large room with a stove, bed, table and work area. Mary picked up the redcoat from the floor and then realised that there was something in a pocket inside. She reached in and found the perfume and sugar.

That was a surprise. Most of the men who had called and the ones that she had entertained, as future prospects and lovers, had little money and certainly not enough to spend on perfume and sugar.

'Those are for you. I forgot them last night in … um,' Williams said.

'Your urgency,' Mary replied.

'My urgency. You weren't exactly eager to slow me down.'

'True. So what happens now Oliver Williams. What happens now?' Mary said. She really liked him; maybe if she dared admit it she even loved him. Please don't let this be a passing thing, she prayed.

'I keep calling on you.'

'Is this what you name it? Calling on me. You mean having me don't you? Is that all you want?' Mary said. She cursed herself, asking why she had to say that, and say it that way. It wasn't enough to just wait and see, she needed to know now. God she really must love him.

'No that is not all I want. I want you now and always.'

'Really,' Mary said. Williams watched her hard front dissolve away, like it did that first night at the King's Arms. She had come in with a few women. They had soon spread out amongst across the tavern, some to their men and a few, like Mary, to a quiet table.

Nate had been drinking after returning from Madame Brigitte's and was the life of the party. He had set eyes on Mary and dragged Williams, Tom Conner and George Newbank over to her table. She had read Smith easily and turned her attentions to Williams only to put Smith off. She was at first hard and mouthy yet at some point, for just a few moments, she had softened and revealed a little of herself to Williams.

He remembered he had been speaking about his grand plan, which he had revealed to no-one, of saving enough to buy a commission, become an officer and then earn enough to buy land in New South Wales. She had talked about sewing and fine clothes and cloth and the possibility of making a go of it here as a seamstress. In doing so, it seemed to Williams, she had tied a thread between the two of them, one he hoped would never come undone.

They had agreed to see each other the next Friday and he had waited far longer than any reasonable man not in love or lust would wait. She had come in and seen him and known then that this was more than a passing thing.

And now here they were, days later, in the cold light of morning and he was saying he wanted her forever. Maybe this is the one, Mary said to herself. And in the next moment she told herself not to get her hopes up.

'So then Oli, a successful breaching of the defences. I take it you shot straight, which would be a first for you.' Nate Smith said when Williams had arrived back at the barracks.

'Nate, please, you know a gentleman doesn't talk.'

'So you are a gentleman now Oli? Well that is a development.'

'Nate, she is the one. Not a conquest but something far more to me.'

'Oli, that is wonderful. Really that is good news and I am happy for you. Truly.'

'When are you going to settle down Nate. Most of the men have a woman, Tom and George and now me. What about you?'

'I tried that once Oli, many years ago. And you know what she did? I got injured and she found another man to help her heal. Those were her words, to heal her. And believe you me they apparently did a great deal of healing together. So that was the end of it for me. I called him out and there was a duel and he was shot in the neck and paralysed and I was nearly hung. Then I found my way into the army and out here.

'So no more of that for me. I like this army life and Madame Brigitte likes me and we have our fun together and then I am settled for a time.' Nate Smith looked away at some distant hurt. 'That betrayal did it for me Oli. It was too much to bear. I am happy and am glad you are too.'

'Thank you Nate,' Williams said.

'So will you take a house on Soldiers Row, or Pitt's Row? It would be for the best. The women who undertake a serious relationship with a Corps man are best near us and not left alone in the town.'

'Is Mary in danger?'

'No. Having the protection of the Corps is a strong deterrent. But there is also a great deal of resentment and jealousy towards us. Once it is known that you are together she is better here.'

'How do I do that, organise a house?'

'Talk to Quartermaster Laycock. He will arrange things for you.'

George Johnston had ridden into town reluctantly. New reports had emerged of incidents in the Hawkesbury region of problems with the local Aboriginals. Most suspected there was little in it, other than farmers up in that part of the colony not wanting to be forgotten. For Johnston it meant something else, time away from home.

'Lads I am going off on a tour of the Hawkesbury, to reassure the locals that the New South Wales Corp are still engaged with their native problem,' Major Johnston said.

'Didn't you sort that one out Lieutenant Davies?' Private Hutton said.

'No, I sent Corporals Smith and Williams, well Private Williams. I sent them out with the local militia and all they did was shoot up the bush,' Davies replied to laughter.

'There have been a few more incidents mainly around the rivers. In one case a boat was boarded,' Johnston said. 'The governor in his infinite wisdom thinks that a show of the colours, so to speak, will alleviate matters.'

'I think you mean the governor in his finite wisdom. The only infinite thing about Mr King is his continuing illness,' Davies piped in.

'I think I need to get Sergeant Major Whittle to teach a bit of discipline when I am talking,' Johnston said.

'Just give me the word Major and I will have these braggarts sorted in no time,' Whittle said.

'And suddenly there is quiet,' Johnston said. 'Now I know this matter is not at the top of your minds and the Hawkesbury is a way off, but the people are worried and have been petitioning the governor. Either we respond to this or we get off side with the governor and a good deal of the population here and we cannot have both. So I will go and tour and be seen and complement the militia and have tea and cakes and pretend to like it. Lieutenant Minchin and a small detachment will accompany me. The rest of you business as usual.'

The men gradually drifted out of the room until only Johnston and Davies were left.

'Lieutenant, have you seen Mac of late?'

'Sorry Major, but I have not as he is so busy with his sheep. Is everything all right?'

'I am worried for him. He seems a little off since returning from England.

'What do you mean by off Major?'

'He seems a little obsessed with the new governor and his plans to make the colony into a wool exporter. It is as though he thinks himself above us some how; as though he were playing a game of chess and we are all the pieces, if that makes sense.'

'I think I know what you are saying Major. There is a distance and aloofness there that was never so pronounced.'

'Precisely. Well said Lieutenant. Anyway keep an eye on things here while I am gone up Hawkesbury way please.'

'Of course George, I will keep an eye out. Speaking of things did you hear young Williams is moving into Soldiers Row with a young lady, Mary Groves?'

'Good for him, he is a goer that one. Since he got involved in the rum trade things have turned around. We are in as good a shape as we were back in the late nineties, before the governors tried to end our monopoly,' Johnston said.

'This is the one Mary,' Williams said. 'It's not the biggest house but it will do us.'

'Oli it is not the house that matters. What matters is that we are sharing it together. Come on, show me inside,' Mary said.

Mary Groves took Williams by the hand and they walked inside the front door. The single room was large enough with a kitchen, table and bed. Williams had hung an old sheet from the roof to form a cosy space around the bed and had found some flowers and put them in a jug on the table. There were simple curtains covering the glass windows that looked out onto the street.

'It's lovely Oli. So perfect.'

'It is. Now shall we test the bed?'

'Is that all you think about young man. Let me get settled and get my chest and things off the street first,' Mary said. 'Well are you going to stand there or are you going to lend me a hand?'

They spent the rest of the afternoon organising things, rearranging the position of the table, creating a space for Mary to hang some clothes and sorting out the kitchen. Mary was excited to see some pots that looked new. 'I bought them from a trader Mary,' Williams said. 'I wanted as much of our home to be new as possible.'

Williams had noticed that Mary had softened a little, dropping her tough exterior once he had asked her to move in with him. Around the house Mary was more relaxed. He put it down to love, for her it was the security of knowing that she had a good man to look after her.

They ate dinner together for the first time in their new house. 'Oli, can I ask you? Will you be marrying me?"

Williams stared at her. She had a wonderful ability to throw him off. It was one of the things he loved about her. He continued to look at her.

'So you are just going to stare at me in the hope that you don't have to answer,' Mary said.

'No, I just ...'

'So it's no, you won't be marrying me then is it. It's all right for you to move me in here and have me cook and clean for you and put out for you but not marry me?' Mary said.

'That's not what I meant ... I meant ..."

'What? You meant what?' Mary said staring at him. She raised her eyebrow. 'You meant what exactly?' Suddenly she burst out laughing. 'You are so easy to bait. All I have to do is mention love or marriage or your intentions and you become this little boy who has no idea what to do or say. It's very endearing.'

'Are you saying I am endearing? God the lads will tease me mercilessly if they ever hear you say that. Soldiers are not endearing, they are rugged and dashing, not endearing."

'You, Oliver Williams, are endearing, and that gets the girls. Well at least this girl, no others all right.'

'There is only you Mary. And yes, I will marry you.'

It was Mary's turn to look stunned and simply stare at Williams. 'Don't try to be endearing, you cannot do it as well as I can,' Williams said.

Mary tried not to panic, wondering if this was all too soon. She had done this once before and been betrayed so many times. Was this what she wanted, she asked herself. She had always lived as a defacto, lived tally as the women called it, since that disastrous first marriage. That meant in the eyes of the law she was a defacto and could take her things and leave. For Mary that allowed her to be free and to earn a living. And now on her first night in a new house with a soldier she had brought up marriage. And he wanted it.

Then again things could be worse, she thought. She had worked the stores for only a short time, the first job most convict women were assigned upon arrival. It was considered the lowest of the low for Sydney's women. The worst part of it was working the stores made a woman beholden to the government and more likely to follow government orders. The pay was not enough to get by, ensuring those women relied on government rations, further entrenching their reliance on the government. Mary had found a place in an emancipist's home cooking and working as a maid. She worked hard to escape that only to fall for that fool and marry him and watch him drink and fuck anyone but her.

There were women far worse off in the colony, like those in the Female Factory at Parramatta, forced to live and work above the gaol, sleeping next to the looms they worked on during the day, spending their lives in one room. The women who skipped from man to man little better than whores. The luckiest women were those who found love with men with prospects.

And what of this man's prospects? She looked at the man sitting across from her and tried to assess him objectively. He was smart, on his way to wealth and opportunity. He could and would certainly protect her, and how many of the men she had known had bought her perfume and placed flowers on the table. Don't panic she told herself, don't run, you started this conversation. Do you have the courage to finish it one way or another?

Mary heard him say 'Of course I will marry you, you are wonderful.'

Sometimes you just had to stop thinking and leap into the waters and see if you would float or sink.

'Then let's do it.'

The Corps did not have a chaplain and neither Oliver Williams nor Mary Groves attended church regularly. Like much of the colony they saw little value in it. They visited one of the churches and paid a small stipend and the priest conducted the ceremony. The following day Mary put her house up for sale.

'You mean the house you were in is yours, you own it?' Williams asked.

'Of course I own it. I worked hard for it and bought it off Mary Reibey. Mary built it and has built many other cottages and homes. My ex-husband gave me a small cottage which I sold to buy the home I am now selling. You men are prepared to gift houses to your women, we women look after them and make them into our own. You use houses to buy love, we think of them as having real value.'

'Have you thought about leasing it out?' Williams said.

'I did but it is too hard to look after tenants and they always complain. There is always something that needs fixing, so I will be selling it. If you treat me right we can use the money to buy a farm one day,' Mary said. 'Now do we own this home or are we renting it?'

'We own it, I bought it,' Williams said.

'Good. The first thing we shall do is put up a paling fence and then plant the garden to vegetables. Then some new curtains and I will start to sew from here. My dresses are growing in popularity. If you can obtain some finer materials I think we can make a good living from it.'

'No need to go back on the stores or draw government rations for you then Mary,' Williams said.

'No, I have you to support me. Make one thing clear to yourself Private Williams, I will take you to court should you treat me bad or not support me. More women are doing that and more women are winning too,' Mary said.

Marriage laws in England united man and woman as one, including property. If the marriage ended the man retained all property. In Sydney a woman was entitled to retain her share of the property in case of divorce.

Mary had worked hard to have a life she was proud of and she was not shy in letting people know that. And right now Williams was on the receiving end.

'I have it good here in Sydney town, far better than in England. I have a good living and own property. I have friends and I eat well and have rights none of which would be mine in England. So you treat me right or else.'

'Settle down Mary, it was only a joke. I meant that you are far too good for the stores and I intend to treat you the best. I have waited a long time for the right woman to come by and am glad I did. Now you start on the fence and I will start on the rum.'

Mary laughed and playfully threw a cloth at him. 'You were doing so well, saying all the right things. And then you say the ending the wrong way around."

Oli Williams looked at Mary confused. 'What did I say wrong?'

'You should have said 'You start on the rum and I will start on the fence, like a true gentleman.'

'Right you are Mary.' Williams smiled and continued to sit watching Mary. She shot him a look that he could not misinterpret, then he swallowed hard, stood up and headed out to start work on building a paling fence.

Mary let him fiddle around outside a good fifteen minutes before she brought out two cups of wine. Together they paced out the distance of the fence and worked out how much wood they would need. Williams disappeared and came back a while later with the wood and started cutting it into palings.

'Good to see you hard at it,' Nate Smith said as he walked up Soldiers Row. Williams had been so absorbed in the task he had not seen Smith approaching.

'We are building a paling fence, Mary and I.'

'Good for you. Now were you planning on telling me you got married or was that something that slipped your mind?'

'It most certainly did not slip his mind Nate Smith,' Mary said emerging from the house. 'So you have come by with a present then?'

'I swear Oli this wife of yours is too clever and smart-mouthed for me,' Smith whispered. 'Uh Mary I must have left it at the barracks. Can you forgive me?'

'I suppose you will be wanting a drink then?' Mary said.

'I wouldn't say no,' Smith said.

'Well how about you make yourself useful and help us get this paling up. Then you can come into my yard and have a drink.'

Smith looked at Williams, smiled resignedly and took his jacket off. Then he grabbed a shovel and started to dig a hole. Williams laughed. 'You dropped yourself in that one Nate, so no blaming me now.'

'No. I blame her,' Smith said and laughed.

Major George Johnston was struggling through another piece of cake, his third of the day. Yet again he wondered why every farmer he met with had to serve tea. Then he asked himself the same question that inevitably followed, how many farms were in the Hawkesbury region anyway, and was every one going to serve awful, bitter, crumbling cake?

The visit had started well. Johnston had arrived with a small detachment and met Chief Constable Thompson who eagerly paraded his local militia. Almost a third of the militia were ex-Corps men and had welcomed the chance to show their skills to Major Johnston.

Johnston had then inspected the militia troops, saying hello to a number of the old hands, before a reception where old and new war stories were swapped. Thompson had picked Johnston's brains on strategies and tactics. The major had enjoyed talking shop and at one stage had placed cups, bottles, shakers and saucers to reenact the battles of Bunker Hill and Castle Hill and half a dozen others.

And now it had all gone to shit, Johnston thought. At the farms of ex-Corps men Johnston had been able to relax, inspect sightlines on defences and joke with old friends. In Thompson he found a willing ally. But only a few of the farms belonged to the old hands. The rest were eager to make their points and resentments under the guise of cake and tea.

Johnston was beginning to think he was too old for parade diplomacy practiced over bitter cake and bitter tea. God willing for a little action he secretly wished; if only a native war party would show itself. Of course, the natives were smart enough to make scarce while a detachment was itching to show off its prowess.

And then there were the remarks from the locals about the price of just about everything, and the inferences those prices were the fault of monopolists in Sydney. It was the sort of double talk Johnston hated, words that seemed innocent enough yet held a deeper meaning. Old soldiers like Johnston just wanted it straight. If someone had a problem with the price of rum why not just say so, he wondered. Instead farmers talked of the red import tax, referencing the red coats of the Corps, and spoke disdainfully of barrel buyers and bottle sellers.

Worst of all there was Thomas Mulligan, private of the Corps. Idiot more likely Johnston thought. On the first night in the area the man had made mischief with a farmer's wife, fucking her in the alley behind the hotel, and none too quietly either. Johnston knew the Corps had enough of a reputation, some earned, some unwarranted, of being a little too free with other men's wives.

To do that up here, where enough farmers already hated the Corps ... what was the man thinking? The whole region now had no doubt what Mulligan was thinking with. Having one of the Corps caught out and the constabulary called and threats and promises of the worst kind made had reduced a tour designed to boost good will into a confirmation of everything the locals hated about the Corps.

'How is the cake Major?' Mick Watkins asked. 'I would have had me missus make it with sugar but that is expensive. Besides, I sent her off to get some more food. Don't want her getting red-faced out the back cooking up something new. You never know what hospitality some lads are expecting.'

Johnston sighed. 'The cake is excellent. It is the type an old soldier likes. How was the harvest this season Mr Watkins?'

'Alas, it was good but not all it could have been. Floods you see. And native raiders who skive off with a few bushels now and then. It all adds up. Tea, Major?'

'Thank you, just a little.' Johnston said. The last thing he needed was another tea. At his age a full bladder was not the easiest thing to deal with, and he felt awash in tea. 'Are you part of the militia Mr Watkins?'

'That I am. Have to be to ensure we help ourselves up here, 'cause no one else seems willing. Them Sydney types are too soft or not interested in anything but our corn and wheat but only at the prices they set,' Watkins said.

Johnston wondered why the hell Thompson brought him to meet this loudmouthed lout. 'Well the thing is the wheat and corn from here are of such a quality, that is why we in Sydney are so enarmoured by it. As to your native issues, now that the governor is looking to your native problem we are able to do something about it,' Johnston said.

'Was the militia under Chief Thompson that did the most damage from what I hear,' Watkins said.

'That is true and an excellent job the militia did. The role of my troops has been curtailed by the governor but we have broken the back of the rebellion now. I interrogated one of the ringleaders myself, along with the Reverend Marsden at Parramatta.'

'Well bully for you then Major, you sure did your part.' Watkins looked at the small crowd gathered nearby and smirked.

'You told him Mick,' a voice said from near the back of the crowd.

Johnston sighed and placed the cake down. 'Now perhaps if there are any issues around the defences here on your property you may wish to discuss?' Johnston barely paused to allow Watkins to speak. 'No, then we best be moving along. Thank you for your hospitality, I fear we must go before we wear out our welcome.'

'Detachment, fall in and present arms,' Sargent Major Whittle yelled.

The troops moved with impressive speed, ready to depart. They too had long tired of the round of farms and sarcastic hospitality and longed for Sydney.

'Detachment fall out, quick march,' Whittle said.

The detachment moved out quickly followed by Johnston and Thompson. 'That was quite uncalled for from Mr Watkins.'

'No need to apologise Chief Constable. I fear that the delay on the governor's part in getting us up here to begin with has sown a bitter harvest. Even more so for those who have borne the worst of the tension waiting for raiding parties to appear.'

'That's true,' Thompson said. 'Thank you for coming, it does mean a great deal to myself and to some of the locals. I fear however that a dozen of these tours will not change the general mindset that anyone from Sydney looks down upon us.'

'Andrew, that's not true, though I do understand where such feelings come from. So where to next?' Johnston said.

'Sorry but another farm. Perhaps we should call this the apology tour. We seem to have spent much of our time apologising to each other.'

'Sorry I missed that,' Johnston said laughing.

'My apologies, I should have spoken more directly,' Thompson said laughing too. Johnston lent across from his horse and gently slapped Thompson on the back as the two men laughed.

'How was the Hawkesbury Major?' Davies said as Johnston and Minchin sat in the mess hall.

'Somewhat of a disaster Lieutenant. The folk up there are none too disposed towards us. They blame Sydney for everything. And to top it off Private Mulligan was caught in the act with a farmer's woman, and was lucky to escape a lynching. See to it that Mulligan has picket duties for the next two months.'

'Ah sir, we don't actually do picket, given we have the barracks and such,' Davies said.

'Well he can do sentry duty at night. Find him a suitable punishment Lieutenant please.'

'Aye Major.'

'What the Hawkesbury did reveal is that we are not the most popular of groups outside Sydney. The governor, for all his faults, stitched us up nicely by delaying in sending the Corps up Hawkesbury way. Now the locals have decided that we are the problem and there is a large degree of resentment. What about here and at Parramatta, how are we perceived?'

Minchin and Davies both looked at each other, willing the other to answer.

'Somebody, anybody, please tell me your thoughts,' Johnston said.

'I think things are a little different here in Sydney town. There is no doubt there is plenty of opportunity. The monopolists, the likes of ourselves, Dr Balmain and even Campbell and his supporters, are ensuring that. I mean most of the convicts stay on after they have served their sentences or are emancipated,' Davies said.

'There is a feeling of possibility and optimism here, and to an extent at Parramatta too,' Minchin said. 'I think that for the most part the people are tolerant of us and are happy so long as they feel they can have a share of the successes of the rich. And they do have that chance.'

'So it is your assessment that the resentment of our country cousins at Hawkesbury is not shared here?' Johnston said.

'I would say so Major,' Davies said.

'Is it worth doing more to help them out? Do they hold any real power here in the colony?' Johnston said.

'I think we've done enough. Perhaps we could send the odd patrol up, but that may only inflame tensions. They already resent us and what we've made of ourselves, which is ironic as given half the chance they would do the same. So I say let them be,' Minchin said.

'I agree Major, let them be,' Davies said.

'Then we are in agreement. But for all our sakes put it around quietly that the men should pull their heads in for a while and behave. I don't know how many more incidents we can afford before the people here start resenting us enough to want something done about it.'

'Do you really think the people have that power Major?' Minchin said.

'Not the people directly. But certainly some of our competitors. Men like Campbell and his supporters have influence,' Johnston said. 'We have a new governor coming out at some stage and Bligh is no fool. On the contrary he is a disciplinarian. That is no coincidence that we have broken two governors and the next one they send out is a hard man. I suspect that there will be a battle for the hearts and minds of the people. Whoever wins the people wins Sydney.'

'Well we have Mac on our side, our secret weapon. He could sweet talk Saint Peter himself into being allowed into heaven even if he wasn't on the list,' Davies said.

'I hope you are right Lieutenant, I really do.'

November 1805

It had been three months since Mary and Oliver first moved into their new house. The vegetable garden was taking life in the spring sunshine, the paling fence gleamed white and the curtains were thick, lending the house a cosy and private feel.

'Oli, I don't want to alarm you but I am late,' Mary said.

'For what?' Williams took a drink of rum and flicked through a copy of the *Gazette*.

It was a full ten seconds before he realised that Mary had not answered nor was she rushing around trying to leave. He looked across at her and saw the broad smile. 'I'm late!'

'What, you mean late late? Is it a boy or a girl?'

'How should I know,' Mary said, pulling a face.

'That is wonderful Mary.' Williams walked over and held his wife close. 'I am so happy.'

'Do you know that this is the first time I have fallen. They say here in Sydney something magical happens and women who could not fall pregnant in England fall here. I think it is the sunshine, and perhaps the food too. There is enough to eat properly here whereas in England there was never enough.'

'I shall have to be gentle around you I suppose,' Williams said.

'I am pregnant, not an invalid you silly man. Although if you are going to do the washing and cooking that would be nice. Actually that may be so much of a shock as to cause me harm. If I need help I will let you know,' Mary said. 'Now speaking of being late aren't you supposed to be meeting Minchin and Laycock?'

'Bloody hell, you're right.' Williams grabbed his coat and shako hat, and kissed Mary and raced out the door.

'Private Williams, so nice of you to arrive ten minutes late,' Minchin said. 'We can't really demote him any further now can we.' Minchin winked at Laycock, doing his best impersonation of Major Johnston. Laycock simply stared at Minchin until the lieutenant turned red and looked back to Williams.

'My apologies sir, I was attending to a domestic matter,' Williams said blushing.

'How are your domestic matters?' Minchin said. 'I take it all is well at home.'

'Excellent, truly excellent sir.'

'Good, then let's get down to the books shall we,' Laycock said.

'So we are doing very well, profits are up a little on the month compared to the last,' Williams said.

'What do you put that down to Private?' Minchin said.

'Spring most likely. The weather is warmer and people are out and about a little more, and thirstier in the heat too I imagine. It was the same this time last year,' Williams said. 'We are also holding our own against Campbell and the government stores, as our sales have increased.'

'Any problems with our suppliers?' Minchin said.

'No. They are all doing well and paying up on time. Corporal Smith, private's Newbank, Conner and myself visit regularly to keep an eye on things. So in short there's really nothing more to report,' Williams said.

'Good. Is it possible to increase our supplies of grog?' Laycock said.

'We have very little in reserves unless we want to push the men to hand over their supplies. Since King stopped some of the monopolists from selling, few are willing to keep a large number of barrels in reserve. Surgeon Balmain was rumoured to have had more than a thousand barrels and had to petition to sell those lest he went bankrupt,' Williams said.

'So tell me why we have a stockpile of wheat then. I notice you have bought up supplies and built a reserve of wheat.'

'When Nate, apologies, when Corporal Smith and I were up the Hawkesbury way last April during the native raids I noticed how high the flood waters were. In many cases farms near the rivers were close to going under. One of the locals, John Cable, told me the floods were not as high as they can go and that it has been several years since they had such big floods.

'Since that time a number of farms have been established near the river and most are growing wheat and most are below the flood lines of the big floods.'

'Right, so why the wheat?' Minchin said.

'Because if a big flood happens then those farms will be under water and the crops will be lost, which means that wheat will be in short supply. And if it is needed for foods then we will have a supply, either for ourselves so we wont have to buy at higher prices, or to sell for higher prices to others,' Williams said.

'That's smart. I hadn't seen that,' Laycock said.

'Or we could be very smart and sell at wholesale and win over some friends,' Minchin said. 'If it comes to that.'

'I hadn't thought of that either,' Laycock said.

'The major will be pleased at how well you have things humming along. So just carry on doing what you are all doing,' Minchin said. 'And we will leave the thinking to Private Williams and myself.'

March 1806

The months passed quickly and summer came and went. Mary's belly grew and grew, the rum trade continued and the halfway governorship of King lingered on. The Aboriginal raids largely ended and the people of Sydney continued to turn out to welcome new ships, wondering if each heralded the arrival of William Bligh.

People throughout the colony had become fascinated by the incoming governor, with his colourful history. There was the famous *Bounty* mutiny. And there was his even more famous voyage across thousands of miles of open ocean from somewhere in the Pacific to Java, after being kicked off the *Bounty*. Stories were swapped of Bligh's return to Tahiti to complete his original orders of taking breadfruit trees to the West Indies.

Then there were the tales of Bligh's battles. At Camperdown captaining HMS *Director* he had engaged three Dutch vessels, defeated them all and captured the *Vrijheid* and the Dutch commander Vice-Admiral Jan de Winter. Even more famously, the taverns were full of the story of how Admiral Nelson had personally commended Bligh after the Battle of Copenhagen, when Bligh's command of HMS *Glatton* had played a pivotal role both in the fighting and in ensuring Nelson's orders were communicated to the rest of the fleet, guaranteeing an English victory.

Beyond the facts there were wild stories of Bligh the man; of a foul temper and mouth to match, and his fractious nature and appetite for confrontation, both with those he commanded and those he saw as his inferiors. How much of these aspects of his character were true no-one really knew, but then the great game of Sydney had become outdoing others in telling over-the-top stories of the new governor.

The only interruption came in March when the Hawkesbury floods arrived in such diluvian quantities as to have farmers suggesting their woes were as great as Noah himself.

Johnston walked into the mess hall, looked around and then called for attention. 'Lads, the Governor has written me,' Johnston said, 'to despair of the flooding in the Hawkesbury. He bids that we should get up there and help out and asks that we assess the damage to the crops.

'Lieutenant Davies, can you take a detachment with Corporal Smith and do what you can to restore order and assess the damage?'

'Aye sir. Right lads you heard the major, jump to it.'

'Private Williams, I am giving you a promotion back to Corporal,' Johnston said. 'Make sure you keep it this time.'

'Yes sir,' Williams said. 'And thank you sir.'

'You have earned it back,' Johnston said. 'Now get to it.'

Williams felt complete again, the way he had when first promoted. Several of the men congratulated him, however, the urgency of the flooding soon overtook any celebrations.

The road from Sydney was completely underwater so the Corps men made the journey by boat. It took three days to reach the Hawkesbury region and Windsor, with flood waters pushing boats downstream and making the course of the rivers and creeks unclear. 'I have never seen so much water before,' Williams said.

'I think I know how Noah must have felt. I think we are several metres higher upon the river than we were last year,' Smith said. 'If we are even on the river.'

Every few metres the captain of the boat, Will Worrell, would stop and drop a weighted line into the water and take depth soundings. On several occasions he muttered an obscenity to himself and then let the boat run with the current towards the middle of the waterway, losing ground. Then he would have the sailors and some of the soldiers row the small ship out of the current towards the far bank. Each time the ship had to lose ground to make ground.

'This is taking far too long,' Lieutenant Davies said.

'We can't make headway against the current of the flood waters, it's too strong. Half the time I don't know where we are in relation to the river. Too often we are straying too close to the banks of the river and whatever debris and land is down there,' Worrell said to Lieutenant Davies.

'I need to get these men up to the Hawkesbury as soon as possible, Mr Worrell,' Lieutenant Davies said. 'Can't you go faster along the banks?'

'Lieutenant if we hit something on the bottom, a submerged tree, or log or goodness knows what, then we will probably lose the boat,' Worrell said. 'How well can your men swim? How well can you swim? I can swim quite well and if I ended up in that water I reckon I would last a minute before I went under. And I don't have your gear weighing me down either. So should I chance it along the banks or keep going slowly? Or would you rather walk?'

Davies looked at Worrell and took his turn to mutter an obscenity under his breath and walk away.

Once night fell Worrell ordered the ship anchored and the men sat and ate a miserable meal and huddled in their jackets and blankets trying to find a warm spot.

'This had better be worth it Nate,' Williams said.

'I don't see how it can be worth it. We'll get up there and the locals will have a go at us for taking so long to get there. And there will be precious little we can do to help and so they will resent us even more for sitting around and doing nothing,' Smith replied.

'Good that you are being positive about this then,' Williams said.

'How can I not be positive? Floating here under the stars, with your lovely eyes to look into. I mean everything is damp and there is no fire, just the chance to huddle together with you and the other lads for warmth,' Smith said. He laughed a dry, mirthless laugh. 'I dream of this.'

Williams laughed. 'Steady on Nate, I think you're going around the bend.'

'Which is more than can be said for this boat. So you just stay over there and I will stay here and enjoy my misery, without the rest of the company,' Smith said. He laughed again, pleased with his joke.

'Works fine by me.'

The next day was a repeat of the last and the ship and its company had only progressed two-thirds of the way to the Hawkesbury settlements. By the third afternoon they were within site of the farms.

'Nate, last year there were farms along this part of the river weren't there?' Williams said.

'Yeah there were. God I think the floods have wiped them out. And the crop land is completely under water. There'll be no crops this year,' Smith said.

'If the rest of the Hawkesbury is like this …' Williams said.

The soldiers looked out at the devastation. Whole farms were gone, vanished under the water. In one or two cases the roof of a house could be seen barely poking out under the flood waters. As far as they could see water dominated the landscape, with trees and small patches of land struggling up from under the inundation.

'I hope the poor buggers got out in time,' Davies said. 'At least the main settlement is built on a rise. Hopefully they are above the worst of the waters.'

'Ahoy there. Ahoy,' came a cry from a small boat on the river.

The men on the boat rowed over towards the ship and clambered aboard. Davies was glad to see Chief Constable Thompson step aboard. 'Chief Constable, I am glad to see you. However this is far beyond what we had been told or expected.'

'The flood peak happened only yesterday,' Thompson said. 'There is still a large volume of water making its way down stream and with so much water ahead of it there is nowhere for the water to go. The outer settlements have been all but washed away. We wont know how bad it is for a few more days at least. Until then there is little we can do but wait.'

'We got here as soon as we could. We've been pushing against the flood waters for three days,' Davies said. 'Is there anything we can do now?'

'Do you have any small vessels aboard that we could use to check some of the outlying houses?' Thompson said.

'There are two we could use,' Will Worrell said.

'Then can we launch them and head out to the houses you can see poking above the flood waters? We'll help too, but I must warn it is hard going,' Thompson said. He paused and looked out over the water for several moments. 'I don't know if we will find any alive or not. We tried to warn as many as possible to get out when the flooding first started but I fear some have chosen to stay rather than come into town.'

'How are things in town?' Davies said.

'Wet and miserable with flood waters around a foot and a half high. Other than that it is bearable,' Thompson said.

The two small dinghies were launched with Williams and Smith commanding one each. Thompson also headed out in his small boat. Four soldiers sat in each of the two dinghies, two men to row and two to give those men a spell. The three small craft headed out in separate directions, like ants spreading from the nest. Each dinghy rowed towards a farm house, visible only from the roof. The waters were tricky to negotiate, with currents and eddies pushing the boats along as if they had a mind of their own. The soldiers on Worrell's ship watched the dinghies get smaller and smaller.

Williams boat was the first to bump into the roof of a farmhouse. Together with Private Hutton they managed to get a rope around the chimney and haul the boat up until it was possible to touch the roof while leaning over from the boat. Williams grabbed an oar and upended it and used the handle end to knock hard on the roof half a dozen times.

'Do you think anyone will answer?' Hutton said.

'Best we be quiet so we can hear Private,' Williams said.

The only sound was water lapping against the roof before it slipped by and continued its journey downstream. Williams knocked again. The soldiers all looked at one another, both willing a sound to come from within while wondering what they would do it if did.

Still no sound came. Williams was unwilling to simply row away and so knocked again. The heads of the soldiers started to drop. The silence was overwhelming. 'Should we head back Corporal,' Private Gillard said. Williams looked at him and saw the fear in his eyes. Being there on such a small boat on a large, moving inland sea was unnerving. Williams feared the men would lose it soon.

'Best we be heading back,' Williams said.

Gillard and Hutton nodded in agreement and quickly helped slip the rope from around the chimney before putting their backs into the rowing. Williams looked around and could see the other two boats also beginning to make their way back to Worrell's ship. There were only soldiers and locals in the two boats, no survivors.

God help anyone caught up in this, for there is no hope of surviving it, Williams thought.

The dinghies returned to Worrell's ship and tied up mooring lines. All the soldiers, local men and Thompson gratefully climbed aboard. Worrell managed to catch a good wind behind the ship and sail the last two miles to where the jetty outside the main settlement was usually found. It was under metres of water and so Worrell again undertook the tedious task of taking depth soundings as the ship edged towards the settlement.

'It looks like a ghost town,' Williams said. 'Where are the people?'

'They're all inside. The waters are carrying a great deal of debris and we've seen the odd snake in the waters too. Most of the locals are trying to stay dry as best they can,' Thompson said.

Finally the ship could nose forward no longer. Still a good fifty yards of low-lying water separated town and ship. 'You will need to take the dinghies and get yourselves across that last area of water,' Worrell said. 'If I take this ship any closer I fear grounding her or holing the hull.'

'Righto lads,' Davies said. 'You heard Mr Worrell, let's get to it.'

It took four journeys to move the men and equipment across the watery divide, but finally the detachment had arrived. They waded through the waters slowly, feeling the footing beneath them lest they fall. Thompson led the way and soon had the detachment at the door to the local tavern. The door was ajar, sandbags forming a leaky barrier between the higher waters outside and lower waters inside.

The soldiers carefully stepped over the barrier and moved their packs inside. A collection of locals greeted the detachment, however there was no sneering or sarcasm, just a muted defeat.

'Mr Thompson, my soldiers are at your disposal. If there is anything we can do other than check more outlying houses please let me know,' Davies said.

'Lieutenant, we have checked all the settlements we can reach. For now there is little else to do other than wait for the waters to recede. There has been enough lost without us risking any people.'

A chorus of ayes came from a number of locals. 'Best to wait,' said one voice from the back.

'As I said, my men are at your disposal, should you need anything,' Davies said.

'Looks like we're here for a while lads,' Smith said. 'Make yourselves useful where you can and stay out of trouble.'

After three days of waiting the waters finally receded enough to send patrols to the outlying settlements. The detachment broke into three groups, each with a dinghy that was carried and dragged from the settlement at Hawkesbury until the soldiers could march no more.

'Okay lads, time to start some rowing,' Williams said. His small detachment had marched only a short distance. They wore makeshift shoes of cloth, britches and old shirts rather than their uniforms. Ahead lay water and the tops of a number of farms down by the river. 'I suggest we row out to the farthest house and then make our way back here. Private Hutton, Private Gillard, you remain here with the muskets and packs. Mason, Gray, Wilford you are with me in the dinghy.'

Williams and Mason made up one team, Gray and Wilford the other. Each team rowed for a short time until finally they reached the outlying house. 'Bump the boat gently up against the house and we will try to tie off and then go inside and check,' Williams said.

Gray and Wilford rowed the last few metres and slowed the dinghy down using their oars. Mason grabbed onto a window-pane and Williams was able to secure the rope around a latch on the door. Wilford then reversed his oar and knocked loudly against the door. He repeated the knocking without getting an answer.

Carefully Williams and Mason climbed out of the dinghy and pushed the door open. It took a considerable effort to force the door open into the hut and a wave of water washed around before flooding out of the door, nearly swamping the two soldiers and knocking them off their feet.

'Okay Private Mason, lets take this carefully,' Williams said. He led the way inside the hut. The water was waist deep and mud stained the walls right up to the top of the ceiling. A table floated slowly towards Williams, with other items - pots, clothing, a small chest - milling around the edges of the watery room.

Williams pushed the table to the side of the room. 'I don't think anyone is here Private.'

A rush of debris came up from under the table. Then a body came floating up from the depths. Williams pushed back in shock and fell into the cold water. Mason spun around and saw the body and recoiled, he too losing his feet and tripping back into the water. A wave rushed out the door and the dinghy bobbed up and down for a few moments. Gray and Wilford held on tightly, wondering what was happening inside.

'God, that scared the hell out of me,' Mason said.

'I hope that was all it scared out of you Private,' Williams said. 'Help me get this body outside. We need to take it back for someone to identify and bury.'

'Do we have to Corporal? I mean can't we leave it and let the authorities up here know?' Mason said.

'No, we need to do the right thing,' Williams said. 'Now grab his legs and let's get to it.'

Together the two soldiers hauled and floated the body across the room and out the door.

'Christ almighty,' Wilford said. 'Is that a body?'

'Of course it's a body,' Williams said. 'Now help me get it into the boat. Wilford get out here and help us push it into the dinghy, Gray you help haul it in.'

'Can't we leave it?' Gray said.

'No we can't leave it. We are taking it back for identification and burial. Now stop whining and get to it.'

Wilford carefully clambered out of the dinghy. Then the three soldiers stood waist deep in the water and pushed the body over the side of the dinghy. For a moment the effort of pushing the body forced the dinghy away from the house to strain against the mooring line, until the dinghy started to swivel and pivot on the line. The soldiers almost lost the body in the water but were able to push the head and torso over the edge of the dinghy and then unceremoniously throw the legs into the dinghy. In the process the legs hit Wilford and he cursed.

'Lads, keep it together. We've seen dead bodies before, this isn't new. Now focus on what we're doing,' Williams said.

They pushed the body towards the rear of the boat with the bloated face downwards. None of the men were keen to see that face looking at them. Then they closed the door and let loose the mooring line and rowed towards the next house.

The next two houses were empty. They recovered two more bodies at the following house and a fourth later in the day. The dinghy was so full of the dead the soldiers took to walking next to the boat, wading through the water while pushing the boat along. By mid afternoon they made it back to where Gillard and Hutton waited.

'Oh god, how many bodies are in the boat?' Gillard said when he saw the men walking up and the pile of bodies in the dinghy.

'Four,' Williams said. 'We'll need a cart of some description to take these bodies to town. Can you see what you can organise Private?'

Gillard ran off towards town and returned soon afterward with Thompson and two carts pulled by horses. Thompson went over and looked at the bodies, carefully searching each face.

'Do you know them Mr Thompson?' Williams said.

'Yes. All local farmers and one convict servant. A grisly day's work. Sadly the other two detachments also recovered some bodies, which brings the total to eight dead,' Thompson said.

'Out of how many farms Constable?' Hutton said.

'Nineteen farms around here. Seven of nineteen farmers and one convict servant dead. What an awful loss. The bend in the river where these farmers worked is rich land, probably from the soils brought down by past floods. We'll have to think about what happens now,' Thompson said. 'All those farms in the way of the floods.'

'How is it elsewhere around here?' Williams said.

'We are still waiting on a few outlying farms but we think we have lost around fifteen lives in total. And that is just this side of Windsor. There are more lost beyond Windsor, all farmers. That will impact up here, not to mention all the crops that have been lost and the money that now won't come from them.'

Williams looked at the constable and wondered if he may cry, and if he did where it may stop. Williams had no idea what else to do. There was so much loss in such a small community. He turned away and walked over to the edge of the water and stared out towards the endless flood.

'I cannot wait to get back to the barracks. To simply walk on dry land again,' Hutton said as the boat the detachment was travelling on tacked towards Sydney Cove. 'All that water, all that ...'

'I think we best focus on what is ahead, not on what we have left behind,' Davies said.

'Sorry Lieutenant, it was just such an awful time.'

'I suggest you think about your own bed, a nice cup of rum and the companionship of a fine lady.'

'Or a comely lady in the case of Corporal Smith,' Gillard said.

'Too right Private. Madame Brigitte will have missed me,' Smith said. 'The poor girl just cannot cope without me.'

'Really,' Hutton said.

'It's true. I am her reason for being,' Smith said.

'And I thought her reason for being was—' Gillard said.

'Careful,' Davies cut Gillard off. 'Sydney Cove looks a treat does she not?'

'Yes she does, she always does,' Williams said.

The boat docked a short time later and the soldiers prepared to disembark. A large crowd milled around the wharves. As the soldiers walked down the gangplank the crowd surged forward.

'How bad are the crop losses up the Hawkesbury,' a voice yelled.

'Will there be grain for winter,' a woman shouted.

'Keep moving lads, best not to get involved in this,' Davies said.

The crowd surged forward, yelling for answers.

'Double-time lads,' Davies said. 'Jump to it.'

The soldiers quickly jogged away from the wharves and up the hill towards the barracks. Some in the crowd ran after them. One man grabbed Hutton and yelled at him, 'How bad is it?'

Hutton tried to shake the man loose but fell. A number of the crowd surged forward.

'Lieutenant,' Hutton yelled.

Davies turned and saw the danger to Hutton as the crowd kept moving forward. 'Lads turn and face, advance march. Hold your muskets across your bodies, use them to push the crowd back.'

The soldiers advanced quickly in line using their muskets to force the crowd back, like a Roman legion of old forcing the enemy back with shields.

Hutton managed to scramble to his feet as the soldiers advanced past him. 'I'm fine Lieutenant,' he said.

'Right lads, retreat slowly and carefully in a line.' Davies began to count out a beat of four. 'One, two, three, four.' The soldiers walked backwards and keeping in time, still facing the crowd which began to thin out. Davies judged that the distance between the soldiers and the crowd had opened far enough. 'Right lads turn and double time, we are almost at the barracks.'

The soldiers ran the last two hundred yards to the barracks.

'Bloody hell that was close,' Hutton said. 'Thanks mates.'

'No problem,' Smith said.

'Are you alright Private?' Lieutenant Davies said.

'Yes sir and thank you sir,' Hutton said.

Once the barracks came into view the crowd following dispersed. The soldiers quickly made their way past the sentry post and headed to their homes or bunk houses. Davies, Williams and Smith went into the mess hall and found Lieutenant Minchin and Quartermaster Laycock inside.

'Back from the Hawkesbury and not before time. Things are a little hairy around here,' Minchin said.

'We just found that out. We were chased by a crowd from the wharves wanting to know what was happening with the crops up in the Hawkesbury. Hutton nearly got trampled after one of the buggers tripped him over,' Davies said. 'Why are they so worried about the crops?'

'The *Gazette* published an article about the floods and detailed the devastation to the crops. People are panicking wondering if there will be enough food for the winter,' Minchin said.

'Well I can tell you that there's nothing left up there by way of crops. And a good quarter of the farmers are either dead or have no homes to return to,' Davies said. 'Things are likely to get more than a little hairy if this continues.'

'We have ordered the men confined to the barracks or home for now, until things settle down a little. There's already profiteering happening with wheat and tensions are running high,' Minchin said. 'We have no intention of getting caught up in it. I suggest you get your men to return to their homes and stay there. For those living here tell them to stay in the barracks for a time.'

'What does the major say on all this?' Davies said.

'He agrees and thinks that we keep a low profile for a while, at least until we know if there will be small or large shortages from the crops lost,' Minchin said. 'He also said to ask Corporal

Williams about how we are placed regarding the wheat supply. Corporal?'

'We bought up quite a bit of wheat over the last few months, so we have a plentiful supply. As I recall we were uncertain what we would do if there were shortages,' Williams said. 'We could stand to make a profit, but then that may also make us unpopular.'

'So that is the question, money or public standing,' Minchin said. There was silence for a time. 'Well no need to worry about that right now. We'll wait and see how bad the losses are,' Minchin said.

Williams walked the short distance from the barracks to his home. He noted that the garden was looking a little shabby in places, and that one of the palings was loose. No doubt Mary was too far along in her pregnancy to do anything physical, he thought.

He walked in and the house was quiet. Mary was nowhere to be seen. For a moment a shot of dread ran down Williams's spine and he shivered, despite the March heat. Steady yourself, he thought. There was no sign of anything being wrong, and the house was in good order.

From outside he heard the gate swing open and close. Mary walked up to the door and he stepped out.

'Well look who is home, my soldier boy. And not before time either,' Mary said. The two embraced and Williams kissed her passionately. 'Not tonight soldier boy. No bayonet practice for you. I am too far along.'

'That's fine Mary. It's so good to see you,' Williams said.

'So how was it? The paper says that the whole area is flooded and the crops are ruined,' Mary said as the two walked inside arm in arm. 'It's all anyone can talk about, which is a change from Bligh but of little comfort.'

'What the paper said is true. There's water everywhere, farms ruined, people drowned. The crops are all gone.'

'Will there be enough wheat for the winter, for bread?'

'The Corps has a stockpile of wheat, so we'll be fine. But please don't tell that to anyone. We don't want everyone to know that we have supplies until the major decides what to do with them. But enough of that, how are you and the baby doing?'

'We're both fine though this is very tiring and I lack the will to do much. The midwife said I should rest as much as I can, which I will now be able to manage since you are back.'

'I'll do as much as I can Mary.'

'Which won't be very much I take it. It's not for long, I should be due within a month or two.'

'That soon. I'd best organise a cradle for the baby, and blankets and...'

'I have done all of that so you can work on fixing a few things up around here. Tell me though, what do you think the major will do regarding the stockpiles of wheat you have?'

'I really don't know. We may sell it at a premium if supplies are low.'

'That wouldn't be a good idea. The people are already panicking about having enough wheat for the winter. The mood in town is volatile and if there's not enough wheat anything could happen. I would counsel that you either keep it for the Corps and families, or sell it to the government stores where it can be handed out as needed.'

'Mary, women don't usually counsel us on what we should do.'

'Which is why you men get yourselves into trouble so often. Profiteering on rum is one thing, but bread is a necessity. It should not be for profit. Anyway, I have said my piece and if you don't like it that's fine, but remember that I have survived on my own for a long time before you came along. I managed it because I am smart enough to know things about people. And I know that people don't like having nothing while others have plenty.'

'Like I said Mary, women don't usually counsel us, but I think from now on I'll listen to you on these matters. Now come over here and give me a hug.'

'Oliver Williams have you listened to me at all? I tell you I am tired and you tell me to walk over to you. You come over here.'

Williams smiled and walked across the room to his wife.

The winter months passed slowly, and while none starved plenty complained of hunger. The government stores were able to keep up a supply of wheat to the people. Major Johnston had spoken to Governor King in late May at a ball held at Government House and offered to provide a quantity of wheat at cost price. The major had been surprised by King's response.

'And what do you want in return for this generosity, Major? A free pass to sell all the rum you desire at hugely inflated prices?' King said.

Johnston looked around the room, where there was a gathering of the elite of Sydney, including the owner of the *Gazette*, traders, land owners and free settlers.

'Why nothing of the sort dear sir. The New South Wales Corps are able to supply this wheat at cost. We do not want to see civil unrest,' Johnston said. 'Our desire is for this colony to grow and thrive, and that cannot happen if the people are hungry and desperate. Consider this an investment in the future of this colony. We know that there is wheat on its way from India and that we can survive. But why simply survive when we as a colony can do so much more.'

It was King's turn to look around the room. Privately he cursed Johnston. The major had chosen his battlefield well and there were too many onlookers to refuse such an offer.

'That is most generous. On behalf of the people of New South Wales I accept. My aide will make the arrangements with you,' King said. Johnston held out his hand and King looked at it for a long moment before reluctantly shaking the hand of the major.

King then hobbled off on his gout-ridden feet. Johnston and the Corps had beaten him, had humiliated him by maintaining their trade in rum, and with the help of Macarthur had ensured his recall to England. He pondered where it had all gone so wrong as he walked out of the room. It was the last time he would be seen in public until August.

Mary and Williams welcomed a son into the world in May. They named him Henry John and he soon had their small house running to his schedule. Williams did what he could to help out but as he said to Mary, 'I have no skills in household matters.'

'I wouldn't argue with that,' Mary said. 'Thank goodness my son is more in tune with the domestic needs of this house than you. He sleeps well enough that things can be done.'

'Your son is it now Mary?'

'Yes my son. When he is a good boy he is my beloved son, and when he refuses to sleep or do what we want then he is your son,' Mary said. 'Once you have that clear things will be even better around here.'

Williams laughed. 'Right you are Mary, right you are.'

The Corps continued to maintain their trade in rum. 'Where are we heading Oli,' Nate Smith said.

'Just doing the rounds of the taverns, checking on how sales are going. Tom and George are doing the wharves and we will do the town,' Williams said. 'Now that there is wheat again the people are reasonably happy and drinking plenty. Life is good is it not?'

'Yes it is,' Smith replied. 'The major was very clever to give the wheat over to the stores house. It will get us all through until the ships arrive from India with more.'

'You have to hand it to him, the major does have his moments,' Williams said. 'And it is nice to walk around the town and have people smile at us and tip their hats and say thank you for a change.'

'It certainly makes a pleasant change from the usual scowling and people crossing the street to avoid us,' Smith said.

'And that's just the ladies you have spoken to the previous weekend Nate,' Williams said.

'There's just too much loving needed and only one of me Oli. I try my best to spread the love around. Sometimes it's hard to reach all those in need of a tender moment.'

'Is that what you are calling it these days? Tender moments?'

'Something like that.'

'The less I know the better,' Williams said.

August 1806

'Righto lads, tomorrow we are to present our best selves, uniforms in mint condition, brass polished to within an inch of its life, muskets clean and faces shaven,' Sergeant Major Whittle said to the soldiers of the Corps.

Every man of the Corps in Sydney had been summoned to the parade ground, where Sergeant Major Whittle was now in full stride.

'We will damn well impress every citizen of this colony with our turnout, marching in order and standing to attention straighter than I have seen any of you manage in a long time, and yes I am looking at you Private Mulligan.

'If you do not have full accoutrements and polished brass and black shakos and bright red uniforms you will find me entertaining you out here for as long as I find enjoyment in it. And we all know that that can be a very long time. Nothing gives me greater pleasure than seeing a proper soldier presenting himself correctly. And I am not looking at you Private Mulligan when I mention properly presented soldier. Is that clear?

'Right now, pay attention to the major, who has important news for all of you. Hutton, Gillard, you had better not be talking back there!'

'Lads, we have had word that tomorrow Governor Bligh will be arriving in Sydney Cove to begin his appointment. We will be putting on a show to impress the new governor, to show him what we are about,' Johnston said. 'The Corps will have all colours flying and show our mettle.

'There will be a welcoming, with Judge Advocate Atkins to represent the civil administration, Mr Macarthur to represent the free inhabitants and myself to represent the military, all welcoming the new governor. We will present him with an official address of welcome.

'Once that is done we will present an official farewell address to Governor King. And then we will march back here and privately farewell the outgoing governor by trading rounds of rum.'

The men laughed and cheered, glad to see the back of a governor who had tried so hard to break their monopoly on rum trading.

Sergeant Major Whittle then issued orders regarding time for assembly and marching orders for the following day.

'Right lads, let's start the show,' Whittle ordered.

A column of the Corps slowly marched out of the barracks, led by two flag bearers, one holding the Union Jack, the other the regimental colours. Behind them two drummers beat time, and two soldiers played fifes. The officers marched out next, resplendent in their hats and red coats.

Finally, a long column of soldiers marched with sergeants and corporals leading each group. The column snaked its way down the hill from the barracks, drawing attention wherever it went. Music played and the soldiers sang in full voice. All around people clapped and cheered, the memory of the wheat the Corps had provided still fresh.

After twenty minutes the column arrived at Sydney Cove. It was a few minutes before 11 am and the boat carrying Bligh was now on its final approach to the wharves. A large crowd followed the Corps, joining those already in place.

Johnston stepped out of the column and walked up and stood next to Macarthur and Atkins.

'A very nice show, George,' Macarthur said.

'Nothing like a little parade to excite the locals Mac,' Johnston said. 'Richard, how are you this fine morning?'

'Well enough George, well enough.'

'So here we go then. Commodore Bligh himself is about to take command. Let's hope it ends better than the *Bounty*,' Macarthur said.

Johnston looked at his old friend. 'Well, if nothing provokes the man I am sure it will,' Johnston said.

Atkins stood quietly by. 'Nothing to say Richard?' Macarthur said.

'I should have thought it would be a welcome change to have a new and strong governor, to get this colony back on track,' Atkins said. 'After all every other man here thinks the governor is to be at his beck and call.'

'By here I assume you mean the three of us? Or are you referring to everyone?' Macarthur said. 'Well it makes no difference to me whether you mean George and I or the thousands now gathered. The Governor's job is to make our lives better and he does that by standing clear of industry and commerce and cutting down the impediments to their growth. Say what you will about King but at least he understood commerce and tried to bring in policies to help grow the colony.

'As I recall John you had plenty to say about King, most of it behind his back and none of good,' Atkins said. 'Is this a conversion on the road to Damascus? Or will you only say good things about him now that he has been recalled and is not present to hear them?'

'Remind me again Richard of who helped you out a number of years ago when you had your money problems? Who bailed you out? Or should that be who gave you the bill of exchange to get you out of your problems? Or better, I could say who gave you a bond out of trouble?'

'Well it wasn't you, and yes it was that trader Bond who helped me out. How do you know his name?' Atkins said.

Macarthur smiled his dazzling smile. 'Oh I know plenty about such things, a great deal indeed.'

Atkins felt a shiver run down his spine. He thought that God himself would not be able to help him against Macarthur if the man knew such things.

'Gentlemen, shall we attend to the business of the day?' Johnston said as Bligh's ship docked and the gangplank was lowered.

William Bligh stepped down the gangplank. His reputation preceded him: master navigator, disciplinarian, fighting sailor. The man himself seemed smaller than the reputation suggested, and older, with a balding head and a slightly hobbled walk. He wore a blue naval dress coat, tricorner naval hat and a sword by his side. The message was clear, William Bligh was still, at heart, a fighting sailor and stood ready for battle, should it come to him.

Governor King stepped forward. 'Your Excellency, may I welcome you to Sydney and as one governor to another say how pleased we are to have a man of such excellent calibre to lead us.' King looked at the crowd and then to Macarthur, Johnston and Atkins. 'You will need all your skills to manage this rabble,' King muttered to himself as Bligh stepped forward.

'Thank you Governor King, I am delighted to have arrived,' Bligh said.

At that moment a short, strikingly beautiful woman emerged at the top of the gangplank and began to walk down. 'Governor, may I present my daughter Mary Putland, who will act as hostess at Government House,' Bligh said.

Proceedings halted for a moment until Mary had completed her descent down the gangplank.

Bligh smiled at his daughter. 'My wife is too ill to make such an arduous journey. She will join us later.'

'Ahem. Governor King, if we may get on with things,' Macarthur said.

'Yes, quite,' King said, seeming to deflate.

'Governor Bligh, on behalf of the free settlers and inhabitants of this colony we bid you welcome,' Macarthur said.

'Thank you.'

'I am John Macarthur and I represent the interests of the free inhabitants of New South Wales. We stand for commerce and progress.'

'So you are Macarthur. Banks told me all about you,' Bligh said.

Atkins and Johnston both stepped forward and introduced themselves, then mirrored Macarthur's words, Atkins for the civil administration and Johnston for the military.

'Thank you both for such kind words. You will find that words are not my strength, actions are. Let me say this however, it is my intention to restore to this colony proper regulations that bring this colony into line with its original purposes.

'There is no reason why such regulations should hinder progress. Instead they should help the industrious settler and merchant to succeed. Success comes in harmony with religion and morality, both of which I shall encourage and seek to inculcate into the daily life of the colony. Together we can reach for and achieve the great goal of setting this colony to the rightful objects and path it was established under.

'To this end I shall personally exercise a close superintendence over this colony, as though a captain on the quarter-deck of this vessel of state. Now Mary is tired, let us depart for Government House.'

Bligh and his daughter stood and waited for action to begin.

'Before you depart Mr Bligh,' Macarthur said, 'we would like to make an address to Governor King.'

'It is Governor Bligh or Commodore Bligh, sir and make it fast.' Macarthur stepped forward. 'Governor King, I shall read the official address to you, on behalf of the civil and military administrations and the free settlers. On behalf of the people of New South Wales our thanks is given for discharging the office of governor under circumstances arduous and difficult beyond what can easily be imagined by any person unacquainted with this peculiar colony.

'Your efforts to open up New South Wales as a trading port, to challenge the monopoly held by the East India Company, resulting in the legitimising of New South Wales as a trading port under the Navigation Act are remembered fondly.

'Free settlers appreciate your efforts to introduce farm stock, initiate use of ploughs and sensibly use public farming. Your efforts to build and enhance trade in the town as a means to supporting mercantile commerce are greatly appreciated,' Macarthur said. King went red in the face at this insult to his efforts to dismantle that same trade in rum.

Macarthur continued for two more minutes, laying insults into the intricately crafted speech. King's efforts to maintain wheat prices at levels of benefit to Hawkesbury farmers rather than to the monopolist traders were mocked. Macarthur wilfully ignored King's early efforts to set the commons aside for public use, instead praising King's foresight in signing over these lands to Macarthur to establish a sheep industry.

By the end King was red in the face and Johnston and Atkins looked at the ground. Finally Macarthur finished, his speech, more a message to Bligh than a farewell to King.

'Now may I go sir?' Bligh said to Macarthur.

'Certainly Captain Bligh,' Macarthur said.

By jove the man isn't wasting any time,' Minchin said.

He was sitting in the mess hall with Davies, Laycock, Whittle, Williams and Smith a week after Bligh's arrival.

'Who's not wasting time?' Davies said.

'Bligh. He has installed Blaxcell as his secretary of the colony. Already he has agreement from the free settlers that they will pay every eleventh bushel of corn into the government stores in exchange for the government grinding corn for individuals in need,' Minchin said. 'Bligh has set a price per bushel for wheat and corn to stop profiteering.'

'That's smart. It will win over the small farmers, particularly those up the Hawkesbury way.' Williams said.

'There's more though,' Minchin said. 'Rumour has it that the free settlers of Sydney and the Hawkesbury presented Bligh with their version of a welcoming address. They have said to Bligh that Mac is the last person they would have chosen to speak for them at the official welcome, if they had been asked.

'They have collectively accused Mac of pushing the price of mutton up by not selling some of his sheep. They accuse him instead of withholding some of his sheep for sale to push for the price he wants. In addition they have complained of the monopolists all but destroying the colony.'

'A few whingers are not enough to divert Bligh's attention. Are they?' Laycock said.

'More than one hundred and thirty Sydney settlers and two hundred and thirty Hawkesbury settlers have signed this. All are free settlers and together they have influence. What they want more than anything is the right to trade on an open market with government price guarantees, rather than one controlled by monopolists,' Minchin said.

'You mean controlled by us, and Mac, and even that conniving Campbell and his fellow traders,' Davies said.

'Do you ever stop to think that Campbell and his fellow traders probably call us conniving. And the Lord alone knows what they call Mac,' Minchin said. 'The point is that Bligh has started off by working to help the small farmers and free settlers and get them on side. If you wanted to break the monopoly that we and others hold that's where you would start.

'The settlers have gathered up all the spare corn and wheat they have and sold it to the government stores for the price they agreed with Bligh. They have made it known that they could have got a better price but are showing their support for returning, in their words, "justice and fairness to the colony". They intend to continue this practice for the good of the colony, not of the few.

'There is more still,' Minchin said.

'Isn't that enough?' Smith said.

'Bligh has the authority to stop the importation of all liquor to the colony,' Minchin said.

There was a long silence in the room. 'That would mean our monopoly would be broken,' Davies said. 'We can't distill enough to keep things going.'

'Word has it that Bligh wants to not only stop importation, he wants to stop the distilling of liquor and the bartering of spirits. In this he has the support of the free farmers who want a proper system of currency established, so as to stop the use of bartering liquor as payment,' Minchin said.

'Where are you getting this from?' Whittle said. 'You seem particularly well informed of the intentions of his high-and-mighty Commodore Bligh.'

The men looked at Minchin. 'Well,' Whittle said.

'I know a lady … well perhaps lady is too strong a word. She knows one of the governor's aides very well, in the biblical sense you could say. Well she is partial to playing around and … well, I think you have the picture now. For a bit of rum she is willing to make a very satisfying trade, and after trading and drinking she is quite talkative,' Minchin said.

'Do you believe her?' Whittle said.

'Do you think, Sergeant Major, I would share that with you if I did not.'

'So then, it seems that Bligh is prepared to take us on,' Davies said. 'Another governor to do battle with.'

'Yes, but this is Bligh. The man is famous for taking discipline to his sailors and for taking on fights. Don't forget he was distinguished at Copenhagen by Admiral Nelson. Things may not be as easy as they were against Hunter or King,' Minchin said. 'I'm worried, the man is clearly here with orders to break the monopolists and return New South Wales to a penal colony of farmers.'

'Well we have a secret weapon do we not?' Davies said.

'And what is that?' Whittle said.

'We have Mac. He'll sweet-talk Bligh round to his way of thinking,' Davies said.

'I hope you are right, I really do,' Minchin said. 'I fear that even Mac is going to find this governor too hard to break.'

'How did it go Mac?' George Johnston said without looking up from the paper. He was sitting in the mess with a group of officers as Macarthur walked in and was still absorbed in his reading rather than listening.

'That fucking rude little bastard. I am going to break him if it is the last thing I do,' John Macarthur said.

'So it went that well,' Johnston said with a smirk. He was about to say something else when he turned and looked at John Macarthur. A cold wave of dread washed over Johnston. He had been right all along in wondering if Macarthur had lost it and that much was clear by the look on Mac's face. Johnston had seen his friend under pressure before but never with this manic look. For a moment Johnston was convinced there was a touch of insanity behind those eyes. He swallowed hard and tried to adopt a gentler tone.

'Mac, sit down. Tell us what happened. Someone get Mac a glass of wine,' Johnston ordered.

'I will damn well break him, just like I did Hunter and King,' Macarthur said. 'I told Bligh about my plans for the wool industry and how the government in Britain was backing it, and the leases on the Commons and other land. And you know what he fucking said to me? To me? He said "Are you to have more sheep than any man before?" He insulted me and my plans to make this colony the leading wool exporter in the world. He dismissed my requests for more land and convict labour. Then that pedantic little shit said that the free settlers do not want me to represent them and that I am hoarding sheep to push up the price of mutton and that the monopolists in this colony are a disease to be eradicated.

'Fuck, I will go and challenge him to a duel right now. I should have done it at the time,' Macarthur said.

All the eyes in the room shifted from Macarthur to Johnston, imploring him to do something.

'Mac, Mac. Tell me who else was there? Who will back up your story?'

'It's not a fucking story George and I don't need backing up,' Macarthur said. 'That gutter-mouthed little rat bastard sailor will not tell me how this colony moves forward. He will not shape its destiny. Only I can do that. That's why I am here. If we let governor bluff-and-bluster run this colony he will take us back to 1788 just to prove that he can. All that I have built will be lost and I can't have that. Why can't I duel him?' Macarthur said.

'Because he's the governor for a start. You can't just challenge him to a duel, especially when there are no witnesses to provide you a justification. You'll look like a man who has been told no and whose only recourse is a gun. Besides you know how the last duel ended,' Johnston said, searching the room for someone to help him reason with Macarthur.

'Yeah, I fucking well put that trumped up fool Patterson in his place,' Macarthur said.

'And then you were sent to England to defend yourself and spent four years away from home. If you do that now Bligh will simply have you charged and sent back, or worse, hung right here without even letting you near him with a gun. Then he'll be here to undo things and you'll be in England — or dead,' Johnston said.

'In England I can lobby Banks and others, I can see the King or the Prince and have him removed.'

'Mac, even if that came to pass it would still be two years before the orders arrived to remove Bligh, and that is the best scenario. You know it took almost that long from the time King was officially ordered home until Bligh arrived to replace him,' Johnston said. 'Are you going to leave Bligh here for that long or more while you're in England? He'll destroy you before you can have him removed.'

Macarthur was silent for a long time. Johnston looked around the room and realised that none of the officers had moved since Macarthur first spoke.

'Then we wait and play him the same way we did King,' Macarthur said. He drained the cup of wine and smiled. 'Sorry lads, didn't mean to give you all a show.'

With that Macarthur stood up. 'Now I must be off to check on my sheep. Bligh can wait and besides, if it comes to it, well we'll just have to march down there and talk some sense into him.' Macarthur turned and walked for the door.

There was silence for a time after he left. The room felt smaller and hotter and the day somehow darker all at once.

'Righto lads, perhaps a spot of lunch is in order,' Johnston said.

There was a murmuring of agreement and the officers quietly went back to their own thinking.

January 1807

Williams and Smith were doing the rounds of the pubs and taverns in the summer heat. A number were owned by non-commissioned officers in the Corps, others by associates who sold liquor supplied by the Corps in return for protection. 'You know I wait all winter for the heat and when it finally arrives I find it harder and harder to bear,' Smith said.

'That's because you're getting old Nate,' Williams said.

'Not too old to put an upstart like you in your place,' Smith replied. 'You know, I remember when you first arrived here, quiet, sensible, willing to follow orders. And look at you now. Knows it all, talks too much, has no respect for his elders.'

'So you admit you're an elder do you Nate?' Williams said.

'So help me God I should have left you to those Irish bastards, or up the Hawkesbury,' Smith said laughing.

'That you probably should have Nate, but I'm glad you didn't.'

'Don't tell anyone but so am I Oli,' Smith said.

'Here's Ravi's shop. Let's see what he's up to," Williams said.

The two soldiers walked into Ravi Chandra's small shop. Chandra saw the two and smiled. He had overcome his nervousness around the soldiers after he found it relatively easy to sell his monthly quota of rum and still make some money on the side.

'How are things Ravi?'

'Mr Smith they could not be better, and Mr Williams it is always a pleasure to see you,' Chandra said. 'How are Mrs Williams and your boy?'

Williams, surprised by the small talk, pulled a face to Smith. 'They are both in good health Ravi, and how about you and yours?'

'I am happy to report that all is well at my home too. Here I have your payment,' Chandra said, pulling out a promissory note.

'What is that Ravi? We said no promissory notes, only sterling' Williams said.

'But Mr Williams this is what people are using. It is legal currency,' Chandra said. 'Mr Bligh the governor has said so.'

'Since when?' Smith said.

'Since the start of the year Mr Smith. Many of my customers pay with these notes. Mr Bligh has said notes of hand must be honoured and are payable in sterling,' Chandra said.

Smith and Williams looked at each other and walked a few paces away. 'What do we do Oli? Do we take it or demand cash?'

'For God's sake Nate I don't know, maybe we take it.'

'Are you saying now that you actually don't know it all?' Smith said.

'Do you really think this the time, Nate?'

'So do we take it? Come on, you're the brains of this outfit.'

'Finally some acknowledgement of the obvious,' Williams said. He looked away for a few moments. 'Alrighty Ravi, we'll take it this time. But next month sterling only, and I don't care what Governor Bligh says.'

Chandra gratefully handed over the note and gave each man a generous tot of rum. The two soldiers drank it and left.

'You know what he is trying to do, don't you Nate?'

'What's Ravi trying to do?'

'Not Ravi, Bligh. You know Governor bluff-and-bluster as Mac calls him. He's trying to make bartering of rum illegal and if he does that it only helps the small merchants, not us. We have enough rum to trade without losing too much, but if rum is no longer the main unit of currency and sterling is then we have real problems,' Williams said.

'Cause we have all this rum and can't use it for currency?'

'Exactly. And if we're not the only ones with sterling then others can buy goods directly from incoming ships. Traders can establish their own networks. Forget the rest of the rounds, let's go straight to the Londoner and see Henry and see what he has to say,' Williams said.

They walked quickly, working up a sweat in the heat. Williams noticed how many of the buildings were having some kind of work done, improvements and repairs.

Henry Adams greeted the two soldiers as they entered the Londoner. 'Henry, back room now please,' Williams said.

Adams grabbed three cups and a bottle of Cape Red and followed the two soldiers into the back room. 'What the hell is all this about promissory notes and the like? Are you accepting them?' Williams said.

'Of course I am. They are the equivalent of sterling and can be used as such. Governor Bligh is intending to phase them out over the next few months as more sterling comes into the colony. That should be in the second half of the year,' Adams said.

'Well you don't have to sound so bloody happy about it Henry,' Williams said.

'Sorry, but it does make life easier. No more drunks begging to trade labour for rum makes for a better experience for all,' Adams said.

'Well at least it's making things better for you. It's going to make life a lot harder for us,' Williams said.

'I didn't make the bloody rules up Oliver,' Adams said.

'But you agree with them don't you?' Smith said.

'Yes I do, it makes things clearer. All the trade and bartering in rum does is make the life of a tavern owner harder,' Adams said. 'Most of the smaller businesses are enjoying the certainty of sterling as currency, and yes I know it is hard on you lads, but I cannot pretend not to be supportive of this change.'

Smith glared at Adams, the promise of violence gleaming from his eyes. Williams went to say something and realised how wound up Smith was. He put a hand on his friend's chest. 'Nate, Henry's entitled to his views, and it's not his policy, it's that of Bligh. So Henry are you going to open that bloody wine or are you expecting a promissory note?'

Adams quickly opened the wine and poured the three cups to the brim. 'To the good old days,' Adams said.

'Let's hope they return soon,' Smith said.

'The same thing is happening everywhere,' Williams said. He had just finished telling the occupants of the mess about Bligh's new rules. 'By banning the trade in rum and reinstalling promissory notes Bligh has got half the town on side. And in a few months there will be no need for notes, they'll all be exchanged for sterling.'

'But why is this so dangerous to us? I really don't think I understand,' Sergeant Bremlow said.

'When we first arrived here,' Johnston said, 'we were the only people getting paid in sterling, in pounds and pence. There were a few administrators but mainly it was the Corps. So we effectively owned and controlled most of the currency in the colony. We could buy for pence and sell in pounds.

'As there was not enough currency, enough coin if you will, rum also became a currency. People tried promissory notes for a short time, but funnily enough, in a colony full of criminals, most people didn't honour them. People wanted payment upfront and rum became the means to do that. Because we were the only ones able to buy large quantities of rum, we controlled the currency and the trade.'

'Alright,' Bremlow said slowly, still not seeing things.

Johnston nodded to Williams.

'Think of it like a game. In effect the Corps controlled the game. We set the rules to ensure we got rich from running the game. Now Bligh wants to control the game. To do that he is saying rum is no longer able to be used to buy and sell goods,' Williams said.

'But there's still not much sterling about,' Smith said.

'That's right, which is why Bligh is using promissory notes. What Bligh is saying is that those notes are legal currency, the same as sterling. Until enough sterling is available people will be able to use those notes to pay for goods as though they were actual coins and bank notes. Bligh will gradually exchange notes for sterling,' Williams said.

'So he will bring more sterling in?' Smith said.

'Yes, and that will mean there are no longer two different markets running. Bligh will run the only game in town,' Williams said. He looked around at the blank faces and quizzical expressions. He saw a deck of cards out on a table.

'Let's put it another way. Say we are playing cards, and betting using coins. What happens if someone runs out of coin, but wants to bet with rum so they can stay in the game? If we can all agree that a bottle is worth, say, a pound, or a cup is worth ten pence then we can play on. But say we can't agree. Some of the players then choose to start another game betting in rum.' Williams said.

'You have two different games,' Bremlow said.

'Exactly. That's what's happening now. There are two different games, or markets, currently running in Sydney,' Williams said. 'One with sterling, and the other with rum. You can get paid in both. Some people can switch between the two markets while others can't because they don't have any money. There is simply not enough about. What Bligh is doing is importing sterling so there is enough about. He is ensuring that there is only one game or market, using sterling, played under his rules.

'People can't drink money. Instead they use it buy food and other things to live. The currency of the market, money, continues to move from person to person, unlike most of the rum where people drink it and then always want more. The crucial difference now is that by introducing more sterling and having only one currency in the colony we no longer hold an effective monopoly. We just lost control of the game,' Williams said.

'Bloody hell, this would call for a drink if only I wasn't so confused about whether I'm drinking rum or money,' Bremlow said.

'There's more to it,' Williams said.

'That's it. I don't care if I'm drinking my savings away. My head hurts from all this commerce and I'm having a drink,' Bremlow said. 'I can do that, have a drink can't I?'

'Yes Sergeant you can,' Johnston said. 'Now explain how it can get worse please Corporal.'

'What Bligh is trying to do is change the game. And his most important rule is sterling doesn't change in value. So goods always cost the same. We can't buy in pence and sell in pounds anymore. That will break our power and allow the small traders and farmers more freedom to trade. By setting prices for say wheat or corn farmers get paid the same regardless of how good or bad a year it is.'

'What do you mean?' Minchin said.

'If a bushel of wheat is valued by the government at three pounds, the price does not change regardless of the strength of the harvest,' Williams said. 'Before Bligh set a price a good harvest of wheat would mean the price dropped because there was more than was needed. But in a bad year when less wheat was produced than the colony needed the price rose dramatically and the people would pay plenty for a bushel. The more available the less people pay for it, but when there is not much available people pay more.'

'Like the women here,' Smith said.

'Trust you to bring that up,' Minchin said.

'No I think I know what Nate means. There are far less women than men, so women choose the men with the best prospects. It's the same with wheat. If we have wheat when no-one else does, we can sell it for whatever price we want,' Williams said.

'Right. So in a bad year where there is not much wheat farmers are in control, but in a good year where there is plenty buyers are in control and can set the price which will be low,' Smith said. 'See, I get it.'

'Care to explain the rest then,' Johnston said.

'Ahh, no,' Smith said.

'Under these new arrangements the farmers can sell to the government store and get a guaranteed three pounds per bushel, where before they may only have got two pound in good years,' Williams said. 'And that means that the government will have most of the wheat and so can set the price, which will remain constant. They will also build up a stockpile for bad years.

'Farmers know that they will always get a minimum of three pounds a bushel. Buyers have certainty of prices too. Remember the panic after the Hawkesbury floods? That will be a thing of the past as everyone will still be able to afford wheat or corn.

'So there is only one currency in sterling, there's no bartering or using rum to make payments and prices remain constant. In other words Bligh now controls commerce, and not us. Bligh now controls the flow of rum and Bligh now sets the prices of goods. It's his game now.'

'The question for us is how we stop the rot?' Johnston said.

'What I don't understand is how this works,' Bremlow said.

'We have just been through that William,' Johnston said. 'Do we really need to start again?'

'No, I mean why are these policies working now when past attempts have not?' Bremlow said.

'Because the constabulary are backing these policies up with warnings and threatening arrests for any use of rum as currency,' Johnston said. He sat and stared out the window for a few moments. 'Sergeant, you just may be on to something there.'

'Am I?' Bremlow said. 'I hope, Major, you don't expect me to explain, because I don't think I can.'

Johnston laughed. 'Tell me this Sergeant, what would you advocate I do against an enemy force, say in the example of the Irish rebels of '04?'

'I would suggest that you use force against them, and if you have the chance kill or arrest their leaders.'

'There you have it gentlemen. Never let it be said Sergeant Bremlow is not a man of great intellectual capacity,' Johnston said.

'I don't think I have ever been accused of that before,' Bremlow said, to much amusement.

'Shall I put you out of your misery and explain my plan Sergeant?' Johnston said.

'That would be much appreciated Major. And can I please have that drink now, I think I have earned it. I have earned it haven't I?' Bremlow said.

'Yes you have Sergeant,' Johnston said. 'Your tactical analysis is correct. We would usually employ force against an enemy and then arrest or kill the leaders, as we did against the Irish. The challenge here is that our enemy is Bligh and we cannot use force against the governor, nor can we use force against his constables.'

'But we could have them arrested,' Williams said.

'Exactly. We go after the head of the snake by having Provost Marshal Gore arrested. That way we break the power the constables have. And we will have the advantage of choosing the battle ground that we control, the courts. In the absence of a real war we must have a proxy war. So it's time to find some information on Mr Gore and to work out some charges. And in the meantime we shall see if we can provoke Mr Gore into doing something foolish.

'And for that purpose I propose that we collectively volunteer Private Mulligan, who has a remarkable capacity for angering people. Lieutenant Minchin, Corporal Smith, can you please tee him up and see what he can do.'

'That's him, the short fellow with the short hair,' Smith said to Mulligan. 'Now remember, nothing too loud or too aggressive, just a bump to start with.'

Mulligan walked out into the street and headed across to where Gore was standing talking with one of his constables. The two policemen started walking slowly along the street towards Mulligan, who moved to be nearer the constables. Then he stopped and looked in a window as the two men approached.

As the policemen were passing Mulligan watched in the glass. He turned blind and bumped the policeman, who turned. 'Watch it,' the constable said.

Mulligan, who had started walking away turned. 'You walked into me and tell me to watch it. Just 'cause you have a constable's uniform on doesn't mean you can do what you want.'

By now the two men were edging towards each other. The constable grabbed his baton and started to raise it.

'Private Mulligan, what the hell is going on here,' Lieutenant Minchin said, appearing on cue.

'Sorry Lieutenant, this man just shoved right through me while I was minding my business. My missus is having her birthday and I was hoping to buy a nice shawl for her and I was looking in the window of a shop and he just shoves me out of the way as he was passing.'

'You liar,' the constable said, 'you turned and hit me.'

'As God is my witness I did no such thing. I was standing still, I never moved,' Mulligan said. 'Nate is here with me. Begging your pardon Sir, Corporal Smith. Look there he is.'

Smith came walking over from the tavern. 'I saw it. That policeman just walked right through Private Mulligan like he wasn't even there.'

'I was beside Constable Hughes, Lieutenant,' Provost Marshal Gore said. 'It was your man that turned blind into my constable.'

'Are you calling me a liar?' Mulligan shouted. People turned and looked from all directions slack-jawed at the possibility of a fight in the street between the constabulary and the red coats.

'I am not calling you anything,' Gore said. 'You did however turn into us.'

'So it's us now. First it was him and now it's us that I supposedly walked into when I was standing still,' Mulligan said. Minchin smiled at the corners of his mouth. Perfect, he thought. Mulligan may be a pest but he did it so well.

'Private Mulligan, stand down. You too Corporal Smith. It appears the words of two soldiers of the Corps is not good enough for our constabulary. It makes one wonder how many crimes they make up and set up, compared to how many they actually police,' Minchin said.

The crowd continued to grow. Gore looked at the growing number of bystanders. Someone shouted something that sounded like 'fight em'. The moment for things to tip over the edge into violence hung in the air. Hughes stood taller and squared his shoulders.

'Lying bastard,' Mulligan said. Then he smiled at Hughes.

Hughes made to start forwards but Gore grabbed him and pushed him back.

'We are leaving Constable. Now lad,' Gore said.

The crowd sensed the possibility of violence passing and began to ebb away.

At that moment Williams led a detachment around the corner and into the street. He had been waiting with six soldiers in a nearby house listening for his cue.

Gore started to say something to Minchin and then stopped when the soldiers entered the street. He and Hughes were now outnumbered ten to two and any further insults would likely result in a fight there and then.

'Constable Hughes, it is past time we left,' Gore said. The remaining crowd started to whistle and jeer, yelling 'cowards' as the constables walked away. Minchin watched them go. Gore was smart enough not to be provoked in the street. Today's work was done.

William Gore was walking home when he realised he was being followed. The Provost Marshal carefully reached for the baton he carried on his belt and secured it in his hand, comforted by the weight of the solid club. He slowed down very slightly and then stopped and bent down to check his boot. He heard a noise behind him and violently sprung up and raised the club, stepping into the space between himself and his attacker. He began to swing the club down and stopped only when he heard the scream of a woman. It was in that moment that he realised his shadow was a woman, small and slim and barely more than a child.

'By God girl, what the hell are you doing following me around?' Gore said.

'She is walking with us,' a woman said from behind the girl. 'Quickly, run and get the constabulary,' the woman said to another young girl.

Within moments two policemen from nearby came running around the corner, closely followed by the young girl Gore had seen run off just moments before.

'That man tried to attack young Jane. We are heading home after work and he just stopped and leapt up and was going to hit her,' the older woman said.

The constables came forward and stopped dead. 'Mr Gore ...'

'Ma'am, this man you accuse of doing this is the Provost Marshal. I think there must have been a mistake,' the taller of the two constables said.

'There was no mistaking what he was intending to do to poor Jane,' the older woman said.

'Best you ladies be on your way and we will deal with this,' the tall constable said.

The ladies slowly walked away heading towards the Rocks. They walked for a minute before doubling back towards Soldier's Row, where they lived as wives and defactos of Corps soldiers. Gore had not done enough to ensure charges could be brought, stopping short of hitting Jane. But Gore's actions could still prove useful to the Corps. Over the next day the women carefully spread the story of the Provost Marshal almost attacking a poor girl returning home from work. The grounds for a possible charge had been laid. Their part of the plan to bring down Gore was finished.

George Johnston, Quartermaster Laycock and Lieutenant Minchin were walking along near the offices of the constabulary when they spied Provost Marshal Gore.

'Mr Gore, may I have a word with you,' Johnston said.

'Major Johnston, always a pleasure. Please speak freely,' Gore said.

'I wanted to apologise for the unpleasantness involving one of my men and your constable the other day. I hope no harm has come of it. Such matters can get heated quickly and we want only to remain on good terms with you,' Johnston said.

'Why George, how are you?' Simeon Lord said, walking up. 'I did not know you were in town, but I am glad to have run across you.'

'Simeon, good to see you too. How is business?' Johnston said. 'Do you know my officers, Lieutenant Minchin and Quartermaster Laycock, and have you met the Provost Marshal, Mr Gore.'

'I do know of Mr Gore. It seems he thinks me a rum trader,' Lord said.

'I can only imagine what he thinks of we soldiers then, given the stories that go around town,' Johnston said.

'We must talk business soon,' Lord said. 'I wonder if we cannot help each other out. Provost Marshal you can stay and chat some business with us if you care to?'

'Yes,' said Johnston, 'after all, we are better friends than not, and well able to put past misunderstandings behind us.'

Gore flushed red, shocked that Simeon Lord, one of Sydney's most prolific rum traders and profiteers, and George Johnston, head of the New South Wales Corps would make such a direct offer for Gore to talk business. Were these men out to tempt him into joining their rum trading.

'I must go, and see where my constables are. There is plenty of work to do policing the governor's ban on rum trading and barter,' Gore said. He turned and walked away.

Minchin sat down in the mess hall, followed by Johnston and Laycock. 'Well that didn't work,' Minchin said.

'Perhaps not, but at least we know the measure of the man,' Johnston said. 'So if he will not join us then we will have to use the Bremlow option and get the man arrested.'

'How do we do that?' Laycock said.

'He didn't take the bait with Mulligan. As to the charges, I take it our ladies had little success?'

'Sorry Major. Gore almost swung at young Jane Hudson but it wasn't enough for charges,' Minchin said.

'But we need to get him up on charges. Once he is before a sitting of the courts he is ours,' Johnston said. 'I can talk to Atkins and get the right panel of officers as the jury and then we can have our day in court. Any other ideas?'

'Evidently Gore does not get along with the gaoler McKay. The two have clashed over how brutally McKay treats prisoners. McKay's woman is the half sister of Private Gillard's wife but that is little known. I shall talk with Gillard and see what can be done to meet with McKay and if he's agreeable to the chance to get rid of his boss,' Minchin said.

'Set it up, but we are not to be involved other than in court. You will need to tread carefully on this one,' Johnston said.

'You the one that wanted to talk to me?' McKay said.

'Yes,' Minchin said.

'Here I am, talk then.'

'Tell me about William Gore.'

'What's to say. The man don't like me and I don't like him. He seems to think those that ends up in gaol should be treated good.'

'And you disagree?'

"They're heres for a reason. Best to give 'em a stronger reason not to want to come back. If beatings do that then I'm doing everyone a good turn.'

'Gore doesn't agree then?'

'That's what I said. So what do you want?'

'To help get rid of Mr Gore and turn the tables. How would you like to see Gore here as a prisoner?'

'I would like that very greatly.'

'Do you have anything on the man?'

'If I did he'd already be here as me guest.'

'How far are you prepared to go?'

'That bastard Gore is threatening to have me removed as gaoler. He thinks I steal from the prisoners. That I take money from 'em and he hates that I beat them.'

Minchin sighed. This was going round in circles and clearly McKay was more disposed to direct physical action against an enemy than he was to thinking his way through the puzzle. 'Is there anything you're willing to accuse him of?'

'Plenty of things. None of them gunna stick in a court,' McKay said.

'What if the court was happy to see the end of Gore's time as Provost Marshal? Would you be willing to prosecute him then?'

'Of course, but how is that gunna happen? Can you rig the court?'

'I wouldn't say rig the court. However, there are those due to sit and serve on juries who would be willing to see Mr Gore taken down. Enough of them to make sure of things, put it that way.'

McKay smiled. 'When do we start?'

'Provost Marshal, I am afraid that we must take you into custody,' Constable Hughes said.

'For what? And on whose authority?'

'Judge Advocate Atkins has two outstanding charges against you, for passing a forged note of hand and for stealing,' Hughes said, unable to look Gore in the eye.

'What nonsense is this?' Gore said. 'My word is good and I don't go around offering notes of hand, nor of stealing. What is it I'm accused of stealing anyway?'

'Sir it's a trinket, a woman's ornament,' Hughes said.

'Well may I at least know who brings these charges?'

'That would be Mr McKay and his woman.'

'McKay the gaoler? By God that man has it in for me. He has done since I threatened to fire him for bashing prisoners and stealing from them. Now he has me charged,' Gore said.

'The trial is set for next Tuesday Mr Gore. I am sorry to take you in, and under the circumstances I will hold you in a cell here,' Hughes said.

'Thank you son. That is decent of you.'

'Can you please do two things for me, if that is permissible by you?' Gore said. 'Would you get me a copy of the charges and could you ask George Crossley to come and see me before the trial.'

'Why do I recognise that name?' Hughes said.

'Mr Crossley was Attorney of the Court of Kings Bench in London before being found guilty of perjury and being transported. I helped him with a matter regarding a convict trying to steal from him last year. If you could ask him to visit that would be appreciated Constable Hughes?' Gore said.

'Major, there is a letter for you, from the Governor, marked most urgent,' Private Gray said. Johnston took the letter and started reading it. The officers in the mess hall had all stopped when Gray had spoken.

'Oh God, he can't do that,' Johnston said.

'Do what? Who can't do what?' Davies said.

Johnston was already on his feet and walking out of the room. Within moments Johnston had marched at a frightful pace out of the gates.

'Do we follow him or ...' Williams said.

'I don't really know,' Minchin said.

'If the major wants help you'll know,' Laycock said.

Johnston marched to Judge Advocate Atkins's house. He hammered his fist on the door which soon opened. 'Where is the Judge Advocate?' Johnston said to the young convict girl that answered.

'He's at the pub,' she replied.

'That would bloody well be right. Well which one girl?'

'Try the Queen's Table down the road,' the girl said, before staring in amazement as Johnston marched off.

The Queen's Table was less a pub than the front room of a house. Johnston saw Atkins sitting with Richard Cornwall, a magistrate. Both were drunk, Cornwall slightly less so than Atkins.

'Why George, what brings you to such a fine establishment this late in the day?' Atkins said.

'It's 2 in the afternoon and we have a massive problem you drunken imbecile,' Johnston said.

'And what would that be? What is so important that my meeting with a fellow Magicstate... Magikstrate... Magistrate, should be so rudely interupced... inrupted... interrupted?'

'Bligh has appointed the panel for Tuesday's hearing of Gore.'

'Gore who?'

'The Provost Marshall, Richard, the bloody Provost Marshall,' Johnston said.

'Wait, are you talking to me or him?' Cornwall asked.

'Him of course, why would I be talking to you? Are you Richard?'

'Well that is me, Richard, and so is he. Richard, Richard.' Cornwall giggled at his little joke.

'More like two limp Dicks,' Johnston said, his anger rapidly turning to fury.

'George, so what if Bligh does that?' Atkins said.

'It means we no longer control prosecutions, and this is one prosecution we need to bring home to a conviction. I may as well give up command of the Corps if Bligh can take command so easily. Get up we are going to see him and protest this,' Johnston said.

Atkins went to stand and instead tipped forward unsteadily. He stiffened and looked around quickly. Johnston stepped back and turned away as Atkins threw up everywhere.

'Bloody hell. Right you, are you a Magistrate?'

'Yes I am Richard Magistrate, Cornwall. I mean Richard Cornwall, Mag'strate.'

'Do you think you can stand and walk without being sick everywhere?' Johnston said.

'Yes I can. Of course I can sir, I am not that drunk.' Cornwall stood and wobbled on his feet before straightening up. 'To battle sir, to battle.'

Johnston and Cornwall walked up the footpath to Government House. 'My God Major you didn't tell me we were going to see the Governor.'

'We are and you will not say a damn word, only nod when I mention that you have advised me. Is that clear?' Johnston said.

'Yes sir,' Cornwall said, before giggling.

The two men climbed the steps with Johnston helping guide Cornwall. They were met at the door by an aide to the governor. 'Tell Governor Bligh that I must see him immediately. It's a matter of the utmost urgency,' Johnston said.

After fifteen minutes of waiting Bligh appeared in the foyer. 'Major Johnston, what is so important that it cannot wait?'

'Sir by what right have you to take command of my regiment?' Johnston said.

'I beg your pardon Major, I don't understand the question. How exactly have I taken command of your regiment? And as governor, should I need to do so by what right have you to stop me?'

Johnston glared at Bligh. 'You have chosen the officers to sit on the panel for Gore's trial. The man is guilty and officers appointed to a judicial panel are by my choice,' Johnston said.

'You are correct, I have chosen the officers that I believe will hear the trial fairly and make a judgement informed by the evidence they hear. Not have a man guilty in their minds before they even enter a courtroom. Do you have a problem with such justice sir? Would you rather justice serve all or just a few?'

'How dare ...' Johnston stopped and looked at Bligh, aware of the line over which he was so perilously close to stepping. 'Mr Cornwall here is a magistrate and he will back me with his judgement, isn't that right.'

Cornwall was silent, staring out the window. 'Cornwall man, dammit, answer.'

Cornwall looked at Johnston and nodded vigorously, then he winked at Johnston, in full view of Bligh. The sudden effort of nodding appeared to take a toll on the magistrate and for a moment Johnston feared he would be sick.

'So am I to appoint the panel or not?' Johnston said.

'It is already done,' Bligh said.

'Then you leave me no other choice than to put a complaint in with the Commander-in-Chief,' Johnston said.

'I would most strongly encourage you to do so Major,' Bligh said.

A side door opened and Mary Putland walked in briskly. 'Father, we have guests and they are keen to share your company. Cannot this wait?' Putland said.

'Mary my dear, you are correct. This can wait. Please tell the guests I will be with them momentarily. In the meantime they will have to content themselves with you as hostess.'

'I am sure that they would prefer to hear from you, but as you wish Father,' Putland said. Mary Putland's skirts swished as she walked briskly back towards the side door where she stopped, turned and beamed a radiant smile at Major Johnston.

'Father, is this the famous Major Johnston?'

'Yes Mary it is and he is about to leave.'

'We must have him at the next ball. A dashing soldier is always needed at any ball,' Putland said. 'Now please excuse me, I have guests.'

Johnston watched the door close behind Putland and then looked back at Bligh.

'Unless there is a genuinely urgent matter you wish me to attend to I shall take leave.' Bligh turned and walked away.

Johnston started to walk out.

'Major, I think you are forgetting something,' Bligh said as he stopped before a side door. Johnston looked at Bligh puzzled.

'Your magistrate Major, please take him and sober him up before he next sits on a bench.'

Johnston grabbed Cornwall and shoved him through the door. 'Major,' Cornwall said before he stopped and vomited.

The mess hall fell silent when Johnston entered. Nobody said a word, all waiting for Johnston to break the silence. Instead the major walked over to the bar stand in the corner, poured himself a large drink, drained it immediately and poured another.

Several of the men present looked to Minchin, willing him to ask the question they all wanted an answer to. Minchin carefully looked away, not willing to place himself in harm's way.

'So that's it then. We had better have a bloody good case against Gore,' Johnston said.

'The case is solid, but the trial panel is ours so ...' Minchin said.

'No, the panel is not ours., Bligh has appointed his own panel and none of the men are ours,' Johnston said.

'Can he do that?' Davies said.

'Apparently he can,' Johnston said. 'Lieutenant Minchin, get this thing sorted and get the people involved water-tight in their evidence. We are going to have to rely on the evidence alone.'

There was a long silence in the room. Smith got up and walked outside, followed a short time later by Williams.

'Oli, what's going on?' Smith said.

'Bligh is turning the screws Nate. He's cut off imports of rum, ended our monopoly. He's backing the farmers and now he's trying to take control of the courts.'

'That's what I don't understand.'

'The civil court is run by the government administration, but the panel that adjudicates is made up of soldiers. If we appoint the panel then we can influence the outcome,' Williams said.

'You mean rig the result,' Smith said.

'Alright rig the result.'

'Sometimes you're so straight and proper. If we're rigging the result just say it. Don't pretend that we are above a little foul play to get what we want.'

'Alright, only now that foul play is not possible because Bligh has appointed the panel of jurors,' Williams said. He paused for a moment. 'Gore is a good man. His only fault is doing what the Governor wants and for that we are prepared to put him in gaol.'

'Oli, I think we are headed for war between us and the governor, and in war there are innocents that get caught up. Gore is one of them.'

'Do you think that it's coming to that?' Williams said.

'The way you just put it, yes. Trust an old soldier, the officers are gearing up for the assault. The problem is that we may have run across an opponent we won't easily break. And when that happens the winner is the one who is willing to go the farthest beyond what is decent and honourable to win.'

'This court will now come to order,' Judge Advocate Atkins said.

The handful of people in the court house sat down, some on boxes they have brought, as the charges against Gore were read.

Deputy Commissary Fitz stood. 'Gore is charged with issuing a forged note of hand the face value of fifteen shillings and stealing an ornament. Who prosecutes these charges make yourself known to the court.'

James Underwood stood up. 'I am prosecuting the forgery charge,' Underwood said before sitting down. He wiped his brow with a handkerchief.

There was silence in the court room. 'Make yourself known if you are prosecuting the charge of theft,' Fitz said.

Again there was silence. Minchin, who was sitting up the back of the court with Williams and Smith looked around. 'Where the hell is she?' Minchin said.

Finally after a delay of too many moments, during which Atkins shifted many times in his chair, Dr Jamison walked in. 'If I may speak to the court,' Jamison said.

'Granted,' Aktins said before shooting a mystified look at Minchin.

'The witness in the prosecution of theft charges against Gore is in the midst of childbirth,' Jamison said.

'The witness or the prosecutor,' Atkins said,

'Er, both,' Jamison said, unconvincingly.

'So is it one woman or two?' Atkins said.

'One woman involved in this prosecution giving birth now is coincidental, two would be fantastic,' George Crossley said from beside Gore.

'Silence Mr Crossley. You are lucky to be here as support for Mr Gore,' Atkins said.

'It's not luck that brings me here. It's the offer of justice for all that has seen Governor Bligh allow me here,' Crossley said.

Atkins chose to ignore this barb. 'Dr Jamison, can you let us know who is in childbirth?'

'The woman bringing the prosecution is in childbirth, the partner of Mr McKay. I have a certificate here for her.'

'Does she have a name, this woman?' Crossley said.

'Er, she is in childbirth, I did not ask it,' Jamison said.

'Yet you have signed the certificate on her behalf. Judge Advocate surely a prosecution cannot go ahead on such basis,' Crossley said.

Atkins looked at Crossley then to Minchin, who shrugged his shoulders. The officers on the panel muttered amongst themselves. 'Is there anyone here who can bring evidence for this prosecution of theft?'

Again the court was silent. Atkins looked around, willing someone to step forward but none did. 'I rule that the second charge against Gore is struck and he is not guilty of theft.'

'As this is a committal hearing to determine the strength of the charges and the charge of theft is struck you cannot say Mr Gore is not guilty when he has not been charged,' Crossley said.

'Well what do I say then?' Atkins said before stopping abruptly. Crossley smiled. The Judge Advocate had just been shown up in his court room not understanding the processes of the law. Crossley leaned across to Gore and quietly whispered something in his ear. Gore smiled a little.

'Right then, to the first charge of forging a note of hand. Mr Underwood you are leading this prosecution. Let's have it,' Atkins said.

'Um, I am prosecuting the charge, but what do you mean by leading?' Underwood said.

At the back of the room Minchin swore under his breath. He had been unable to convince McKay to undertake a prosecution and instead had ended up talking to Simeon Lord, who had suggested Underwood prosecute the charge. The two had agreed and convinced Underwood, a partner of Lord in rum trafficking, to take on the prosecution.

Underwood had been jailed the previous year for writing an insolent letter insulting the governor. The prosecution had been sold to Underwood as a means of taking revenge against the establishment. Underwood could still hear Minchin's words. 'It will embarrass Bligh and the administration by having their man Gore thrown in jail.' Now Minchin realised, the only people likely to be embarrassed, were Atkins and himself.

'I am able to provide the details of the prosecution case,' Deputy Commissary Fitz said.

'Now this is beyond unusual. It is outright corruption if an officer of the court involves himself in the prosecution,' Crossley said. 'It is immediate grounds to appeal for a new hearing or appeal against any findings of the court.'

Atkins shifted in his chair yet again, glaring at Crossley. He was tired of hearing Crossley speak. The man knew the usual tricks and worse, knew how to stop them.

'Judge Advocate, your ruling please?' Crossley said.

'Sorry, what?' Atkins said.

'Your ruling on this matter please,' Crossley said.

'Deputy Commissary you cannot lead this prosecution,' Atkins said. Atkins saw Minchin throw his hands in the air at the back of the court, saw Crossley smile and lean across and say something to Gore who smiled a little more broadly than before. The officers of the panel were scowling and muttering to themselves and Atkins wondered how he had managed to get himself pulled into this farce.

'Mr Underwood, are we doing this or not?' Atkins said in desperation.

'So Mr Gore, this false note you passed me, what possessed you to write it?' Underwood said. Atkins looked at Underwood and wondered what possessed him to open up the prosecution with so direct a question.

'I have never written such a note and as you well know I have never had any business dealings with you that would necessitate the writing of notes of hand,' Gore said.

'So you deny the writing on the note is yours?' Underwood said in a moment of desperate inspiration.

'If you would show us the note,' Crossley said, playing a hunch, 'we could advise you on the writing.'

Underwood stared at Crossley and Gore. He looked at Atkins and then around the court.

'Fuck us all,' Minchin said quietly to Williams and Smith. 'He doesn't even have a note to show. We're sunk lads.'

Underwood continued to stare blankly around the courthouse. 'Do you have the note to show us?' Crossley asked.

'Mr Underwood, the note please,' Atkins said.

'Er, um, I appear to have misplaced it,' Underwood said.

'It is the key piece of evidence in this case that you were provided with,' Atkins said. 'Provided with by Mr Gore of course.'

'I have lost it,' Underwood said. 'Perhaps I can bring it in tomorrow?'

'Where were you when Mr Gore supposedly gave you this note?' Crossley said.

Underwood's expression became even blanker. His jaw fell open a little. Crossley repeated the question and Underwood's mouth opened but no words came out.

One of the officers on the panel stood and approached Atkins and spoke to him. The blank expression on Underwood's face seemed infectious as Atkins's jaw fell open and he too stared into space.

'I have no choice but to throw this charge out,' Atkins said. 'Mr Gore you are free to leave.'

Gore stood and shook hands with Crossley, then turned and walked out of the court. Crossley approached Atkins and spoke loudly. 'This is the most ridiculous farce I have seen in a courtroom.

'You, sir, should be ashamed for allowing such a prosecution to proceed when it's clear that such charges are completely false. You should never have allowed this to committal in the first place. Good day to you.'

Crossley walked out of the court smiling. He would meet with Bligh later in the day and provide a complete report. The panel of officers also walked out, suggesting that Atkins not waste their time on such matters again. Jamison, Underwood and Fitz stood in a small group staring at the floor. Minchin, Williams and Smith quietly disappeared through a side door. Atkins still sat in his chair staring into space.

Minchin, Williams and Smith were in no hurry to return to the barracks. The court case had been a debacle and Minchin knew that he would wear a fair proportion of the blame. 'Why the hell was Underwood so unprepared?' Minchin said.

Minchin led the two corporals to a tavern near the wharves. At the rear of the tavern in a private room he found Simeon Lord. 'I have heard. Why was Underwood not properly briefed?' Lord said.

'That's what we were going to ask you,' Minchin said.

'When you first came to me and told me your plan I agreed to it to get Gore off my back. It made sense to all the rum traffickers,' said Lord. 'And then this McKay was not sure he wanted to carry out the prosecution and I knew Underwood could be the man. He detests the government and Gore was the man who arrested him. But he was told that all he had to do was show up at court and say he was the man making the charge. No one told him he would have to present the case.'

'Who did he think was going to do that?'

'He thought McKay would do it, and this McKay did nothing of the sort,' Lord said.

'Why the hell would he think that when McKay said he was not willing to carry out the prosecution?' Minchin said. 'This is a colossal mess. And the worst of it is we can't get to Gore now.

He is effectively untouchable. Another prosecution will make us all look completely desperate,' Minchin said.

'We are completely desperate,' Lord said. 'Bligh has all but stopped the trade in rum. His prices for goods like wheat are breaking the power of all the leading traders. The only place we have left to make some headway against the man is the courts. There is no other place to air public disputes or to mete out justice here. And now he has control of the heart of this colony, the courts.

'Make no mistake, there is little we can do now other than wait this bastard governor out,' Lord said. 'And then there is no guarantee that a new governor will be any better. It appears Banks and his cronies in London would have us a penal colony and nothing more.'

Lord took a long drink. 'See, I am forced to drink my own profits, for that is the only value left in rum now, easing the pains forced on us by Captain bloody Bligh. To Fletcher Christian, at least he escaped Bligh's clutches.' Lord laughed bitterly and poured himself another drink. Minchin stood and walked out, followed by Williams and Smith.

Minchin walked into the mess hall and sat down. Williams and Smith followed, both looking as dejected as Minchin.

'So it went that badly?' Johnston said.

It took Minchin less than a minute to outline the sorry story. 'And at that point one of the officers stood and walked to Atkins and said something. I imagine "End this farce now," and that was that,' Minchin said. He then detailed his visit to Simeon Lord.

Johnston, Davies, Laycock and a number of other soldiers eased back in their chairs. All waited for the major to speak. The sorry tale of the Gore prosecution had taken only a few minutes to be told and in that time the mess hall had gradually cleared. At first all the men had gathered hoping to hear the tale of a famous victory. Instead what they got from Minchin was exactly the opposite.

'So Underwood and McKay have let us down,' Johnston said. 'Then for now there is little else we can do. We must be patient and wait for the right battlefield to present itself, if or when Bligh makes a mistake.'

Minchin started to breathe a little easier. He had feared that the failure of the prosecution may come to rest on him.

'Who were the officers of the panel?' Johnston asked.

'They're all Parramatta men under Captain Abbott,' Minchin said.

'That's all I need to hear,' Johnston said. 'Abbott and his mob out there at Parramatta have been keeping their distance ever since Bligh got here.'

'Do you think Bligh has got to them?' Davies said.

'I'm not sure,' Johnston said. 'You know Abbott though, he flies his flag up whatever ship's mast is sailing strongest. The man is anyone's if he thinks it will credit him.'

The soldiers were shocked to hear Johnston talk so badly another officer. 'I am certain that…' Minchin said.

'Certain of what?' Johnston cut him off.

'Abbott is probably keeping his head down, worried about how effectively Bligh is achieving things,' Minchin said.

'Well it would be easy to be effective against such a disorganised rabble,' Johnston said. He looked at Minchin and saw his head drop. 'So you say that Lord is now in his cups and lamenting what's happening. Perhaps I need to see him and talk some fire into his belly. And I should see Mac too. It is time we started to fight back against Bligh don't you think Lieutenant?'

'Yes sir it is.'

February 1807

Johnston drove his buggy at speed towards Elizabeth Farm. His thoughts were usually few on such occasions, content to thrill at the speed and the air rushing past, happy and energised. Today that rapture was far from his mind as he wondered how to fight Bligh when the man was in control of so much of the battlefield. Bligh had won over the small farmers, the smaller traders were supporting him, much of the administration was on his side and Kemp and his soldiers at Parramatta had gone to ground.

Simeon Lord had been of no help. Lord's answer to the Bligh conundrum was to wait it out. Yet if Bligh was successful it could be years before he returned to England and if London thought he had done good job why not send another of the same ilk to replace him?

The buggy was coming up to a tight corner. Johnston pulled on the reins and slowed the horse down, easing through the corner. Had it come to this, easing up when things got a little hairy. By God there was a time when he would have accelerated into that corner. Bligh really had got him rattled.

He crested a small hill and Elizabeth Farm came into view. The house stood a considerable distance from the river, with its elegant columns holding the blue verandah roof, multiple chimneys and two-storey living rooms at the rear. The grounds were beautifully manicured, with a line of low trees in the distance creating a wind break, taller trees lined behind the house and other trees standing in small groups of two or three, spread evenly across the property.

Country estates in England may have been bigger and grander, but few were as well maintained or perfectly set into the landscape as Elizabeth Farm. Johnston ran the buggy down the hill and swept leisurely into the long driveway to the farmhouse; if you could really call something so grand a house.

Even at a decent pace it still took more than a minute to reach the house. Mac was standing out on the verandah watching Johnston. 'Every time I see you in that buggy George I am conflicted. I think that I must get myself one and yet worry that it does not befit my status as the leading man of the colony,' Macarthur said.

'Well why not set a new fashion? After all isn't that what a leading man of the colony should be doing?' Johnston replied climbing out of the buggy. A convict worker took the horse by the reins and led it and the buggy away.

'So I got your note George. It seems we need a council of war and a plan of action. Well you are in the right place,' Macarthur said. He led Johnston into the house and to his study. Papers were sprawled over the desk.

'Are those promissory notes?' Johnston asked, looking at the pile of papers on the end of the desk.

'Every one. I've been collecting them for quite some time. You never know when they will come in useful. Which brings me to my plan of attack. I am intending to start calling these notes in, beginning with that leading figure of authority at the Hawkesbury, Andrew Thompson.'

'Thompson signed a promissory note to you? I thought he had more sense than that.'

Macarthur laughed. 'Of course he does, he signed it to another. I just happen to have bought it from that third party. Now this note is special as it's a promise of wheat in bushels or its equivalent monetary value at the time the note is called. At most times it would be of little interest but I have asked Thompson to pay it at the current market value of wheat, which as you know is quite high.'

'Bligh has set the price for wheat.'

'Yes but the small farmers are allowed once a week to sell wheat on an open market where the price that Bligh has set is only a base price. If they can sell their produce for more they are allowed to do so. I've asked Thompson to pay in cash at last Wednesday's market price, which was two pounds eight above the government price.'

'You've already gone ahead with this?'

'One cannot wait for incompetent men like Lord and Underwood and that dimwit McKay to fumble about in the courts. I will either get my price from Thompson or sue him in the courts and show everyone how things are done and done properly.'

'Thompson's a good man Mac. He was invaluable in ending the Aboriginal raids and returning peace to the Hawkesbury and he helped pull the place together after the floods.'

'Yet he is Bligh's man and that makes him our enemy George. Have you noticed that we are growing fewer, those of us willing to take on Bligh and keep this colony as a mercantile port. If we have to break a few good men to send some important messages to the small farmers in the Hawkesbury and elsewhere so be it.

'This is a war George and you know better than most that in war decisive action allied with effective strategy and tactics are what matters. We will break Thompson and others and doing so dismantle Bligh's web of sycophants and bullies. George you are very quiet. Are you ill?'

'No Mac, it's just that if we do this we are all in. We can't declare war on Bligh and not see it through.'

Macarthur smiled. 'Yes George, that's the fun of it. We get to go to war against another governor and break him too. Then London will understand that I'm the power here and that they need to heed what I expect. Now let us toast our next engagement, may it be short and overwhelmingly one sided in our favour,' Macarthur said before he drained the glass in one gulp.

It was five days before Johnston saw Macarthur again, this time at the barracks.

'Thompson has refused to pay me the full amount owing. He insists on paying on the price of wheat at the value when he signed, which is almost fifteen pounds less than I have demanded,' Macarthur said. Johnston leaned back in his chair in the mess hall.

'So, I take it you are here in town to begin proceedings against Thompson?' Johnston said.

Macarthur smiled a wicked smile. 'Of course dear fellow. It's time that Bligh's supporters learnt their place in my colony.'

Johnston saw Minchin and Davies look up at Macarthur in astonishment. The major ignored them. 'What if you lose the case Mac? There's always that possibility.'

'I don't expect to lose, but should that happen then I'll have an avenue to appeal to Bligh. The man does not seem to want to see me so this is a way to achieving that end. Besides if Bligh sides with Thompson then that will certainly clarify where he stands and who he stands with.'

'Well then, when does this trial begin?' Johnston asked.

'In two days' time before the Civil Court. Until then I am in town and shall be consulting with Simeon Lord and others in terms of mounting a defence against Bligh's impositions on us,' Macarthur said.

'You are welcome to bunk down here at the barracks should you wish,' Johnston said. 'It could be like the old days.'

'My dear George, those days are long gone. It would not befit the leading man of the colony to be seen bunking down with the common soldiers. I shall stay at my new accommodation in town. Now I'd best be off and get Lord and his group of smugglers to work,' Macarthur said.

When he had left Davies spoke what many had been thinking. 'Major, is Mac alright? I mean all that high and mighty leading man of the colony talk. Have things got to him?'

'And he refuses to stay with common soldiers yet in the next breath talks of meeting with smugglers,' Minchin said.

'Mac is a little more highly strung than usual. He has a lot riding on the colony being able to trade with the world, and is worried that Bligh is going to stop that. He'll come good, just give him a little time.' At least Johnston hoped he'd come good.

It was three days before Macarthur once again visited the barracks. 'He didn't even listen to me, to me of all people. That fucking sailor. He just dismissed my request out of hand and when I tried to talk to him he said he had more important matters to deal with. As if anything in this perfect hell is more important than me,' Macarthur said.

'Mac, slow down a little. What's happened?' Johnston said.

'The fucking court fucked me over. They sided with the Hawkesbury man Thompson. A Hawkesbury settler is more important than I to those idiots,' Macarthur said.

'So the court will make Thompson pay at the value of the wheat when Thompson signed it?' Johnston said.

'Yes. I didn't care too much about that, as it was an avenue to appeal to the Court of Civil Appeals, which is overseen by Bluff and Bluster Bligh himself. And his high and mighty sailor dismissed my claim out of hand, and when I approached him after the session he said he had more important matters to attend to and left. He just fucking walked out on me,' Macarthur said.

The mess hall was quiet. After a pause that seemed as tense as waiting for a hanging Johnston finally spoke.

'Well you wanted to find out where Bligh stands, now we know. There's no turning the man and our tactics that worked with Hunter and King have let us down. So we need some new ideas.'

'Here's an idea, how about we march up there and kick him out of Government House and run this place ourselves,' Macarthur said.

No one dared move let alone speak. Had Macarthur really suggested overthrowing the Governor? Minchin's eyes darted to Davies, who shot back a look of horror. Such an act was treason, punishable by hanging. Usually such an outlandish statement would be followed by a joke. Instead Macarthur got up and walked out of the room, leaving the dreadful idea floating in the air.

'You have to hand it to Mac, that may be his best joke yet,' Laycock said.

'I would call it gallows humour myself,' Johnston said. 'For that is where such jokes lead, to the gallows. Let us not speak of this again and chalk this up to Mac being off colour. I think I shall head back to Annandale.'

Once Johnston left the room cleared almost immediately.

Oliver Williams told Mary about the visit from Macarthur over dinner. 'I know the major said not to speak of it but Macarthur's mood was terrifying. Yet I can't imagine him trying to lead a force on the Governor.'

'You stay clear of this nonsense Oliver Williams. I don't need you hung. You have a boy and me to support and doing something mad like marching up to Government House will have you hung.'

'The major wouldn't go for something like that, and Mac is almost manic in his hatred for Bligh. It's idle talk that's all.'

'That's how stupidity starts Oli, with idle talk from men who have lost the ability to know better. You steer clear of this Macarthur, do you hear me.?'

'Yes my dear. I think most of us will be steering clear of Mac from here on, at least until he regains his senses. Mind though, he has a point in regards to Bligh. Things are not the same without the trade in rum and other goods.'

'Those are games, well-paid games, but games none the less. I know you enjoy that side of your work but for now Bligh is winning over a lot of people. It's only the rich that are unhappy. The majority of the people seem to think Bligh is doing a good job.'

'Are you complaining about having some of the finer things my dear? This is a side to you that I hadn't expected to see,' Williams said.

'I am simply saying that there are many people in Sydney who feel that life is a little easier and more secure since Governor Bligh took over. It provides the average person with a degree of power that they previously lacked.'

'So you're agreeing with Bligh then?'

'I am saying that when the governor serves the interests of a few, and when those few are wealthy and getting wealthier, then life for the ordinary person is hard. They are dependent on the rich dropping scraps from their table. That's when people resent the wealthy and the government, when the two are seen as the same. When a government helps the people things are a little easier for the ordinary folk and they like that.'

'Why shouldn't government serve the wealthy?'

'Because then things are like they are in England, with ordinary people stuck with their lot in life and unable to improve themselves. That's what keeps people here, the chance to make something more of themselves. A better chance for them and their families, a chance that in England is not possible. In England to improve yourself means stealing bread just to feed the family.

'I think you've forgotten that for some people life is not all rum and trade and fun. For some life is serious and choices have to be made. You men of the Corps love to chance your arm and make money and have your adventures. For many that is not possible without some help from the governor. You should remember that. Why do you think your father did what he did?'

'You leave my father out of this Mary.'

'No Oliver I will not. Your father did what he did to help his family out. He would have wanted a better life for you and would have hated working for rich men who paid him a pittance.'

'You never knew him, how can you say why he did what he did? You never even met him.'

'No I didn't meet him. I know him because I know you and I've heard you talk of him. You are a good man, you work hard for us and treat me properly. I love you for it, but please remember that many of the people are here because, like your father, they wanted something more and could not find the way to reach it. All that was left was to steal.

'There are people here who say that is what the Corps does. It robs the people for no greater cause than money, only here it's legal because you have power. There are people here who say you want to be the new aristocrats. If Bligh is bested and the Corps and others like Macarthur and his ilk are allowed to run this place people may as well be back in England forced to live by the leave of those who think themselves our betters. Remember these things Oli when you have to make a choice between the Corps and me.'

'What do you mean, make a choice?'

'Don't you see, Macarthur wants to control things and make himself a king here. He wants to own the land and the people. He sees the Corps as his to direct. As his own army. He and others like him would have you at Bligh's throat before you fully know what you are all doing.'

'Mary, I think the baby has kept you up too many nights. It will not come to that.'

'When men fight over power it always comes to that. You'll have to make a choice Oli.' Mary walked to the other side of the room and picked up her son.

April 1807

Lieutenants Minchin and Davies were looking at the horse in the way that men do when they are uncertain of what they expect to see, yet don't want that known. 'So she's fast?'

'Very fast. What do you intend to use her for?' Barnes said. The man knew little about horses himself, but he fancied himself an expert on people and understanding what they wanted. It mattered little what he was selling. Instead it was his ability to manipulate people that counted, and that began with reading them. And Barnes's reading of the two Corps officers told him they knew even less about horses than he did.

'We want to race her,' Minchin said. His face broke out into an unprompted smile and he flushed red. Minchin and Davies had been talking about entering a horse in the Hawkesbury races for almost a year and finally they were acting on the dream.

Barnes smiled just a little, seeing Minchin blush. 'In that case you cannot go wrong. This horse is fast and she loves to gallop. She'll not let you down,' Barnes said, using the same line he always used. The fact he had no idea of what the horse could do, whether it was fast or slow, or how far it could run was unimportant. What sold the horse was his apparent sincerity.

Barnes started playing out the usual routine and both men looked ready to commit. Time for some insurance he thought. 'Of course that is if you train her right.'

'Train her? What does that involve?' Davies said.

Barnes tried hard to suppress the smile but he could not. How could he have been so lucky to have these two find their way here, Barnes thought. 'Well you have to ride her hard, keep her strong from running every day.'

'Oh so that's all that's involved. Well that sounds easy,' Minchin said. 'So how much for her?'

'Seven pounds,' Barnes said.

'Make it five pounds and you have a deal,' Minchin said.

'There's another interested party, a wealthy trader who also wants to run a horse at Hawkesbury,' Barnes said. 'I could do six pounds three shillings but no less.'

Minchin and Davies huddled together, talking quietly while sneaking looks at the horse. They were more than happy with the price but did not want to be seen to accept any offer immediately. Corps men did not do that.

'Alright, how about six pounds and leave the shillings out of it,' Davies said.

'I am sorry I cannot. The wealthy trader will be by later today,' Barnes said. He paused for several moments. 'Perhaps he'll buy this horse and turn her into a winner.'

'Then six pounds three it is,' Davies said.

'Righto lads, line up by height and size,' Minchin said, quickly and excitedly.

The troops looked at each other unsure what was meant. 'Smith, what's hi-asize? Is that some new kind of formation?' Mulligan asked.

'I don't bloody know,' Smith shot back.

The soldiers started to move about without the slightest idea of how to form up. Men began bumping into one another and Hutton and then Newbank and Conner started to laugh. Soon the men were milling about trying to suppress laughter while experimenting with new formations.

'Good God men, is it really so hard to line up?' Minchin said. 'Perhaps I need to get Sergeant Major Whittle out here.'

Gillard and Conner tried to blend into the background. As Gillard stepped back he put his foot onto Private Gray's foot and fell backwards. 'Timber,' Hutton yelled as Gillard landed heavily on his backside. By this time most of the men were laughing uncontrollably.

'Watch yourself,' Gillard said to Gray.

'You trod on me. Why should I watch myself?' Gray said.

'For God's sake men, height order, and size. Line up from tallest to shortest,' Minchin yelled.

A dozen men realised what they were supposed to do and order was returned. Minchin and Davies looked at the line of men and walked towards Hutton and Gillard, who stood at shortest end of the line.

'Righto then, can either of you ride a horse?' Minchin said.

Hutton and Gillard looked at one another and then to Minchin. 'No sir,' both said in unison.

'Bugger,' Davies said. 'Well perhaps they can learn?' he said to Minchin.

'We can't have our jockey learning as he goes. Righto lads, step forward if you can ride a horse.'

Private Mulligan stepped forward. He was fourth from the end of the line and lightly built.

'Congratulations Private, you are going to be the jockey of our horse in the Hawkesbury races this weekend,' Minchin said.

'Three cheers for jockey Mulligan,' Smith said. There was an explosion of yelling and laughter as the soldiers stepped forward and mobbed Mulligan.

'Corporal Smith. You and Corporal Williams see to it that Mulligan gets some practice on the horse,' Davies said.

Davies and Minchin looked at each other and grinned. This horse racing was a lark and just too easy. If only they had known what was in store for them.

'So whose going to tell them?' Smith said. He was helping Mulligan up off the ground for the fourth time in the past few minutes. Each time Mulligan had fallen from the horse as soon as it broke into a trot.

'Bloody hell, I just wanted to curry some favour with the officers,' Mulligan said.

'By lying to them?' Smith said. 'I know what you were thinking. I can ride a woman so how is a horse any different? Well I guess you just found out.'

Williams looked at the other men. 'Can any of you ride at all?'

No-one said a word. Riding was the domain of the wealthy in England and none of the soldiers fit that class. In New South Wales people walked or went by boat.

'So no riders then Nate. What do we do?'

'Don't ask me Oli. You're the brains of the outfit.'

'We'll just have to get Mulligan used to riding.' Williams looked at the horse then to Mulligan. 'Could we tie him on so that he doesn't come off?'

Smith looked at Mulligan and then the horse. 'You know that just may work.'

'Righto Private Mulligan, back in the saddle. Hutton, Gillard, get some rope, we are going to secure our jockey to his mount,' Williams said.

Mulligan immediately started backing away. 'I don't think that's a good idea. It's not much of a idea at all,' Mulligan said.

'You volunteered for this. Or would you rather go tell the lieutenant's that you lied to them? I dare say that they may second our idea anyway. And besides, this way you wont fall off,' Williams said.

Hutton and Gillard returned with the rope and together helped Mulligan up into the saddle. They then tied the rope around Mulligan's waist, across his legs and around the horse.

'There you go. That should be a slip knot so if things get too hairy you can pull this end of the rope and it'll come undone,' Hutton said.

'I didn't know you knew how to tie knots,' Mulligan said.

'I don't really, just a slip knot.'

'Righto Private, let's go again. Give some encouragement lads,' Smith said.

Gillard took that to mean slapping the horse on its rear. Hard. The horse reared and then ran and horse and jockey hurtled out of the barracks and into the street. Mulligan yelled something that sounded like a scream for help before he and the horse disappeared from view.

'Oh shit,' Williams said. 'Come on lads,' he yelled before sprinting after the horse and the hapless Mulligan. Together Williams, Smith, Gillard, Hutton, Conner and Newbank raced into the street, only to catch a glimpse of the horse racing around a corner. There were screams and a loud crash.

'Dear God we've killed Mulligan,' Conner said.

'Pray to God that the horse is all right. I think Minchin and Davies can live without Mulligan, but if that horse is hurt we're in it up to our eyeballs,' Williams said.

They finally reached the corner and rounded it. A cart lay on its side with produce scattered across the road. Two women sat on a step holding each other, both looking pale.

'What happened?' Williams said. 'Are you all right? Did the horse hit you?'

'We're fine but that ruffian riding the horse, well, the language he was using. I have never heard such vulgarity in my life. He was swearing like a trooper,' one of the women said.

'That's because he is a trooper,' Gillard said.

'Shut up you fool,' Smith said.

'Is he a trooper?' the other woman said.

'No he's not. He went riding past the barracks and we thought it best to chase him,' Williams said. 'Come on lads follow the trail.'

The six troops raced off. 'Why shouldn't I tell them he's a trooper then Corporal?' Gillard said.

'At the rate he's going Mulligan will wreck half of Sydney. Do you want everyone to know that he's from the Corps?' Williams said.

'Oh I see,' Gillard said, not really seeing at all.

Williams led the group on, following a trail of minor destruction. Soon the soldiers came across boxes stewn over the road and people wandering around dazed. 'That bloody idiot. He's trying to ride the horse sideways,' a man said.

Williams skidded to a halt. Smith crashed into him followed by the other soldiers, who all collapsed to the ground. 'Well praise be, the Corps is here to save us all,' someone said to much laughter.

'What do you mean riding sideways?' Williams said once he regained his feet. 'Do you mean side saddle?'

'No, he was kind of hanging off the side of the horse, like he was sitting but on the side of the horse,' the man answered.

Williams had a picture in his head of Mulligan strapped to the horse and having slid down so he was riding horizontal to the road, clinging on for dear life as the horse galloped on. He won't be able to stop it like that Williams thought.

'Come on lads, get after it,' Williams said.

They followed the trail of broken boxes, upturned items and dazed people for what felt like an eternity. By the time they saw the horse it was meandering near the governor's mansion. Mulligan was not in sight.

'Slowly now lads, we don't want to spook it,' Williams said. 'Spread out and surround it and we will walk carefully in and get it under control.'

Williams began to circle the horse with Hutton and Newbank following. As he rounded the back of the horse Williams saw that Mulligan was still strapped to the horse, sitting on its side, just as Williams had pictured. Hutton saw it too and got a fit of the giggles. Newbank asked what the joke was and Hutton merely pointed to Mulligan. Newbank too started to laugh, as did Gillard, Conner and Smith as they saw Mulligan hanging in space.

Mulligan looked at the approaching soldiers. He saw Hutton. 'Slip knot my arse you fucking idiot,' he said, before the horse reared and took off again.

'Who's the idiot now? Hutton yelled, as the horse raced away again.

'Well I will say one good thing — at least the horse is fast,' Smith said.

This time the horse did not travel far. It still took the soldiers ten minutes to catch up and finally secure the horse.

'Now Private Mulligan, you promise not to harm any of us?' Smith said. 'After all you did volunteer for this.'

'Alright, just get me off this bloody thing,' Mulligan said.

Hutton reached around to the knot and pulled on the loose end of the rope. 'It doesn't work,' Mulligan said.

'Are you sure?' Hutton said.

'I've been yanking on it for the best part of an hour and it is still tied you idiot,' Mulligan said.

Hutton looked at the knot again. 'Oh my mistake, it's this end,' he said pulling the rope at the other end of the knot.

'Wait,' Mulligan screamed, before the knot came loose and he crashed to the ground. He slowly stood up swearing. 'I'll fucking well kill you you bloody idiot.' He lunged at Hutton. Smith, Conner and Newbank restrained him as best they could. Still he made ground on Hutton. Gillard and Williams stepped in to help and in the tangle of legs the soldiers crashed to the ground for the second time since the horse escaped.

'I'm really beginning to dislike horse racing,' Conner said from the bottom of the pile.

'How do you think I feel?' Mulligan said.

Two hours later the dishevelled soldiers walked back into the barracks leading the horse. Minchin and Davies were waiting.

'Have you been out training her? Is she fast?' Davies said.

'Very fast and strong on her feet. It takes a great deal to stop her,' Smith said. The seven soldiers exchanged glances.

'Wonderful. And how is Private Mulligan at riding her?' Minchin said.

'He seems to have found the knack to getting the best out of her,' Williams said. Smith sidled up next to Mulligan and nudged him.

'Um, that's right. I have just about figured her out,' Mulligan said.

'Excellent,' Davies said. The two officers strolled away. 'That would be a first,' Davies said. 'Mulligan actually figuring out a female, even if she is a horse.'

'Well said. You know I didn't realise that it took so much effort to train a horse. The men looked very tired,' Minchin said.

'Well that's good they're taking it seriously,' Davies said.

'So how are we going to make this work? I mean, we can't just tie Mulligan to the horse again, can we?' Smith said.

'You have to admit, it would've been hilarious to see him bouncing along tied to the side of the horse,' Conner said. 'You can see it now can't you, the horse galloping around the corner with the rider coming into view a second before the horse. It would have looked like he was flying.' Conner tried to straddle a chair and then lean sideways but the chair started to topple. He fell to the ground laughing.

Smith couldn't resist any more and started laughing. Soon all the men were laughing. 'We need to take this seriously. Minchin and Davies will have our guts for garters if we don't get this right,' Williams said.

'To tie our guts up with a slip knot that doesn't slip?' Newbank said laughing.

'Come on, we have to get serious and work this out,' Williams said.

'We'll have time on the trip up to Hawkesbury, perhaps we can test a few ideas then,' Conner said.

'And what ideas are those Tom?' Williams said. 'Other than tying the rope better does anyone have an idea?' There was silence in the room. Conner again tried to sit sideways on the chair which fell, prompting more laughter. 'I have an idea. Let's have a drink and think about it,' Smith said.

'That's your answer for everything,' Williams said.

'Yes it is. Not having your brains I am forced to deal with problems in other ways, like drinking till I forget what the problem was. Now who wants a drink?'

Two days later the soldiers were still drinking, only this time up in the Hawkesbury. They had walked there over two leisurely days and come a little closer to solving the problem of how to turn Mulligan into an accomplished jockey. Or even a jockey capable of sitting on a trotting horse.

On the first morning Smith and Williams had sat Mulligan on the horse and left him in the hope that several hours may get him feeling more comfortable. By lunchtime it was clear things had not gone to plan. As the soldiers sat and ate Mulligan paced around.

'Sit down and join us, you're making me tetchy,' Hutton said.

'I can't. My arse is so bloody sore from sitting on that monster,' Mulligan said.

'I hardly think she's a monster,' Smith said.

'She may well say the same about you, what with you sitting on her all morning,' Williams said.

'It was your idea Corporal,' Mulligan said, drawing out the word corporal to somehow sound like an insult. 'Only it's my arse paying the price. So typical behaviour for the army.'

'You'll certainly have a price to pay with Minchin and Davies if you can't pull this race off,' Smith said. 'It will be more than your precious arse that ends up sore.'

'We're all in this together lads, so we had better get something sorted out,' Williams said.

By the time they reached the Hawkesbury Mulligan had spent several short spells in the saddle and was starting to feel more relaxed. On two occasions he had even managed to stay on the horse while she extended into a gallop. So the first night in the Hawkesbury they had found a pub and in a state of over confidence about Mulligan's abilities settled into a night of drinking.

'By God lads, you just have to hear what is happening here later,' Gillard said. He stared at his fellow soldiers, willing them to ask him. None did.

'Its a kangaroo fight,' Gillard said, beaming.

'What on earth is a kangaroo fight?' Smith said.

'A fight between two kangaroos,' Gillard said. 'What were you thinking it meant?'

'I don't know, it just sounds so … I don't know what?' Smith said.

'It's like a cock fight, only with kangaroos. We have to see this,' Gillard said.

'Sounds like it could be fun,' Hutton said.

'I'm in,' Mulligan said.

Conner and Newbank looked at each other. 'By God, it sounds better than sitting here and drinking with you sorry lot,' Conner said.

'Alright where's this happening?' Smith said.

'There's a barn just up the road. See that fellow over there, he knows,' Gillard said and pointed to a shifty looking man near the back door to the pub. The man nodded to Gillard.

'Alright lads we go, but be alert. This could be more than it seems,' Smith said.

'How can anything be more than two roos fighting?' Gillard said. 'This sounds like the best thing possible.' The soldiers quietly moved to the back of the pub and the shifty looking man walked out the back door.

'Up from Sydney are we boys?' Shifty said.

'Yes we're from …' Gillard said.

'We're here for the races,' Williams said, keen not to reveal that his group were from the Corps. He had not forgotten how unpopular the Corps was up in the Hawkesbury region.

'Well, we have a little pre-race entertainment in store. Couple of the local lads caught two roos and were gunna fight them,' Shifty said.

'Wait, I thought the roos were going to fight each other, not you fight the roos,' Gillard said, sounding disappointed.

'That's what I meant. The roos will fight each other,' Shifty said. 'God, a roo will do you real damage. They're bloody dangerous to go up 'gainst.'

'We're in,' Gillard said.

'Then this way,' Shifty said. He led the soldiers towards the outskirts of town. They rounded the corner of a shed and a group of men were standing waiting. Williams and Smith both tensed, ready for an ambush.

'Righto then all of ya.' Shifty said. 'Let's have this fight then.'

Williams reached into his pockets searching for anything he could use as a weapon, convinced this was an ambush. He saw Smith glance at him with a look of alarm before he looked at the other troops. Conner, Newbank and Hutton were all standing warily, fists clenched and expecting trouble. Mulligan and Gillard were already walking over to the main group of men.

'This way then,' Shifty said. He strode out in front of the men and headed towards a barn nearby, a few hundred yards from the outskirts of town. Williams relaxed a little, but tugged at Smith's sleeve.

'Be ready for anything, I don't trust this man,' Williams whispered.

'Don't worry, I already am,' Smith said.

As the men walked up the road there was a hubbub of noise and laughter coming from the main group. Mulligan and Gillard were right in the midst of it. The other soldiers followed cautiously.

The further from town they got the more Williams started to worry. It was one thing to rumble a group of soldiers on the outskirts of town, quite another to do so half a mile away. In town it would be easy to scatter and hide. The barn up ahead had no cover anywhere near it, the ground around having been cleared.

Smith glanced at Williams again, a clear sense of alarm in his expression. The soldiers were well outnumbered. Williams looked at Conner and saw a similar look of concern. Newbank too looked deeply worried. Hutton, now seemingly oblivious to the danger, had walked ahead to join Gillard and Mulligan.

The group reached the barn and began to walk inside. Hutton, Gillard and Mulligan all headed in. Williams stopped for a moment and knelt down, pretending to look at his boot. Smith stopped by him and asked if he was alright. Then he too knelt down.

'Come on, you'll miss the fun,' Shifty said. Light poured out through the door as Shifty opened it and beckoned the soldiers in.

Smith stood and carefully removed a knife from his boot. He nodded at Williams and then the two walked slowly inside, tense and ready for trouble. There was a great deal of noise to be heard. That made it harder to coordinate an ambush, Williams thought.

Williams saw a makeshift boxing ring marked out by ropes. A few men taking bets and two crude cages stood near the ring. He breathed a little easier. This was too much trouble to go to for an ambush. Gillard and Mulligan both had a drink in their hand. Hutton and Conner were in line near a bench, set over two barrels, waiting to order drinks. Smith looked at Conner and grinned. Newbank stood nearby smiling too.

'This promises to be some sport,' Newbank yelled at Williams and Smith over the noise. 'I may even put a bet on.'

'I wouldn't do that George. How do you even know which roo to bet for when you haven't seen them,' Smith said loudly, leaning in near Newbank.

'I hadn't thought of that,' Newbank yelled back.

Smith leaned in close again. 'Keep your wits about you.'

'As you wish Corporal,' Newbank said.

Behind Smith one of the locals turned quickly at hearing the word corporal. He looked at Smith and Newbank, trying hard to place their faces. Then he moved quickly over to a group of the locals.

Williams said something to Conner who moved off through the crowd towards Mulligan, Hutton and Gillard. When he found them he spoke to them and headed back to where Williams stood.

Mulligan, Hutton and Gillard wandered over to join the other soldiers. The group stood near the door, ready to make a quick exit if needed. Shifty climbed onto the ropes of the ring and a hush swept over the crowd. He stood up on the ropes.

'Ladies and gentlemen,' Shifty yelled.

'There ain't none of them here tonight,' a wag at the back of the barn yelled.

'You mean ladies?' Shifty said.

'Or gentlemen,' the wag said prompting raucous laughter.

'So now we get to it,' Shifty said.

A handful of men stepped forward and lifted the ropes in front of the two cages while others slid the cages forward. The makeshift doors at the front of each cage were levered open and the two roos came out into the ring. There was an explosion of noise as the room roared out in anticipation of the fight.

The two roos stood on either side of the ring, facing one another while the crowd goaded them into conflict. Williams felt Gillard inhale and then freeze. For the briefest moment he thought about checking to see if the soldier was still breathing but could not avert his eyes from the ring. Smith grabbed Hutton on the shoulder, half pushing him out of the way, half in solidarity at the spectacle about to unfold. The din was astonishing in such a small space. So many of the men were wound up in anticipation, scarcely believing that what was before them was real.

And yet not a one of them had realised the flaw in Shifty's plan, even as it began to unravel. The larger roo simply jumped over the low ropes and into the crowd seeking a way out. The smaller roo followed.

At that moment Williams heard one of the settlers yell 'That's him!' and turned to see the man pointing at Mulligan as a dozen locals rushed at the soldier. In the moment before they were set on Williams realised the shouting settler was likely the man whose wife Mulligan had slept with during the major's visit.

The soldiers reacted to the rushing group of settlers and within moments punches were being thrown left, right and centre. Others in the crowd, drunk on booze and disappointment, took the idea of throwing punches on board and soon the whole room broke into a series of rolling brawls.

Smith knocked out the first settler who charged at him, and then another, before a group brawling nearby crashed into him and sent him sprawling across the room and onto the bare ground. He grabbed at a man above him and began wrestling him. Conner and Newbank fought back to back, each instinctively protecting the other from assault. They were holding their own moving towards the door.

Gillard had been flattened in the first wave of settlers and lay motionless on the ground, with Hutton standing over him, valiantly trying to protect his friend. Mulligan took the worst of it with four settlers all launching themselves headlong at him. Williams saw him crash to the ground under the settlers before fists started flying in every direction.

Williams had managed to sidestep the first wave and was fighting his way towards where Hutton stood over Gillard. He sensed a presence behind him and turned with his fists raised ready to fight. Stunned, he froze as he stared into the eyes of the larger of the two roos and watched as the roo reared up and readied to attack with his powerful legs. This is it, thought Williams, as the roo began to kick its legs forwards.

Then Williams was hit from the side as a group of settlers wrestling with Conner and Newbank crashed into him. As he fell he witnessed the comical sight of the roo, having rocked back on its tail and thrusting its legs forward, find no target and simply continue to fly forward until it overbalanced and it too fell on top of the group of men.

The door of the barn was pulled open from the outside and several constables tried to rush in. They were met by the smaller kangaroo racing out and fell over themselves trying to get out of its way. Now two piles of men lay on the ground both with a kangaroo on top, flailing about.

Two men went crashing into the side of the barn and the whole structure lurched sideways. For a moment everything stopped, as though an artist had carefully staged the whole event and had called on every man to stop and stay motionless. At that moment another constable entered the barn and yelled for everybody to stand still to a room full of men already motionless. Every man held his breath for an instant in the hope it would stop the whole structure from coming down.

There was a loud creaking sound and the whole barn lurched further sideways breaking the spell the room was under. Men began breaking away from the fight, disentangling themselves from one another, and trying to get out. A number of wall panels were broken and shoved out and aside as men sought a way out and the whole barn lurched even further sideways only accelerating the egress.

The constables managed to push the roo that was on top of them towards the door while the constable who had yelled watched as the roo bounded towards and then past him out the door.

Williams managed to collect himself from the floor and with Conner and Newbank went and helped Hutton drag Gillard out the door. Smith followed. The group began retreating away from the barn.

'Where's Mulligan?' Williams said.

'I don't know,' Hutton said.

He might still be in there,' Conner said. 'Do we go back?'

They stopped and saw that the constables had given up on trying to detain the large number of men running from the barn. Then with a creak the whole structure lurched even further sideways and began collapsing.

'Christ, I hope Mulligan isn't in there,' Newbank said.

'I didn't even think you liked him,' Smith said.

'I don't. But if Mulligan is buried under that then someone else has to ride that bloody horse tomorrow.'

All the soldiers turned and looked at Newbank. 'Fair point,' Williams said.

The larger of the two roos went bounding past and the surreal nature of the evening struck home.

'Over here,' a voice said and the group turned and saw Mulligan emerging from the tree line a short way distant.

'Praise be to that,' Williams said. 'We still have our jockey.'

A carnival atmosphere and unusually warm autumn weather mingled together to make race day feel as if the Lord himself had reached down and blessed the Hawkesbury. This contrasted with the large cohort of men attending the races who felt much the worse for wearing the bruises of the previous night's brawling.

'What on earth happened to you lot?' Minchin said when he and Davies arrived and met up with the soldiers.

'We went to a kangaroo fight,' Gillard said. Williams shot him a displeased look.

'Well clearly the kangaroo won,' Minchin said. 'And do you think that good preparation for today's race?'

'We got jumped by a group of locals who recognised Mulligan from his past nocturnal activities up here. Don't worry they got the worst of it,' Williams said.

'So is Mulligan alright and will he be riding?' Davies said.

'Oh he's fine, and ready to race,' Williams said.

'Good. I hope you have the horse in good shape and we put up a good showing,' Minchin said.

'You can count on us,' Williams said, not making eye contact with Minchin.

The race itself was over two miles, running from a post set up on the main road outside town, across a roughly drawn course that looped back past the post. The rule was simple, the riders had to stay within the marked course. The sheer number of people lining the course, many from Sydney and Parramatta, meant that any attempt to cheat would be immediately recognised.

Race time was fast approaching so the two lieutenants, along with the soldiers, went to see Mulligan, who looked very nervous. Only Conner and Newbank were missing, having been given the task of having the horse ready.

'Righto Mulligan, time to show us how well you can ride. I suggest you stay with the main group of horses until the run back into town and then let her sprint to the win,' Davies said.

Minchin nodded agreement with the strategy. The two officers walked away looking very pleased with themselves.

'Now listen Mulligan, first of all don't fall off the bloody horse,' Williams said. 'Do we need to tie you on again?'

'No, please don't do that,'

'Alright, so do you think you can make the turn?'

'I hope so.'

'This is going to be a debacle,' Smith said.

Ordinarily Mulligan would have said something back, but now he was quiet. Williams began to worry. 'Just try to be with the main group of horses at the turn and hopefully the bloody animal will just follow the others round. Then do as the lieutenants suggest and let her run on the way back. Can you manage that?'

Mulligan nodded. Smith took a step back, afraid Mulligan may throw up everywhere. Williams tried to think of something to say to gee the soldier up.

'Just hang on and think of how happy the officers will be if you win. All of the past troubles may just disappear,' Williams said.

'And if I lose?'

'Maybe just keep riding,' Smith said.

'Come on it's time to mount up,' Williams said. He and Smith began walking towards the start line.

'Er Corporals ...,' Hutton said.

Mulligan had not moved a muscle. He was rooted to the seat he sat on and staring blankly into space.

'What do we do?' Gillard said.

'Come on Mulligan, get it together,' Hutton said.

'Private, get up and ride that damn horse, that is an order,' Smith said. 'Now soldier, move!'

Something inside Mulligan recognised that an order was an order and he stood and walked slowly to the horse. Conner and Newbank had the animal saddled up and ready to go and helped shove Mulligan up and onto the horse. Conner then led the horse to the rope that stood at head height across the course, from the post on one side to a group of men standing on the other side.

Horses jostled for position crowding each other. Mulligan lent over the side of his horse and was sick. Horses shuffled sideways and there was a space next to him. Then the rope went taut and a starter yelled something incoherent. A gun was fired as the rope dropped and the horses were racing.

All but Mulligan and his horse, which stood still at the starting rope. Conner, standing near the start, looked at Minchin and Davies and the sunny day was momentarily replaced by the look of thunder on their faces. He turned and looked at Williams who was frantically motioning with his hand to slap the back of the horse.

Conner couldn't understand what Williams was signalling. He looked at Gillard and then in a moment of inspiration remembered how the soldier had slapped the horse that first day in the barracks. Without thinking he slapped the horse on its rear as hard as he could.

The mare reared up and began galloping rapidly after the other horses with Mulligan screaming, having woken from his reverie. Minchin and Davies yelled at seeing the horse sprint towards the pack of horses. 'We're going to win this,' Minchin yelled.

When Mulligan caught up with the animals at the rear of the pack he tried frantically to slow the horse but she was having none of it. The mare sprinted straight through the middle of the pack and within a hundred yards was easily leading the pack by several lengths. Mulligan yanked back on the reins as hard as he dared.

The mare skidded to a halt as Mulligan went flying over her head and fell hard to the ground. Within moments the chasing pack was on top of the mare and Mulligan and rode past.

Watching from the start Williams dropped his head in his hands. Smith turned and looked for Minchin and Davies and saw the two yelling and gesticulating. They turned and looked at the soldiers and for a moment Smith wondered if they could be court-martialled. He imagined himself and the other men before Major Johnston, while someone read out 'Charges of gross incompetence in the training of horses.'

Mulligan recovered his feet and struggled to clamber up the side of the horse, finally managing to do so by grabbing a clump of its mane. That seemed only to enrage the horse, which shot off again after the chasing pack. In no time at all she had caught the pack only this time Mulligan managed to keep her running with the main group. When asked afterwards how he had achieved that he said simply 'Buggered if I know.'

For a few hundred yards the pack of horses stayed together. As they neared the tree that marked the turn several horses raced out in front. Mulligan managed to keep the mare in the main pack of horses and round the turn without incident.

The smaller group of horses pinned their ears back and started to run harder and harder once they cleared the turn, immediately putting some fifty yards between themselves and the chasing pack.

Williams watched the race while every so often glancing across at Minchin and Davies. The two were yelling at Mulligan to move it. There was so much noise from the mass of humanity watching that they may as well have been silent, such were the chances of Mulligan hearing them. Slowly the leading group moved closer to the finish, everything taking more time than Williams imagined it should.

Then Mulligan and his mare, along with another horse separated from the chasing pack and began to make up ground on the leaders. Williams tried to calculate how far they had to go to catch the leaders and measure that against the distance to the finish. It was going to be awfully close, he thought.

Still the leaders kept coming as Mulligan and the other rider urged their horses on, closing the gap. Then one of the leading group slowed down, the horse clearly in distress. The two remaining leaders seemed to be slowing too, while Mulligan's horse and the other horse were holding their pace.

'By God, I think he might actually do it,' Smith yelled.

The leading horses were now two hundred yards from home but slowing all the time. The horse that was running next to Mulligan's horse appeared to be slowing too, and then Williams saw one of the leading horses quickly fall away.

'Come on Mulligan you bastard,' Williams said. He was surprised that he was so animated, but then the whole crowd were. There was something about seeing horses in full flight running to be first to the post that was universal.

Williams glanced at Minchin and Davies who were jumping and yelling like men escaped from an asylum. Then Williams looked around and realised he was one of the few not acting in the same way. Men and women everywhere were screaming and yelling and jumping and dancing and waving their arms at the horses as though each were riding their favourite home.

The lead horse was now one hundred yards from the post with Mulligan's mare closing rapidly. If anything, Mulligan's horse was still accelerating while the other horse barely hung on.

Then Mulligan brought the mare up beside the leading horse. It would be tight, Williams thought. It would be very tight. Only then did Williams realise that he was screaming along with the rest of the crowd. There were only a few yards left, a few strides to go, the two horses next to each other, both covered in sweat.

Williams screamed 'yes' as Mulligan and the mare kept surging forward, now edging in front. The other horse bobbed its head forward but Mulligan and the mare were unstoppable and moved further in front, passing the finishing post first.

Bedlam broke out. Williams saw Minchin and Davies grab each other and hug each other while jumping up and down. Such behaviour at the barracks would have men shunned with questions raised about their sexual preferences, but Williams knew this was pure elation on the behalf of the two officers. Then he looked and saw Smith — of all people Smith —hugging Connor and Newbank and jumping up and down. Gillard had found a fence post and had half climbed it, yelling at the sky in delight while Hutton just stood grinning.

Williams turned and looked for Mulligan and the horse. He realised that the horse was still running with Mulligan clinging to its back, the two quickly disappearing into the distance. Williams laughed aloud at the sight of it and then jumped into the group hug with Smith, Conner and Newbank.

'Bloody hell lads you did it. You did it,' Minchin said. The four soldiers stopped jumping and disentangled themselves from each other.

Davies ran over and used two of the soldiers as a launch pad to jump into the air. 'Lads you bloody marvels. You'll get extra rations of rum for a week ... no, a month,' Davies yelled.

Gillard and Hutton reached the others and Minchin turned to them. 'Oh lads you are wonderful. All of you. Thank you so much.'

In the delight of victory and mutual praise none of the group thought of Mulligan and the horse. Then the organisers of the race came over. 'Are you gentlemen the owners of the horse?' an older man said. He was one of a group of four who introduced themselves as the committee responsible for the race.

'We most certainly are the owners and trainers too. Our fine lads here from the Corps did the training,' Minchin said. He was too excited to see the glances the committeemen exchanged when he said 'Corps'.

'Your prize is here. All we need is to see the horse and jockey. Are they here?' another of the group said.

'Yes, that's good, I mean right. We must see the horse,' said the first committeeman. The others nodded in sudden agreement, starting to smile broadly.

'Where is Mulligan?' Davies said.

The men began looking around for him. Williams stared off into the distance where he had last seen Mulligan and the horse heading. There was no sign of horse or rider.

'We must see the horse and rider before we present the purse,' the eldest of the committeemen said. Two of the remaining committeemen looked at each other and nodded.

'Is Mulligan here, can any of you see him?' Davies asked.

'He kind of continued past once the race finished, heading thataway,' Gillard said, pointing in the direction that the soldier and horse were last seen headed. The soldiers all craned their necks and stood on toes looking in the direction Mulligan had headed. There was no sign of him.

'Without the horse and rider we will not present the purse,' the eldest man said.

'Now hang on a minute, every person here saw our horse win,' Minchin said. 'You had better give us that purse or else.'

'The rules of the race are clear. The winning horse and rider must be present and the rider must collect the purse,' one of the committee men said.

'Where are these rules? Show us where that is written,' Davies said.

'The by-laws of the race are not here. We have them at, we have them elsewhere,' the older man said.

'If you think you are going to rob us of our victory you have trouble coming your way,' Minchin said. 'You do know who you are dealing with, members of the New South Wales Corps.'

'The rules are clear, you must ...' the older man said before being cut off.

'The only must that needs to happen is you must give us our purse now, or else,' Minchin said.

'Or else what?' a man watching nearby said. Williams looked at him and recognised him as one of the men who had first rushed the soldiers the night before.

'Or else what?' the man repeated. 'Let me make it clear to you; there are eight of you and a coupla hundred locals. I wonder how many men a Corps man is able to take on? Five each? Ten, fifteen, more? Perhaps we should find out?'

'We're with you,' another man said. Others quickly joined the chorus,moving threateningly towards where the soldiers and committeemen stood.

'Your rider is not here to claim the purse so your position in the race is forfeit,' the older committee man said.

'Best be on your way boys,' the man from the crowd said.

Minchin looked at the man and for a moment Williams thought that the lieutenant may actually lunge at him. Davies sensed it too and grabbed Minchin and started to haul him away. Williams stepped between the man and Minchin and grabbed Hutton and started to follow Davies as he forced Minchin away. Smith then rounded up the others and together they slowly walked away, keeping a wary eye on the crowd.

'Where the bloody hell is that fool Mulligan?' Minchin said. 'I'll have him on stockade for the rest of his fucking useless life.'

'Let's just get out of here as quick as we can,' Davies said. 'Corporals, find Mulligan and our horse as soon as you can and meet us on the road to Sydney.'

'Aye sir,' Smith said.

Smith and Williams waited a few moments until the group was entering town and then one by one used the buildings as cover to break away from the group. Minchin and Davies ordered Conner and Newbank to collect the soldiers' gear from their lodging and soon the group were on the road to Sydney. They walked a little while until the town was out of sight, and then they retreated from the road to a copse of trees and waited for Williams and Smith.

Once they had detached from the main group Smith and Williams quickly rendezvoused behind the pub. They watched for a short time in the hope that they may see Mulligan but the volume of people coming and going after the races was enormous. They headed back past the finishing line and followed along the line on which Mulligan and the horse were last seen.

They were almost a mile away from the finishing line when they heard voices. The two quickly ducked down and found cover and carefully began edging towards the noise.

A small group of men stood over a mound. To his horror Williams recognised the mound as the mare and soon saw that Mulligan was lying nearby. Williams glanced at Smith. 'I only have a knife,' Smith whispered. 'You?' he said.

'Not even that. Well at least we know why Mulligan didn't make it back.'

'Oh for a musket and ten armed men from the Corps,' Smith said.

'Not helping Nate. Let's just figure out what we can do ourselves.'

'It probably wouldn't make a difference if you had a musket anyway, the way you shoot.'

'Not now Nate.'

One of the group of men turned and Williams recognised one of the attackers from the previous night. 'What about him, do we kill him like the horse?' the man said.

'Might be the man whose wife Mulligan fooled around with?' Smith said.

Williams felt his stomach churn. It all made sense. The locals had taken the chance to get their revenge on both Mulligan and the Corps.

'We can't take them all on,' Smith said. 'We need a plan.'

'Can you circle around quickly without being seen?' Williams said.

'Yes, why?'

'If we can make them think they are surrounded they may scatter.'

'So yet again we're about to be dropped in it up to our eyeballs,' Smith said. Then he began quickly moving to circle around the group.

Williams watched him, grateful that the attention of the men was directed at Mulligan and not on the surrounding bush. Finally he saw Smith take up position.

'Hands up we have you surrounded,' Williams yelled.

'Hands up, all of you.'

Williams quickly rolled and crawled a few metres sideways. 'Move it, hands up now or we open fire,' he said in a dodgy Scottish accent. 'Take aim men.'

One of the group started to run, then others began to scatter.

'Hold your fire. Chase them, round them up,' Williams yelled.

'That way you two, You others with me,' Smith yelled. He carefully followed the main group, yelling orders to the imaginary pursuers.

In moments the clearing was empty. Williams quickly raced in and rolled Mulligan over. He had taken a savage beating; his face was raw and bloodied and bruising already.

'Mulligan, it's Williams. Can you hear me? Can you walk?'

Mulligan tried to focus and slowly moved to look at Williams. He grabbed Williams and pressed his body against the Corporal. 'Dear Christ I'm glad to see you,' Mulligan said. For Williams the words were almost unintelligible such was the beating that Mulligan had taken.

'Come on, get up,' Williams said.

A man raced into the clearing. Williams tensed but saw it was only Smith.

'We don't have long. We have to go now or stand and fight,' Smith said.

'Mulligan's a wreck. He can't fight. Help me support him.' Smith and Williams hauled Mulligan to his feet and shuffled and half-ran as quickly as they could retreating from the clearing and then moving back towards town. They managed to make it halfway back to town before they stopped to rest. The last thing Williams saw as they left the clearing was the bloody carcass of the mare on the ground.

Williams and Smith skirted around the settlement at Hawkesbury to avoid raising questions about Mulligan's appearance. The beating the soldier had taken would take a long time to heal, though Williams was more worried about Mulligan's state of mind. Mulligan had clung to Williams almost the entire time as though seeking some form of comfort in being held by someone he knew.

When the three had first stopped Williams and Smith had done what they could to stop the bleeding and assess Mulligan for any serious injuries. The two suspected that Mulligan may have a broken jaw but otherwise no other bones had been broken. 'We need to get him back to Sydney and get Doc Wentworth to look at him and patch him up,' Williams said.

The three managed to skirt past the town without drawing attention to themselves and find Minchin, Davies and the soldiers on the road out of town.

'What happened to him?' Davies said.

'And where is our horse?' Davies said.

'The best we can understand it, some of the locals grabbed the horse after the race and led it away with Mulligan on it. They then dragged him off it and knocked him out and killed the horse,' Williams said. He looked at Minchin. 'Sorry Lieutenant.'

'The horse was already dead when we found Mulligan. There was a group of local men surrounding him and deciding if they would kill him,' Williams said. 'We managed to spook them and they ran off and we grabbed Mulligan and hightailed it out of there.'

'Do you know the men?' Minchin said. 'Could you recognise them?'

'They were some of the men who attacked us last night,' Williams said. 'One of them may be the husband of the woman who Mulligan had his fun with last time around.'

The group were silent for a while.

'Lieutenant, shouldn't we head for Sydney as soon as we can?' Williams said.

'Those bastards killed our horse,' Minchin said. He stared back down the road towards Hawkesbury.

'Not to mention almost killed Mulligan too,' Williams said.

Minchin started to head up the road to the settlement. 'Will, where're you going? What do you think you're going to do?' Davies said.

'I'm going to report what happened to Chief Constable Thompson. Williams, Smith you're with me. I intend to get those men up on charges, get the purse for winning the race and then we can return to Sydney.'

Davies ran after Minchin and grabbed his arm. Minchin pulled it away and turned squaring up to Davies with a wild look in his eye. 'Let it go Will,' Davies said. 'Half the town is drunk. Too many know who we are and want to do us harm. The only thing you will manage is to get yourself killed.'

'They killed my horse and stole the purse,' Minchin said.

'Yes they did, but how is getting yourself killed going to make that right?'

'At least I'll be doing something. What do you want to do, turn tail and run?'

'No. I want to get back to Sydney and then we talk to the major and take the appropriate action, with the full force of the Corps behind us. This way we are walking into a fight outnumbered maybe one hundred to one. Remember what the major says, pick your battleground carefully. Think your strategy through.'

Minchin glared at Davies. He looked at Williams who still stood with the other soldiers. They looked tired and small, too small in number to achieve any good.

'Our time will come, but it's not today,' Davies said. He motioned along the road towards Sydney. 'Come on, let's go home.'

Minchin stood still. Davies took a step towards Sydney and waved his arm at Minchin. 'Come on Will, now's not the time.'

Reluctantly Minchin started walking after Davies. The rest of the group slowly followed, Conner and Williams helping Mulligan along.

Major Johnston was sitting in his chair in the mess hall when Minchin and his group returned.

'So the racers have returned. Good, we have work to do,' Johnston said.

'Major, those bastards up the Hawkesbury cheated us out of our winnings and killed our horse,' Minchin said. He had barely calmed down since his confrontation with Davies on the road.

'Not to mention beat Mulligan nearly senseless,' Williams said.

'Well that wouldn't take much doing. After all, Mulligan didn't have much sense to begin with,' Laycock said.

'Major, we need to get back up there in force and set things right,' Minchin said.

'Sorry gentlemen but we have bigger problems to deal with,' Johnston said.

'They robbed us and attacked us and killed our horse. What could be bigger than that?' Minchin said.

'Not to mention beat Mulligan,' Smith said.

'I really don't care too much about that, assuming of course that Mulligan will recover,' Johnston said.

'But Major, this is an insult to the Corps,' Minchin said.

'Then we will deal with it when appropriate," Johnston said. 'Right now we have a far bigger problem. Bligh is out to stop us using convict labour supplied by Wentworth.'

Minchin was about to launch into another impassioned plea for action. Upon hearing Johnston speak he stopped.

'We are to hold a court-martial of Doc Wentworth for disobeying orders from Captain Abbott about treating ill convicts,' Johnston said.

'I don't understand,' Davies said. 'What's going on?'

'While you were away playing at being horse owners Abbott sent two convicts from Castle Hill to the hospital at Parramatta. He ordered Wentworth to treat the two,' Johnston said. 'Wentworth refused to do so, because as he said, Bligh had previously ordered him to get convicts out of the hospital and so he can only accept new convict patients on the approval of Governor Bligh. So Abbott decided to press charges against D'Arcy for disobeying orders.'

'What on earth is Abbott thinking?' Davies said.

'Fortuntely its not Abbott doing the thinking. Its all part of a plan. The idea is that we hold the court martial to make it clear that Bligh is issuing orders to the military that are unclear and unknown to many of the officers,' Johnston said.

'I see. We can say Bligh is not discharging his role as head of the military clearly, for only some of the officers get certain orders,' Williams said.

'Exactly, but that is only part of it,' Johnston continued. 'So we hear the charges, decide the whole thing has been the fault of the Governor, then dismiss the case against D'Arcy and put the whole thing back to Bligh as a message that he needs to send clearer orders.'

'So what has this got to do with convict labour?' Smith asked.

'Ah yes, thank you for reminding me,' Johnston said. 'Earlier this year Bligh refused permission when Wentworth asked for the use of two convicts for labouring at the hospital. So in effect Wentworth will be arguing that Bligh has stopped him from being able to do his job properly, as Wentworth does not have enough manpower to get everything done. That is why he needs the convicts. Bligh is determined to say where convicts work and ignore the Assistant Surgeon.'

'So the case is really about who controls the convict labour, the governor or Wentworth,' Smith said.

'Yes. If Wentworth can keep control of the convicts at the hospital he can loan those convicts out to us,' Johnston said. 'If Bligh can kick those convicts out of hospital as he demands then he stops us using convicts.'

'So Abbott is not really angry at Wentworth?' Davies said.

'No. He's following a plan devised by Mac,' Johnston said.

'I thought Abbott was on Bligh's side,' Minchin said.

'Well that was last week. Now that Mac has sweet-talked him he's back on our side,' Johnston said.

'So when does this all happen?' Davies said.

'As soon as we have a panel to convene the court martial. And now that our resident horse owners are back, and assuming you are both happy to return to being officers, we begin tomorrow,' Johnston said.

'Order. The court will please return to their seats,' Johnston said. The court martial had been hearing evidence for less than an hour and already the room was overflowing. People sat two to a chair or box, others stood, both inside and outside craning their heads to peer through windows. Johnston had not only ordered that the proceedings be open to all, he had issued orders to a number of soldiers to round up as many people as possible and to have them attend.

Johnston sat as President of the Court Martial with Richard Atkins acting as Deputy Judge Advocate.

'So your position is that unless Governor Bligh ordered it, you could not take the convicts into the hospital?' Atkins said to Darcy Wentworth.

Wentworth smiled a little. 'That is the nub of it. I wished for the governor to satisfy me for what cause he had taken them away.'

'Them being the convicts?' Atkins said.

'Yes, the convicts.'

'So the governor ordered you to remove the convicts?'

'Yes that is correct.'

'Yet the Principal Surgeon of this colony, Mr Jamison, told us earlier he had no knowledge of this order.'

'That is true. Mr Jamison knew nothing of this.'

'And Captain Abbott, did he know of this order?'

'It would be a strange thing to know of the order and then send convicts to the hospital. I assumed that he did not know of the order either.'

'So you admit that even though you are part of the military here in this colony, and are aware of the chain of command, you disobeyed Captain Abbott's order?'

'I prefer to think of it as following an order from the military commander of the colony, the governor. But yes I did disobey the order.'

'Does that not put you in a difficult position, receiving orders that contradict other orders?'

'Yes it does. But above all I am most concerned about the care of the convicts. The two who I sent away were sick and should have been admitted as patients.'

'They were sick?' Atkins said.

'Yes they were.'

'That is your medical assessment and opinion?'

'It is. But that is where such orders from above are difficult. I am dealing with patients not on the urgency of their case but on bureaucratic orders. I find this difficult.'

'You find it difficult to do your job because of this order from His Excellency?'

'I find it difficult because my superior officer, Mr Jamison, did not know of this order of His Excellency nor did Captain Abbott. But Captain Abbott, in ignorance, sent those convicts. That is an order. But to to obey Governor Bligh I have to disobey Abbott. So yes my job is difficult.'

'And what of those who say that you abuse your position by offering out the labour of convicts at the hospital?' Atkins said.

'That does happen and I'm sure I'm not alone in using convict labour off the books. But I would contend that in order to assess when a fellow is fit to return to labouring; the best way is to build him up to it with some light labour where I know what he will be doing.'

'So you lend out convicts while they are convalescing to assess their health and fitness to return to work?'

'Yes. If I send out a convict to, say an officer, I can advise what that convict can do, and the officer can ensure that that labour is all that is done. Then he can report back to me. If I release a man who has been laid low with fever to a farmer and the farmer works him too hard the convict will fall ill again even quicker. By doing it my way we get them working quicker and doing more for everyone and get them back to the farmers quicker too.'

The courtroom erupted with many of the locals cheering Wentworth. A few, friends of poor farmers, looked darkly on this statement. They had heard too many stories from farmers unable to contract convict labourers who were instead working delivering rum for the Corps.

'Order, order,' Johnston said. He looked at Atkins.

'I have nothing to add Mr President,' Atkins said.

'Thank you, and in the absence of any other witnesses we shall close this session and deliver a verdict shortly,' Johnston said.

'It is the verdict of this court martial that D'Arcy Wentworth, assistant surgeon, has breached one of the articles of war, by disobeying an officer. The sentence is Wentworth be publicly reprimanded,' Johnston said.

The officers on the panel had already agreed with Wentworth on the sentence and had spent the rest of the day, following the adjournment of the court, drinking with the guilty man. Captain Abbott had put an appearance in and been given a rousing reception. Wentworth and Abbott had joked about the court martial and its outcome.

'So tell me again George,' Abbott said to Johnston, 'why we are finding D'Arcy guilty?'

'So Bligh can sign off on the sentence and agree to it. By doing so he also agrees with the trial and the finding that Wentworth and Jamison had unclear orders. He also concedes their medical authority was being undermined by the Governor. It makes the man look like a dictator ready to ignore medical advice and other expertise,' Johnston said.

'Right,' Abbott said.

Johnston wondered, not for the first time, how Abbott had managed to get where he was. He knew men like Abbott who used money to buy their commission, that he understood. What he could never fathom was how a dullard such as Abbott had managed to scrap together the amount to buy a commission in the first place. Johnston contented himself that at least Abbott was always at Parramatta and not at the barracks.

The following day Johnston ordered the troops in Sydney on parade. A light drizzle fell as Johnston stood up to speak. Sergeant Major Whittle came out of the mess, followed by D'Arcy Wentworth and Quartermaster Laycock. Both walked to the parade ground and stood before Johnston and the troops.

'Righto lads,' Johnston said. 'It is my duty, ordered by His Excellency the Governor, to upbraid Assistant Surgeon Wentworth for disobeying an order from Captain Abbott. Mr Wentworth was doing so to uphold an order from Governor Bligh. The governor considers his orders, be they never so bounteous or Christian, to be required to be followed no matter how pigheaded or wrong.

'Assistant Surgeon you have been a disrespectful and naughty fellow. Consider yourself upbraided before the men. Does any man wish to address the Assistant Surgeon?'

Quartermaster Laycock stepped forward. 'Sir!'

'Proceed Quartermaster,' Johnston said.

'Lads, let's give it to Doc Wentworth. Three cheers.' The troops yelled their pleasure loudly.

'Now don't do that again, or you might just find yourself back here. Is that clear D'Arcy?' Johnston said.

'Yes sir,' Wentworth said smirking.

'Now lads let's get out of this weather and have a drink,' Johnston said.

Bligh struck back at the Corps a week later.

'What do you mean suspended? I ordered him back to work yesterday,' Johnston said. He was sitting quietly reading the *Gazette* when Minchin came into the mess hall.

'Bligh has ordered that Wentworth be suspended until the King's pleasure is known,' Minchin said.

'Known about what? Is Bligh bringing new charges or contesting the finding of our court martial?'

'That's what D'Arcy is trying to find out. He doesn't know himself. D'Arcy asked Jamison why he had been suspended and what fresh charges may have been brought. After all, he cannot be found guilty of disobeying Abbott when he has already been reprimanded for it.'

'So what did Jamison say?' Johnston said.

'All he got out of Jamison was that the governor disapproves of Wentworth's conduct,' Minchin said.

'I'm sure that is a general view Bligh holds about the entire Corps, so why single Wentworth out? What has he done?'

'That's it, no-one seems to know excepting Bligh.'

'Well that's no way to run a colony. Bligh is setting himself up as judge and jury on each man's conduct while he also holds the power to enact the sentences he judges fit,' Johnston said. 'That is dictatorship. So what's D'Arcy going to do?'

'He has asked to be allowed to return to England and evidently Bligh has already refused the request,' Minchin said. 'This reeks Major, this is wrong.' He was silent for several moments then he looked directly at Johnston. 'Bligh means to break us entirely, doesn't he George?'

It was the first time that Minchin had used Johnston's given name and he was unsure of what the response would be.

'I think you are right Will, and it concerns me. Bligh is not like the other governors we have seen come and go. He means to break us and nothing we do seems to have an effect on him.'

For a moment Minchin saw Johnston deflate and seem to give up. The major changed before his eyes as in some strange picture, the military bearing and authority vanishing to be replaced by a man looking lost in delirium, before Johnston visibly pulled himself together.

The whole time Johnston seemed to be looking through Minchin, towards some distant and future place that he shrank from.

May 1807

Mary Putland looked over the dancefloor and the couples spinning elegantly, most in time to the music. Around the walls of the room groups stood talking. Free settlers mixed with bureaucrats and soldiers, women chatted and smiled, men talked business over the music. The entry foyer to Government House was too full, but there were few other places to hold a ball and none with the credibility of the governor's residence.

The music swelled and the couples on the dancefloor finished their dancing. Men graciously bowed to their partners, who in turn courtsied. The small band that was seated on the terrace of the stairs put down their instruments and were grateful to the waiter who offered them drinks. Despite the cool evening outside the heat in the crowded foyer was ever present.

Mary Putland carefully made her way across the room to a group of men including Robert Campbell, Chaplain Henry Fulton, Lieutenant Minchin and Major Johnston. 'Gentlemen, it is a pleasure to see you. And Major Johnston I am thrilled that you are gracing us with your presence here. I know what a coup it is to have you in attendance and I am grateful for it.'

'Mrs Putland it is difficult to refuse the first lady of the colony when she singles me out as, what were your words, "Essential to the ball's success," I think you said.'

'As I once said to you in this very room, every ball needs a dashing soldier. Perhaps later you will dance with me, if your wife does not object.'

'I am afraid that my dancing days are over. And I am far less dashing than you would credit me for. These days I am content to live a quiet life with my Esther.'

'Were that it was so,' said a loud voice behind Johnston. He turned, as did many others.

William Bligh stood glaring at Johnston. 'But you are hardly content to live a quiet life. Instead you seek to stand against the progress that is being made here in this colony. Since I arrived morality has been restored, public drunkeness is all but a thing of the past and we live as civilised Englishmen.'

'Governor, I apologise if I have said something untoward, however, I think this is neither the time nor place to discuss such matters,' Johnston said.

'Why, sir? Are you afraid to speak against those gentler aspects of civil society that I have restored? Or to speak for the venality that you have long championed? It surprises me, for it has been you and your men that have driven so much of the liquor-fuelled stupidity for so long. You have been content with trading in rum and trouble for years and now, when you have the chance to debate the matter before the leaders of our colony, you demure. I thought better of you, sir, than you deserve.'

Johnston looked around, conscious of the sweat beading on his forehead. Everyone was watching, surprised at what they were seeing and delighted by the prospect of what may unfold.

John Macarthur walked over and stood beside Johnston. 'Governor, you have ...'

'Mr Macarthur, you are only here at my daughter's insistence. Were I to have my way you would never tarnish this place with your presence. But such is the weakness of a father for his daughter, that I relented and allowed you here tonight. So you will remain quiet or I will have you removed before all these people.'

'You wouldn't dare,' Macarthur said.

'Mr Gore, if you please,' Bligh said loudly.

Gore and several constables entered the room via a side door and marched over to Macarthur. 'Sir, you may leave unattended or I will have my constables attend to you. And believe me they are primed and ready to offer you very close attention.'

Macarthur stared at Gore, then turned to Bligh. 'I have had enough of playing gentlemen, so I shall happily leave. George, are we done?'

'John, I do believe we are.'

'Major, you cannot leave yet, we have not had our dance,' Mary Putland said. 'Father, if you do not object I shall like to dance with the Major?'

'Mary, you may when we have finished our conversation. Still here Macarthur, I thought you were leaving?'

Macarthur looked around the room, saw the smiling and leering faces enjoying his humiliation and turned and walked out.

'Major, the floor is yours. This is your chance to put forward the case for rum trading, for drunkeness and stupidity. I assure you that if you carry the argument here and now I shall cede the public direction and morality of this colony to your view. All you have to do is convince these fine people that your view of the colony is superior.'

A long silence filled the room. Johnston looked around for an escape. He saw none.

'I will take your silence as your rebuttal of my argument. And as support for my policies, support I expect to continue beyond tonight. Mary, I shall pass Major Johnston over to you. You may have your dance with the dashing Major,' Bligh said and nodded to the band. They struck up a waltzing tune. Before Johnston could do anything Mary Putland took Johnston by the arm and began walking out onto the dancefloor. Mary put her arms out waiting for Johnston to lead. No-one else made a move to join in the dance. Johnston smiled grimly and tried to do his best waltz, watched by the leading lights of the colony. Twice he stepped on Mary's toes. Then the music stopped and Johnston got out of there as fast as he could.

Oliver Williams and Nate Smith were sitting on the verandah of Williams's house. Ever since the ball the talk of Sydney had been about the confrontation between Bligh and Johnston. The major had not been seen at the barracks since that night. To make matters worse Minchin had quietly told Davies, Smith and Williams about his own conversation with Johnston prior to the ball and his fears for the future. Smith, a man of direct action, a soldier by nature and trade, disliked politics, yet sought to understand it.

'So what happens now?'

'I'm not sure Nate. What we've done in the past is ignore what the Governor wants and do what we want. We've been able to get under their skin and then show them up as weak. As a result past Governors have just let us be.'

'But not Bligh?'

'Bligh is different. His reforms are working and the people like what he is doing. And more than that he intends to fight us.'

'Okay, so we fight back.'

'Well in a way we have been. That's what the major and Mac have been using the courts to do. But Bligh is on to that too. Maybe Bligh is just too strong and smart for us?'

'And the major believes that Bligh has it in for us?'

'That's right.'

'I said it was coming to war between us and Bligh. Sides will have to be taken. Either we oppose Bligh, or we give in and do as Bligh wants.'

'I think your right Nate,' Williams said. He looked away from Smith, glanced at his drink and then at the road. He remembered what Mary had said about choosing sides. For the first time in a long time he felt lost, unsure what to do. If Johnston did not know the road ahead then things looked bleak. Williams emptied the rest of his drink over the verandah railing into the garden.

Smith went to say something more, then looked at his drink and downed the remainder. He too looked out from the verandah, lost in his own worries.

The noise from the mess hall rose and fell like a heartbeat. For the first time in days the room was crowded again, the word spreading quickly that Johnston had put in an appearance. When Johnston had first arrived none of the soldiers knew what to say, but they all wanted to crowd around the major. Minchin had taken the lead, playing joker. Now the officers and men were sitting in the mess hall listening to the end of a poor joke by Minchin.

'Corporal, I think you should take Lieutenant Minchin into custody while I convene a court martial on the grounds of inability to tell a good joke,' Johnston said to Williams. 'Davies and I will sit on the panel. The rules will be simple, Minchin tells us a joke that actually makes us laugh and he gets off."

Williams looked at Minchin, then to Johnston. 'Well that's condemning him right now Major, but if you insist.'

There was a commotion outside then Macarthur burst into the room. 'George, I need to talk to you alone, now.' Macarthur looked dishevelled, his shirt untucked and buttoned wrong, with a tear on the left leg of his riding britches.

'Mac you can talk to me here.'

'Bloody hell George, the future of the colony is at stake. You and me in private now,' Macarthur said.

The officers stared at Macarthur and then watched as Johnston stood and slowly walked into a side room used for storing wine barrels and other goods. Macarthur followed and slammed the door.

'Mac, what's going on?'

'I need you to find someone for me now. He is a convict named John Hoare.'

'What's so important about him and what does it have to do with the future of the colony.'

'I can't tell you that now. Just find him please.'

'Mac, I can't just order the Corps to find someone. That's not our job. Now if it is important enough…'

'Important enough? Dear God, important? Important, George? The man may have escaped on board one of my ships bound for Tahiti. If he has then Bligh has me over barrel and can have me arrested. Me George. That fucking useless man will win and who will fight for the colony then? Who will look after my sheep and the wool industry and who will ensure that that fucking bastard sailor doesn't win? Who George, who? Find this man now. Prove to me he's still here and not in Tahiti. Oh Christ George it can't end like this, it mustn't end like this.'

Then just as suddenly as he had burst in Macarthur turned, opened the door and walked out. 'Thank you George, owe you one. Lads,' Macarthur said and walked out with a beaming smile.

Johnston raced out of the store room and followed Macarthur outside. 'Mac, I don't understand? What does it matter if this man Hoare has escaped?'

'George, each ship's owner is required to pay a bond for out-going ships leaving the colony. So Blaxcell and I have paid £800 each to ensure that our ship does not carry away convicts. This Hoare has me in breach of that bond.'

'So you lose the bond,' Johnston said. 'Yes it's a blow but surely one you can still afford.'

'Of course I can afford it, but how does that look if I am said to help convicts escape? Me, George, the leading man of the colony is helping convicts escape. It jeopardises everything else. It leaves me at Bligh's mercy.'

'Alright, but how do you know this man Hoare is aboard, or suspect it?'

'The master of the ship, a fellow named Glenn, was ashore and seen with this Hoare on several occasions. Hoare did not show up for his work detail the last few mornings so his convict supervisors went to find him and could not. When the constables were sent they found no trace of him.'

'He could have gone bush. More than a few convicts try that and we both know that a small number either die out there or go native. Can't you just say that's what he's done?'

'There is allegedly a witness who saw him near the *Parramatta* before it sailed. There's more, I'm sure of it, but I can't find out. If you can find him then this is not a problem. If you can't then we know and I need to figure out what happens next, what moves I make.'

'Alright we'll look for him, but we'll do it quietly and carefully. In the meantime keep yourself together Mac, so things appear normal. If anyone asks say nothing. Can you do that?'

Macarthur smiled one of his most dazzling smiles and laughed. 'Of course George.'

Johnston watched him go, shaken by how quickly the man changed character. It was as if the last few minutes had been imagined, another of Minchin's bad jokes.

As he walked into the barracks Johnston saw the worried looks on the faces of the officers. The murmur of conversation dried up into nothingness leaving an anxious pall in the room. The men wondered who would be the first to break the silence, to ask the question on every man's mind. None spoke.

Johnston sighed. 'So, Mac has lost a convict, and you know how Mac gets when something bugs him. He wants us to have a sniff around the town and nearby areas out in the bush and see if we can find this convict.'

They're not buying it, Johnston thought. Even for Mac that performance was too much, too far into mania and madness to be anything other than unsettling. They were tied together, the Corps and Mac, and each man knew it.

'As to the rest of it, the future of the colony and the like; well let's just say that Mac needs a little more sleep than he's getting.'

There was a subdued chuckle that Johnston couldn't place to any one man.

'Righto lads. You heard the major, we have a convict to find,' Minchin said. Johnston was thankful the lieutenant was willing to play along and grateful that all the eyes in the room were no longer on him. He felt tired and unable to shake the idea of giving up his place in the Corps and becoming a farmer at Annandale.

Williams watched the major as all the other men turned to look at Minchin. He felt a shiver shoot down his spine.

For a moment he thought Johnston's bearing changed, but he could not be sure if it was something he imagined or had been real.

'The name of this convict Major?' Minchin said.

Johnston was uncertain who had asked the question. 'Yes, Hoare, John Hoare,' Johnston said vaguely. 'Hoare,' he repeated.

'So I think we do this in the shadows lads. Not upfront but quietly and out of uniform,' Minchin said. 'Corporal's Smith and Williams, perhaps you take a few trusted men and lean on a few people in the usual places. What say you?'

'No problem Lieutenant. Leave it to Nate and I. We'll take Tom and George with us, visit a few pubs and see what we can find,' Williams said.

The four soldiers set off quickly in civilian clothes, heading for The Londoner. They had briefly chatted with Quartermaster Laycock who had filled the soldiers in on what he knew of Hoare and the *Parramatta*. Other than gleaning that Hoare was transported for life and a few scant details about the *Parramatta* including the name of the ship's master, Williams and Smith had little to go on.

Henry Adams was behind the bar at the Londoner when he saw the four soldiers come in and immediately felt a shot of worry course through his body. What did four soldiers want with him, and this late in the day? The bully boys of the Corps usually visited when times were quiet, not now as the afternoon was gearing up into the evening.

'Nate, Oliver, what can I get you? And for your friends something too?'

Williams motioned Adams to head to the back room. Adams swallowed hard. Business had been down since Bligh's crackdown on rum and he had not seen any of the Corps for a couple of months. He feared this was the start of a push from the bully boys to get him to sell more of their rum. Not for the first time he was conflicted about what that meant. In recent months less rum had been available, with the Corps and other suppliers unable to meet demand. People were complaining, but for Adams not having the Corps as suppliers meant no-one from the Corps telling him what to do or visiting threats on him. More rum meant more profit but feeling free from the harassment of the Corps had a lot going for it too.

'Henry relax, we want some information is all,' Williams said. Adams tried to appear calm and relaxed. He hated how Williams could read him so easily.

'Do you know a convict named John Hoare, a lifer?' Williams said.

'Gentleman John. He comes in on Saturday nights. Quiet type. He seems a little out of sorts, like he hasn't come to terms with being here for life.'

'So what does he look like?'

'Thin, really skinny from what I recall. Looks like you could never feed him enough. Funny thing is it is always the skinny ones that can drink the most and stay relatively sober.'

'Anything else you can tell us about how he looks?'

'Dark hair I think, with a receding hairline, maybe around thirty years old but it's always hard to tell. He looks clean shaven, like he could never grow a beard even if he tried.' Adams looked at Williams who encouraged him to tell more.

'Er, his clothes are shabby but he tries hard to look his best in them, if you know what I mean. He's not too tall.' Adams was quiet for a moment, as though trying to picture Hoare. 'The funny thing is, he is not really the kind of man you remember much ... bits and pieces only, not the whole. He could be sitting out there now and you would look past him half a dozen times even if you were looking for him. So why are you after him anyway? Has he crossed the Corps?'

'That's not for you to worry about,' Williams said. 'So each Saturday night he comes by. Do you know if he drinks anywhere else?'

'Not sure about that, but he wasn't here last Saturday for sure and maybe the one before that too.'

'Does he have any friends he drinks with? Any men, women, anyone at all?'

'Not usually, but the last time he was here he was sitting with a sailor, a ship's master. What's his name?' There was a long pause. 'Sorry I can't place the name.'

'Had this master been in before? Had he met with Hoare before?'

'Not for a long time. I only know he is a ship's master because he comes in every six months or twelve months or so, spends up big and then is gone again. He tried to court one of the convict women. Matt Roy's woman, think her name is Kate. Spent big on her but got nowhere.'

Williams stared hard at Adams, enjoying watching the publican squirm under his gaze. He watched a few moments longer and satisfied that Adams had told all he knew, smiled at the publican. 'Thanks Henry, very helpful.'

Then Williams spun on his heel and led Smith, Conners and Newbank out of the back room and into the pub. They were opening the door when Adams yelled. 'Glenn, it could have been Glenn.'

'Glenn?' Williams said.

'The ship's master, it could have been Glenn was his name,' Adams said.

'Thanks Henry,' Williams said.

'There is one more thing,' Adams said following Williams out the door of The Londoner. 'I don't really want to mention it, but, well, a lot of people are complaining about, well you.' 'Me?'

'No, the Corps. They want to know why you've slowed the trade in rum, and other goods too.'

'It's not us, we still want to trade. It's Bligh. He thinks drinking is bad and encourages poor behaviour. As if that ever happened,' Williams said, with a smirk. 'We want to trade, but we can't, at least while Bligh is governor. Tell that to people.'

Williams thanked Adams again and walked away. 'Bloody hell, Adams said the ship's master who Hoare met was Glenn. That's the master of the *Parramatta*. And since he last met Hoare the convict has disappeared. I'd wager Hoare is on that ship and Glenn has taken money to get him safe passage.'

'So what do we do now?' Conner said.

'We see Matt Roy and his woman, see if they know anything,' Williams said.

Roy lived outside of town on a small farm. The four soldiers took more than an hour to make the walk. 'So Adams is saying that people are blaming us for the lack of rum around at the moment,' Williams said as he finished telling the others about his conversation with the publican.

'But that's all Bligh's doing. How is that down to us?' Newbank said.

'We've been the main suppliers and traders in rum for almost two decades. When supplies dry up people don't ask why, they remember who's been involved, who's led the trade. They add it up and say the Corps must be the ones responsible,' Williams said.

'So what do we do about it?' Conner said.

'I think we need to let people know just why supply has dried up,' Williams said. 'Blame the Governor and put it on him.

Make him the face of the rum shortage. We do it quietly, telling the bar keepers and publicans and shop owners who we trade with. We tell a few people who are influential. We maybe tell the *Gazette* and see if they can publish something.'

'Sounds like a plan to me,' Newbank said.

'This is it, Matt Roy's place,' Smith said.

'How do you always know where to go, where everyone lives?' Connor said.

'Old soldier's trick,' Smith said.

'Well aren't you going to tell us the trick?'

'I just remember, that's the trick.'

'Help you boys?' a voice said from near the side of the small farmhouse.

The soldiers spun around and looked in the direction the voice came from. At first they could not see anyone, then slowly Matt Roy stood up from behind a pile of weeds and rubbish. He held a pitchfork loosely in one hand. Smith was not fooled by the loose grip.

'Steady on Matt, we just want to have a chat is all,' Smith said.

'That you Nate Smith?'

'It is,' Smith said. 'I got a couple of me mates with me. How about me and Oli Williams here come over. Tom and George will wait back on the road,' Conner and Newbank didn't need any further instruction and headed back to the road.

'How are you Matt?' Smith said.

'Things are good. Would like them to stay that way too,' Roy said.

'Matt this is Oli Williams, he's my best mate.'

'Good day Oli,' Roy said. 'Still in the Corps Nate?'

'Yes, still in the Corps. Oli here is too. Mind if Oli asks a couple of questions?'

Roy nodded slowly. 'Don't mean you'll get any answers if I don't like them questions.'

'Ever run across a John Hoare,' Williams said.

'I ran across him. He stood by while his mate, some ship's master called Glenn, tried to steal my Kate he did. Calls himself Gentleman John but doesn't act like a proper gentleman. Why you ask?'

'We're trying to find him,' Williams said.

'Well he ain't here. You can be on your way then.'

'Thing is Matt, this Hoare got in some trouble and we want to square things up with him. Anything you could tell us to help find him. And I don't mind saying we don't like men that stand by while their mate's try to steal a man's girl, so we would be happy to give him a few pointers on manners on your behalf,' Williams said.

'Ask me, I reckon if he can't be found it's because he's done a runner. Always talked to Kate about getting out of here, out of Sydney and the colony. Used to talk about getting to America.' Roy was quiet for a moment. 'I'll take your offer. You find him give him more than a few from me, and a couple from Kate too. He liked drinking at The Londoner and the Queen Bess too sometimes. That's all.'

Roy turned back to the pile of rubbish and dug the pitchfork in. Smith nodded to Williams and turned and walked back to the road. Williams followed.

'So the Queen Bess it is then,' Smith said. He and Williams walked up to Conner and Newbank.

'Fancy a drink boys. We're off to another pub,' Williams said to Conner and Newbank.

Smith smiled and licked his lips. 'I don't mind this searching if it keeps leading to more pubs. Let's hope this Hoare has been on a weeklong bender and tried every pub in town.'

The Queen Bess was several rungs lower down on the list of watering holes than The Londoner, looking more like a home temporarily converted into a pub. As Williams and Smith walked in they noticed a number of sailors drinking. The owner was a woman called Patricia, who looked like she was more than capable of handling a drunk, or awkward questions.

'Nate, hang back a bit and let me do the talking, okay,' Williams said.

Williams ordered two rums and sat on a wobbly bench near the rear of the place. Williams noticed that a number of items of old and broken furniture were stacked in the corner near where he sat with Smith. Definitely a house that doubled as a bar.

A waitress came over. 'You lads new in town?'

'Just landed off a boat and looking for someone. Told he wants to talk about taking a sailing trip,' Williams said in a broad English accent.

The woman sat down. 'Maybe I can help you with that and any desires you may not have had met at sea,' the woman said.

'That may be very nice but me ship's master wants us to find this fellow, a convict I think named Hope, Hoare or Hones or something.'

The woman looked around carefully and then motioned for Williams to follow. Williams hesitated a moment. 'Don't worry, I ain't going to roll you. Your friend can come too. The more the merrier.'

'Willing lass, isn't she?' Williams said softly to Smith as they headed out the back.

'I think she's a bit old to be called a lass, but I might still have a crack,' Smith said. 'Just to keep up appearances as it were.'

'Just to keep up appearances is it. What will Madame Brigitte say?'

The woman stopped and Smith walked up to her and she kissed him vigorously.

'Before you two get started me master needs to know about this Hope or Hoare fellow,' Williams said.

'He came in here looking for passage out of the colony, before he came in here too,' she said pointing at her groin and laughing hard. Another kiss for Smith followed. 'But he met someone from a schooner, a master named himself Jones, but other times he been here he was called Glenn or Glynn. That was a couple of weeks ago and then he disappeared and none have seen him since.' The woman started kissing Smith again.

'Hoare or Glenn?' Williams asked.

The woman slowly extracted her tongue from Smith's mouth and disentangled herself. She looked surprised for a moment. 'Both of 'em actually,' she said.

'Well I better get back and tell the master this news. You coming Nate?" Williams said.

'He soon enough will be,' the woman said. Smith waved a hand and Williams quietly slipped away. He met up with Conner and Newbank who had been checking other drinking holes nearby. 'Where's Nate?' Conner asked.

'Trying hard not to blow his cover,' Williams said with a smirk. 'Any luck?'

'A man down the road at the dive we passed walking here said he knew Hoare. Called him Gentleman John. He said Hoare always talked about getting out of here, going to America, which for a lifer sounded odd. Reckoned that Hoare had found passage out. Hoare went from being downcast to very cheerful a couple of weeks back. The man hasn't seen him since. No-one's seen him,' Tom Conner said.

'The serving lady at the Queen Bess said that Hoare had met up with Glenn recently, a couple of weeks ago. I think our man

Hoare has done a runner on the *Parramatta*. Mac is going to be inconsolable when he hears this.'

'Tell Oli the other thing Tom,' Newbank said.

'The man we spoke to said we weren't the first to ask about Hoare. Seems the constables have been sniffing around too.'

'Then looks like Mac has a much bigger problem than he feared,' Williams said. 'If the constables are asking questions then they're on to this too.'

'Did you say that Mac paid a bond of £800?' Conner asked.

'Yeah, £800 to ensure that no convicts could get passage on the *Parramatta*. Looks like he's just blown that money.'

'Can he afford that?' Newbank said with shock.

'Yes. Quite easily,' Williams said.

'Then what's he so worried about?' Conner said.

'The governor finding out, and with the constables on the case it looks like that's going to happen very soon.'

The notices informing the people of Sydney of Hoare's escape went up two days later. By then Williams and Smith had reported that Hoare was in all likelihood on the *Parramatta* bound for Tahiti.

'Well that's not good enough, do you hear me? Look again,' Macarthur shouted at Williams and Smith as Williams concluded his report.

'Mac, they are only reporting on the task you wanted carried out. It's hardly their fault,' Johnston said.

'It fucking well is their fault. If they had found this Hoare I would be free and clear. I ought to have them pay the bond. That will be £400 each of you. Come on now.' Williams and Smith looked at Johnston who waved them out of the room. 'Where the hell are they going George? I want my money.'

'Well you don't think they have that money on them now do you?'

Macarthur burst out laughing. 'Nice joke George that is quite unlike you. So now we start to get down to it eh, me and Bligh. I wonder if that trumped up little sailor really has it in him to come for me, especially with you and the Corps standing behind me.'

'I guess we'll see then,' Johnston said. 'So what will you do about this Hoare and the *Parramatta* Mac?'

'I have a few strategies already in place which will end the matter. Now what really interests me in the report your fine lads just gave is this idea the people are angry about less rum flowing. Good of Williams to start spreading the story that it's Bligh behind this and not us.'

'You realise you just asked my fine lads, to borrow your phrase, to repay you the bond on the *Parramatta*. And that was after blaming them for Hoare's escaping,' Johnston said.

'Did I? I suppose I did. Well they know me enough not to take that seriously. Now we have a few months grace until the ship returns. I suspect closer to December, so plenty of time to prepare.'

'Prepare for what Mac?'

'Why the war with Bligh. In a way I am relieved that this is happening now as … well deep down I knew it would come to something like this.'

A thought crossed Johnston's mind. Surely Macarthur hadn't let the convict escape aboard his ship just to engineer such a situation. Not even Mac could be that brazen. Surely not.

'Really, what I have in mind for the colony and what Bligh wants to do are completely incompatible, so it's time to let the future take its shape. Do you know George that I really do think we need to keep telling all and sundry that Bligh is behind the rum shortage, that Bligh is willing to cruel all trade and will pour more and more convicts and dull farmers into the colony. He is pulling down houses that have not been properly approved, so we need to make something of that too. We have till December and the *Parramatta's* returns to win over the people.'

'Well and good that may be Mac, at least here in Sydney but elsewhere Bligh is winning the people over. In the Hawkesbury and outside Sydney the small farmers are enjoying set prices for their produce. They are free from our control. And unlike here they don't have the free time to drink themselves senseless so the price and supply of rum matter less.'

'They don't matter George, it is Sydney that matters. Sydney decides the colony and its fate and we rule Sydney, so let Bligh come. Let him try to rule us while we win over the people. He tried once before to stand before the will of those under him and failed, let him try and fail again.'

'Are you talking mutiny John? That is dangerous ground to tread.'

'It won't come to that George, I know it. Bligh will fold when the people of Sydney turn on him.'

Johnston watched as Macarthur walked away. He knew with all his conviction that Macarthur was wrong, that Bligh would never fold. This was the man who had refused to stand down on the high seas when the crew of the *Bounty* had threatened mutiny. When he had almost no support from his crew. Why would Bligh quit now when he was so close to winning.

Johnston stared into space, wondering if this life — the intrigue, the plotting — was what he wanted anymore. Maybe his day had passed. He sighed and walked out to his buggy.

'Major, about Mac?' Williams said. Smith stood nearby.

'We don't have that money sir,' Smith said.

'Forget it lads, Mac wasn't serious. Go home and forget it.'

Johnston liked the sound of that. Going home and forgetting, just for a little while. He climbed into the buggy and slowly walked the horse to the barracks gate.

'Be seeing you again soon Major?' Private Gray asked.

'Sorry Private what did you say?' Johnston said, having been lost in his reverie. Then Johnston gee'd the horse and rode out of the barracks. It would be months before he returned.

July 1807

'I've been thinking about what Adams said, about people blaming the Corps for there being less rum to drink,' Williams said. He was sitting with Minchin, Davies and Smith discussing recent events.

'What of it Corporal,' Lieutenant Minchin said. 'Surely we're more popular than Bligh.'

'Well that's just it, maybe we aren't. So either we win this battle for the heart of the people or Bligh does,' Williams said. 'We've asked a number of our associates to put the word about that Bligh is the one stopping the trade, not us. Yet it hasn't really changed anything. The people are still blaming us.'

'Do you have an idea of what we should do then Corporal?' Minchin said. Williams hated the way that Minchin used Corporal rather than his given name when in the barracks. He felt as if the Lieutenant was talking down to him, reminding him of his place all while expecting Williams to solve the problems.

'Other than keep telling people about Bligh's role, no, I don't know what else to do.'

'Well that's a first for you Corporal,' Minchin said.

'Come on Nate, we'll go see Henry Adams and have another chat with him.'

Davies watched the two junior soldiers walk out of the room. 'You were a bit hard on the young lad Will.'

'Sometimes he annoys me. He has the major's ear and runs the books and gets all the plum assignments. It just irritates me is all.'

'He's a very smart lad and uniquely qualified for the role of keeping the books. He had the trading side of things humming along delightfully until Bligh cruelled it. Just because he's smarter than both of us doesn't mean you should hold it against him.'

'Well I do hold it against him.'

'So you admit that he is smarter than you?'

'Shut up Robert,' Minchin said. 'And by the way where's the major? Haven't seen him in days?'

'I think he is taking a bit of time out at Annandale with the family."

'And leaving us here in charge then?'

'Well there's not a great deal to do these days,' Davies said. He stared into space for several moments. 'I miss the old days.'

'Next thing you will be lamenting the colonel and pining for England. Get yourself together Robert.' Minchin sighed and looked out the window. 'Perhaps I should become a gentleman farmer and part-time soldier like the major. At least it would alleviate some of this boredom.'

Williams and Smith were sitting in the back room of The Londoner with Henry Adams. Barrels of wine and bottles were neatly stored and the room was cool but not cold. All three men sat on small barrels with a glass of rum in hand.

'I have been telling people that it's Bligh whose behind the shortages,' Adams said. 'That it's the governor who controls imports of rum and wine. I have said he's the one who has banned stills and sets limits on prices. The people don't really care about those things.'

'Do they still blame us for the shortages?' Williams said.

'Some do, some don't.'

'How can they blame us? It's so clearly Bligh even I get it,' Smith said.

'Because in the past when Hunter and King were in charge and trying to ban rum you Corps men still came up with the goods. You kept supply going and the whole town was awash in rum. Now the only thing some people see is far less rum flowing. People don't care about the policies of the Governor. Instead they wonder why the Corps that was once so fearless and able to keep the rum flowing now doesn't do so.'

'So what do we do about it?' Smith said.

'I don't bloody well know,'" Adams said.

Williams looked at Adams and Smith and was keenly aware that the two had turned to him to solve the problem. 'I don't really know either. With rum no longer a currency and the Governor cracking down on controls I don't see a way around it.'

'So for now the best thing to do is probably drink up,' Smith said. He swallowed down the last half of rum in his glass. 'At least that is one small amount that has escaped the Governor.'

Williams and Smith left and headed to Ravi Chandra's shop. Chandra was closing for the day when the two soldiers arrived.

'Ravi our good man, how are you?' Smith said.

'I am well. How is trade with you? I have not seen you around for a while. You know that I always have customers wanting more rum. Can you help out in this please?'

'We don't have any rum for you,' Williams said.

'Some supply now would be easily sold for a great profit. It's the same everywhere since your supplies have dried up. Except of course in some of the outlying areas.'

'What does that mean Ravi? What do you know of it?'

'One of the farmers from on the Cumberland Plain was here recently and told me that there is illegal distilling going on. He said some government men are also supplying rum, only they have shifted their enterprises from here in Sydney to the farms and small communities.'

'Does Bligh support this?' Smith said.

'The Governor doesn't know what is happening.'

'So he is probably popular out there then?'

'The farmers when they come to town do not complain about the Governor like others here do. They have little reason to. The people in those communities are happy with things as they stand.'

'Ravi, you said that the people here in town complain about the Governor?' Williams said.

'That is right, he's not a popular man. He demands respect without having properly earned it, if you ask me. I have heard it said that he swears a great deal and is now intent on tearing up illegal land grants and houses built without permission.'

'You hear that from who Ravi?'

'I would prefer not to say.'

'Who Ravi?'

Chandra looked around, swallowed hard and then looked around again. There was no one else nearby. Williams wondered who Chandra thought might overhear the conversation. When Chandra looked around again Williams realised that the Indian shopkeeper was not worried about being overheard, he was hoping for someone else to come by to rescue him from answering the question.

'Ravi!' Williams said harshly.

'Do you know the Chief Commissary, Clerk Mann? Governor King allowed him to build a house next to Government House, so he could be close to work. This was when he was personal secretary to King and often was called on to work all odd hours. Well Bligh has begun ordering buildings that he considers unfit or illegal to be torn down. One of those is Mr Mann's house. When Mann spoke to the Governor and explained that under English laws his house was legally built he said Bligh shouted "Damn your laws of England. Don't talk to me of your laws of England! I will make the laws of this colony, and every wretch of you, son of a bitch, shall be governed by them." Mann now faces losing his house.

'To make matters worse Mann says that Bligh has stopped handing out land, that new settlers and freed convicts cannot now build houses unless the Governor allows it. Yet he will not hand out land to them to build on.'

Williams looked in shock at Chandra. 'Please do not tell anyone I have said of this,' Williams heard Chandra say.

'No, I won't tell of this,' Williams said.

Smith and Williams left feeling shaken. 'The way Ravi puts it makes it sound like Bligh is doing what he wants?' Smith said.

'That's what concerns me so much Nate. He seems hellbent on running the colony how he sees fit. We need to talk to Minchin, he has a contact in the Governor's mansion. Let's see what she knows.'

Minchin listened to the report by Williams. He too looked shaken. 'Surely not even Bligh is so willing to put people offside. Pulling down houses, refusing to hand out new land grants, stopping trade in rum. Mac is right, he wants Sydney as a penal colony and to undo all that has been done. I will see what I can find out from my lady friend.'

The following day Minchin returned shaken. 'It's much worse than we thought,' Minchin said to the gathering of officers. 'Bligh has it in for us, for the Corps. He blames us for what he calls the evil tendencies of many as we supply the rum that lets those tendencies out.

'Bligh's view is that we are becoming a dangerous militia and associate with too many convicts and ex-convicts. He is against some of our non-commissioned officers owning and running pubs.'

'So what's he intending to do about this?' Sergeant Major Whittle said.

'He wants to rotate other regiments through here, a year or two for each regiment.'

'Where does that leave us?' Smith said.

'If Bligh has his way either sent to England, and then God alone knows where, or forced to resign. Make no mistake gentlemen Bligh is out for us and he wants to remake Sydney into a penal colony. He alone sees himself as the law here, the man to make the laws and the rules and the man to enforce them. If he breaks us then he will be the law here.'

'So what do we do about it?' Whittle said.

'What do you mean Sergeant Major when you say "do about it"? Do you have something in mind?'

'No sir, that's why I'm asking you?' Whittle said to Minchin.

'How much longer is Bligh here for?' Quartermaster Laycock said.

'That's the problem, no-one seems to know. Unless a new governor appears soon then it is safe to say a couple of years at least. He has not even been governor for twelve months, so unless he is recalled ...' Minchin said, trailing off into his own thoughts.

'Can we write to England, seek his removal?' Davies said.

'On what grounds? That we don't like him?' Minchin said. 'We would need to have solid evidence of wrongdoing.'

'What about his tearing down Mann's house and other houses?' Williams said.

'We can't go into bat for Mann. That's his call not ours. Do we know the names of others whose houses Bligh has ordered torn down?' Minchin said.

'I'm just trying to think of ideas,' Williams said.

'Do you have any better ideas?' Laycock said.

Minchin spun around and glared at Laycock. 'I don't like your tone Quartermaster.'

'Careful,' Davies said. 'Everyone calm down a little.'

'I don't think I need to calm down, Robert,' Minchin said to Davies.

'Does anyone have any ideas?' Davies said glaring at Minchin.

'I don't think you are going to get any takers,' Laycock said.

'That is twice now Quartermaster. Watch yourself,' Minchin said.

'Right everyone is dismissed. Go home and calm down,' Davies said.

Smith was the first to reach the door where he ran into one of Bligh's messengers. 'From the governor,' was all the man said before he quickly disappeared.

Smith turned on his heel and walked back in to the mess. 'I thought I told you to leave Corporal,' Davies said.

'This just came from the Governor,' Smith said handing over the missive to Davies. All the officers stood and watched as Davies opened it.

'We ... we are confined to quarters for the remainder of the week, at the order of the Governor,' Davies said.

'He can't do that,' Laycock said. 'What about all the men who live nearby?'

'Oh he is clever,' Minchin said.

'Whose clever?' Whittle said.

'Bligh. Don't you see what he's doing? He's ensuring that we must follow his command. If we leave the barracks we are disobeying a direct order from the Governor, which would be grounds for court martial. He's imposing his will on us.'

'You don't have to sound so admiring,' Whittle said.

'I am not admiring him, but it's a clever tactic. And it stops us trading and being seen around town. And as Williams said the other day there are many people asking where the Corps is when it comes to supplying rum. Now we won't even be seen around town.'

'So what do we do about it?' Smith said.

'Unfortunately we follow orders,' Minchin said.

'What about our families?' Williams said.

'What about them Corporal? They will have to stay at home.'

'Sergeant Major we may have to sound the general assembly,' Davies said.

'I don't think we need bother,' Laycock said. He was standing at the door of the mess watching soldiers heading into the barracks. 'I think the message is already out there.'

'How much longer must this go on?' Smith said. 'It's been a week and still no word on when we can get out of here.'

'It's alright for you. You don't have a wife and children out there like some of us do,' Conner said.

'So that makes my misery here less than yours does it?' Smith said.

'That's not what he meant Nate, is it Tom?' Newbank said.

'Don't tell me what I meant and what I didn't mean, you don't speak for me,' Conner said.

'Since when, Private, did I give you permission to call me Nate?' Smith said glaring at Newbank.

'Begging your pardon, Corporal,' Newbank said before walking away muttering to himself. 'High and mighty for a whore's friend.'

'What precisely was that statement Private?' Smith said standing and walking towards Newbank.

'Well if you think that was directed at you perhaps you agree with the description,' Newbank said.

'For God's sake that is enough, all of you,' Minchin said. 'One week in here and everyone is at each other's throats. We're better than this.'

'Are you saying that or ordering it,' Conner said.

'Damn it Private I will have you up on charges if you're not careful.'

'Have you ever stopped to think this is exactly what Bligh wants. All of us fighting and to have charges laid and to drive wedges between us,' Davies said. 'Think about it, if someone ends up on charges then we will have to convene a court martial.

'If we find one of own guilty then that proves that we have lost our discipline and Bligh has grounds to send us to England or God knows where else. There is talk that the English may side with Spain and Portugal in fighting Bonaparte or it could be India or who knows where we end up. If we have a trial and let one of our own off then that proves the point that we are corrupt and unable to instil discipline and the same thing happens. Bligh has a case for shipping us back to England. So everyone just shut up, make the best of things here.

'In fact I have a better idea. Corporal Smith, you want some action? Let's have a drill on the parade ground. Make some noise and show Bligh that he cannot lock us up here for a week and break us. We'll show him how disciplined we are. Sergeant Major Whittle, if you please, let's have some drill work on the parade ground.'

'With pleasure Lieutenant,' Whittle said smiling.

The drills lasted an hour and a half with the Corps attracting a large crowd. Minchin and Davies passed along each row with the same message.

'Go to the fence and tell the people that we are doing as ordered by the Governor. We're confined to barracks and not currently able to have the freedom of the town. Pick your targets, the gossips and rumour mongers and tell them quietly that the Governor does not approve of our trading in liquor. Tell them Bligh wants to send us back to England so that no-one opposes him. Tell them we are obeying orders out of respect to His Majesty and not to the Governor,' Davies said.

For the next hour a range of conversations were held beside the fence with people drifting off in ones and twos, many with a clear idea of who wanted to end the flow of liquor.

'So how many do you think heard us and liked what they heard?' Minchin said. He was sitting in the mess hall with the officers and non commissioned officers following the drill.

'Quite a lot I think Lieutenant,' Williams said.

'I would agree with that assessment,'" Laycock said. 'I personally spoke to three gossips and they will already be out tattling about what is happening.'

'Good, then let's see what happens from here,' Minchin said. 'Perhaps the governor will get the message and let us out again.'

'Do you think Bligh will do that? He seems intent to have us disbanded or back in England?' Laycock said.

'Well he can't keep us confined to barracks forever. There are things that need to be done by the Corps,' Minchin said.

'You know if the major were here things could be different. He would not stand for this,' Williams said.

'The point is he is not here like the rest of us, and why that is I do not know,' Minchin said.

'What exactly are you suggesting here Lieutenant, that the major is in on this?' Laycock said.

'I'm not suggesting anything Quartermaster and I don't wish to get into another argument with anyone. I'm sick to the stomach with arguing,' Minchin said. 'All I know is that while we have been here the major has been noticeably absent.'

'In fact the major has not been here for some time, even before this confinement to barracks,' Whittle said.

'Well good luck to him I say,' Laycock said. 'Hopefully he is working on the outside to get something done.'

'That is if he even knows we're stuck in here,' Minchin said.

'You keep saying, Lieutenant, that you don't want to argue with any one,' Laycock said, 'and yet you continue to try to provoke some of us. Why is that?'

'I don't like your tone,' Minchin said. 'Maybe you need to be up on charges.'

'We just went through this didn't we?' Davies said. 'Do I need to get you all out on the parade ground again?'

'So now you're in charge are you?' Minchin said.

'I have had enough of this,' Davies said walking out of the mess hall, followed by Laycock, Smith and Williams. Whittle and Minchin watched them go.

'Well that at least clears up who's on my side then,' Minchin said smiling at Whittle. The Sergeant Major stood from his chair and walked to the door.

'I thought it was us against Bligh, Lieutenant, or have you forgotten that?' Whittle said. He slammed the door behind him as if to punctuate his query in the loudest way possible.

A messenger arrived at midday the following day. Without saying a word he handed a dispatch from the Governor to Private Gray who stood on sentry duty. Normally Gray was content standing at the gate but over the last few days he had been grateful for the respite from the constant bickering and arguing.

Gray looked around and saw Connor walking nearby. 'Tom, a message from the governor. Better get it inside quick.'

Conner grabbed the envelope and walked quickly inside, hoping that the message would end the confinement. He walked into the mess hall and handed the envelope to Davies. 'Lieutenant, it's from the Governor.'

All conversation in the room stopped. Men shuffled forwards in their chairs, not daring to look at one another. 'What does it say?' Smith said.

Davies opened the letter and read it quickly, aware that the men were watching him. Despite the attention he could not help but look in disgust at the letter.

'It's bad news isn't it?' Smith said. Someone groaned and several of the men shook their heads in disgust.

'Its England isn't it, we're being sent back to England,' Newbank said.

'The Governor has ordered that regular patrols of the colony outskirts be undertaken by the Corps, and that at all times half the men be at the barracks and ready for action.'

'Action against what? And what are the patrols looking for?' Laycock said.

'At least it's not England George,' Conner said to Newbank.

'The Governor does not specify, other than to remind us that we in the Corps are responsible for the security and safety of this colony. His lordship seems to think he is still at command at sea,' Davies said.

'So what do we do?' Smith said.

'We do as we're ordered. We conduct patrols of the outskirts, and we rotate two duty shifts, one at the barracks, the other off duty, changing over as often as we can,' Davies said. 'We will try to ensure that each man has an opportunity to be at home or off-duty every second day and night.'

'So who gets to be off-duty first?' Smith said, voicing the question each man was asking in his head.

'Married men get the first night off, we'll make that tonight,' Davies said.

'Of course the married men get the night off,' Smith said.

'Corporal, I am trying to do this as best I can,' Davies said. 'Would you rather we draw lots? Or would you prefer that I change the shifts from daily to weekly? For now this is how things will be. And I would note Corporal Smith that the married men are here until 6 pm tonight. The rest of you had better be back by then or I will lay charges,' Davies said. 'I would've thought with the pent up frustration of a week in here six hours is far more time than you need.'

Smith stood looking at the Lieutenant, grinning.

'Well you are wasting valuable time Corporal standing around grinning like an idiot. Mind you it is something you do well,' Davies said.

Smith turned and grinned at Williams on the way out. 'Looks like you are about to get dropped right in it. Have fun Nate,' Williams said smiling.

'Corporal Williams, Quartermaster Laycock, please let the men know of the arrangements,' Davies said.

Williams and Laycock quickly left the room and started informing the men of the changes ordered by the Governor. 'How about I get a few of the married men and we run a quick patrol now, just to be seen to be doing the right thing by the Governor,' Williams said. 'Besides, it will be a change just to be out.'

'Good idea young man,' Laycock said. 'I'll let the Lieutenant know.'

The routine for the next few weeks was set. The two shifts of soldiers worked to meet the Governor's orders while doing their best to convince the people of Sydney that the bans on rum were the doing of the governor.

That night Williams returned home. 'So finally the brave and handsome soldier returns home to his beloved wife and child,' Mary said.

'Mary I missed you so very much,' Williams said.

'Like fun you did. I wager you spent each night in the barracks drinking and roughhousing with the lads. Oh what a terrible burden it must have placed on you,' Mary said laughing. 'It's good to have you home. You know the baby is asleep and if we stay quiet…'

'Since when have you ever been able to stay quiet Mary?'

'Well if you are going to insult me I'll just have to go out to the pub and leave the baby with you. Don't worry he is growing up fast and probably more mature than you already. So I'll leave him in charge, unless of course, you want to apologise?'

'Mary, I humbly apologise and promise to do my best to keep you happy.'

Later the two lay in each other's arms. 'You know Oli maybe being confined to barracks is not so bad, if you are going to be so loving when you see me.'

'Mary it was awful.'

'Oh thank you very much you ungrateful …'

'Not you, now. The barracks was awful. The men were at each other the whole time arguing and bickering. And the shadow of Bligh was cast over us the whole time. He wants to rid the colony of the Corps, send us to England or who knows where else.'

'Well he can't send you away Oli, this is our home now.'

Williams was quiet for a time.

'Tell me he can't send you away Oli?' Mary said, sitting up and pulling the blanket up over her body. 'You can't go.'

'It hasn't come to that yet. However if the Corps are ordered to leave I am a part of it and would have to go or face court martial. The penalty for deserting is death.'

'No, I love you, and refuse to let you go.'

Mary rolled over and began sobbing. Williams reached for her but she snatched the blanket away and walked over to the cot where Henry lay sleeping. Gently she pushed the child over to make room and lay down beside him, crying softly.

Not for the first time Williams heard Mary's words 'You will have to choose sides, between us and the Corps'.

August 1807

The convict work crew arrived at the end of Soldier's Row early in the morning. A rough looking convict named Clemson thumped on Private Gillard's door. Gillard opened it. 'What on earth are you doing here,' he said to Clemson. 'This is the Corps's part of town and this is my house. Now get the hell out of here.'

'Got our orders to bring this house and those two there down today,' Clemson said.

'Orders? What do you mean orders?' Gillard said.

'Its all in here,' Clemson said handing over a written document with the governor's seal. Gillard opened it up but could read almost none of it. As he looked up Clemson was already stripping down to his shirt sleeves.

'Right lads, let's take her down,' a voice said. Gillard looked and recognised the speaker as Martin Miller, one of the convict supervisors responsible for handing out work assignments and ensuring the work was done. Miller had been transported for life for killing a bailiff in a brawl, and was known around Sydney as a hard man not to be crossed.

'Joanna, run up to the Williams' and get Oli down here and then go to the barracks and get Lieutenant Minchin or Davies. Go now, quickly,' Gillard said to his wife.

The convicts watched Joanna go as they started taking out their tools. Gillard went into the house and emerged again with his musket, glaring at Miller.

'What are you doing with that soldier-boy,' Miller said. 'We have orders direct from the Governor. This house was illegally built and must come down. Are you gunna dispute that? Maybe Clemson should go get the constables, tell 'em someone is defying the Governor's orders? Or maybe we can just sort it out ourselves.'

Miller and Gillard looked at each other, the former standing on the road, the latter on his verandah. Miller smiled a leering smile, goading Gillard into action. 'Don't worry lads,' Miller said, 'soldier-boy here doesn't have the balls to do anything without an order from his officers.'

'Well look here, if it isn't one of those very same officers. Now things could get interesting lads,' Miller said as Williams arrived.

'What's this all about?' Williams said.

'Orders here from the Governor condemning this house to be knocked down. We have it on our list for the day,' Miller said. 'So here we are ready to knock it down.'

'May I see that order please?' Williams said.

'You accusing me of lying?' Miller said.

'No, I am simply asking to see the order please,' Williams said.

Joanna came running back down the road, still in her night clothes.

'Don't worry sweetie, once your house is knocked down you can stay with us,' Clemson said walking towards Joanna.

'Back off,' Gillard shouted advancing into the street.

'Just offering the lady something better than being a dirty Corps whore,' Clemson said. 'What are you afraid of? Afraid that she might like it with us? I bet I could give her a better fucking than you ever managed. She'd probably like it too, right sweetie.'

'Convict scum!' Gillard yelled, lifting his musket and aiming it at Clemson.

Williams raced forward and knocked the gun upwards as Gillard discharged his Brown Bess, the lead ball flying just over Clemson's head. Convicts ducked for cover and Miller screamed something at Gillard that sounded like murderer, though Williams could not be certain of what he heard.

Joanna screamed as Clemson tried to grab her. Gillard raced forwards and Williams followed. Clemson threw Joanna to the ground and reached for a club he had concealed on him, leering at Gillard as he swung the club menacingly from hand to hand.

Miller yelled 'At 'em boys' and the convicts all produced clubs and truncheons, readying for a fight. Williams grabbed Gillard by the arm and screamed 'Get Joanna' in his ear. The two soldiers dodged the first wild swings of clubs from the convicts and grabbed Joanna, hauling her up and moving quickly backwards until they all tumbled over the fence into Gillard's yard.

Clemson and another convict raced ahead of the others, jumping the low fence and then stood over Gillard and Williams, each preparing to swing a club downwards. Williams managed to kick at and hit the knee of the convict above him, causing the man to stagger and drop down onto the hurt knee. He screamed in pain before again raising the club. Williams covered his head and face with an arm, trying to push Joanna back with the other hand.

Clemson stood over Gillard. 'I am going to enjoy this,' he said. Gillard yelled something defiant to Clemson and Williams was surprised at the soldier's fight. Then Clemson smiled.

The volley of shots that rang out was deafening. Everyone froze and then bodies scrambled in every direction trying to get to cover.

'Patrol front rank, reload. Rear rank step forward and take aim,' Minchin shouted. Williams rolled over and grabbed Gillard and Joanna and together the two soldiers tried their best to cover her body with their own, waiting for the shout of fire.

Clemson and the other convict nearest Williams tried to jump back over the fence looking for cover. Convicts scattered running in low crab-like lines for the security of houses and trees, desperate to avoid the volley aimed at them.

'Now that I have your attention, you can all back off, now,' Minchin said. 'Miller you rogue bastard, you had better show yourself now and get this convict rabble under control or else so help me God I will order my men to do their worst.'

'If I come out you'll kill me,' Miller said.

'Ain't so brave now you cowardly little bastard, are ya?' Gillard yelled.

From behind a fence Miller peaked around and looked at the Corps soldiers still standing and taking aim. The rear row of soldiers had finished reloading and stood ready to step into line and take their shots.

'Miller I see you. Now stand up and get these men under control,' Minchin said. 'Do it.'

Slowly Miller stood up and then ordered the convicts to assemble by him. Williams and Gillard were close enough to see Miller trembling.

'We was only doing what we was ordered to do,' Miller said.

'Be that as it may, your orders apparently were to dismantle a house, not some of my soldiers. You, Clemson, I'm not surprised to see you at the centre of this. Sergeant Major Whittle, please take Clemson and the other man attacking our soldiers into custody. We will turn them over to the constables in due course.'

'You can't take my men into custody,' Miller said.

'Try and stop me Miller. Oh please try and stop me. Nothing would give me greater satisfaction right now,' Minchin said.

'We have orders from the governor,' Miller said.

'This is military land, handed over to the Corps by Governor Philip. Everything built here is legal, so go back and tell that to the governor,' Minchin said.

Miller looked at Minchin. 'But my orders ...'

'I will give you until the count of five. After that I will consider that you are defying me and trying to stop my men from taking violent criminals into custody.'

'You wouldn't ...' Miller said.

Whittle led half the first row of soldiers forward to where Clemson and his fellow club man were standing.

'One, two, three, men take aim, four ...'

'We're going,' Miller said, backing away quickly. A number of the convicts were already running off. Whittle's party secured Clemson and his compatriot.

'You two,' Minchin said, pointing at two of the convicts slowly backing away, 'stand where you are. You will not be harmed. You will witness that these two arrested men will be treated decently by the Corps, despite what they were willing to offer my men. Miller you agree to that?'

Miller nodded and continued to back away lest he also be singled out to remain behind. He waited until he was close to a group of the convict labourers and quickly jumped behind them, using them as cover as he walked away as fast as he dared.

'Are there no lows that he will not stoop to?' Davies said. He was standing outside a hut beside the parade ground at the barracks, with Minchin and a handful of Corps men. Clemson and the other convict were inside the hut. The other two convicts selected by Minchin were standing nearby talking to Hutton and Conner.

'He is supposed to be the governor, applying the laws fairly, not a despot bending the rules to his needs. At this rate he'll have us all begging for his leave to do the most basic of things,' Davies said.

'Can he just order houses be torn down?' Smith said.

'If a house has been built illegally, on land that is not owned by the builder then yes. But Philip gave us this land almost twenty years ago. In that whole time not one complaint has ever been made of houses being built illegally. This is tyranny,' Minchin said.

'Here are the constables,' Williams said.

'So what's all this about then?' Constable Oakes said.

'The two men inside the hut attacked a woman and the two soldiers who came to her aid,' Minchin said. 'Had my men and I not intervened I believe that all three would have been injured or killed.'

Oakes looked in the hut. 'Clemson, I might have known to expect you.'

'I was shot at Oakes.'

'That's Constable Oakes to you. So who shot at you and what exactly did you do to deserve that? And please don't say nothing. With you it's never nothing.'

'Private Gillard shot at me only 'cause I made a suggestion to his woman,' Sewell said. 'Is that now outlawed here?'

'He was going to tear down Gillard's home, Constable Oakes,' Minchin said.

'Well I know Clemson is a reprobate and cause of a great deal of trouble but I doubt even he just decides to tear down a house,' Oakes said.

'It was on the order of the Governor,' Clemson said. 'Miller was our supervisor, ask him.'

'Is this true?' Oakes said to Minchin.

'That house is built legally on Corps land. This man had no right to tear it down and besides he was armed and attacking unarmed men and women,' Minchin said.

Oakes rubbed his face with both hands. Watching from a distance the action may have appeared prayer-like, but up close the groan that accompanied it said something altogether different. Here we go again, Oakes thought. He was tired of being caught in the middle between the Corps and the governor, with hired hands acting as proxy for the governor.

'Right, well clearly these men can't stay here,' Oakes said. 'And these two, what about them?' Oakes said pointing to the two convicts standing watch nearby.

'We asked them to come along to ensure that no harm was done to Clemson and his associate. They are free to go,' Minchin said.

'You two up and let's go,' Oakes said to Clemson and his associate. 'I will have to talk to the Governor's office about this and figure out just what we do. My best advice to you all is to forget this happened and move on, lest Private Gillard be charged for shooting at these men.'

'You weren't even there and already you have him guilty on the say-so of convicts,' Davies said.

'I don't have him guilty at all, that is the lot of the courts. But you can see where this is going to go unless someone backs down and the other side agree to do the same. Besides, if Gillard is charged you lot will probably try him and we all know how that ends. Thank you and you are free to go Private. Why not let these two go now and we all just move on with matters?' Oakes said.

'I thought you were impartial in such matters, letting the courts decide?' Minchin said.

'Usually I am, but today I'm tired. If you lot here want to go to war with Bligh so be it, it will end badly for all. But does it have to start here today?' Oakes said.

'What do you mean go to war with Bligh?' Davies said.

'It is hardly a secret that Bligh has it in for you lot. Or that you lot have it in for Bligh. He wants to run this colony his way and you want the good old days back. So do you think it a coincidence that Bligh sends these men here today to start up trouble? He will tell me you have defied him and his orders. You will say that it is not his place to act here and then the whole thing just escalates. Do any of us really want that?' Oakes said.

'What about my house?' Gillard said.

'I don't know. Take it to court like everyone else whose house has been ordered destroyed,' Oakes said. 'That should buy you some time. Now am I going to be able to go and deal with all the other things that need my attention? Or do I arrest these two on your say so, arrest Gillard on their say so, and wait to see what happens next?'

Minchin looked at Davies who nodded. 'All right they can go but if they show up here again things are going to get very serious,' Minchin said.

'I think shots being fired and men locked up is serious enough, don't you Lieutenant?' Oakes said. He turned and walked away, followed by Clemson and the other convicts.

'How dare he do this to us,' Minchin said. 'He has no right to send convicts here to our turf. We ought to march down to Government House and tell him how we feel.'

'Do you think Bligh would care, or do you think he would welcome it as further evidence that we need to be sent back to England?' Davies said. 'He's trying to provoke us into doing something stupid and he nearly succeeded today. We must be careful from here, do as we are asked and run these patrols and keep our heads down. Soldiers are not to go out alone, they must move in small groups. No carousing or fraternising with convicts and no incidents of any type. I will send a messenger to Mac about Gillard's house and see what he recommends.'

'What about the major?' Minchin asked. 'It's beyond time that he put in an appearance, don't you think?'

'I agree. Perhaps I will see if Mac knows what's going on there,' Davies said. 'Right who's leading this afternoon's patrol?'

'I am,' Williams said.

'So before you head out call on me, I'll have a message for Mac. You are to deliver it yourself.'

'Yes sir.'

It was mid-morning before Williams, message to Macarthur in hand, led the patrol out of the barracks. They turned and headed slowly out towards Parramatta. Tom Conner walked next to Williams.

'Oli, things are starting to get out of hand. How does this all end if Bligh has it in for us?'

'I don't know Tom.'

'Jess, my missus, is worried that we will be recalled to England. She likes it here and says that if I am ordered back I should resign and stay. But I can't just do that and when I told her ...'

'She didn't take it too well?' Williams said.

'She took it real hard. Complained that I had misled her. She said that she will be left here with our child and nothing else while I spend most of a year getting to England and then who knows. And her here alone. I'm afraid she might leave me, find another man to support her,' Conner said, looking at his feet and struggling to hold in his emotions. 'Oli, I love her and don't want to lose her and yet if Bligh has his way then I fear I will.'

'Tom, you're not the only one in that boat. I am and so are more than half the men. Mary will not go back, nor Jess nor most of them. The women have a freedom here undreamt of in England. And Lord knows they would not be short a suitor or two if we weren't here. I wish I knew how this ended but I don't. All I know is that Mary has said I will have to choose between the Corps and her, as if I have an actual choice. I don't know what to do about it any more than you do.'

'So you two have had the discussion with your misusses as well,' George Newbank said from behind Williams and Conner.

'If we go back will Rebecca stay here or go with you?' Williams said motioning for Newbank to join him and Conner in the front ranks of the patrol.

'She wants to stay here. When she got transported she thought it was the end of her life. Then a while later she got a letter from an aunt telling her that her mother had died so she really has no close family in England. Here and now she has a wonderful life compared to before. Do you know that in England she could not fall pregnant, yet here she has fallen twice for two healthy babies. The women say it is the air and climate and soil that does it, though I'm not so sure.

'Personally I think that here we eat better than any of us could ever have hoped for in England. When I was back there I didn't know what most vegetables even looked like and mainly ate bread and sometimes mutton gruel growing up. Here the markets have so many vegetables that I still have to ask what some of them are, so I reckon that is something to do with the babies.'

'You done philosophising George, fascinating though it is?' Williams said.

'Well it's better than thinking about having to go back while Rebecca and my children stay here.'

'Out of curiosity just how many of the men with wives and girlfriends have had the same discussion about staying and going? Do either of you know?' Williams said.

'I don't know for certain but my reckoning would be most,' Conner said.

'I agree with you Tom, most of the men I know are keen to stay on here,' Newbank said.

Williams sighed. 'Well for now enjoy the walk and the fresh air and not living at the lower rungs of society.'

They marched on for some time, joking and laughing about silly things, occasionally picking up stones and seeing who could hit some nearby object. Williams always judged how well the men were travelling by the level of banter and the tone of the discussions and gradually he felt the mood lighten.

For the first time in weeks it felt as though there was more to the future than Bligh and what happened with the Corps. He missed Mary, who had been remote and had shared little, and wished that she were there with little Henry and they could amble along and enjoy the sunshine.

Looking out over the landscape still reminded him of a country estate in England. His thoughts turned to owning a piece of land, perhaps running some sheep and cattle. He told himself he had no grand plans, yet he doubted he could bury his ambitions and resign from the Corps.

A thought that had long lain dormant suddenly surfaced again. Would he get promoted beyond Corporal if he wasn't here with the Corps? Was he only a Corporal due to his skill in managing the rum trade, in keeping the books? Did he have what it took to be a soldier under different commanders?

He felt at home in Sydney with the mercantile bustle of the wharves, the warehouses and shops. What were his options? Run some imports using the money he had saved, take a share in a boat and bring in some trade goods, use his contacts with the Corps to buy and sell rum and make more money? So much for no grand plans you fool. And how would that work under Bligh? Would the man allow such trade? There was only one alternative.

Commanding soldiers in the field, the privilege of rank and the ability to make good money from trade — he did not want to give it up for something else. The money he had saved could buy a commission. Would he do that in England were he to return? Could he convince Mary to leave Sydney, to live as an officer's wife? They would have to hide the fact that she was a convict, that could never be tolerated or accepted. Hardly acceptable for an officer and gentleman to have a convict wife, to have a child that was half the making of a criminal.

A shadow passed across the sky, covering the sun and taking its heat away and with it the optimism and joy that Williams had so recently felt. The doubt about his promotion rushed in. Did he have it in him to make it as an officer outside the Corps? When the cloud moved and the sun beamed its warmth and hope again Williams could not take it in. Mary or the Corps. Damn Bligh and damn it all he thought. All he wanted to know was what his future held.

He looked out again at the landscape and then thought of Mary. It was time to ask her about the future.

'Mary I am home,' Williams said walking into the house. Mary sat in a chair, Henry asleep in the cot near her. Williams looked at her. She looked tired. The stress of recent weeks, not knowing her future, was beginning to show in her face.

Mary slowly stood and walked over and kissed Williams on the cheek, more out of routine than affection. 'I have made some dinner for us. Eat while Henry is still asleep.'

Williams swallowed hard. He had rehearsed this speech in his mind most of the afternoon: how he would begin, what arguments he would use, and the resulting reconciliation with Mary. What he said and how it ended were not even close to his imaginings.

'Mary, we need to talk about the Corps and us,' Williams said. In his rehearsal he had begun by professing his love of Mary and Henry and had not even mentioned the Corps until later.

'What about the Corps?' Mary said sharply.

'I didn't mean it like that, but Mary I can' just up and leave the Corps. I have obligations.'

'And what do you have here? Hopefully something more than obligations, although we wouldn't know it from the time you spend with the Corps men. You will run off and defend someone else's house or travel halfway across the colony for a horse race, but too often of late you're not here, not ready to defend us should we need it.'

'That is not fair Mary and you know it.' 'I know it, do I? What else do you want to tell me I know? That I should follow you and the Corps to England? Here's something you should know. Everyone believes that Bligh has it in for you all, and that his solution to the problem that you soldier boys have created is to ship you off. We all know it, all of us women here. And what do we get for it? Not support from our men. Instead we are told to pack up and follow you all. Well it's not that simple.'

'It is if you love me.' Williams immediately regretted his words.

'Oh I love you, more than you probably realise, but my life is here now. I have Henry. I have a home here that in England I could only dream about. I thought I had you but now I'm not so sure. My love for you is real whether I choose to follow you or not.'

'I don't understand? How can you say that? If you loved me you would follow me.'

'And leave all that I have here, to be what? A camp wife following a soldier around, mending your uniform while you stay late in the mess? Do you think you will get anywhere when your wife is an ex-convict? I will be shunned and you will have to make choices. Where am I in that? Who am I in that world you want?'

'But, what, what if we stayed here?'

'And how does that happen if you stay in the Corps and it gets sent back to England? I told you a choice is coming, between Henry and me or the Corps and the men who back it. Why is that so hard? Don't I matter to you?' Mary began sobbing.

Williams walked over to her and placed his arm around her. She shrugged it off violently and walked over to stand beside the cot, staring down at her child, still sobbing. Williams looked at his wife and realised that for the first time he did not know what he wanted. The choice between the Corps and a military career, and Mary, was not one he had seriously contemplated until now. Once it had been so clear, yet that time felt distant, as great as the distance he felt between himself and Mary now.

Williams looked at her and waited for something. Instead Mary climbed into the bed and rolled over, alone with her thoughts.

September 1807

'So I visited the Major yesterday,' Minchin said. 'I felt that I could no longer just sit by, that I needed to know why he has not been around.'

Davies leaned forward in his chair in the mess hall. 'And what came of it?'

Minchin was aware that all the conversation in the room had now stopped. A dozen eager bodies leaned forward mirroring Davies. They all wanted to know, Minchin thought, so here goes.

'Two of the major's children have been very ill and he has been staying at home in Annandale to help manage the situation,' Minchin said, repeating the line he had agreed with the major. The truth, Minchin knew, was far less palatable, that the major had lost the appetite for the fight and sat brooding at home.

'Fortunately the children will recover, although for a time the major believed he would lose one of them and possibly both,' Minchin said. 'Despite this he is aware of Bligh's dictates to us, of the Governor's orders. The major has written to the Duke of York, the commander in chief of the army about Bligh. The details of the letter he wished to remain private, however he asked that I share some of his words. In relation to Bligh's order the major has said to the Duke that Bligh's "abusing and confining the soldiers without the smallest provocation" was outside the chain of command or law.

'The major writes that Bligh's "casting the most undeserved and opprobrious censure on the Corps were example of his indecorous and oppressive" conduct towards us. The major concluded by saying that "Governor Bligh seems ignorant of any instructions or rules whatever, but such as are dictated by the violent passion of the moment". Major Johnston is fighting for us as best he can under the circumstances.'

'Do you know when the letter was sent?' Whittle asked.

'Some time soon after we were ordered to remain in the barracks. It will still be on the seas to England but it's on its way. For now the major asks that we keep ourselves from trouble and do our best to make this current situation bearable.'

'It's good to know that the major is still fighting for us,' Whittle said.

"I would expect nothing less from him,' Laycock said.

'There is more that I need to share, that the Major told me. Some of the wealthy traders have had enough of Bligh's favouring of Robert Campbell and others who would tell Bligh what he wants to hear. They are suffering from Bligh's policies and believe that the colony cannot grow while Bligh is governor.

'Together they have gathered a fund of £1,500 to send Mac to England to lobby the Home Secretary for Bligh's removal. This is a serious undertaking that these men are making, such is the precarious nature of the future of the colony,' Minchin said.

'When does Mac leave?' Davies asked.

'Soon. Once the *Parramatta* is returned he will sail out. The message from Mac and from the major is clear; we will be under Bligh's tyranny for some time yet, but a new day is coming and with it a return to our standing and mercantile pursuits. For now we must be patient.

'I know that many of you are having a hard time with the rumours that Bligh wants to send us back to England and what that means for you at home … well I know that it's not easy. The Major is in this position too, and keen to let you know that he and Mac and others are doing what they can to ensure that we remain here and the old and good days return once Bligh leaves. So let us do what we can to make the best of this, knowing that in time the tyrant Bligh will leave.'

'That day cannot come soon enough,' Laycock said. 'I was speaking with Doctor Arnold, the former naval surgeon now here and he told me of Bligh's manner. He said Bligh was "overpowering and affrighting every person that might have dealings with him, expecting from all a deference and submission that the proudest despot would covet".'

'What exactly does that mouthful mean?' Smith said. Several of the men laughed.

'Translate it into English,' Hutton said.

'That is His Majesty's English in its purest form, but since you lot are far from pure I will translate it into terms you understand,' Laycock said. 'The power has unhinged him and he wants everyone to bow before him as though he were king here.'

'Right, well that is a fine translation,' Hutton said. He leaned across to Smith. 'At least now I know what he is talking about.'

Smith smiled and nodded. 'So for now we just carry on doing as we have been, keeping our selves out of trouble and doing as ordered?'

'Correct Corporal, and hopefully Bligh will be recalled and we will stay and not the other way around,' Minchin said.

The patrol was skirting along a road running south from Sydney near Botany Bay when the movement first attracted Williams's attention. He stopped the small column of troops and they quickly cleared the road, the left line of troops ducking down into the trees on the left of the road, those on the right moving to the right side of the road and taking cover.

'What is it?' Gillard whispered.

'I'm not sure,' Williams said. 'I saw movement, I think it was a person.'

The troops stayed in their positions, crouching and lying on the ground below the trees for several minutes. There were few sounds: a rustle of wind in the trees, a bird calling, somewhere far off an animal making a snorting whistling sound.

Williams looked at Gillard who lay next to him. Gillard looked back and shrugged. 'Maybe it was a roo.'

'Maybe I just imagined it,' Williams said, searching the terrain ahead.

'Corporal, on the left about a hundred and fifty yards ahead,' Newbank said quietly from the other side of the road. Williams looked at Newbank and saw the soldier pointing into the distance. He followed the line of Newbank's hand but could not see anything. Williams make a gesture of questioning to Newbank.

'Come here. You can see them from here,' Newbank said.

Williams looked across the road and noticed a number of the troops quietly adjusting their weapons, loading muskets and fixing bayonets. Someone was out there. He looked at Newbank and indicated that the soldier should signal when it was safe to cross the road.

Newbank waited several moments then motioned with his hand. Williams raised himself to his feet and keeping as low as he could while still being able to run raced across the road and dropped down beside Newbank.

'There Oli, a few of them. Do you see them?' Newbank whispered, pointing his hand at a copse of trees nearby.

For a moment Williams wondered if everyone was seeing things and then he saw the shapes of two men move across a clearing behind the copse, their fleeting images fading and then reappearing between the trees.

'Maybe an illegal still,' Newbank said.

'I think you're probably right,' Williams said.

'Do we take them, or send a runner back to alert the constables, or leave 'em be?' Newbank said.

Williams looked at the copse and the occasional glimpses of men amongst the trees. It was tempting to simply leave the area quietly, report the whole thing to the constables and be back home in time for tea.

'We could just slip away and report them,' Newbank said, seemingly reading Williams' mind.

'That sounds good George,' Williams said. 'However, maybe we can win a little favour with Bligh, show him we are worth having around.'

'You thinking to taking them and breaking the still up?' Newbank said.

'When I was on the other side of the road that slight rise up ahead kept me from seeing the same thing you were, so let's use that to advantage. I will slip back over the road and take half the patrol to circle around behind. You take our soldiers on this side and move carefully forward and we should be able to surround them.'

'Okay Oli, sounds like a good plan. I'll let you make the first move, as it should take you longer to get into position.'

'Good man,' Williams said placing a hand on Newbank's shoulder. Then Williams raised himself and raced back across the road. He explained the plan and together with Gillard,

Hutton, Gray, Conner and Mulligan they began the careful task of flanking the men ahead.

'Do you think there'll be shooting?' Gillard asked.

'It's a chance,' Williams said.

'Just remember lads if there's any shooting make sure you stay behind the Corporal,' Conner said.

Gillard and Hutton chuckled.

'That's enough. Time to shut up while we get into position,' Williams said blushing at the insult to his shooting ability.

Williams led the way, crouching low and treading slowly, sometimes stopping to test his footfall lest it break a branch or disturb a rock and betray the patrol's presence. The soldiers with him were concentrating hard on trying to place their feet into the same location as the man in front, while keeping low and barely breathing.

The going was slow. Williams grew anxious that Newbank's men would be seen before he had his troops in place. He gradually started to push the pace, still trying to be careful in his tread while also gaining time. Twice he slipped, landing once in grass that masked the sound of his fall and a second time landing hard on a rock, but despite the noise the men around the still remained oblivious to the approaching troops.

Slowly sounds from the men working the still became clearer, wood cracking in fire, the sizzle of steam and snippets of conversation. Williams tried hard to count the number of voices and was sure there were at least four men ahead. Each time he searched through the trees to the clearing he had to stop and he would begin to panic that they would not make it in time.

Finally Williams judged that his column of troops had flanked the still and were on the far side of the clearing. He signalled to the men to begin spreading out. Conner went left from Williams's position with Gillard and Mulligan following.

Hutton and Gray went right. At intervals of around two yards one of the troops would drop down and find a covered location with a view of the clearing.

There were now seven men in the clearing, Williams counted, but he could not be sure if more were obscured from his view or even located nearby. It was not uncommon to set up a camp near the still for a second shift of men to sleep so the still could be run as much as possible.

Carefully Williams pulled out his powder for the musket and arranged it on a rock in front of him. He poured some powder down the barrel and then dropped a lead ball wrapped in paper to sit on the powder. Slowly Williams withdrew the ramrod from its holder under the barrel and rammed the ball down into the muzzle to drive the lead ball into position.

He looked up checking the position of his troops while occasionally glancing at the clearing. In the quiet he could hear the fire warming the still crackling and the gurgling of the liquor as it distilled. Wary of making too much noise Williams carefully placed a small amount of powder into the flash pan of the musket, located above the trigger, and pulled the cocking mechanism back until it clicked, halfway towards full extension.

Next Williams pulled the frizzen into position to cover the pan and then clicked the cock back to full extension. The rifle was now ready to fire. Once he pulled the trigger the cock would slam forward, the flint attached to the head of the cock would strike the frizzen, pushing it back from the pan holding the powder. This would create a spark that lit the powder in the pan, allowing the lit powder and spark to burn through a vent in the barrel to light the main charge, sending the deadly lead ball to do its worst.

Unlike some of his fellow soldiers Williams was careful to keep the barrel as clean as possible to ensure no build-up of powder and residue in the barrel. He had heard stories of soldiers who did not clean their muskets. Such men had been injured when the powder in the barrel ignited behind a lead ball that was caught in powder residue and refused to eject from the muzzle. All that energy was in turn expelled in a small explosion of wood and metal centred around the trigger. Occasionally soldiers died from their wounds. Most ended up scarred, disfigured and blinded in at least one eye when the barrel exploded.

Williams meditated for a moment on such a possibility and put the idea out of his mind. Time for action he thought.

'You by the still, we have you surrounded. Come out with hands held high,' Williams yelled as he stood and started forward.

For a moment he heard nothing but the crackling fire and then the still began to hiss as though in warning. Williams looked for a moment to his right and Hutton stared back, a confused look on his face.

A shot came whistling past leaving a snapping sound ringing in Hutton's ears. Hutton fired a moment before he heard Newbank yelling 'At 'em boys' from the far side of the clearing. Williams was already a pace ahead, with Gillard, Conner and Mulligan ahead of him and moving into the clearing.

The explosion was deafening and the shockwave that followed knocked the breath from the men's lungs. Hutton fell to his knees and half slumped over struggling to stay upright. His chest felt empty and for several moments he struggled to get any air into his lungs. Finally he managed to stand and take a couple of breaths. Somewhere he heard screaming and urgent voices snapping out words that the ringing in his ears overwhelmed.

Hutton stared at his musket for a second convinced it had exploded but the flintlock mechanism was intact and the barrel still whole. He touched his face and felt no pain and convinced himself it was because his face had been blown apart. He lifted his hands before his eyes but they were dry and there was no blood.

Someone blew up the still, Hutton realised. And Williams and Conner and the others were heading towards it. Hutton stood and started to run towards the clearing. Screaming was coming from up ahead.

Finally Hutton made it into the clearing. Some of the soldiers were stamping on small fires with their feet. Williams and Gillard knelt over a body on the ground working furiously.

'Who is it? God did I kill one of us?' Hutton said.

As Hutton ran up to the body he heard Williams say 'He's dead' and felt a wave of revulsion rip through his stomach and head up his throat. Finally he reached the burnt body and unable to recognise a face because of the burns he turned and threw up.

'Who is it? Please tell me it's not one of us?' Hutton said.

'We don't know who he was, probably an escaped convict. Best guess is someone accidentally hit the still and it blew up spraying this poor bastard with burning liquor. He never stood a chance,' Williams said.

'So it's not one of us?' Hutton said.

'No it's not, everyone else is fine,' Williams said.

'I ... I fired because someone shot at me. You heard the shot didn't you Corporal?'

'Yes I did, but none of these fellows has a weapon,' Williams said.

'I think that was probably my shot,' Newbank said. 'We heard your call Corporal and when nothing happened we started to run in. One of the men lifted a piece of wood and I thought it was a gun so I fired.'

'Well you nearly hit me,' Hutton said.

'And so you decided to return fire knowing we were in the firing line?' Newbank said angrily.

'Only after you did the same,' Hutton said.

'That will do,' Williams said. 'Let's get these men tied up and clear the area and get back home.'

Newbank walked towards Hutton. 'Sorry, I think my aim was no better than the Corporals.'

Hutton smiled at the joke, accepting the apology. 'Yes, well don't make a habit of it.'

The soldiers set about checking the pile of barrels stacked nearby. 'All empty,' Newbank said. 'Looks like they were just starting operations.'

'Break them up and then let's get out of here and turn these men over to the constables,' Williams said.

'And what about him?' Conner said pointing to the dead man.

'Bury him here,' Williams said.

For the next hour the soldiers worked to break up the barrels that were to hold the distilled liquor. The prisoners were ordered to dig a grave for the dead man. When the work was done Williams walked over to the five men sitting with their hands tied.

'Any of you know who he was?'

'Fuck you Corps man,' one of the men with a bald head said.

'I just want to know his name so we can bury him and leave a cross marking his passing.'

'Duncan Porter, his name was Duncan Porter,' the man furthest from Williams said.

'Was he a convict or free man?'

'How should I know. But he was good at manning a still and brewing good liquor. You may want to mark that on his grave major arsehole,' the man said.

'Thank you, and I am a corporal, not a major,' Williams said.

Two of the soldiers lifted Porter's dead body and half-carried, half-dragged him to the grave where they dumped him. One of the soldiers had found an old piece of canvas and threw it over the body.

'Anyone want to say anything?' Williams said. He turned to the prisoners who remained seated. 'At the very least you could all stand.'

The prisoners remained sitting staring sullenly into the bush.

'Fine,' said Williams. 'Lord we commend this man Duncan Porter to you. Amen.' Then Williams nodded to the prisoners. 'Cover him over.' Slowly the prisoners stood and began kicking and pushing dirt into the grave. 'Use the bloody shovels,' Mulligan said.

'I'll use a bloody shovel on ye skull Corps man if you give me half a chance,' the bald prisoner said.

'If you think you are quick enough to beat my shot give it a go,' Mulligan said unslinging his musket and pointing it at the bald prisoner. The two eyed each other across the barrel of the musket, assessing their chances. Then the bald prisoner slowly raised his hands and grinned at Mulligan.

'Another time Corp man,' the bald man said. 'You better sleep with an eye open cause when I find you …'

Mulligan smiled and pulled the trigger.

Williams turned from where he was talking with Conner, Hutton and Newbank and saw the bald prisoner crumple to the ground. The soldiers raced over and Williams grabbed the bald man and rolled him over.

'Oh God he's dead too,' Williams said. 'What on God's earth were you thinking Mulligan?'

'He rushed me,' Mulligan said.

'No he didn't,' one of the prisoners said. 'You just murdered him cause ya could.'

'That's what happened Corporal,' said the prisoner who had earlier volunteered Porter's name. 'He just shot him for no good reason.'

'Mulligan, get over there,' Williams said pointing to a tree on the far side of the clearing. Williams looked at the prisoners. 'Start digging another grave.'

Williams followed Mulligan to the far side of the clearing. Newbank and Conner watched from near where the prisoners were beginning to work on a second grave.

'Jesus, what the hell happened Mulligan?' Williams said.

'I didn't like the way he looked at me and then he threatened me, said he would bash me skull in with a shovel. I told him to back off. Then he said another time, like he had marked me and would find a time to do me in, just like those bastards up Hawkesbury tried. Ain't no-one going to ever get the better of me Corporal. You cross me you die.'

Williams had noticed that ever since the Hawkesbury, when the locals had nearly beaten him to death, Mulligan had changed. But this, this was beyond the pale. 'I need your musket Private. There will have to be an inquiry about this.'

'So you too Corporal?. Always thought you were a suck up and not one of us. Here have it.' Mulligan lifted his musket and gripped it in both hands holding it across his body horizontal to the ground. He shoved it at Williams, letting it go with force. Williams reacted too late and was hit hard. Then Mulligan turned and ran into the bush disappearing from view.

Watching from the far side of the clearing Newbank and Conner saw Mulligan throw his musket and then sprint off into the bush. They in turn ran across to where Williams stood.

'What happened Oli?' Conner said.

'I told him we couldn't let this rest and that there would be an inquiry and he ran.'

'Do we follow him?' Conner said, looking into the bush.

'No, let him go. I doubt he'll last long and when he comes back to town we'll round him up then.'

'Bloody hell, you've had a very adventurous day indeed,' Lieutenant Minchin said. Williams had just finished briefing Minchin, Davies, Laycock, Smith and Whittle on the events of the day.

'So come on. While it's all still fresh in the mind let's go to Government House and you can brief Bligh himself,' Minchin said.

'Are you sure that's such a good idea?' Laycock said. 'I mean do you think Bligh will be that interested?'

'We need to win him over somehow and this is as good a start as any,' Minchin said. 'We show him we're doing what he wants, breaking up stills and cutting liquor supply and carrying out patrols that are helping implement his policies. What's not to like?'

'How about Mulligan murdering a convict in cold blood and then escaping?' Whittle said.

'Well, we leave that bit out,' Minchin said.

'Actually Sergeant Major, we don't even know who the man was, let alone if he was a convict,' Williams said.

'Wait, what?' Davies said. 'What about the other one who died?'

'His name was Porter, though what he was we don't know?' Williams said.

'Interesting. Very interesting,' Davies said. Then he stood and walked out of the room.

'What's he up to?' Laycock said.

'Never you mind,' Minchin said, wondering the same thing himself. 'Now young fellow, off to Government House.'

An hour later Williams found himself finishing his briefing for the third time that afternoon, this time before Bligh himself.

The second briefing had been given to one of Bligh's aides half an hour before. Minchin and Williams had arrived at Government House and asked to see the Governor. Instead they were ushered into a small room and presented with one of the governor's many aides.

'One does not simply invite oneself to see the Governor. On what matter does such importance attach itself?'

Minchin looked blankly at the aide, then to Williams. 'Er we have some information regarding illegal distilling of liquor. Is that of enough importance in its ... ah ... attachment?'

'Tell me,' sighed the aide. So Williams had provided a brief of events, leaving out the murder of the second prisoner by Mulligan.

'Let me see if the Governor considers this of sufficient importance to be interrupted from his duties,' the aide said, before heading off to find Bligh.

'Did you get his name?' Williams said to Minchin.

'No. They never seem to have names up here,' Minchin said. 'Perhaps they're not important enough to have such attachments.'

'Or we are not important enough to know such attachments.'

Within a few minutes the aide returned. 'The Governor is keen to hear your report. Please wait in the foyer.'

So Minchin and Williams had waited for half an hour until a door opened and Bligh appeared. Williams looked at Bligh. The man had a high forehead with a receding, curly hairline, and round almost cherubic face. He was shorter and less imposing than Williams imagined such a tyrant to be.

'So tell me about this still,' Bligh said.

Williams repeated his briefing, omitting only the murder of the second convict by Mulligan. When he finished he looked at Bligh, who in turn looked at Minchin.

'Where is Major Johnston?' Bligh said.

'Pardon?' Minchin said.

'Pardon Governor,' Bligh said. 'And Johnston?'

'He is indisposed at his farm Governor,' Minchin said.

'He is always indisposed on his wretched farm. One would think him a farmer rather than a soldier.' Minchin shifted uneasily, uncertain what to say.

'Now as to this still. It just shows that I have been right to have you pathetic lot out earning your pay doing some good, rather than doing the public mischief supplying liquor,' Bligh said. 'And when can we expect you to start selling the rum you no doubt confiscated?'

'We did not confiscate any rum Governor. None had been properly distilled,' Williams said.

'Don't you dare address me you insolent little prick,' Bligh shouted at Williams.

Minchin placed a hand on Williams's shoulder.

'Begging your pardon Governor, the Corporal meant nothing of it. He is correct in that no rum was seized.'

'No it was probably drunk on the spot. So the real question here is this; why are you not discovering more of these stills and putting them to fire? And I wager that it is because you are running many of them yourselves and only putting the odd competitor out of business.

'So bloody well get out of my sight and get out there and find more of these damn stills, including any of your own, and break them down until there are no more in my colony. Well, why are you standing in my foyer? Get the hell out and get to business. And consider yourself all under curfew again unless running patrols. The Corp is confined to barracks until advised otherwise. Patrols to be doubled and at least two damn stills a week broken up or else I will advise their Lordships that you are ready for duty in Wellington's impending peninsular war.'

Bligh turned and walked off, quickly disappearing through a side door. Minchin stood looking after him. Williams didn't know where to look.

'Still here?' the aide said, amused by his pun on stills. Minchin grabbed Williams by the shoulder and spun him around, then turned and shoved the Corporal towards the door.

'The conquering heroes return,' Laycock said to Minchin and Williams as they walked back into the mess hall. 'So how did it go?'

'Oh just great. We are confined to barracks again and ordered to double our patrols and break up at least two stills each week,' Minchin said.

'Is that all,' Laycock said smiling. 'So it went that well.'

'Quartermaster I am not joking. Those are Bligh's orders to the letter. So you and Sergeant Major Whittle had better start rounding up the troops and organising some more patrols. And for what it's worth Bligh thinks we are running illegal stills and has threatened to send us to help fight

Bonaparte unless we find and destroy at least two stills per week.'

'Aye sir,' Laycock said sighing. He and Whittle stood and left the room. Williams followed. Minchin picked up a glass and filled it to the brim with rum before downing half of it in one go. He looked at the glass and swirled the rum around inside it, wondering if rum were more trouble than it was worth.

Slowly the troops returned to the barracks having said good-bye to loved ones. Whittle and Laycock organised the men into patrol groups and set up a roster for each group. Once all the troops were back Minchin ordered Whittle to have the men assemble on the parade ground.

'Now lads, even if you don't find a still, report back that you had some level of success. Perhaps following some reprobates into the bush to establish where a camp may be or that you broke up a consignment of barrels heading into town,' Minchin said.

'And if we don't find anything?' Smith said.

'Then we may end up finding ourselves marching off to fight Bonaparte in Portugal or Spain, so bloody well find something to report back,' Minchin said.

A murmur went through the ranks of troops. So it was true, Bligh really was out for the Corps. 'He'll see us shipped off to war,' someone said. Half a dozen men all started to talk about their family, friends, businesses, investments. The noise grew.

'Shut up! No-one gave you permission to speak,' Whittle bellowed at the men.

'Thank you Sergeant Major,' Minchin said. 'For now we stay disciplined. We run patrols and find stills and things to report. We do as the Governor has asked and we do not give him a reason to send us away. Is that clear?'

There was a hollow sounding yes from a handful of the troops.

'Is that bloody well clear?' Whittle yelled.

'Yes,' said the Corps.

'Dismissed.'

Instead of the usual rush of men leaving the parade ground small groups milled about talking. 'Bligh really wants us out of here doesn't he?' Conner said.

'Do you think so?' Newbank said sarcastically.

'Steady on lads, no need to start anything,' Smith said. 'What do you think Oli, you met Bligh?'

Williams sighed. 'Bligh thinks we are little better than convicts. He blamed us for supplying rum and called us a mischief to the public. So yes he wants us out of here.'

'But can we change his mind, if we find these stills and do as he wants?' Conner said.

'I don't think it matters what we do, Bligh is determined to run this colony, or "my colony" as he called it, as he sees fit. I had the impression that no matter what we do it will never be enough,' Williams said.

'So where does that leave us?' Newbank said. He glanced around. By now almost two dozen soldiers were listening.

'Hoping Mac can convince the powers that be in London to get rid of Bligh. So for now we wait until the *Parramatta* returns and he can get to London,' Williams said.

'So up the harbour without a ship,' Conner said.

'Something like that,' Williams said. Quietly the group of men walked into the mess hall and found seats and began drinking.

It was some time later when Davies strolled back into the mess hall with a broad smirk on his face.

'What are you looking so happy about?' Minchin said.

'I just solved a very big problem for Mac,' Davies said. He looked around the room and realised that it was mostly full. 'Why is everyone here?'

'We are confined to quarters,' Minchin said.

'When did that happen?' Davies said.

'Earlier today after the lieutenant here dragged young Williams to Government House to brag to Bligh about breaking up a still,' Laycock said. 'And Bligh asked why it was only one still and threw one of his tantrums and here we are confined to quarters unless running patrols.'

'Shut up Quartermaster,' Minchin said.

Laycock smiled at Minchin. "Did I get that wrong? That is what happened isn't it? When you decided to speak to Bligh.'

'What the hell is that supposed to mean?" Minchin said.

'Nothing,' Laycock said, smiling.

'Be careful Quartermaster,' Minchin said.

'So does anyone want to hear what I have cooked up with Mac?' Davies said.

'Even if we don't want to hear it I assume you'll tell us anyway,' Minchin said.

'Yes I will,' Davies said. He smiled at Minchin and looked around the room. 'I have solved the problem of Gentleman John.'

A series of blank faces looked back at Davies. 'Gentleman John, the convict who absconded on Mac's ship the *Parramatta*. Or at least that is the rumour doing the rounds. The truth is that he is buried in a grave out in the bush having been shot point blank in the face by Mulligan earlier today.'

'That wasn't Hoare and you know it,' Minchin said.

'Ah but does Bligh know that? Do the courts know that?' Davies said.

'Do the four convicts now in the custody of the constables know that, or will they say that it wasn't Hoare?' Laycock said.

'Are you and Mac seriously going to try to pull this off? All it would take is for one of those four to contradict you and the whole charade is blown.'

'Or one of the crew of the *Parramatta* to confirm that Hoare was on board,' Minchin said. 'I don't even know who that poor bastard was that Mulligan shot but he is going to be missed somewhere and then what happens? And if this goes to court do we stand and say that we had the one man who can clear Mac of this problem in our hands and we shot him in the face? Isn't the whole thing just a little too convenient?'

'Not to mention that any number of people were saying that Hoare was keen to escape the colony, was seen talking to Glenn, the master of the *Parramatta* and was seen at the wharves when the *Parramatta* was due to leave,' Williams said.

'All this is going to do is dump us in it with Bligh even more,' Minchin said.

'That's a strong statement coming from you, given your outstanding efforts in that area this afternoon' Laycock said.

'Quartermaster I have told you to shut up once already today. Perhaps we need to escalate things to charges of insubordination,' Minchin said.

'What happened earlier today?' Davies said.

'Ask him,' Laycock said, pointing to Minchin, who glared back at Laycock.

There was silence in the room for several moments. 'Will someone tell me what on earth is going on?' Davies said.

'We went to see Bligh to report about the still and he said we were not doing enough, that we need to break up more stills,' Williams said.

'More stills?' Davies said. 'And where are we supposed to find these stills?'

'Bligh doesn't care where, just that we do,' Minchin said. 'He accused us of only breaking up stills belonging to our competitors and said we are a public mischief by supplying rum. The long and short of it is that we are confined to quarters and have to double our patrols and destroy at least two stills a week.'

'That will teach you to run off and brag to the governor,' Davies said.

'Better that than suck up to Mac and try to pass off ill-conceived schemes for his benefit while we wear all the risk,' Minchin said.

Davies walked towards Minchin, who stood from his chair. The two eyeballed each other from too close a distance to provide any degree of comfort to those watching. Men all around the room tensed their muscles and edged up out of their seats.

'For Christ's sake everyone stand down now,' Whittle bellowed in his parade ground voice. 'We are not going to do this again. Every time we are confined to quarters things start to go awry. Well not this time lads, not this time. Anyone that wants to start something outside on the parade ground now, and we will have this out once and for all. If not bloody well grab yourself a drink and shut the hell up, is that clear? Lieutenants, is that clear?' Whittle said.

Both Minchin and Davies looked in shock at Whittle calling them out.

'Well are we having a stoush with you two on the parade ground or are we having a quiet night in enjoying one another's company?' Whittle said menacingly.

Minchin turned and walked to the bar table at the end of the mess. He poured himself a drink and downed it in one go. 'Goodnight all, and make sure the patrol is up and out early tomorrow.' With that he walked out of the mess as the men slowly returned to their seats or wandered to the bar.

November 1807

For the next two months the Corps spent all but two weekends confined to quarters. Many of the married men and those with defacto partners chose to stay in the barracks. Several of the men who went home were back before the night was through. Quarrels broke out between soldiers over the smallest offences and slights and often led to pushing and shoving.

After each patrol the non commissioned and commissioned officers sat and wrote reports filled with fictions; of stills being discovered and shipments of illegal liquor seized and destroyed. The continual fictions placed further strain on the officers.

Life in Sydney echoed the life of the confined soldiers. Each day was the same. Everyone was on edge waiting for something to give in the cold war between Bligh and the Corps. Some people backed the Corps, others Bligh. Most remained undecided, waiting to see what would happen next and what that would mean for the people of Sydney. And for many that something was the answer to the mystery of where John Hoare might be. Answering that question would signal a path ahead and whose side to go all in on.

The *Parramatta* could not dock soon enough. Most of Sydney was abuzz with rumours surrounding the ship and the truth of where Gentleman John may be. One rumour suggested that John Hoare was in Tahiti living the high life, another that he was buried in a grave in the bush, another that he was living with Aborigines near Manly.

Each new ship entering the harbour caused a tumult of rumour and gossip. Crowds thronged at the wharves to see if the arrival was the *Parramatta*. At each false alarm tempers frayed.

The constables mounted regular patrols at the wharves once a signal from South Head suggested a ship was running towards the harbour. Two boats that tried to sail out to the heads to see arriving vessels capsized and two people drowned.

Day by day the anticipation reached a new height until it seemed impossible that the mood for the *Parramatta* to show her sails could swell even more. And yet with each new day the anticipation grew. Spring had come and almost gone. The wags and gossips fed the rumour mill offering expert opinions that the longed-for vessel must be due any day.

At the end of November a rumour began that the *Parramatta* had sunk on her return voyage. The fate of Gentleman John would never be known. Within hours all of Sydney were caught up in conjecture and analysis. Macarthur would get off the hook on which he was so close to dangling some said. Others hoped that the fate of Gentleman John would remain a mystery.

Conspiracies began to grow. Bligh was behind a plot to get rid of Macarthur and then the Corps and had Gentleman John in chains at Coal River. Bligh was framing Macarthur to break the Corps so he could cut the liquor consumed and run the colony as though a ship of the line. Others suggested that Bligh had let John Hoare escape on the *Parramatta*, still others offered that Macarthur had Hoare in safekeeping and would present his prize as the *Parramatta* sailed up the harbour, so as to humiliate Bligh.

Sides were being drawn and most of Sydney preferred a larger supply of rum and freewheeling commerce. To stand with Bligh was to stand for austerity and homes being demolished at the whim of a governor for whom the law was a plaything.

Talk began to fill the pubs of the need for a change of governor without any idea of how that may be possible. One afternoon Anthony Kemp, a captain in the Corps, based at Parramatta barracks, was in Sydney on business. When that was concluded he spent a good part of the afternoon drinking. He knew of the plan to send Macarthur to London to lobby for Bligh's removal. In the way of all unfulfilled men who know a secret and believe that sharing it will boost their standing Kemp was easily coaxed into telling that secret. Kemp's newly minted drinking mates suggested he share this news with Bligh himself. Drunk on liquor and false admiration from the roustabouts at the pub Kemp marched up to Government House and wrangled an audience with Bligh, but was soon back at the pub.

'So I told him,' Kemp said to his new mates, 'I told Bligh himself that Macarthur was going to London to have him removed and you know what Bligh said? He said "I am as irremovable as Ararat". As Ararat himself.'

'Isn't Ararat a mountain, where Noah's ark washed up? That is what Bligh means doesn't he?' said one of Kemp's drinking mates.

Soon enough the story was being shared, of how Bligh believed that he could not be removed from his post, of his scorn for Macarthur and the odds of London having Bligh removed.

Within days people were being asked to declare who they backed in the battle, the farmer at Cow Pastures or old Ararat himself. Often these questions resulted in sharp tongues cutting others off, in scuffles and occasional brawls. Sydney was being pushed apart into two camps with no middle ground. One was either for the Governor or for Macarthur and the Corps. With liquor in short supply and the governor having a stranglehold on its supply many wanted a return to the old days of trading by the Corps. Too many had seen their houses knocked down at Bligh's whim and others just didn't like being told what to do.

Sydney was rapidly turning on Bligh and his austerity measures. Visitors to the barracks where the Corps were confined continued to grow. People brought food, papers, gossip and pledges of support for the Corps though what this meant none seemed too sure of.

The only thing most people agreed on was that Bligh had to go. Every wag and blow hard had an opinion on the government and why it was failing the people. These were spiced with stories of Bligh's temper and foul language and played nicely into the narrative that the tyrant now saw the people of Sydney as he did the *Bounty*: a crew to be broken at all costs.

'Have you heard the news?' Hutton said rushing into the mess hall. 'A message has come from Tahiti. Gentleman John was seen leaving the *Parramatta* when she was anchored. He got himself passage on a ship headed to America.'

'Who said that?' Davies asked.

'Everyone. A ship docked this morning with the news. The Governor is more than happy to have the people spreading this rumour," Hutton said.

'So who told you then?' Davies said.

'My missus, she dropped by earlier to tell me.'

'Bloody hell, this could be it for Mac. It's what Bligh has been waiting for, something to hold Mac over the barrel with,' Davies said.

'So much for your grand plan to pass off that convict as Hoare,' Laycock said.

'Well at least I'm trying to solve the problem rather than sitting around gossiping about it,' Davies said.

'Is there any news on when we should expect the *Parramatta*?' Williams said.

'Within the week,' Hutton said.

'What will Bligh do?' asked Smith.

There was a long silence. 'So for all the gossip and rumour no-one actually knows what Bligh is going to do?' Smith said. 'Oli, you are the brains here, say something.'

'Allow me to fill in the blanks,' Minchin said from the door. He had been standing quietly listening to the conversation. 'In all likelihood the only thing Bligh can do is enforce the bond.'

Again there was a long silence and a number of blank stares directed at Minchin. 'That means all Bligh can really do is make Mac pay the bond. And Mac has the money to do that, so I am really not sure what all the fuss is about.'

'Yes but this is Mac we're talking about,' Davies said. 'The only thing he loves more than his sheep is his money. He's probably at home buried in his legal books trying to find a way out of paying up.'

There was a general round of laughter. 'So are you saying Mac loves his sheep more than Mrs Macarthur?' Smith said grinning.

'Not in that way you pervert,' Davies said with a wink. 'But if I know Mac he'll have a plan to wriggle his way out of paying. I am willing to wager that he's already tried to get Blaxcell to buy out his share of the ship.'

'Not even Blaxcell is that stupid,' Minchin said. 'But I'm inclined to agree with you. Mac will find a way out of this. Lads top up your glasses. To Mac. May he show up Bligh and get off the bond.'

When asked later if he would have proposed the toast in the full knowledge of what support for Macarthur would lead to, Minchin thought for a moment and said yes, anyone in Sydney would have at that time.

December 1807

The morning of December 6 was cloudy with showers regularly passing over the harbour. This made it difficult to see the lighthouse on South Head so many missed the signal that a ship was entering.

The *Parramatta* was halfway up the harbour when word began to pass around. Cries of 'She's here at last' rang out over the town. People climbed windmills and raced to Observatory Hill to watch the ship tacking back and forth across the harbour. A large number of constables gathered on the docks to keep the people well clear.

Robert Campbell, Bligh's appointment as Naval Officer led a small deputation of men down to the wharf. The *Parramatta* finally nosed her way to the anchorage just beyond the main docks and lowered her anchor. Campbell and three men climbed into a tender and were rowed out to the ship that was the centre of attention.

Despite the Corps being confined to quarters Laycock, Williams and Smith mingled with the crowd that was now being held back by the constables. Minchin and Davies wanted a first hand account of what happened when the *Parramatta* arrived and had ordered the three to quietly slip out of the barracks and keep a watch.

The usual procedure was for a ship to drop anchor, a tender to row out with a representative of the Naval Officer and for the ship to present its papers, outlining the nature of the cargo it held, ownership and port of origin.

The Naval Officer was responsible for sighting these papers, directing the ship to a dock and issuing instructions about the cargo; which warehouse it should be sent to and what cargo may not be unloaded, such as supplies of liquor. The whole process usually took an hour. People in the crowd settled in for the wait, assuming a search of the ship and its crew would take place.

Less than five minutes after the tender pulled up alongside the *Parramatta* it started heading back to the shore. 'Something is up. Campbell and his cronies are already on their way back,' Williams said.

The crowd started to press forward, eager to know what was happening. A rumour swept over the people: they have found Gentleman John. From one end of the mass of people to another the words flew. Within moments the tender reached the dock and Campbell and his compatriots climbed up to the dock.

'Is Gentleman John with you?' someone cried. The crowd started to press forwards, a woman screamed and then a chant of 'Show us John' started. Constables struggled to maintain their footing as the crowd swelled forward. 'Show us John, show us John.'

Campbell stood on a crate and yelled for silence. Slowly the chant died down and Campbell felt the noise was low enough for his voice to carry. 'I have placed the *Parramatta* under arrest on grounds of allowing a convict to escape. John Hoare is not aboard the *Parramatta*, having taken passage on another vessel in Tahiti, bound for America.'

The crowd, just a moment before so certain that Gentleman John was about to appear, started to boo. Campbell and his men were escorted away by a number of constables. The remaining constables yelled orders for the crowd to clear. Laycock, Williams and Smith did not wait around to see anymore and made their way back to the barracks as fast as they could.

'So that's it for now, the ship is under arrest and the next move is over to Mac,' Williams said to the men in the mess hall.

'What will he do?' Smith said.

'We can only wait and see,' Davies said.

The following day came news of Macarthur's big play.

'So Mac has relinquished his ownership of the *Parramatta*,' Davies said. 'He wrote to the master of the ship, Glenn saying "I have abandoned the said schooner and that neither you nor them are henceforward to look to me for pay or provisions". Mac is justifying this on the grounds that the arrest of the ship by the Naval Officer has dispossessed Mac of his ship.'

'Can he do that, just abandon the ship?' Whittle said.

'Legally he has a right to do so. The real question is what does Bligh do?' said Davies.

As it turned out Bligh did nothing other than wait.

'The papers are saying that by abandoning the ship Macarthur is no longer duty-bound to feed the crew,' Williams said to the men lazing in the mess hall. 'How long can they hold out before they decide to come ashore?'

'Ah that is the thing Corporal, the crew are unable to legally leave the ship and come ashore without breaching local regulations. Bligh would know that having been a ship's captain. I suspect that he is waiting until the crew can no longer manage and decide to try to leave the ship,' Davies said.

'And then what?' Williams said.

'Then it becomes a question of who is responsible for the crew and if charges can be laid if they breach the regulations and come ashore?' Davies said.

'You are remarkably well informed on such matters,' Whittle said. 'Are you thinking of becoming a lawyer? Or are you in contact with Mac?'

Davies smiled. 'Wouldn't you like to know Sergeant Major?' Davies got up and left the mess hall.

'Yes I most certainly would like to know, because I see nothing but trouble ahead. This is the end game and only one of Bligh or Macarthur will survive it.' Whittle muttered to himself.

A week after the *Parramatta* anchored the crew jumped ship. A number of constables were running patrols day and night at the docks. When the crew lowered a tender and rowed ashore the constables stood ready for a confrontation. Instead they got a big surprise.

'I am master Glenn of the *Parramatta*. We hereby surrender ourselves to you, left with no choice by the owner of the schooner, Mr Macarthur.'

'Mr Macarthur says that he has abandoned the schooner and is no longer responsible for you,' Chief Constable Oakes said to Glenn.

'You do not understand. We have not been given supplies for a week and have nothing aboard left to eat. 'Tis Mr Macarthur's actions in depriving us of food that have brought us ashore and nothing more. Even if a ship is arrested or impounded it's the responsibility of the owner to feed the crew. Macarthur has not done that. I would request an interview with Governor Bligh to let him know of our position and the role of Mr Macarthur in bringing us ashore,' Glenn said.

'Camberwell, get yourself to Government House and let them know of the situation here and the master's request to interview with the Governor. Then get back down here and let us know what we do about it,' Oakes said.

Camberwell took off up the hill from Sydney Cove towards the Governor's residence as fast as he could.

'Right then gentlemen,' Oakes said, 'in the interim we will get depositions from each of you about John Hoare, and about what happened in Tahiti. Then you can try to justify why you have breached regulations and come ashore despite your ship being under arrest.'

Oakes was skimming through the depositions taken from the crew of the *Parramatta* when Camberwell returned. 'The Governor said he does not wish to interview with Glenn. Governor Bligh is content for us to take depositions from each man and then turn these over to the Naval Office for a decision on forfeiture of the bonds,' Camberwell said.

'The Governor does not wish to see me, despite what I have to say about Mr Macarthur?' Glenn said.

'The Governor is not in the habit of meeting with those complicit in a crime, as you likely are given the assistance you offered a convict to escape the colony,' Oakes said. 'Gentlemen let us take these sailors to the station and give them accomodation while Mr Campbell decides what the Naval Office will do.'

At midday the Naval Office announced that the bond payable on escape of a convict from the colony was forfeited.

News reached the Corps' mess hall soon afterwards. 'So Mac is off the hook then, the bond is forfeited?' Gillard said.

'No you fool, quite the opposite. The bond being forfeited means that Mac has to pay it. And to make matters worse he and Blaxcell each threw in an extra £50 surety so both men owe £900,' Davies said.

'What will they do?' Smith said.

'No-one really cares what Blaxcell does, it's all down to what Mac will do,' Williams said.

'How about we consult the oracle of all things Mac,' Laycock said. 'Lieutenant Davies, what do you divine Mac will do next?'

'That's not funny,' Davies said.

'Actually it is funny,' Minchin said. 'I take back most of what I have said about you Quartermaster.'

'Well?' Laycock said to Davies.

'Mac and Blaxcell will appeal having to pay the bond,' Davies said.

'Appeal to who and how do they do that?' Minchin said.

'They'll need to petition the Governor,' Davies said.

'Does anyone else see a flaw in that plan?' Minchin said. 'Bligh is hardly going to let them off now is he?'

'Bligh will have to be careful to ensure that procedural fairness is followed lest he be accused of having it in for Mac,' Davies said.

'Do you make these terms up?' Laycock said. 'I mean procedural fairness, it sounds like one of the silly French names the whores at Madame Brigitte's use doesn't it.'

'It means that Bligh has to do everything properly, following the law. Everyone knows that Bligh has it in for Mac and for us for that matter,' Davies said. 'So he can't just make decisions, he has to be seen to be doing the right thing legally.'

'Or else what? Someone will complain?' Minchin said.

'Yes, like Mac when he goes to London,' Davies said.

'You mean if he goes, don't you?' Williams said. 'How can he leave the colony when he is obligated to pay a bond?'

'I am sure he has a plan,' Davies said. 'I will see him tomorrow when I take a patrol out past his place.'

'So that's why you have been leading patrols,' Laycock said.

The soldiers stayed at the end of the long driveway that led to Elizabeth Farm, the Macarthurs' home near Parramatta. Davies was so familiar with the long walk that he fancied he could have walked it blind-folded, so many times had he been there in the past few months.

Macarthur was not on the porch as usual and so Davies knocked and waited for a reply. Eventually a servant girl answered and ushered him into Macarthur's office. Legal books were spread all around the room, some opened, others closed with multiple bookmarks.

'So Bligh is having me investigated by that shit Atkins, who has decided to side with Bligh,' Macarthur said. 'Atkins is saying that the master and crew of the *Parramatta* have violated the conditions of their arrest coming ashore. Which is something I think everyone knows. Trust Atkins to make the obvious sound even more so.

'At the heart of it is the idea that the crew justified their actions by alleging I had given them no means of subsistence aboard the ship.' He absently waved the letter at Davies. 'Read the final lines.' Davies grabbed the letter and scanned it till he located the final lines. "In consequence of such their representations I request your attendance at Sydney tomorrow morning, at 10 o'clock to shew cause for such your conduct".

'What will you do Mac?' Davies said.

'I have already drafted a letter to Atkins. I have reminded the dullard that as the Naval Officer illegally detained the vessel I have declined any further ownership of the ship and that as such I am justified in not paying or feeding the crew. I have reminded Atkins that he has already been informed of this and the whole affair now has nothing to do with me. Of course I have dressed that up with words that it will take Atkins a good few hours to understand with the aid of a dictionary.

'And to end the letter and turn the screws on Atkins a little I have referred him to the Naval Officer for what further information he may require. None of this has anything to do with me and that is made sufficiently clear.'

'So will that be the end of it Mac?'

'Oh good lord no, Bligh will push this as far as he can. The fool seems to think if he can get me to pay £900 I will be bankrupted and he will be rid of me. Let me tell you that is far from the case and as far as I am concerned breaking that foul-mouthed sailor is the only thing that currently occupies me. And if it takes ten times what I owe on that bond it will still be a worthwhile investment.'

'So it really has come to that. It's you or him and only one of you can continue on here?'

Macarthur smiled a dangerous smile. 'Absolutely, isn't it fun?'

Davies swallowed hard. He had grown used to Macarthur's moods over the past few months and once he had seen beyond those had grown to admire the man's intellect and tenacity. The qualities that made him a fine officer also made him a fine business man, Davies thought. What scared Davies was Macarthur's appetite for risk; for all-out war with Bligh. It chilled Davies to the bone, yet he could not step back from it, from the secret thrill of having a ringside seat to the contest.

'And the best part of it all, Robert, is knowing that you and the Corps are behind me the whole way. Now let's have a drink and you can get back to playing soldiers and I will get on with running my colony.'

'By Christ I am growing to hate that man,' Atkins said to Chief Constable Oakes. 'Macarthur seems to think we are all here to serve his needs. He thinks he knows what is best for us and we really only matter when he needs something from us.'

'Some might say the same of the Governor,' Oakes said.

'Yes they may. We are surrounded by high and mighty men who each have a view on what this colony should be, yet none seem to want to hear from us as to what we want.'

'It's the way of government, Mr Atkins. They all know best even when they don't have an idea of who it is they are supposed to be helping. Still you didn't summon me here to ruminate on the ways of the world now did you?'

'No I summoned you as I need you to present this warrant to Macarthur. Complaints have been made on oath that Macarthur illegally stopped providing for the crew of the *Parramatta*, which incited the crew to violate colonial regulations regarding unauthorised landings. Furthermore I issued an official letter to Macarthur summoning him here to appear before me regarding these matters. He refused to do this so you are to deliver this warrant to Macarthur personally. It requires Macarthur to appear before the magistrates on Wednesday 16 December at 10 am. I should then like you to return here to let me know what happened.'

'As you wish Mr Atkins. I will head out there now.'

John Macarthur looked at Oakes, standing on the porch holding the warrant. 'What do you want?' Macarthur said.

'Mr Macarthur I am asked by Chief Magistrate Atkins to provide to you this warrant, requiring you to …'

Before he could finish Macarthur snatched the warrant from Oakes's hand and turned and walked inside, slamming the door. Oakes turned to leave when the door opened and a servant girl asked him to wait. 'The Master will be out shortly to see you.'

Oakes looked out over the gentle sloping ground that meandered to the river. The playing of lords and ladies and manor houses were a part of England, not this new colony. And now Macarthur had his servants calling him the Master. The man's ego knew no end, thought Oakes. Perhaps it came from living in isolation in the country, but then again, perhaps seeing so much land only spurred Macarthur on.

A few minutes later the door was opened by the servant girl. 'The Master will see you now.'

Oakes waited several moments and then started walking towards the door when Macarthur came out. 'Here is my response. Take it to Atkins and show it to him, but you must keep this paper as it constitutes my justification for my actions.

'I have considered what is asked of me here and reject any such notion that this situation can rest on me. Tell whoever is behind this that if the persons directing that warrant had served it I would have spurned them from my presence. If you come a second time come well-armed for I will never submit until there is bloodshed.

'These people have robbed me of £10,000 and now they maintain to lay upon me their own folly. They are fools and you and I should leave them alone for they will soon find a rope to hang themselves. Now be gone from my premises and remember I will never submit short of bloodshed and then much of it if needed.'

Oakes stood rooted to the spot, trying to understand the wild-eyed man before him, promising bloodshed. It was not until Macarthur turned and again went inside the house and slammed the door, leaving the servant girl outside with Oakes, that the Chief Constable thought again on the promise of bloodshed. The hairs on his arms and neck raised up as his mind raced. Then Oakes left the porch and walked as quickly as he could to his horse and mounted the animal and trotted down the long driveway to the road.

Only when he was well away from Elizabeth Farm did he stop and open the paper from Macarthur. The words were written in a messy script that reflected the hint of madness that Oakes had seen in Macarthur.

Mr Oakes - You will inform the persons who sent you here with the warrant you have now shewn me, and given me a copy of, that I never will submit to the horrid tyranny that is attempted until I am forced; that I consider it with scorn and contempt, as I do the persons who have directed it be be executed.

J. McArthur
Parramatta 15 December, 1807

Oakes reread the letter again. 'Horrid tyranny, scorn and contempt...never will submit...until I am forced'. Macarthur had to be mad or playing a very dangerous game. He was clearly in breach of the bond of £900 and there was a sound case that the crew of the *Parramatta* were his responsibility. A ship's owner could not simply abandon a ship while in safe anchorage. To force the crew to violate the laws of the colony regarding illegal landing by not feeding them was on Macarthur's shoulders. What on earth was the man attempting? Did he think he was above the laws of the land.

By the time Oakes had recounted his meeting with Macarthur Atkins's mouth was agape. Initially the chief magistrate had stopped Oakes to ask questions, by the end of the report Atkins was dumbfounded.

'What on earth does he hope to achieve by this?' Atkins said after a good minute's silence. 'His actions amount to sedition, refusing to recognise the authority of the law in His Majesty's colony is ... well it cannot be anything other than sedition. By God the man could hang for this.'

'So what do we do?' Oakes said.

Atkins looked at Oakes but his mind was in another place. For the best part of twenty seconds he was quiet. 'You will please summon the remaining magistrates of the colony, Major Johnston, Mr Palmer and Mr Campbell, here as soon as possible. Do not accept any excuses, they must all come at once. What time is it?' Atkins said.

'It is after four in the afternoon, should I summon them all here today?' Oakes said.

'Ask them all to be here tomorrow morning at 10 am, no excuses. They must all come.'

'Right you are Mr Atkins.' Oakes left and rode hard to the constables' offices in Sydney. Riders were sent to relay the messages to Johnston at Annandale and to the other magistrates.

At 10 am the following morning Atkins, Johnston, Palmer and Campbell sat in Atkins's office. 'Gentlemen, what I have to tell you is both alarming and of extreme importance to this colony.'

Palmer winked at Campbell and slyly muttered 'Here he goes again,' under his breath. Campbell chuckled to himself. Atkins was well known for over-egging the pudding, with a reputation for turning the ordinary into an emergency from which only Atkins himself could save the colony.

'Yesterday a warrant was issued to John Macarthur regarding his need to appear here on 16 December to answer questions regarding the recent events that occurred on the *Parramatta*, and the violation of colonial landing orders,' Atkins said. 'Chief Constable Oakes, will you please relay to the magistrates your meeting with Mr Macarthur.'

Oakes repeated the story that he had told Atkins the previous afternoon. Once again when he finished there was a long silence. Palmer and Campbell exchanged a glance then looked at Johnston. Atkins too looked to the major, uncertain of what the soldier would say.

'There is no choice but to issue a warrant for Mr Macarthur's arrest for a hearing to determine if he should stand trial,' Johnston said.

'On what charges would you prefer this hearing put forward?' Atkins said.

'For goodness sake Robert dispense with the silly legal talk,' Palmer said. 'It is clear that the charges must include sedition. We all see that so just speak it plainly.'

'Alright then, there is no doubt in my mind that in refusing to submit to the warrant that Oakes delivered him, Macarthur is defying the law of the land. His reference in the letter to Oakes of horrid tyranny is aimed at the Governor,' Atkins said.

'What letter?' both Campbell and Johnston said at the same time. The two men, often opposed on matters of trade, looked at one another, surprised by this momentary alignment in thinking.

'Mr Oakes, do you have a copy of the letter for tabling?' Atkins said.

'Here you are gentlemen. This is what Mr Macarthur handed me yesterday in response to my giving him a copy of the warrant.'

The magistrates read the letter in silence which lingered for several moments after each man had finished it.

'Good God, what is he thinking?' Palmer said. 'This amounts to a statement of utter contempt aimed at Bligh and the law of the land. It cannot go unchallenged. Macarthur has to know that.'

'I think that Mr Oakes should be provided with a warrant as soon as possible and get out to Elizabeth Farm with a group of constables and arrest Mr Macarthur,' Campbell said.

'You know he will post whatever bail is necessary for his freedom,' Johnston said.

'So are you saying your old mate should be allowed to sit in his manor house and ignore the laws of the land?' Campbell said.

'You know I am not saying that Robert. I have already said we have no choice but to issue a warrant for his arrest. We need to be aware that while he is on bail Macarthur does not abscond or gather supporters to him. So I would suggest we sit tomorrow morning to hear the committal case against him. This needs to be done properly or else we will completely divide the colony into the pro-Bligh camp and the pro-Macarthur camp. That, gentlemen, is the worst possible outcome.'

'Mr Oakes, how long do you need to gather a sufficient force of constables to arrest Mr Macarthur?' Campbell said.

'I can have that done within an hour, then another to ride out and execute the warrant.'

'Good, please see to it,' Campbell said.

'Wait,' Palmer said. 'I want to hear it from each man here that they are in agreement.' Palmer looked at Johnston.

'I agree,' Johnston said.

'Then get it done Mr Oakes,' Atkins said.

So much for each man agreeing, Johnston thought.

Four hours later Oakes arrived at Sydney police station with John Macarthur under arrest. 'That took longer than you anticipated,' Atkins said. 'Did he try to live up to his promise of bloodshed?'

'No, we had to change our plans. Macathur was out visiting. We arrested him at the home of the surveyor-general, Mr Grimes.'

'Pity, a part of me was hoping he would honour his promise and you would do us all a favour and shoot the bastard dead,' Atkins said. Macarthur, who was nearby, glared at Atkins, who returned the stare with a smile.

'Do you wish to post bail Mr Macarthur?' Atkins said to Macarthur.

'Bloody silly question Atkins, but then I wouldn't expect any other type of question from you,' Macarthur said.

'£500 bail then,' Atkins said smiling.

'I was expecting more,' Macarthur said. He quickly handed over the sum. 'I am expecting that back.'

'Well then you best be here tomorrow morning at 10 am for your committal, otherwise you can wave this money and your freedom goodbye,' Atkins said.

'I look forward to it,' Macarthur said. 'Just spare us all your high-handed legal terms. I expect a great deal of the colony will want to watch and it would be best if they actually understood what you are trying to say. Of course the assumption in that argument is that you do understand what you are trying to say, which is why one never assumes anything.'

'What does that mean?' Atkins said.

'Tempting though it is for the defence to rest here, I will help illuminate your sorry condition by answering you. There is a rumour around that you are quite an accomplished legal mind, but of course that is the beauty of most rumours, they aren't true.'

Oakes and several of the constables smirked, and one even laughed aloud.

'What does that mean? What's so funny?' Atkins said.

'Now the defence rests dear boy,' Macarthur said.

'I am hardly a boy,' Atkins said.

'Hmm,' Macarthur said absently. 'I was referring to your intellectual prowess when I called you dear boy, dear boy.'

There were more laughs.

'Get him processed and out of here,' Atkins said, his cheeks going red with the sting of a humiliation he felt yet did not fully understand. That only made him blush even more.

'Ah, the first tomato of summer blooms,' Macarthur said. Atkins walked out with the laughter of half a dozen men ringing in his ears.

The next morning the committal hearing was over and done within half an hour. Judge Advocate Atkins kept a tight rein on proceedings.

'Ladies and gentlemen, and the rest of you,' Atkins opened, unable to keep his favourite jest from slipping out, 'this is a committal hearing only, to determine if the charges against Mr Macarthur will go to trial. There will be no noise from the audience, is that clear?'

'Mr Oakes, will you please tell us of your efforts to arrest Mr Macarthur,' Atkins said.

'Before we do I wish to object to the panel of magistrates here today,' Macarthur said.

'You don't really have that right,' Atkins said.

'Then if you are prepared to continue and to give me a reason to have this charade shown for what it is and declared a mistrial, by all means continue,' Macarthur said with a leering smile.

There was a buzz of laughter and voices from the audience. Atkins turned and looked at Campbell and Palmer, then to Johnston and Captain Abbott who had been coopted to the hearing. All of the magistrates shrugged, making it clear the decision was Atkins's alone.

'Very well then Mr Macarthur on what grounds do you object?'

'Well given this case is about the *Parramatta*, the ship that I abandoned following the unauthorised arrest by the Naval Officer, I object that the same Naval Officer, Robert Campbell, sits as a magistrate on this hearing today. One can hardly expect a fair trial when the cause of this problem is going to judge me.'

More noise came from the gallery. A voice near the back said 'That's a good point'. Another added 'It can't be a fair trial with Campbell up there'. Macarthur leaned back in his seat and turned and started talking to someone in the audience, after which a ripple of laughter rolled outwards from where Macarthur was sitting. Atkins flushed red in the face, looking up from his discussions with the magistrates.

An impromptu vote was quickly taken by Atkins. Campbell abstained, with the remainder of the panel splitting two and two on the matter. Johnston and Abbott were in favour of the objection and wanting Campbell removed, but Palmer sided with Atkins to keep Campbell on the bench.

'Silence please,' Atkins said. 'The panel is equally divided on the issue so we will ...' Atkins looked desperately for some guidance. 'We will ...' 'In that case I withdraw my objection to Mr Campbell sitting on this hearing.'

If Atkins looked desperate before now he looked thoroughly confused, unsure if he should let Campbell sit or tell him not to. Conscious that the eyes of hundreds of people were on him Atkins flushed red in the face again.

'Under the circumstances I believe that the panel can make an informed judgement of the matter before it and decide if a trial is warranted, without my input,' Campbell said.

'So you are not going to sit on the panel?' Atkins said far too quickly and loudly, flushing red in the face. 'Thank God for that.'

'You realise you said that last bit aloud?' Palmer said quietly.

'Oh God did I?' Atkins said. He flushed even redder in the face.

'I say Mac, looks like you are being put on trial by a tomato,' someone yelled from the back of the gallery. It took two minutes for Atkins to stop the laughter directed at him and get the room back under control.

Chief Constable Oakes was finally asked to repeat, under oath, his meeting with Macarthur two days previously. There were gasps from the large crowd as Oakes laid out the words Macarthur had used.

Atkins quickly found a prima facie case existed and the four remaining magistrates committed Macarthur to stand trial on January 25th in the Criminal Court. For his part Macarthur remained calm. Atkins ordered the court to rise and the session was over.

Crowds buzzed with analysis and conjecture outside the courthouse. Macarthur was surely finished, for none could willingly defy the law of the colony on such tenuous grounds, some said. The affront to the law of the land was also an affront to Bligh, others said. Some speculated the war between the two men was nearing its end. Gradually the sport of speculation and what-ifs turned tedious as people contemplated a trial still more than a month away.

Back at the Corps' mess word was slow to filter through. 'So Mac has been committed to stand trial,' Davies said when he entered the mess. He had been at the committal hearing along with a couple of convicts whom he knew. 'Still there was some good sport. My convict mates stitched Atkins up well, questioning the legitimacy of the trial and calling Atkins a tomato every time the man blushed.'

'Plan that in advance did you?' Williams said.

'A little something Mac and I cooked up,' Davies said.

'Be careful Lieutenant. We'll likely have officers sitting on the panel for Mac's trial and we need to ensure things appear to be done properly,' Major Johnston said, walking into the room.

Every man rose as one and pushed forward, wanting to see the major and shake his hand. 'My apologies, it has been so long since I was last here,. Things at home have kept me busy.'

'That's fine major. Now don't all crowd the poor man at once,' Laycock said. 'We have been muddling through without you.'

'As I knew you would. I suspect you sell yourselves short gentlemen. Now if the officers could brief me on the activities of the last few months please.'

Johnston listened to the tales of stills and false paper work and the meeting of Williams and Minchin with Bligh. He apologised that he was not able to defend the men before Bligh, but as one they waved their hands and said don't worry. All was forgiven now that Johnston was back.

'Major, we heard that you wrote to the war office regarding Bligh and his behaviour towards us,' Smith said. 'Has there been a response?'

'I fear that my message is still at sea and will be for some time to come, and then there will be the bureaucratic delays and politicking. It will be many months before we hear anything on that front,' Johnston said.

'Its just ... the continual confinement, men sneaking out and risking being discovered,' Smith said. 'It's wearing us down. And all the time the men talk of being forced to leave. This is our home, we don't want to leave. What becomes of us with a powerful enemy like Bligh at our door?'

Johnston looked at the floor for a long time. The officers waited fearful that Johnston did not have an answer. Johnston knew he had to say something, anything to offer reassurance.

'It will not come to that. One way or another it will not come to that. I'm in the same boat as all of you. I have family here and land and now regard Annandale as my home for as long as the Lord grants me breath. No we won't leave without a fight.'

Johnston looked at the men, saw the grins and nods of approval. Johnston wondered if he could back up his words, for he had no better idea than anyone else on how to defeat an opponent as ruthless and resilient as William Bligh.

John Macarthur opened the gate to Judge Advocate Atkins's house and walked through the small but pretty garden. He strode up to the door and knocked loudly, whistling a tune. A woman opened the door. "Can I help you?"

'Please tell the Judge Advocate that John Macarthur is here to see him.' Macarthur smiled to himself as the woman gasped at his name. He still loved the thrill when his name drew a clear response.

A minute later the woman returned. 'I am afraid Mr Atkins is out and will not be back before dark,' she said.

'In that case I will wander a while in this pleasant little garden and wait.'

Almost an hour later the woman opened the front door. 'I am instructed to tell you that Mr Atkins is not at home to you sir and cannot be spoken to.' Once she had finished speaking the woman took a couple of steps backwards, fearful of what Macarthur may do.

'Very well dear girl, tell him, when he returns home of course, that I shall write him.'

Macarthur wandered slowly away, heading to the Corps's barracks. He sauntered into the mess hall and poured himself a generous drink. Minchin looked up from his paper and watched Macarthur. Davies walked in several moments later and stiffened in alertness when he saw Macarthur.

'Mac, what're you doing here? Can we help you?' Davies said.

'Not at present. I thought I should stop by and whet my whistle.'

'Well you are always welcome here,' Davies said.

'Yes, too welcome,' Minchin said quietly under his breath to himself.

'Well that hit the spot nicely, I must be off,' Macarthur said. 'Robert, a moment of your time if you please?'

Davies nodded and walked out with Macarthur. 'I now have something over Atkins that I think will help immeasurably in my case, as insurance if you will,' Macarthur said.

'Oh and what is that?' Davies said trying to sound casual and disinterested.

'Robert, don't play coy with me. I know you are desperate to find out.' Macarthur paused for a good ten seconds before talking again.

'I have in my possession a bill of exchange drawn up 15 years ago by Mr Atkins for £26. Now that is hardly an inconvenient sum even to a dullard like Atkins, but with interest, well then it does get interesting. That interest allows me to up the bill, let us say to £82. That should extend Atkins and make him pliable to my needs without the amount of the bill seeming unreasonable.'

Davies was quiet wondering, not for the first time, if he had made a pact with a devil in siding with Macarthur.

'Are you listening?' Macarthur said. 'Atkins cannot and I suspect will not pay the bill with interest. So this will allow me to write to Bligh. Here read this,' Macarthur said handing a letter to Davies. The soldier took it and saw that it was only partially complete.

...the unhappy effects it might produce on the morals of this colony if it should appear that a judge resists the payment of a just debt, without any other reason to offer in his defence than that he chose to take advantage of the merciful and indulgent spirit of his creditor.

'So Atkins refuses to pay you and you petition Bligh who will do what? What will Bligh do?'

'Robert, that is why I like you,' Macarthur said. 'You realise that to win in such matters a man must be several steps ahead of his competition, yet you cannot always envisage what those steps must be. Let me tell you. Bligh will no doubt direct the matter to the Civil Court, and who sits on that court? Why Atkins of course. So either he must step down from the case and lose or sit and bring judgement on himself.'

'So now both Campbell and Atkins will be excused from any trial, leaving a jury made up of officers and then you are acquitted,' Davies said.

'And there is more too. Atkins will do his damnedest to find a way out of this. When he does I will write to Bligh who will again refuse to make Atkins pay. At that point I shall trouble Bligh no more. I shall simply let him know that I will ask for the matter to be heard via memo by the Secretary of State for the Colonies. So with this I get two birds with the one stone, Atkins compromised and Bligh seen to side with him. It all builds the case to have Bligh removed. And with that I can continue to remake this colony from what Bligh has turned it into to become the great wool production house for the empire.'

'And this will work as you foresee it?' Davies said.

'Yes, Atkins is a dullard and predictable as a result. Bligh's predictability comes in his animosity to me and his devotion to his duty. Use your enemies' weaknesses to your advantage, just like the major in battle my dear Robert.'

With that Macarthur walked away whistling a tune.

Davies walked into the mess hall looking distant. 'What's up with you, and Mac for that matter?' Minchin said.

'I fear that I may have got myself in too deep with Mac. He has a plan to rig the jury on his case, so that it is Corps men only. Then it will be up to us to decide his guilt. How do we find him innocent when he refused to obey the law? Once you go down that path there is no return, surely.'

'Robert, you knew how devious Mac was before you got all friendly with him. We all know that the man has few scruples when it comes to getting his way. So he's going to rig the jury, haven't we done similar things? Stop acting so precious and hope his plan works.

'So I hear that you have been having problems with your house,' Macarthur said to Gillard. Before leaving the barracks Macarthur had searched out the private. 'Have you thought of transferring the deed, perhaps to the major? I have suggested the same thing to Sergeant Major Whittle and a few other soldiers, along with a few private citizens. All face losing their homes because the Governor sees fit to change the rules as he wishes.

'You see the Governor wants to turn back the clock to the old days of Arthur Philip, when no leases were available on Crown land here in Sydney,' Macarthur said. 'But Governor King relaxed that rule and allowed limited leasing, with the idea that the lease would then turn over. Do you follow?'

Gillard had a pained expression on his face. 'I think so.'

'The point old friend is that I too am in the same position. Bligh, the bastard, wants this land taken from me, despite my paying for it, just as you paid for the land for your house. We are not alone in this, there are many in the same boat.'

'Okay,' Gillard said slowly. 'So what would transferring the deed to the major do?'

'Ah well, the major is too well respected for Bligh to tear down a house on land that the major owns. You would not pay rent, rather you would have a gentleman's agreement and when Bligh is sent home the land would revert to your name.'

'Can that be done? He would own the land but not the home? Why not just sign the whole thing over to the major?'

'One of your fellows, Blakemore, a soldier like you, was questioned by Bligh some time ago. Seems that Blakemore made the mistake, in Bligh's eyes at least, of building a hut alongside his house, on land that Blakemore owned. And Bligh said that no man should have two houses when others go without. And yet Bligh has a house in London and lives here in Government House which he considers his own. Then he has the other Government House at Parramatta. You see, he has one set of rules for himself and different rules for others.

'I say we ensure that we beat him at his own game, that we all unite as landowners to ensure that our rights are not rudely trampled by the Governor. So now that we are united in this cause all I ask is that should the time come you and some of your fellows assist me in fencing my lease here in Sydney. In turn should you have need I will swing my considerable resources behind you. Are you in agreement?'

Gillard nodded, not entirely sure what it was he was getting himself into, but glad to have the backing of Macarthur. The two men shook hands and Macarthur strolled away.

'How many stills did you break up today laddie?' Whittle said to Williams as he returned from another patrol.

'Oh dozens Sergeant Major. It's nothing but wall to wall stills out there. Where once trees and scrub grew now it is stills and barrels as far as the eye can see.'

'So we will have our work cut out for us to get rid of all of these barrels and stills. Just as well we are running patrols all the time. Before you do your paperwork your missus is here to see you. She's in one of the huts out back.'

Williams quickly took off his armament belt and washed his face and hands in the latrines before racing out to the huts. The married and attached men had taken to using the huts for conjugal visits during the long days of confinement. It was not uncommon to hear raised voices coming from the huts, both in the throes of passion and in heated argument over the future of the colony and the Corps's place in it.

'There is daddy,' Mary said to young Henry as Williams walked over. Henry toddled and wobbled a few feet until Williams scooped him up.

'Look who's walking,' Williams said, hugging Henry closely to him. He walked into the hut and closed the door, his excitement tempered by realising that with Henry present there would be no intimacy with Mary.

'So how goes it soldier boy?' Mary said.

'Good as can be, but all the better for seeing you,' Williams said. He leaned in close to Mary unsure if she wanted to be kissed or not. To his surprise she reached up and kissed him passionately. It did nothing to ease his excitement but he felt relieved knowing that Mary still had strong feelings for him.

'Oliver, there is much talk about town of the war between Bligh and Macarthur reaching a conclusion. What does that mean for us, and for your Corps?'

'No-one seems to know. Mac has a plan in place that he believes will see him freed, and then he will head to England to fight for Bligh's removal.'

'That may not be as easy as it seems. Here in Sydney everyone is sick of Bligh and his high-handed morality. But outside Sydney the people support Bligh, particularly in the Hawkesbury region. There have been fights and brawls in town between the Sydney-siders and the country people. Things are getting out of hand. Do you know what will happen to you?' Mary said, coming to the heart of the matter.

'All I can say is that we will not be recalled immediately, That order would need to come from London, and then new troops would need to be sent out. There's no word of any of that happening.'

'But Bligh still has it in for you all does he not?'

'That he does. However, the colony can't be left without troops, and we would not be relieved without orders from the war office. The major doesn't believe that such orders are coming any time soon.'

'Can you come home then?'

'Bligh has us almost constantly confined to quarters, as punishment for some slight or other. Our hope is that things will change soon.'

'I miss you Oli. We both do,' Mary said starting to tear up. Henry looked at his mother and said 'Mummy'. Williams looked at his son astonished.

'How long has Henry been saying that for?'

'A few days now,' Mary said wiping away a tear. 'What happens if Bligh sends you all to England?'

Williams let the doubts about his promotion and its implications for a military future come rushing in. It helped give him the courage to say what Mary wanted to hear.

'I will resign and stay here with you Mary. There are men who are working to remove Bligh, some of them would take me on I am sure.'

'So you would give up on your dream of becoming an officer?'

'For you Mary I would.'

Mary launched herself into Williams's arms and clung to him. 'I love you Oli, thank you.'

'I love you too Mary,' Williams said. He did not have the heart or courage to tell her that he wasn't sure he could simply resign. Or that he was not entirely convinced of the idea. There had to be a way, if it came to that, to stay in Sydney and in the Corps.

January 1808

'So Bligh wants me to relinquish my land here in Sydney,' Macarthur said to Davies, who had stopped by Elizabeth Farm at the end of his patrol. The troops were sitting under a tree in the shade enjoying a rum provided by one of Macarthur's servant girls. Davies and Macarthur were sitting on the porch enjoying the view down to the river.

'What will you do?' Davies said.

'Bligh thinks he has outsmarted me by offering to swap my land for another parcel of similar character.'

'What does that mean, similar character?'

'My land was originally set aside for a church near the Cove. I intend to take the Governor up on his offer and ask for similar land that is part of the government reserve for wharfs.'

'But the Governor will not allow that, will he?'

'Of course he won't. That's the point. Bligh did offer me the chance to have the Colonial Secretary rule on the issue, however first I want to show that I can play the game. Hence my choice of land that Bligh cannot cede to me. Once Bligh says no I will write him and let him know that I beg leave to retain the lease I already possess. Then it will be Bligh who will be forced to write to London for an answer, at which time I will advise my friends there that Bligh is seizing land and tearing down houses already built for no other reason than he can. And of the land that Bligh has given out, half has gone to himself and his daughter. Half. He will look unreasonable and greedy and I will look like the wronged party.'

'Mac, that will all take a year or more. Can we all wait that long?'

'No, but rest assured I have written to or discussed this issue with a great many men here. Most have homes that are on leases of Crown land dating from when Governor King was in power. If Bligh tears down one house he can tear down all the houses, and that means most are now worried for their homes. And what happens if they lose their homes and land? They are then reliant on Bligh for other land and old bluff and bluster is not handing out much land. This is tyranny and these men all have a hatred of tyranny. For what makes a man a tyrant more than his willingness to threaten the very homes of so many and for what? A whimsy for the past. Because he can and none will stop him. Bligh has with these actions united the town against him.

'Do you know Robert that a number of the soldiers in the Corp are also in this position, and have had their homes threatened? Whittle for one, and Gillard and Blakemore and a dozen others I could name. And if Bligh can win on this issue then what next? The Corps being sent away no doubt and good men that remain put at the peril of the constables. We are all that stands now between Bligh's tyranny and oppression.'

'Mac that sounds a little fanciful does it not, the constables acting as Bligh's own private police force?'

'Tell you what, let's put it to the test shall we? I intend to fence my lease in town as a first step to constructing a home there. The times being what they are I feel the need to have a safe place in the town to reside with my family. I have spoken to Private Gillard, who as you know nearly had his house torn down recently. He has agreed to help me, as have others from the Corps. Put the word about when you return that I am offering free rum to any man of the Corps who tomorrow attends me at my town residence and helps erect a fence around the property.

'If nothing comes of it then I am proven wrong, but I wager that Bligh will send his constables around to break down the fence, thus proving my point. The land is mine by lease for fourteen years to do with as I wish. Who could find erecting a fence around their legal property a threat worthy of the constables other than a tyrant like Bligh.'

Early the next morning more than two dozen soldiers from the Corps arrived at Macarthur's Sydney leaseholding. Davies, together with Williams and Smith, stood close by watching.

'Lads, it's so kind of you to come and help me secure this lease. For your kindness I will give each of you a barrel of rum for your own uses,' Macarthur said.

A cheer went up from the soldiers adding to the attention that was already being directed to the site. The work proceeded quickly.

Macarthur for his part chatted to every person who stopped to ask what was being built. The words varied but the story was the same, 'I am securing my legal lease hold in preparation for building a home here'.

Like moths to a night-time bonfire more and more people came and soon the whole town was alight with the news that Macarthur and the Corps were defying Bligh. Crowds gathered and wagered on how long before the constables arrived and what would transpire when they did.

Shortly before lunch a commotion occurred to the west of the property. The fencing posts were already in place and the first cross slats were being hammered in near the ground when the crowd was ordered to part. The constables had arrived, in force. At least two dozen constables and acting constables were marching towards the property being led by Constable Gore.

'They don't march in time do they,' Macarthur said to the soldiers who stopped their work. 'Perhaps we should teach them a lesson.'

Gore heard the latter statement and immediately ordered the constables to action. 'Take out your batons and subdue any man that causes you trouble. Mr Macarthur I hereby, on order of the Governor, demand that you stop this illegal work.'

'What illegal work? I have leased this property fairly for a period of fourteen years. And while you are at it have your men put their batons down, we will not cause a problem.'

'You just threatened to teach us a lesson Mr Macarthur.'

'In how to march in time you clod and for that you bring out the batons in front of all these people.' Macarthur turned to the crowd. 'Did I not suggest to these generous men of the Corps, helping out an old friend in return for some refreshment, that we could teach the constables how to march in time?

The crowd roared and laughed. 'That you did,' a dozen different voices yelled.

'So Mr Gore, batons down if you please. Now I assume you will do what the Governor orders, even though this is my land by right of law.'

Gore looked around at the crowd. 'Batons away boys. Take down this fence.'

'Sorry lads to have wasted your time on this. I maintain that I legally own this land and can do on it as I will. However, rather than have a confrontation I suggest we stand aside. I will give you each an extra glass of rum as compensation.'

'Mr Macarthur, paying in rum is no longer allowed,' Gore said.

'Mr Gore these men are my friends helping me as a favour. In my world such generosity of spirit is returned in kind, in this case with a few tots of rum for their hard work. That is hardly payment, it is simple common courtesy, or is that too now banned by the tyrannical Mr Bligh?'

Gore swallowed hard. 'Boys, the fence please and quick to it.'

Macarthur wandered over to where Davies stood with Smith and Williams. 'Well Robert, I rest my case.' Then he turned and wandered back to his property. 'Mr Gore please make sure your men are careful with my property, as I expect to be able to use that fencing wood again one day.'

Slowly the crowd started to disperse with the possibility of violence now gone. Many though had marked what they had seen; constables acting to enforce the will of Bligh on land that had been legally leased from the Crown by a man as powerful as Macarthur. If he could not stop the Governor's constables who could.

That afternoon and evening in pubs all over town the talk was of Bligh's program to tear down houses and remake Sydney into something of the past. The future was at peril from a Governor determined to undo all the freedoms the people had and restore the town to a penal colony. Listening quietly in a number of pubs members of the Corps smiled and occasionally fuelled the fire of discontent. Sydney was now almost completely united against Bligh. Macarthur's gambit had paid off handsomely.

'So what did Mac mean when he said "I rest my case"?' Williams said. Davies, Williams and Smith were ambling back towards the barracks, having watched the constables stop work on the fence at Macarthur's property.

'Yesterday I stopped by Mac's farm on the way back from patrol,' Davies said. 'Mac told me that the constables would come and take down the fence because Bligh wants to control everything. Mac straight out called Bligh a tyrant.'

'I think he may have a strong case if that's his argument,' Smith said.

'So what now?' asked Williams.

'Back to the mess, we need to talk with the officers,' Davies said.

'Why, what's the urgency?' Williams said.

'Mac said that if Bligh can do this, can use the constables to rule Sydney as his own, then the only thing that stands in his way is us. The Corps. So Bligh's next step will be to get rid of us as soon as he can and then he controls Sydney. We need to let the others know what's happening and work out where we go from here,' Davies said.

'What do you mean by that?' Smith said. 'If Bligh orders us away what can we do?'

'What we've already done, appeal to the war office,' Williams said.

"And in the meantime? We can't simply sit and defy Bligh for a year or more while we wait for an answer from England. What if it goes in favour of Bligh? We would be considered mutineers and could be hung.'

'You're right, but that's why we need to talk to the officers and come up with a plan,' Davies said. 'What that plan is I don't know, but the time for waiting is gone.'

'Seems events are going too fast, aren't they?' Smith said to Williams.

There was no answer from Williams, who stared at the ground and thought of Mary and Henry and William Bligh; a problem that had no solution.

When the three men walked into the mess hall they were greeted with little enthusiasm. That diminished further when Davies asked for the attention of the men and set about addressing the issue everyone wanted an answer to, but few wanted to discuss.

Johnston opened the floor to debate following Davies's report on the constables actions and Macarthur's prediction of what would happen.

'What do we do then gentlemen?' Johnston said.

'What is there to do? We are bound by our duty to the Crown to do as we are ordered,' Minchin said.

'So you're just going to give up and let Bligh send us to England or who knows where else?' Davies said.

'Well what's your idea, or should I say what idea has Mac put in your head?' Minchin said.

'At least Mac is still fighting Bligh, unlike most of Sydney, and more than a few around here,' Davies said.

'And for all that you and Mac still have no better idea than sail back to England and beg, cap in hand, for someone to listen when we all say we don't like the Governor,' Minchin said

'Well what better idea do you have?' Davies said.

'I don't, that's why I don't want to talk about it. Its all anyone wants to talk about,' Minchin said.

'Its all there is to bloody well talk about,' Smith said.

'Has anyone got any ideas,' Johnston said.

'Let's talk about it, shall we,' Hutton said.

'Talking hasn't got us anywhere, other than confined here,' Minchin said.

'And who's fault is that William. Who thought it a good idea to march up to Government House and brag to Bligh about blowing up one still,' Davies said.

'Gentlemen, we don't need this sort of quarrel between us,' Johnston said. 'I am seeking ideas of what we can do, other than wait to hear from London.'

'Well perhaps we should write something first and send it,' Davies said.

'I think you're forgetting that the major has already done that, yet the reality is that such matters take time,' Laycock said. 'I see no other action than continuing what we're doing. It would be difficult for Bligh to mount a case to send us to England when we're doing all that he orders us.'

'Don't underestimate the man,' Davies said. 'He intends to take control of Sydney and the only thing standing between that end and Bligh achieving it is Mac and us.'

'So you're advocating we stand strong before him and do what?' Laycock said.

'Maybe we should oppose him more actively, refuse these ridiculous patrols and confinements,' Davies said.

'That is dangerously close to mutiny and sedition Lieutenant,' Johnston said.

'Perhaps, but then Bligh is no stranger to pushing his subordinates to such lengths is he?' said Davies.

'Good God man are you suggesting we mutiny against Bligh?' Laycock said.

'No, but can't we oppose him in some way that isn't mutinous?' Davies said.

'Well if you can figure that one out you're a smarter man than me,' Laycock said.

'You'd be smarter than all of us,' Minchin said. 'Which is highly unlikely.'

'I don't think myself smarter than you, but I know one who is,' Davies said. 'Mac is smarter than all of us in these matters. Perhaps we should talk to him?'

'Just a few days before he is going on trial before a panel of Corps officers you're going to suggest we consult with Mac?' Laycock said.

'If I may Major,' Williams said, 'perhaps that is the answer. If Mac is acquitted what message does that send Bligh, given the panel is made up of our men?'

'It says that we are united against him and that the Corps will not fold to his whims,' Smith said.

'Exactly,' said Davies.

'Or it says that we are so corrupted that we can no longer tell right from wrong,' Minchin said. 'And I'm one of those officers, along with Quartermaster Laycock there, and Kemp, Brabyn, Moore and Lawson. It is not your arse on the line is it Corporal?'

'Sorry, I'm only trying to help,' Williams said.

'Well it's one idea more than we had a few minutes ago,' Davies said.

'Are you saying that as a Corps man or as Mac's man?' Laycock said.

'Careful Quartermaster,' Davies said.

'It's a fair question,' Johnston said. 'And it's the one we'll all have to answer sooner or later, given that Mac and Bligh are at each other's throats and only one can win. Either we stand with Mac or let Bligh do as he wants.'

'Exactly what are you saying Major?' Whittle said, from his chair in the corner.

'That we are now at the point where things can't easily be put back the way they were. There is no more middle ground here gentlemen. We choose a side or one will choose us. And if we wait we lose any initiative that may be gained.'

'That sounds like battle tactics Major,' Smith said.

'Yes it does. Because that is all that's left. From where I sit the moment for confrontation is very soon. And in battle the winner is the side that seeks the initiative, the side that chooses the location and terrain, the side that strikes early with a plan. The way I see it we are now in the last moments before the battle begins, so it's time we choose a side. And I think it high-time we were all reminded of who and what we are, that we are soldiers. So we shall have all soldiers here on Saturday by noon and a mess dinner on Saturday night.'

'Sounds like a good idea,' Minchin said.

'It's not an idea Lieutenant. I am issuing an order. Everyone will attend, even the officers from Parramatta. In the mean-time I want you all to think about the future, your homes and what you want to have happen here. It is time we concluded this matter with Bligh, one way or another.'

'Major, are you sure that ...' Minchin said.

'Spit it out William, or remain quiet.'

'The words you are using, talking of choices and battles ... are we there now? Out of options and well ...'

'Well then present me with options. In the absence of those, yes we are there. So each of you go away and think about it. And if there are no better ideas then we'll have to make that choice.'

The room fell silent and gradually the men drifted off to find the time and space to think. Johnston sat in the corner nursing a rum, swirling the dark red liquor in a glass as if a prognosti-cator of old, searching for the answer in the currents and flows moving in the glass.

'Sir, can I beg permission to speak freely?' Minchin said. Johnston looked up and realised that he was alone in the room with Minchin.

'As you wish William.'

'I am confused by your sudden transformation. For months you have been a stranger here brooding at your farm. That day I visited you I believed that ...' Minchin paused and swallowed hard.

'Go ahead and say it William, you believed that I'd given up.'

'Yes, I thought that you'd given up, that Bligh had broken you. Yet now here you are practically goading the men into rebellion. I need to understand that change sir, to make sense of it.'

Johnston paused a long time and again looked at the rum in his glass while he swirled it around. 'I am at heart a soldier William. I need a fight that is real, an enemy at my gates. Before I did not know how to fight Bligh, and with so few standing up to him, it overwhelmed me.'

Again there was a long pause. 'Forgive me that I ran away from a situation that I could not figure out, and sought the comforts of home. I did give up for a while and believed that I could forget all of the damage Bligh has done to the colony. And to my shame I abandoned you and the men to that conflict.

'Recently my son asked me why I was not spending time here and I said to him that perhaps I had had enough of soldiering. And he said fine and walked away to play. That was when I realised that I was doing the same, walking away from a fight that is mine. For whatever reasons Colonel Patterson has abandoned the Corps and left me in charge. And now with Bligh threatening to send us away from our home, and tearing down our houses and imposing old fashioned morals on us, I realise that I cannot stand by and watch. Does that make sense, for it is the best I can do to explain it?'

Minchin smiled. 'Old soldiers don't lose the stomach for battle.'

'You are absolutely right William. I have the appetite for a fight and by God I shall bring the battle to Bligh.'

Minchin grabbed a glass and poured himself a rum. 'To one last battle.'

Johnston raised his glass, tapped it against the glass Minchin held out and drained the rum. 'To one last battle.' Then he smiled, stood and walked past Minchin, placing a hand on the lieutenant's shoulder. 'Thank you William. Now please excuse me, I have things to organise,' he said and walked out of the mess.

'What mischief are you lads about to get into,?' Davies said to Smith and a handful of the single men in the Corps who were gathered in the mess. All were dressed in civilian clothes.

'Well sir, we are going visiting in town. We checked with the major and he said that we could have a night in town, to clear our heads as it were regarding the choice we have before us,' Smith said.

'And which heads are you planning on clearing?' Davies said. 'The ones you use for thinking or the ones you use for loving.'

'Is there a difference? We are going drinking Lieutenant. Nothing like a good drinking session to clarify ones thoughts, is there?'

'Try not to get into too much trouble, and be back by morning' Davies said.

'Righto lads, hop to it,' Smith said.

Davies watched them walk out. As they left Johnston entered the mess hall. 'Major, do you think it wise to let that lot off the leash?'

'No doubt they will get themselves into all sorts of mischief, but that will send Bligh a message that we have reached the limits of his overbearing authoritarianism.'

'That will be some message,' Davies said.

'I hope so Robert, I really do,' Johnston said.

Smith lay in the arms of Madame Brigitte. 'My dear Beth, that was wonderful.'

'As always Nathaniel you were true to your soldier's nature: head straight for the main target and seek to bombard it with heavy artillery.'

Smith laughed. He loved it when Beth used that line. He had begged her to use it the first time they had met, when she was still a common whore.

'Do you remember when we first met?' Smith said.

'Of course, you were such a handsome young soldier, eager to fuck but not to talk,' Beth said.

'You were almost as beautiful as you are today,' Smith said.

'You say the sweetest lies with such conviction. What has you all melancholy for the past?'

'Things were simpler back then,' Smith said. He sighed and looked at the small window on the other side of the room. 'We are heading for a confrontation with Bligh and I don't know how it ends. I like a fight as much as the next soldier, but maybe some of those we are fighting will be friends. Some may even be Corps men. I like a clear enemy to fight and it's all so messy now.'

'Times change and so do people Nathaniel, it's the way of things.'

'I know, but over the past twenty years the two things that have stayed the same for me are the Corps and you, and now things with the Corps are changing.' Smith looked away and Beth caught the same lost little boy look on Smith's face that had first attracted her to him. She had seen that look on almost every man she had slept with, to the point she often wondered if they practiced it.

'In all those past years you have stayed loyal to me, and helped me to buy this place and run it. Is that why, to keep things as they were?'

'I love you Beth, in the only way I know how. Back in England growing up in Cheapside I never knew men and women to stay together. The men whored and took what they could from whichever woman gave it, and the women did much the same. So when I met you and found a common history, I knew you were the one.'

'So I was the one and you let me whore away for ten years before you offered to buy this place with me and let me run it? Such deep love.'

'Now wait a minute, you make it sound like I was pimping you out?'

Beth laughed and hit Smith with a pillow. 'I'm teasing you. We both chose the paths that have led us here and we both did so knowing neither of us could be faithful to the other. It doesn't mean I regret my choices. I wouldn't change things Nathaniel, nor would you.'

'I know Beth, but soon everyone here will face a choice. Either Bligh wins and we will be treated like convicts or we win and we can keep things as they are. If Bligh wins I fear what becomes of you, but I will look after you, I promise.'

'I don't need looking after Nathaniel, but I love you for promising to do so. Now are we going to keep talking or are you going to get the full value out of your investment?'

'Full value Beth,' Smith said as he pulled her to him and kissed her.

'What are you writing?' Mary said to Williams.

Williams and many of the married men had been given permission to spend a night at home. While Henry slept Mary and Williams made love. The two had fallen asleep beside each other. Mary woke to find Williams missing from the bed and had noticed the candle burning over by the table.

'It's my resignation from the Corps. I intend to give it in after the weekend. On Saturday we are having a full mess dinner, the first of the Corps for many years. I think that would be a fitting last hurrah before I resign.'

Mary hugged Williams around the shoulders. 'I know how hard that will be for you Oli, thank you.'

'You know that it is up to the major as to whether he accepts it.'

'He's a good man. I'm sure he will understand.'

'It's Nate who I hope understands. He's always been a soldier and will always be a soldier. It suits him to the ground. I'm not sure he will understand my reasons.'

'It suits you too, but you have skills in numbers and trade and could make a fine living for us working with any number of men here.'

'I had thought about talking to Mac.'

'Must it be him? You know my thoughts on him.'

'I think that he could at least help me find something with someone else.'

'Yes that would do. Come back to bed. You're here so rarely and it is comforting to know you are beside me.'

Mary grabbed Williams's hand and started towards the bed. He stood and followed her and lay down beside her. Mary was asleep within minutes but Williams lay awake thinking of what was ahead. He had begun to convince himself that his promotion back to Corporal was due to his improving skills as a military man. The doubts about his promotion were becoming less resonant, easier to subdue. How could he leave the Corps when they were about to confront Bligh? He decided he would wait until the confrontation with Bligh was over before he resigned. He rolled over in the hope that his mind would stop and sleep would come.

The following day the Corps devoted to reestablishing the rituals and traditions that had faded in recent years. During the morning the soldiers drifted into the barracks, taking their time to get organised before they assembled on the parade ground. At high noon Sergeant Major Whittle stood before the assembled men. Quartermaster Laycock, Corporal Smith and Private Gillard stood between Whittle and the men. The regimental drummer beat time as Lieutenant Minchin proudly walked before the assembled ranks with the regimental flag.

Carefully Minchin gave the flag to Smith and Gillard who rolled it up and then Laycock manoeuvred a casing over the flag. Whittle then called the ranks to arms while Laycock took the cased flag and worked the bottom end of the flagpole into a specially made hole in the ground.

'For the Corps,' Whittle bellowed in his finest parade ground baritone.

'For the Corps and the Crown,' the assembled ranks roared back.

The men were dismissed to assigned tasks to prepare for the dinner. Some cooked, others set up seating and tables in the hall, others cleaned and polished equipment. A party led by Minchin in his role as artillery officer manoeuvred the cannon to look over the parade ground. By afternoon all was ready for the dinner.

'This is good,' Smith said to Williams as the two directed soldiers to finish the last few jobs. Already soldiers were wandering in and getting themselves a drink. 'It feels like the old days again, the Corps as one united and working for ourselves, doing as we wish.'

'I must admit it's good to be part of this again. It reminds me of when Tom and I first arrived. God remember that, marching off to quell the Irish rebels.'

'The good old days. Its the major, whenever he's here things go our way. He's our talisman.'

Williams laughed and pointed a soldier to deliver chairs to the far side of the mess hall.

'Speaking of the major he will be here soon. Word is he has a surprise for us, something he and Mac cooked up.'

'Is Mac joining us for dinner?

'No. He intends to be seen around the town, to deny any involvement with us prior to the trial.'

'Smart idea. After all drinking with the same officers who are going to sit in judgement in his trial in a couple of days is not going to go down well.'

'So he's sending his son instead.'

Smith laughed out loud. 'How funny is that. Mac not showing up but his son coming instead.'

A rumble came from outside. The noise inside the mess hall died down and the men realised the rumble was Sergeant Major Whittle shouting. 'Parade ground now.' The soldiers moved as casually as they dared. The mood was already festive yet the men did not want to fall foul of Whittle, who owned the parade ground. All knew that Whittle would happily make an example of any who contravened the solemnity of the Sergeant Major's hallowed land.

Within minutes the soldiers had assembled before Whittle. 'Now lads tonight the Corps comes together as one. All that we are missing is the major. So lads right turn.'

The soldiers turned in unison away from the mess hall so that they were now facing the road and the front gate. On cue Major Johnston sped in on his buggy.

'Three cheers for the Major. Hip, hip.'

'Hooray, hooray, hooray,' came the collective cry.

Johnston stopped the buggy and secured it and strode across to stand next to Whittle.

'Thank you Sergeant Major, thank you lads. Quartermaster Laycock, if you please.'

Laycock marched over to the cased flag of the Corps and carefully removed it from its slot in the ground. He then marched the flag across to Johnston and Whittle. Johnston pulled the casing from the flag and then Laycock nodded and Smith and Gillard marched forward to collect the flag. Gillard took the flag and held it high on its pole and marched along the rows of soldiers. As the flag passed each group of soldiers they snapped to attention and saluted the flag. Finally once all the men stood at salute the flag was returned to Laycock who marched to the mess hall. He proceeded inside and the soldiers ended their salute and returned to ease.

Laycock was met inside by Hutton who helped the quartermaster secure the flag at the far end of the mess hall.

'Company, file inside for dinner,' Whittle bellowed.

Each line of soldiers began to march inside, with those nearest the hall leading the way. Once they were in the officers, led by Johnston, walked inside and sat at the main table. Then all the soldiers who had been standing sat too. Within minutes the formality had gone as the first drinks were finished and conversation spread in waves, rising and falling.

'A wonderful display Sergeant Major, thank you for that,' Johnston said.

'A pleasure. There's always a thrill deep inside to see the troops turned out in uniform on the parade ground.'

'That there is Sergeant Major, that there is,' Johnston said. 'Before things get too loose perhaps we should inform the men of Mac's surprise. I shall let you do the honours Sergeant Major.'

Whittle stood and within seconds a silence fell over the room, the drill sergeant still able to instill fear and intimidation into the men.

'Lads, I shall be brief. Firstly I welcome to the mess hall James Macarthur, tonight representing his father, who felt it best not to dine with a jury of his peers.' There was widespread laughter. 'Mac has instead offered as consolation for missing his sparkling company rum for each man, at three barrels apiece.'

A roar broke out. Men cheered and clapped as they calculated the profits to be had in selling such large quantities. Johnston smiled, both at the reaction of the men and the outright provocation such a large quantity of rum represented to Bligh's hopes of instilling greater sobriety in the colony.

'Now lads that is hardly a fitting way to thank Mac,' Whittle said once the cheering and laughter had subsided. 'All upstanding and raise a glass. To Mac, friend of the Corp, long may he enjoy his freedom.'

'To Mac, long may he enjoy his freedom,' the men echoed Whittle.

Johnston wondered, as he downed his drink, what an independent observer would make of the six officers who were to preside over Mac's trial in two days time toasting his long-term freedom.

The men sat and Whittle joined them. Only Johnston remained standing.

'Lads, the past few months have been difficult, but tonight a new time starts for the Corps. I have asked you to think about what you are willing to do to defend the town and ourselves. To defend our homes. Tonight I answer you. As soldiers we are at our best when defending our homes. So make no mistake we will do what is necessary to defend our homes and our way of life, regardless of who threatens us.'

For a moment the room was quiet, many of the soldiers stunned at the major's words, each wondering far would they would be willing to go. Then someone cheered, and then another and within moments men were standing and applauding and chanting 'For our homes'.

Johnston looked at the men and knew they were his to command again.

'Dear God, my head,' Smith said. 'I think Bonaparte invaded my skull last night and has his entire artillery letting off fusillades.'

'Please don't speak so loudly,' Gillard said from nearby. 'Every … word … hurts.'

From nearby the sound of someone vomiting and retching could be heard. A soldier stood and staggered from the room and added his own notes to the horrendous chorus of bile.

'Why is it so bright?' Williams said from the other side of Smith. 'And where are we?'

'Again with the speaking. Please don't,' Gillard said.

Smith very carefully and slowly sat up. 'Oh, either the world is spinning or my head is.' He slowly dropped his head forward and held it in his hands.

'Nate, where are we?' Williams said.

'You open your eyes and look. I can't keep mine open,' Smith said.

Williams tried hard for what felt like an eternity to open his eyes and adjust to the light. Finally he was able to focus on an upturned table, another on its side and two broken chairs. 'Did we get into a fight?'

'I would fight you right now if it would shut you up,' Gillard said.

Behind them there was a groan and then more retching. 'Who's that?' Williams said.

'Turn and look,' Smith said, looking at Williams through one half-opened eye.

'If I turn I think I'll be sick. Did someone poison us last night?' Williams said.

'I think it was self-administered,' Smith said and managed a lame grin.

'Who's back there?' Williams said.

'Its me, George. Tom is here too, a lot the worse for wear.'

'I think that is rather a large group,' Smith said. 'God, if something happens in the next hour or four the people of Sydney will have to deal with it on their own.'

'Shut up please,' Gillard said.

'I think we're still in the mess hall,' Williams said.

'Now I know why they call it the mess hall,' Smith said, looking around at the chaos of bodies and furniture standing at all sorts of angles. 'You know it's a good night when you ended where you started and don't remember a thing.'

'It's not last night that worries me, it's the next few hours,' Williams said. He finally managed to stand but the world was spinning and his stomach was heaving. 'Excuse me lads.' Williams staggered outside and threw up.

The parade ground and areas nearby had become temporary sleeping quarters. Soldiers were strewn around in all sorts of places and positions, every man seemingly struggling with a hangover at least as bad in magnitude as that of Williams.

Lieutenant Minchin came wobbling over, placed a hand on Williams's shoulder and simply grinned a lopsided grin. Minchin held his hand there for a long time before he finally managed to remember where he was going and staggered and wobbled away.

Williams laughed out loud watching Minchin stagger away.

'What's so funny?' Whittle said from behind Williams.

Carefully Williams turned. 'I was thinking that we may have drunk Sydney dry last night. And then I thought that's one way to show Bligh we're doing the right thing.'

Whittle started to laugh too. 'The problem lad, is I don't think we can do this every night.'

'I agree Sergeant Major. Perhaps we are better off resisting Bligh in other ways rather than supporting his push for sobriety.'

Williams staggered off and found a patch of grass under a tree. He closed his eyes and hoped the nausea would go away. When he woke the sun had shifted far higher in the sky. His mouth felt dry as if it were closing up. He staggered back into the mess and found some water and drank a long pull from a jug.

Looking around he saw that there were still a number of men asleep on the floor. Gillard, Hutton and Conner were still in the same spots as earlier though Smith was nowhere to be seen. Williams drank as much of the water as he dared then poured the rest over his head. He immediately regretted the decision as the cold dank water flowed down under his uniform.

Carefully he made his way back to his temporary accommodation in Smith's hut. As he walked in he saw Smith sitting on the bed reading something.

'So you're resigning from the Corps?' Smith said.

Williams looked at Smith but could not hold the older man's eyes with his own. He looked away from Smith.

'Just tell me why Oli, that's all I ask?'

'Mary wants me to,' Williams said looking at the floor.

'So you're doing it for the right reasons?'

'Yes. I thought you would be disappointed with me.' Williams felt the doubts rise again, the questioning tone of Smith's words opening a lid on thoughts he had hoped were suppressed and forgotten.

'Only if you don't do what you want Oli. Mary is a wonderful woman and you are so well suited. And we both know that if you were to stay in the army and she follow, you'd be judged for having a convict wife. All that hierarchy and officer bullshit carries a lot of weight in England.'

'And you Nate, what if we're recalled? Will you go or resign and stay?'

'I think given what the major said last night about taking the fight to whoever challenges us, that it won't come to that. At least I think I remember the major saying that.'

'I think he did. I remember that too, which is about all I can remember.'

The two men laughed awkwardly and Williams lay down on the camp bed in the corner. 'Thanks for understanding Nate.'

'You're my friend, why wouldn't I?'

'Its just that, well I wasn't sure how you would take the news?'

'Well who knows, when I sober up I may not even remember this conversation and you'll know how I'll react if you tell me again.'

'Thanks Nate,' Williams said to Smith who was already snoring.

Williams rose from the bed and walked over to Smith and gently took the letter from Smith's hand and looked at it for a long time. He would hand the letter to Major Johnston once things settled down.

'All rise for Judge Advocate Atkins,' the bailiff said. Very slowly most of the public gallery stood, many waiting a good few seconds after Atkins had entered the room until they stood. Most of the gallery were soldiers of the Corps. A few members of the public sat in too, but most had seen the soldiers marching up and moved aside. Outside the court room people huddled close to windows, hoping to hear what was happening. Those further back in the crowd waited until whispers flowed back to them for an idea of what was happening.

Atkins finally sat down in the central chair behind the high bench at the front of the court. To his side sat the six officers sworn in as magistrates: Anthony Fenn Kemp, Thomas Laycock, William Minchin, William Lawson, John Brabyn and William Moore.

Atkins picked up the gavel resting on the bench before him and banged it down. The sound was tinny and hollow. Macarthur smirked and many of the soldiers in the gallery chuckled.

'Mr Macarthur,' Atkins said. 'I understand that you have been busy petitioning Governor Bligh for my removal from this bench. The Governor gives his reply here and now with my presence.'

'In that case Judge Advocate I object to your presence again, on the grounds that you owe me money, you have spread malignant falsehoods against me and behaved with vindictive malice,' Macarthur said.

'Are you done Mr Macarthur?' Atkins said.

'On the contrary I have barely begun. I also object on grounds that I'm completely unaware of the charges against me, you not having provided them to me. Is it usual practice to allow a poor defendant to have no idea of what it is he's supposed to have done? I object on the grounds of your bias against me. How is a man in this land to defend himself when the Governor's own man will act in judgement? In addition, I have it on excellent authority that the charges that have been cooked up against me were done so by yourself in conjunction with George Crossley.'

'Mr Macarthur it is part of my job to prepare the warrants against you. How can you object on that ground, or on grounds that independent legal support has been provided by Mr Crossley?'

'You have had a bias against me from disputes dating back many years to the time of Governor King and you and Crossley, who is also set against me, are in fact conspiring to ruin me.'

'Oh for goodness sake, this is ridiculous. Let's get on with things.'

'Again I object. Sir, you have already had me in custody, such that if this trial fails to convict I will have grounds for a suit for false imprisonment against you. Therefore it is in your interests to convict me to avoid this suit, making you biased against me.'

At this the gallery applauded.

'Silence,' Atkins shouted, banging the gavel on the bench to almost no effect on the crowd.

Macarthur stood and raised his hands appealing for quiet, which followed almost instantly. Who is in charge now you useless bastard, Macarthur thought to himself.

'Finally, I object on grounds that you have already declared publicly on occasion that independently of the criminal court, the Bench of Magistrates possesses power to imprison and fine as means of punishment.'

'What are you expecting the court to do if you are found guilty Mr Macarthur? Give you a pat on the back and a warning and send you on your way?'

'That is how one treats a child. This is, however, business for adults. You have the eyes of an anxious public upon you, trembling for the safety of their property, their liberty, and their lives.' The public gallery erupted into cheering.

Atkins stood bolt upright. 'I will commit you to jail sir!'

'No sir, I will commit you,' Kemp said leaping to his feet. Applause burst out from the gallery at the sight of one of the six officers, sworn in to act as magistrates, threatening to jail Atkins.

'You see this is my point, you are willing to jail me without even trying me,' Macarthur said.

Atkins and Kemp ignored Macarthur, with both remaining on their feet, staring at one another. Then Atkins turned and walked out of the court, muttering that the court could not function without him.

Kemp remained on his feet. 'In the absence of a member of the civil magistracy I propose that Mr Macarthur be bailed until a replacement for Atkins be found. All in favour?'

The other officers loudly agreed and fifteen minutes later Macarthur walked out of the courtroom surrounded by members of the Corps. Crowds cheered, yelling 'Down with Bligh'. As he left the courtroom Kemp secured the official papers for the trial that Atkins had left upon his abrupt departure. When a deputation of constables arrived and requested the documents Kemp refused to hand them over.

The imagery for those members of the public watching was unmistakable. The Corps and Macarthur had soundly rejected Bligh's authority and that of his man Atkins. There was little doubt now about who was running the courts and by default the colony.

'What is our next move?' Kemp said loudly to Laycock and Minchin as the two walked amongst the large and boisterous crowd.

'We are to write to Bligh and ask for a replacement for Atkins,' Minchin said, 'and we must do this now.'

At 11.15 a letter arrived at Government House requesting the replacement of Atkins by an acting judge advocate. Bligh consulted Campbell and Palmer, who along with Johnston had acted as the official magistrates during Macarthur's committal hearing more than a month earlier.

Members of the Governor's Guard, made up of Corps's soldiers, watched the governor's residence, hoping for signs of chaos or panic. Instead the mansion was quiet. The only activity occured when a courier left and walked across town to the barracks where he handed a letter to Minchin, who was relaxing in the mess hall.

'What does it say?' Kemp said.

'Bligh has refused our request and states that under Imperial Statute there is no court without the judge advocate. Bligh also wants the official documents of the court back. You didn't expect that Bligh was going to let us win so easily?' Minchin said.

Minchin quickly wrote out a reply and handed it to the courier. 'For the Governor if you please.'

'What did you say in reply?' Laycock said.

'We are refusing to sit with Atkins on the grounds that he is not capable and has lost the court. Nor will we in future sit with him. It is for these reasons that we have also secured the official documentation of the court until such time as we can return it to a newly appointed acting Judge Advocate.'

'So what's next?' Kemp said.

'Next we send Bligh Mac's formal deposition that he believes his life is in danger,' Minchin said. 'In this we, and Mac, state that he is still under the authority of the court and we and he still recognise the authority of the court. As such he is to be bailed under either our protection or those we deem fit to carry out the task.'

'Do we need to say all that?' Laycock said.

'Yes, it provides us, and Mac, with the legal protection of the court.' Minchin turned and smiled at Macarthur, who sat nodding.

'Now, Mac, having done as you suggested, to whom do you wish to have yourself bailed?'

Macarthur smiled. 'I think Blaxcell and Bayly will be adequate, don't you?'

'A fine choice. Let's get it done.'

'And remember, don't send my deposition to Bligh until around 3 pm. That should ensure he does not have enough time to organise anything in reply.'

'As you wish.'

Macarthur left with Lawson and Braybyn accompanied by a patrol of soldiers from the Corps. They walked Macarthur to Blaxcell's house and the soldiers remained nearby while the officers returned to the barracks.

Johnston stood gingerly on the verandah of his farmhouse at Annandale, looking at the orderly standing before him. 'You must tell the Governor that I cannot travel. To do so is a matter of life and death for me.' The orderly had ridden from Government House to Annandale with orders for Johnston to visit the Governor immediately.

'As you can see from the arm,' Johnston said, trying hard but unsuccessfully to lift his right arm and the sling in which it rested, 'I am unwell.'

'The rumour doing the rounds is that you fell from your buggy on Saturday night. That is hardly life-threatening,' the orderly said.

'Are you a doctor or one of the Governor's helpers?' Johnston had almost said lackey but caught himself, knowing that every detail of the conversation would likely be relayed back to Bligh.

'I am one of his orderlies.'

'Then you are no doctor, unlike the one who attended me earlier today. He has forbidden me to travel for several days lest it cost me all. When I am able to I shall visit the Governor.'

With that Johnston closed the door hard on the orderly, who was forced to return to Bligh without procuring Johnston.

January 26 1808

'All rise, this court is in session,' the bailiff said.

Kemp, Minchin, Brabyn, Moore, Lawson and Laycock walked in and sat in the same seats they had occupied the day before. Kemp smiled and looked at the seat where Macarthur had been seated the day before. It was empty. 'Where is Mr Macarthur?' Kemp said to the bailiff.

'Provost Marshall Gore arrested him earlier this morning for breaches of bail,' the bailiff said.

A look of panic shot from Kemp's face and seemed to be contagious as it passed along the group of officers. 'Where is he?' Kemp said.

'Who?' the bailiff said.

'Macarthur, who else would I be referring to?' Kemp shouted.

'He's in the town gaol. And if Mr Atkins and the Governor have their way you lot are likely next.'

'What on earth does that mean?'

'Have you not read the paper this morning? Mr Atkins has written a letter to say that your actions are, and I quote,' the bailiff said pulling out a copy of a newspaper, '"a usurpation of His Majesty's Government, and tend to incite or create rebellion or other outrageous treason in the people of this territory". Should I read more?'

'Shut up and get out,' Kemp said.

'Treason. That's a hanging offence,' Lawson said.

'By God we're all going to be hanged,' Laycock said.

'Steady on. Nothing of the sort is yet determined. We must stay our course of action,' Minchin said.

'I'm with the quartermaster on this one,' Lawson said. 'Bligh will do us over like he did Dwyer. Remember how the court found him not guilty which should be the end of it. Then the Governor hand-picked a bench of his magistrates and Dwyer was found guilty and hanged. I bet even as we speak Bligh is rounding up his magistrates.'

'Relax. Any court must be made up of six officers of the Corps, which keeps us safe,' Minchin said. 'Besides, there are only eleven officers eligible to sit, we're safe.'

'Weren't you listening to me?' Lawson said. 'Bligh will use his own magistrates. He'll find a way to do it and then we're done for.'

'It won't come to that William, trust me,' Minchin said. 'The major won't let it. Remember what the major said at the mess dinner. We will fight Bligh on this.' This time there was no going back.

Bligh's chosen magistrates filed into Government House watched by Ensign Archibald Bell, commander of the Governor's Guard. The Guard posting was a prized one amongst the soldiers for it mainly consisted of sitting around and watching. Bell had the role of daytime commander due to his compliance with orders and his rather portly physique. It would be early evening before the magistrates left Government House and by then the world around Bell would have shifted entirely. For now Bell grazed on a plate of food and watched.

A few minutes after the magistrates arrived an orderly ran down to the front gate, opened a smaller side gate that stood by the larger ceremonial gates, and raced out. He was in such a hurry that he did not even secure the gate properly.

Within minutes the orderly raced up to the Corps barracks and handed a letter to Private Gray on sentry duty. Gray took the letter and delivered it to Minchin, who sat in the mess hall with his fellow officer judges.

'Dear God, he's actually done it,' Minchin said reading the letter.

'A little enlightenment please William?' John Brabyn said.

'Bligh has summoned us to appear before him and a panel of magistrates tomorrow morning,' Minchin said.

'We're all going to be hanged,' Laycock said.

'There he goes again,' said Kemp.

Watching from nearby Whittle said, 'Why so?'

'Why so what, Sergeant Major?' Lawson said.

'Why are you going to be hanged?' Whittle said.

'Old Bligh has summoned us to appear before him,' Laycock said.

'If you're afraid I'm not, and will find a way to cool him,' Minchin said.

'Precious good that does,' Brabyn said.

'What does?' Lawson said.

'Words like that, I will find a way to cool him,' Brabyn said.

'If not we are going to be hung,' Laycock said.

'It won't come to that,' Kemp said.

'Why not,' Laycock said.

'This is Bligh after all. The man isn't going to back down now. He wants blood,' Brabyn said.

'We will stop him,' Minchin said.

'How? He's the bloody Governor,' Laycock said.

'By arresting him before he arrests us,' Minchin said.

'Are you joking?' Laycock said.

'What are you saying William?' asked Lawson.

'What I said. We arrest him before he arrests us,' Minchin said.

'Well if there was a doubt we were going to be hanged for treason this will surely do it,' Brabyn said.

'Why not?' Kemp said.

'Why not get hanged?' Brabyn said.

'Why not go and arrest Bligh?' Kemp said. 'He's had it in for the Corps since he arrived and now he is striking at us. Don't you see if we are found guilty there are not enough officers to effectively run the Corps. That renders us all as useless.'

'We can appoint more officers,' Whittle said helpfully with a smirk.

'Not helping Sergeant Major,' Minchin said.

'The point here is that we are the breach in the ranks that Bligh has been searching for. With this Bligh can rout the Corps,' Kemp said. 'It's a clear danger to us. We stand and fight or we surrender to the tyrant.'

'Careful with your language, that's sedition,' Moore said.

'We are going to be tried for treason and you're worried about sedition. Have you seen the forest for the trees Will?' Kemp said to Moore.

'So what do we do?' Brabyn said.

'Tell people. Tell everyone that Bligh is trying to take down the Corps,' Minchin said.

'What good will that do?' Moore said.

'Oh that is brilliant,' Lawson said. 'If the people think that Bligh is going to rid Sydney of us then their last hope is gone. It will unite the people in fear of Bligh.'

'Quickly, go and spread the word, tell as many of the men to do the same. Tell them to say that Bligh intends to destroy the Corps through a series of show trials. Do it,' Minchin said.

The officers left the room. Only Whittle stayed. 'You're not that smart?' Whittle said to Minchin.

'Thank you Sergeant Major for that commentary,' Minchin said.

'This is Macarthur pulling the strings isn't it?'

'Do you have a problem with that?'

'Far less than if it were you trying to manipulate things.'

Within minutes soldiers began leaving the barracks and heading out across Sydney. The Corps had a long established network of fellow traders, pub and tavern owners, shop keepers and family and friends. Men were told to make that network talk for them. Williams made a beeline for The Londoner.

'Henry my favourite publican, how are you travelling? Listen I can't stay but I need to talk to you.'

'Come out the back Oli,' Adams said.

'No need, here will do,' Williams said looking around at the large number of drinkers. 'It's about Bligh.'

The room fell silent and Williams smiled a little. It was the reaction he had been hoping for.

'The Governor is moving against the Corps. He intends to try and judge some of our officers for the crime of wanting a fair trial for Macarthur. Nothing more, nothing less, only a fair trial. All we're trying to do is ensure that the court system remains fair. Remember how Bligh re-tried Michael Dwyer? Now say what you will about that rebel but the point remains, Dwyer was found not guilty by his peers and Bligh used his own magistrates to get the result he wanted. Dwyer was found guilty and hanged, and now Bligh intends to do the same for us.

'Imagine Sydney without the Corps. There'll be no balance against the constables that Bligh employs. The courts that will be loaded with magistrates loyal to Bligh. Anyone that gets on the wrong side of Bligh will face the Governor's magistrates and the Governor's justice. The Governor's campaign to end drinking will gather momentum. People who previously had permission to build houses will see them torn down. The Governor will control the stores and the flow of goods and will have everyone working for next to nothing. Convict labour will dry up and business will come to a halt. We'll all be forced to live as peasant farmers labouring in the fields for a new Lord.' Williams paused and looked around the room, seeing the fear and uncertainty infect most of the drinkers.

'Henry, I wanted you to know that this is what's ahead. You've been a good friend and I don't know when I'll see you again, perhaps never if Bligh has his way.'

Williams held out his hand and Adams slowly grabbed it and shook it, bewildered by what he had just heard.

'Henry, do you understand, I am saying my goodbyes because I believe that Bligh will destroy the Corps and send all of us soldiers away. So goodbye old friend.'

'Is there anything I can do Oli?'

'Just remember the good times.' Williams turned and headed for the door, then stopped. 'Henry, maybe tell the people what's going to happen.' Williams turned and walked out, delighted at the look of fear on many faces.

By the time Williams returned to the barracks he had seen Adams, Ravi Chandra and Will Worrell. Already people were stopping each other on street corners, in pubs and by the wharves, all talking about Bligh taking over Sydney. A sense of panic was in the air and people began running towards their homes, shutting their doors as they would if a fierce summer storm were approaching.

George Johnston opened the door of his farmhouse shortly after noon and saw Surgeon Harris standing before him. If Harris was a more observant man he may have wondered why Johnston was in uniform, or queried the sling holding Johsnton's arm. Instead Harris was preoccupied when Johnston greeted him. 'John, what brings you out here?'

'George, Sydney is in an uproar. Bligh has summoned the six officers acting as judges on Mac's case to front a panel of magistrates tomorrow morning. Atkins has already publicly accused them of treason. The rumour is that Bligh is going to have them tried and found guilty.'

'If he does he will halve the officers of the Corps,' Johnston said. 'By God, it's outrageous. It's illegal and flagrant. He cannot be allowed to get away with it.'

'George, the people are saying that this is Bligh's chance to be rid of the Corps, to destroy it. I genuinely believe that an insurrection of the inhabitants of Sydney is to be feared.'

'Is it that bad?' Johnston said.

At that moment a rider came up to the house and dismounted. Johnston recognised him as Charles Whalley, a sergeant in the Dragoons, seconded to act as orderly for Bligh.

'Orders from the Governor,' Whalley said.

'You see George, orders from the Governor now. He intends to do us all in,' Harris said.

Whalley stood by waiting. 'Thank you now go back to the Governor, I shall be along presently,' Johnston said.

Once Whalley rode off Harris asked Johnston what the missive from the Governor said.

'Bligh is informing me of what you have just said, that the officers are summoned to appear before him tomorrow morning. He suggests if I am too sick he will send for Captain Abbott in my absence. That fool Abbott isn't going to take command

and idle around trying to work out how to suck up to Bligh while my officers hang. John, we are going to town and will make whatever mischief we must to stop this tyrant.'

'Good, first to my house and we can work out a plan from there.'

'I think you will find, John, that things are already underway.'

'What does that mean? What are you up to George?'

Johnston smiled at Harris then turned and walked to his buggy.

'How many of the men are still unaccounted for?' Minchin said to Whittle.

'Around thirty. I have Williams and Smith out now trying to round them up,' Whittle said.

'And they are doing it quietly I take it?'

'That's why I sent them. They know how to remain discreet.'

'Good. We leave the recall until the last minute. Now I have received a note to meet the major at Harris's residence. We will be back here soon afterward.'

'I'll keep the men under close watch and have them ready themselves as they come in,' Whittle said.

Minchin strode off towards the gate, where sergeants Bremlow and Johnston waited. 'Right sergeants, to the guard house at the Governor's mansion, by different routes please. Once there order Ensign Bell to have the men stay out of sight. They are to fix bayonets and ready themselves to secure the front gates of the mansion, but not until time, is that clear?' Both sergeants nodded and quickly set off.

Half a dozen soldiers came wondering up the road to the front gates. 'You men, go to your quarters. Put on your accoutrements and come quietly into the barracks through the back way,' Minchin said. The soldiers looked at each other in confusion. 'Now,' Minchin said and smiled in satisfaction as the soldiers ran to their quarters.

'Gray, I will be back soon. No-one from outside the Corps is to come into these gates, and there are to be no exceptions, do you understand?' Minchin said to Private Gray standing on duty at the sentry box.

'Yes sir,' Gray said.

A few minutes later Minchin knocked on the door to Harris's Ultimo residence. He was quickly admitted to find Johnston and Harris finishing a quick meal.

'William, how goes the preparations?' Johnston said.

'All but done. We are ready Major.'

'Preparations, for what?' Harris said.

'As I said to Whalley, tell the Governor that I shall be along presently,' Johnston said. 'Sorry but this was on a need to know basis and best for you if you are at arms length.'

'Good God, you're going for Bligh aren't you?' Harris said.

'Yes. William, you have the papers?'

'All signed and ready to go. The letter from the officers of the Corps, and another from a handful of leading citizens. We can fill it up with more once Mac is out and able to tap into his networks.'

'May I see them?'

Johnston studied the letters for a few moments. The first was from the officers imploring Johnston to put Bligh under arrest, stating that Bligh intended to ignore their requests regarding the rule of law and use the magistrates to put them in harm's way. The second was from the leading citizens of Sydney including D'Arcy Wentworth and Simeon Lord begging Johnston to act to avoid an insurrection and massacre of the Governor and his staff.

Johnston smiled and looked at Minchin. 'Excellent work William.'

'Right then John, thank you for your warning and for the meal. When next we meet it will be under better circumstances,' Johnston said. Then he and Minchin left.

Ensign Bell peered out the window of the guard house. 'Nothing doing out there, all quiet at the Governor's.'

'Good,' Bremlow said. 'Right lads, check your weapons. Make sure the flint is shiny and you have your powder and shot.'

'What exactly are you expecting Sergeant?' Bell said.

'I'm expecting the major at the head of the Corps, come to set Mr Bligh away from putting some of our officers on trial.'

'Putting who on trial for what?'

'You really need to poke your head out of your guard house more often Archibald. As you are hopefully aware Mac is on trial. At the start of the trial that grub Atkins walked out when Mac accused him of bias. Our six officers on the panel refused to finish the trial with Atkins. In retaliation Bligh, who wants to see Mac hang, has charged our officers with treason and is set to put them on trial tomorrow morning. So the major is going to march here with the Corps and have a chat with the Governor.'

'Dear God. And our role?'

'We are the vanguard. Now lads fix bayonets.'

Nicolas Bayly and Garnham Blaxcell walked up to the gates of the barracks.

'Halt, you cannot enter,' Gray said.

'It's alright Private, they can come along with us,' Minchin said as he and Johnston walked up from the other direction.

'You have the warrant?' Blaxcell said.

'It's in the commandant's quarters waiting for the major to sign,' Minchin said. 'Follow us and we will get you on your way.'

A few minutes later Gray watched as Minchin walked to the gates with Blaxcell and Bayly, who continued on in the direction of the town gaol.

'Those two gentlemen will be returning soon with a third gentleman. When they return admit them to the mess hall immediately,' Minchin said.

'Yes sir,' Gray said.

Minchin then turned and walked purposely towards a group of soldiers standing nearby. 'Private Gillard, would you and the other gunners take the cannons from the front gate, load them and return them ready for action.'

Gillard led a small party of artillery men, all of whom volunteered to earn extra rations and an extra pair of boots each year. The men quickly ran to the front gate, pulled the chocks out from under the wheels of the cannons and started rolling them towards the powder store. Hutton pushed a corkscrew-shaped rammer down the barrel of each canon and twisted it as he removed it, cleaning the barrel of any powder residue. Then Gillard rammed the powder charge into each of the two cannons, while Hutton then rolled the shot balls into each barrel before pushing them hard against the powder with the ramming stick.

Once the cannons were loaded Gillard and the gunners pushed the cannons back into position beside the gate.

Gray watched on quietly. Gillard saw the quizzical look on Gray's face and simply smiled and winked at the sentry.

Moments later Blaxcell and Bayly came striding up with a tall, dark-haired man walking between them. Gray's eyes widened when he recognised their companion as John Macarthur.

'Evening Private Gray,' Macarthur said as the three civilians walked through the gates.

'Mac,' was all Gray could stammer, bewildered by the cannons, Macarthur fresh out of gaol, men in uniform readying weapons and orders for none to enter. Then as he often did when things were happening, Gray chose to look out towards the harbour and admire the view.

'George, good to see you,' Macarthur said.

'You too Mac. Trust Mr Reilly looked after you well?' Johnston said.

'Yes. He is a good man Reilly, took wonderful care of me. You know it almost felt like I wasn't in gaol, but it was necessary of course to mask my role in preparations.'

'All of which are now complete. Sergeant Major please sound the recall and assemble the men on the parade ground. You may let them know the peril some of our own are in. We will be out shortly,' Johnston said.

Whittle walked out and Johnston looked at Macarthur. 'There is no going back from this Mac.'

'No major there is not. Or should I say Lieutenant Governor.'

'Why Lieutenant Governor?' Blaxcell said. 'Why not Governor?'

'Under the articles of law establishing the colony, if the Governor dies or is unfit to discharge his duties the commander of the New South Wales Corps assumes the position of Lieutenant Governor. We are removing Bligh only until a new governor can be put in place. It is not our intention to break away from England, only to remove the tyrant from our midst,' Macarthur said. 'Lieutenant Governor signifies that the position of governor is vacant due to Bligh being unfit to carry out the duties of governor. This is only a temporary fix until England sends a suitable replacement. Nothing else will change.'

Outside, Private Gray stood to attention as lieutenant's Minchin, Lawson, Moore and Kemp walked out the front gate, along with Lieutenant Cardwaller Draffin. The five men turned and headed for the Tank Stream. Gray watched as they crossed the bridge and headed up Bridge Street, straight towards Government House.

Whittle strode onto the parade ground and nodded to the regimental drummer who began to beat the recall and a handful of soldiers came running up to the barracks. Seeing the majority of their peers already gathering and in uniform they ran as quickly as they could to the barracks to dress.

Finally all the soldiers of the Corps stationed in Sydney stood on the parade ground. Sergeant Major Whittle used all of his forty-two years' experience in the army to address them.

'At ease lads. We are now in harm's way. Governor Bligh has summoned six of our officers to attend a hearing before himself and his chosen magistrates, tomorrow morning. It is Bligh's intention to have our men charged and tried for treason, and we all know Bligh. Once he is set on the idea that those below him are engaged in anything other than following his orders to the letter he finds them guilty.

'It is the Bounty all over again and our officers may as well be named Fletcher Christian, for the tyrant sees them as no different to Fletcher. The tyrant Bligh sees them as meat for the Governor to grind and then hang out to dry. You have seen the Governor, sworn to uphold the laws of this colony, shit all over those rules. He has torn down houses, including going after some of our own, ain't that right Private Gillard?'

'Yes Sergeant Major,' Gillard yelled.

A chorus of boos and hisses rang out from the Corps.

'Well this tyranny ends today and we are the ones to end it. Bligh is not going to arrest our officers. If he does then who will be next, who will he come for next?'

'Us,' the men of the Corps bellowed.

'That's right us, and that will not happen under my watch nor under the command of the major. We are going to put on a show lads, marching up through the town, drums beating time, fifes playing, singing and looking fine gentlemen. We are going to put the minds of the people of this town at ease, for many right now are fearful. Terrified. Afraid in their own homes. Fearful of Bligh and fearful that we have been cowed and broken.

'We will show them the mettle of the New South Wales Corps. We will show them the finery of British soldiers marching to stare down their enemy. We will show them that they have nothing to fear. So lads, stand to attention.'

The Corps snapped to attention as one. Johnston walked out followed by Davies, Brabyn and Laycock. Laycock walked to where the flag of the Corps was on display and carefully removed it from the ground, then with the officers he marched to the gate. Whittle issued the order and the drummers beat time. The fifes began playing 'The British Grenadiers' and the long column of troops, resplendent in black shako hats, red coats and gleaming polished brass belts, with Brown Besses standing above them like a forest in winter, marched towards Government House.

Ravi Chandra was pulling a bag of flour down off a high shelf for a female customer when a man burst into the store. Chandra turned and walked quickly to the small counter and reached for the thick club that he kept under the counter. The lady he was serving backed away. Something was wrong thought Chandra, the man was not drunk like such fools who tried to rob him were. And what was the faint echoes of music that he could hear from outside. Drums and fifes playing.

'The Corps, the Corp are marching on Government House, they are marching on Bligh,' the man said before racing back out the door. Chandra exchanged a confused and shocked glance with the woman, who promptly dropped what she was carrying and raced out the door before turning and heading in the direction of Government House.

Usually Chandra would have stopped and cleaned up the mess, but instead he walked to the door, carefully locked it behind him and followed the woman towards Bligh's residence.

Henry Adams's few customers heard the music and watched astonished as the New South Wales Corps, in full regalia with flags flying, drums beating time and fifes playing marched past headed east, towards the Tank Stream bridge. Beyond lay the government quarter and Government House.

Voices from outside were shouting and yelling and whooping. It sounded like a party. Adams opened the front door and windows. 'What's happening?' he yelled to no-one in particular.

'The Corps are marching on Bligh. We're all saved,' a voice yelled back.

A huge cheer went up from the few customers in the pub, before most ran outside. Only the hardened drinkers stayed put. They downed their liquor before standing and wandering outside. A long snake of people followed the Corps as they crossed the Tank Stream and turned towards Government House. Then in the distance a woman's scream could be heard from the Governor's mansion.

As the Corps started marching Minchin, Lawson, Moore, Kemp and Draffin had arrived at the guard house at Government House and quickly entered. They found Sergeant Bremlow quietly urging his troops to focus on the task ahead. Minchin called for attention.

'Righto lads, this is it. We're going to enter the Governor's mansion and secure it. Our first target is the front gates. We get in, open the main gates and then split up and enter the mansion via the front, side and rear doors. No harm to anyone inside unless it is in defence of your life. And for God's sake no-one attack the Governor. He is to be taken unharmed and treated with the utmost courtesy. Sergeant, if you please?' Minchin said, motioning to begin the action.

Quickly the soldiers led by Ensign Bell raced from the guard house. The officers ran behind them. Bell reached the main gates puffing heavily, well behind the soldiers he had only moments before led from the guard house. The gates of the Governor's mansion were usually open and Bell expected to find them so. The gates were closed. A small woman armed only with a parasol stood behind the gates. She held the parasol as a man would hold a sword and waved it at Bell.

'Stab me to the heart, but respect the life of my father,' Mary Putland said.

Bell simply stared at her, astonished. His men, uncertain how to handle the situation, stopped and watched the strange confrontation.

'What the hell is going on?' Minchin said. He looked up and recognised Bligh's daughter, Mary Putland, standing behind the gates. Ensign Bell stood rooted to the ground.

'Bremlow, get up there and sort that out. This whole bloody thing is not going to fall apart because one woman is standing in our way. And Bremlow don't hurt her,' Minchin said.

Bremlow ran up and shoved Bell out of the way. 'Mrs Putland, I admire your spirit but we are coming in. If you do not stand aside we will force the gates open.'

'What brave soldiers you are rebelling against the Governor and the Crown,' Putland said. Her words did nothing to make the rebels stop.

'Lads shoulders to the gates and push, now,' Bremlow yelled, assuming the gates to be locked.

The soldiers raced forward and lined up against the gates. 'Together lads, shove,' Bremlow said. The soldiers were surprised when the unlocked gates were easily pushed aside. As the gate forced Putland back she screamed.

The column of troops was now more than half-way to Government House. Walking at the rear of the column Sergeant Major Whittle urged the troops on. 'You will do your duty, regardless of what you face,' Whittle said.

A number of children were darting in and out amongst the civilians following closely behind Whittle. John Macarthur led the civilians, with Blaxcell and Bayly on either side, like a private honour guard.

By now almost two hundred and fifty people were following the column as it marched up Bridge Street. A few stragglers fell away as the road gained in elevation, but most were now eager to see what would happen.

'You children watch yourselves,' Whittle said to the children making sport of running at the rear of the troops. 'You may be in the line of fire and get yourself killed.'

'For God's sake Whittle you fool, you'll have half the town stampeding away from us. Do shut up,' Macarthur said.

Whittle turned and realised that Macarthur was close behind and from that point on remained quiet.

Further ahead Williams and Conner marched next to each other. 'Are we doing the right thing?' Conner said.

'It seems both the right thing to do and a step too far all at the same time.'

'Exactly. Do you think we'll get away with it?'

'Bligh is no longer respecting the rule of law. He is out to be rid of us so we must act.'

'And don't forget it's Bligh, the tyrant of the *Bounty*. He has form with this,' George Newbank said from behind Williams and Conner. 'That is our best defence.'

Williams turned around looking for Smith, who was marching behind in the next company. 'I know Oli, we are all dropped in it now,' Smith shouted smiling. Williams laughed.

'What's so funny?' Conner said.

'An old joke,' Williams answered. Then he swallowed hard and looked ahead. A distant memory stirred of another march, soon after the Irish rebellion at Castle Hill. A memory of Smith asking what it would take for the Corps to rebel.

At that moment up ahead Mary Putland screamed and Williams and Conner exchanged worried glances. 'This all goes wrong if civilians start getting hurt,' Williams said. 'I hope Bremlow and company have things under control.'

Bremlow had very little under control. The delay in opening the gates had bought Bligh precious time. 'Will someone secure that bloody woman,' Bremlow said to his men. Mary Putland was now stuck behind one of the front gates as it swung towards her, the soldiers having shoved it hard with their shoulders, expecting the gates to be locked.

Putland screamed again as the gate swung towards her. The gate was heavy and not well finished, having a few jagged barbs and edges. At the last moment, as the gate raced towards her, an arm grabbed Putland and pulled her to safety. She looked up and saw Robert Campbell.

'It is no use getting yourself hurt here Mary. Come back to the verandah where you will be safe.'

Campbell led Putland away from the gate. 'This should be interesting,' he said.

'What should be interesting?' Putland said.

'Watching these bumbling fools trying to enter Government House and find your father,' Campbell said. Then he ushered

Putland up the steps and sat her down next to John Palmer's wife Susan, while he left his brother-in-law John Palmer to stand guard over the women.

Campbell then ran to the front door and knocked, yelling 'It's Robert, let me in.'

The door flew open and Chaplain Fulton and Provost Marshall Gore quickly slammed it behind Campbell. At the back door Tom Arndell slid the bolts to lock the door. Government House was now secure.

Outside Ensign Bell stood still, completely unsettled by his encounter with Mary Putland. Around him Minchin was issuing orders. The guard was divided into five groups, with one group to stand at the gates with Bell.

'Sergeant Sutherland, you take the rear, Draffin, you are with Sutherland. Moore and Sergeant Hall you take the north side of the house. Secure the rear gate and search the outside buildings. Lawson you and Kemp can have the honour of opening the front door. I will watch the side door,' Minchin said.

Quickly the soldiers broke up into their assigned groups and scattered around the grounds. Minchin glanced back down Bridge Street and saw the long column of soldiers only moments away. He knew they would then separate into various platoons and surround Government House.

Minchin was sweating by the time he reached the verandah and ran past Mary Putland and Mr and Mrs Palmer. His main task was to ensure no one escaped via the side doors. Minchin was close to panic. It had taken too long to secure the house and given Bligh too much time in which to escape. In all the preparations one point had been drilled home again and again, Bligh could not be allowed to escape.

Minchin wondered if it wasn't already too late, if the Governor wasn't already on horseback charging west and then northward to the Hawkesbury. A group of more than eight hundred settlers of the greater Hawkesbury region had signed a petition which they delivered to Bligh at the start of the year, thanking the Governor for his good governance and pledging their loyalty.

The worst-case Minchin knew, was if Bligh made it up north and raised a citizen's militia from the Hawkesbury. If that happened the chances of the Corps winning were gone. It was one thing to shoot Irish rebels, quite another to have a civil war in the colony with Bligh and the country settlers pitted against the Corps and Sydney.

Kemp and Lawson strode up the steps of Government House, hands caressing the pommels of their swords. Chaplain Fulton peered out from a window beside the door.

'Open the door please,' Kemp said.

'My apologies, I cannot do that,' Chaplain Fulton said.

'Who is inside?'

'It's Chaplain Fulton.'

'Chaplain, please open the door, we wish no harm.'

'Yes, open the door sir,' Lawson said. Kemp looked at him wondering if that contrubution was really necessary.

'I will not open the door. You may drive your bayonets into me, a man of God and the cloth, but you will not get in,' Chaplain Fulton said.

Campbell leaned in close. 'Well chosen words with the man of God and the cloth, Chaplain,' Campbell said.

'Yes I thought so too,' Fulton said.

From outside there was a rumble on the steps as half a dozen troops rushed up.

'Want us to stick 'em with a bayonet Captain?' Campbell and Fulton heard a voice say from outside.

'No I bloody well don't want you to do that,' Kemp said.

There was a pause of half a minute before Fulton and Campbell heard Kemp speak. 'I say Chaplain, would you mind letting the Governor know that Captain Kemp and Lieutenant Lawson are here to see him.'

Fulton peered out the window and saw Lawson shoot Kemp a look.

'Gentlemen, I think the Governor is well aware that you are here. Why not come back in the morning when you are due to meet the Governor in more civilised circumstances,' Fulton said.

Campbell smiled at Fulton. The Chaplain was the epitome of grace under pressure.

At that moment there was a thump at the rear door. Provost Marshall Gore raced to the door and found Arndell backing away as the door was smashed open.

'Stand aside,' a soldier said pointing the tip of his bayonet at Gore. The Provost Marshall contemplated the sixteen-inch-long blade and knew that it would run him through if thrust into his chest.

Gore folded his arms and stiffened up, raising himself a good centimetre in height. Before he could say anything a second soldier drove the butt of his rifle hard into Gore's chest. 'He said get out of the way,' the soldier said. Then stepping over Gore the soldiers burst into the house.

At the side door Minchin was wondering why it was taking so long for the soldiers to enter the house. His visions of Bligh fleeing on horseback were becoming more vivid by the second as he heard snippets of the standoff at the front door. He needed to get into the house.

'Mrs Putland, by chance would you have a key to your side door?' Minchin said.

'No you scoundrel I would not.'

Minchin looked around for something heavy to use on the glass and was shaken as Putland seemed to read his mind.

'If you break the glass to my room you will pay for it, in more ways than one,' Putland said. Then she smiled a cold, hard smile. Minchin felt a shiver go down his spine.

'Someone find me an axe or rock or something,' Minchin said to the soldiers who stood idly behind him. Several of the soldiers ran off, three stood staring at Putland unwilling to move.

A few moments later a soldier ran up and handed Minchin a large rock.

'I am warning you Lieutenant Minchin,' Putland said.

He tried to defiantly return her stare but could not. It took all the courage he had to grip the door handle and swing the rock back. As he shifted his weight backwards the door handle turned in his hand. The bloody door had been unlocked the whole time.

As he entered the house Minchin caught a glimpse of Mary Putland's face looking distinctly unimpressed and heard her say 'dullard' quite loudly to Mr and Mrs Palmer.

Minchin raced through Mary's sitting room and opened a door and spilled into the main foyer. He saw Chaplain Fulton and Robert Campbell still standing behind the locked front door. From the rear of the house there was a commotion and Minchin raised his hand and the troops immediately behind him followed suit and lifted their rifles and extended them at the threat. At that moment Draffin and his men burst into the room. The two parties faced each other for a second before they all relaxed.

'Why are you holding a rock,' Draffin said laughing. 'A sword would be a better option.'

Minchin had not realised that he was still holding the rock that he had intended to use on Mary Putland's door. He dropped it, the sound of the heavy rock thudding into the floor resembling a shot going off. More than a dozen armed and confused men looked in alarm for the source of the noise, several trying to raise muskets, others shouting to hold your ground.

A voice from behind Minchin spoke.

'Chaplain I suggest you stand clear of the door and open it before those fools outside do you a mischief, they are inside already.'

Minchin and Draffin both spun around expecting to see Bligh and were surprised to see Mr Palmer.

'How in God's name did you get in here,' Draffin said.

'By following him,' Palmer said pointing to Minchin.

At that moment Fulton unbolted the door and stood back. With a huge cheer six soldiers shoved the door open and raced in, only to come up short at seeing Minchin, Draffin and twelve other soldiers. Kemp and Lawson raced in and stopped dead too.

'Where is Bligh?' Kemp said after several moments. Campbell, Fulton and Palmer stared back without answering. Soldiers milled about uncertain what to do.

'You,' Kemp said pointing at Palmer, 'where is Bligh?'

'I really couldn't say. The last time I saw the Governor he was putting his uniform on.'

Minchin looked about wildly, a panicked vision of Bligh riding away, grinning as he turned to take a look at Sydney, filling the lieutenant's head. Kemp and Lawson groaned while Draffin, whose sanity many of the men doubted, laughed.

Moments later Major Johnston walked in the front door, his right arm in a sling, his left holding his sword. Johnston looked around at Palmer, Campbell and Fulton, his officers and soldiers all standing slackly.

'Does anyone know where the Governor is?' Johnston said.

For a long few moments no-one answered.

'Well find him, now,' Johnston said before quickly walking out, a worried look on his face.

Lieutenant Moore walked out of the front door of Government House and down the steps and the long drive to the front gates. He had the air of a condemned man when he told the major the bad news.

'What do you mean you can't find him?' Johnston said urgently.

Moore looked at the major and shifted continually on his feet. He had drawn the short straw when the officers had finished searching Government House and been unable to find Bligh.

'We have searched the house, he's not in there,' Moore said.

'Laycock,' Johnston roared, 'take a party and search the grounds, every house and structure on them and find me Bligh. Lieutenant Moore, organise some soldiers to search every government building within a half a mile of here, and do it very quickly,' Johnston said.

Macarthur walked over. 'Jesus George, if we don't find Bligh this whole thing is over with.' Macarthur looked at the large crowd still standing nearby.

'You, me, Blaxcell, Bayly, Simeon Lord, James Badgery, the Blaxland brothers. All standing out here like shags on a bloody rock while Bligh is nowhere to be seen. There will be no doubt in the minds of the people who is behind this. Bligh will have a hundred or more witnesses to put us all here at the scene.'

'This was your bloody idea Mac,' Johnston said. He realised that he was still holding his sword in his left hand and slowly and awkwardly reversed his grip on it and managed to put it back into its scabbard.

Macarthur walked away muttering. Johnston, a man of action, stood and waited for a report from one of his men. There was nothing else to do beside supress the thought that they all might hang.

Johnston looked at Macarthur and his fellow conspirators and watched as the minutes ticked by and the group became more agitated. Voices began to be raised, harsh words said. The major looked at the crowd which was growing in number. He half expected a 'We want Bligh' chant to start at any minute.

Finally Laycock came rushing over.

'There's no sign of him Major, it's as though he's disappeared.'

'Are you sure he isn't in the house?'

'As sure as we can be. It has been searched twice as have all the outside buildings.'

Sergeant Major Whittle came over. 'Nothing from Lieutenant Moore's groups, they have checked all the nearby Government buildings.'

'Get all the officers who led the vanguard here now,' Johnston said.

A few minutes later an argument was underway between Minchin, Kemp, Lawson, Moore and Draffin.

'It was two minutes at the most from when we left the guard house until we were at the front door,' Kemp said.

'And the rest,' Draffin said. 'That stupid harpie at the gate slowed us down by quite some time. I reckon it was more like three or four minutes.'

'No one got past me,' Minchin said.

'Nor me,' Moore said.

'But how would you know, given the time it took for us to get into position?' Draffin said.

'Wait, what did Palmer say?' Minchin said.

'He said the last he saw of the Governor he was getting into his uniform,' Kemp said. 'So he must still be in the house.'

'Sergeant Major Whittle, get inside that house. Find Bligh's servant Dunn and his secretary Griffin and threaten them until one talks. No violence, just the promise of it,' Johnston said.

'So where is your master?' Whittle said to Dunn.

'I don't know. When the shouting started he disappeared,' Dunn replied.

'Do you think he looks suitably afraid Mr Griffin?' Whittle said to Edmund Griffin, Bligh's personal secretary.

Griffin trembled but said nothing.

'See Mr Dunn, that is how you should be looking,' Whittle said, pointing to Griffin who was still trembling. 'Now who is going to tell me where the Governor is and avoid a more direct approach when next I ask?'

Both Dunn and Griffin looked at each other. Yet neither man said a word.

'Then we will have to see if we can extract some conversation from you another way,' Whittle said. He walked over to where Corporal Michael Marlborough and Private William Wilford were sitting.

'May I borrow a bayonet please Private,' Whittle said.

Wilford unscrewed the bayonet from his Brown Bess. 'Sergeant Major, this isn't going to be like last time is it? It took me a whole day to get all the blood and gore off of that?'

'Tell you what Private, the one who speaks last will be assigned the task of cleaning up your bayonet, that sounds only fair,' Whittle said. 'Now gentlemen, when the bayonet was first introduced as a weapon of war some said it would end all war, given it was such a terrible weapon.

'Do you know why it is so terrible? Let me tell you. It will go straight through a man with only a small amount of force behind it. A tiny amount of force and it will easily go through an eye. Of course the trick is not to push too hard or else it slips effortlessly into the brain, either killing a man or rendering him retarded for the rest of his life.

'So who is first,' Whittle said sunnily.

Dunn whimpered and turned his face away.

'Looks like Mr Dunn volunteered lads,' Whittle said, as Malborough moved behind Dunn and grabbed his head. 'Of course you could just tell me where Mr Bligh is?'

'So this is the liberty you bring, torture of innocent men? And how long did that take, an hour?' Griffin said before Dunn could let slip anything. 'Do you think that this won't be made known to the public out there? And then your new republic will be shown to be no better than that of Bonaparte, a tyrant's playground, the people fearful of their turn with the torturers.'

Whittle stopped and put the bayonet down. He was smart enough to know that the game was up. He looked at Marlborough, who released his grip on Dunn. 'Get Sutherland, Hutton and Newbank in here now.'

Within moments Marlborough returned with the other soldiers. 'Right lads, two groups. Hutton and Newbank with me, Sergeant Sutherland take the others. We search this place. I will take Griffin, you take Dunn and turn the ground floor upside down. Look for hidden doors and secret chambers, Bligh must be in one of those,' Whittle said.

Forty minutes later Whittle stormed back into the foyer. 'Damn my eyes, I can't find him anywhere.'

Sutherland walked into the foyer and held out his upturned hands to say no luck. He looked upstairs and Whittle nodded. Marlborough shoved Dunn towards the stairs. 'More work to be done yet so let's go.'

After fifteen minutes of searching rooms Marlborough came upon a door built into the wall. 'What is behind that?'

'My private room,' Dunn said.

'Well are you going to open it or should I order Corporal Marlborough here to kick the door in. He is looking suitably frustrated to do it,' Sutherland said.

Dunn opened the door. The ceiling sloped down sharply from the door to the far wall. Inside was a stack of firewood and a small bed. The wood was piled high and there appeared to be no space behind it.

'What, our generous governor sticks his firewood in your bedroom? Some master he is,' Marlborough said.

Then without warning Marlborough shoved his rifle, bayonet end first, under the bed and whipped it from side to side. Sutherland watched Dunn for a reaction but there was none. Then Sutherland grabbed a small log and tossed it over the top of the wood pile. It hit the far wall and landed very quickly on top of the pile.

'Well certainly no room behind there for a governor to hide,' Sutherland said.

In frustration Marlborough shoved his rifle under the bed again.

'Wait, what was that?' Marlborough said. 'I thought I heard a boot scuff the floor.'

'Grab the bed and haul it up,' Sutherland said in excitement.

'It's too tightly wedged, we can't lift it,' Marlborough said.

'Corporal' you have your bayonet, stick it under there until something squeals or it hits a target,' Sutherland said.

'Wait,' a voice said from under the bed. A moment later a round, almost cherubic face topped by curly, receding hair poked out from under the bed, next to the wood pile. Bligh had to squeeze himself out from the far side of the bed and crawl over it to escape his hiding place.

'Mr Bligh, so nice of you to join us,' Sutherland said. Then he walked out the door and shouted 'Its him, we got him.'

Within moments Whittle came running over followed by Hutton and Newbank. They all crowded into the room along with Sutherland, Marlborough and Wilford, and Dunn and Griffin. In the tiny space it was almost impossible to move.

'Hutton, let the major and the men know we have our prize,' Whittle said.

Hutton raced down the stairs, yelling to the troops in the house 'The Governor is found'. He continued the cry as he raced past Minchin and outside and across Bridge Street to where Major Johnston and the civilian leaders stood.

'Major, the Governor is found,' Hutton said. Macarthur clapped Blaxcell hard on the back and whooped. Laycock breathed a deep sigh of relief, Moore and Lawson smiled and Kemp nodded. Johnston then carefully removed his sword with his left hand and reversed his grip on it. To the cheers of the crowd he marched up through the gates, along the driveway and up the stairs to the front door of Government House.

Minchin was standing in the foyer with Palmer, Campbell and a few troops when he heard shouting from upstairs. He looked up to see Griffin screaming. 'They are going to kill the Governor.'

Pushing past the soldiers and ignoring Campbell and Palmer shouting about no harm befalling the governor, Minchin sprinted up the stairs. Griffin pointed him to the room where Bligh was found. Minchin ran to the door but could not get in. Five soldiers as well as Dunn were in the way. He dropped onto his hands and knees and crawled and shoved his way on all fours past the soldiers in the room, only to see Marlborough with a bayonet to the throat of Bligh.

'Take your hand out of your jacket. He has a pistol,' Marlborough shouted.

'Sergeant, keep the man off, I have no arms,' Bligh said while kneeling on the bed.

'Corporal, stand down now,' Minchin yelled from on all fours.

Sutherland looked around to see where Minchin was and at that moment Wilford moved and stumbled over Minchin, who was below him. Men and bodies fell in a tangled heap on the floor.

'For God's sake get off me,' Minchin said.

'He has a pistol, take care,' Marlborough said struggling to get back to his feet.

'I have no arms,' Bligh said desperately.

'Sergeant, get the men to stand off. The Governor is not armed, he is not armed,' Minchin said. 'I will take responsibility for him.'

As if to prove the point Bligh very slowly removed his hand from his jacket to show it was empty.

Slowly the gaggle of bodies separated and one after another the soldiers withdrew from the room. Marlborough was the last to leave, backing out while keeping his musket raised and pointed at Bligh. As he exited the room Marlborough turned to Minchin and pointed under the bed. 'We found him under there sir.'

Minchin nodded and then stepped forward offering Bligh a hand down from his position on the bed. 'I am extremely sorry you suffered yourself to be found hiding under a bed,' Minchin said loudly for all to hear. 'A brave man would have come forward in the first instance to meet the officers at his front door. Now Mr Bligh, Major Johnston wishes to see you. If you would accompany me please,' Minchin said.

Minchin walked through the door first and waited until Bligh came up beside him. In front of him stood a large number of soldiers who parted and stood to each side. As Bligh walked past the soldiers jeered and hissed.

The long line of red coats parted before Minchin and Bligh as they walked down the stairs and into the foyer. Like an undoing of Moses parting the Red Sea, Bligh was delivered before his enemy.

Lieutenant Moore watched Bligh descend the stairs, the Governor's arm resting on Minchin's arm for support. Once at the foot of the stairs Bligh looked around to see red coated Corps men standing in front of the walls and looking in from the windows outside. Moore walked up to Bligh and handed him a letter.

Bligh opened the letter and quickly read its contents. Minchin did not look to see what it said. He knew it accused Bligh of crimes that rendered him unsuitable to govern, and asked Major Johnston, on behalf of the colonists and officers of the Corps, to arrest Bligh and ask that the Governor resign his authority and submit.

When he had finished reading the letter Bligh carefully folded it and handed it to Griffin who had followed Minchin and the Governor down the stairs. Minchin thought it an odd thing to do, rather than scrunch the letter up and throw it away.

Bligh looked around and saw Major George Johnston enter the room, sword in left hand and looking elegant in his red uniform. Bligh then surprised Minchin again by striding across the room and holding out his right hand to Johnston.

'You are to be congratulated Major on the clever manner in which you have executed the wishes of the inhabitants of this colony,' Bligh said. Still he held his right hand for Johnston to shake, but the major would not remove his arm from his sling.

'Mr Bligh, will you resign your position and authority as Governor, as requested by both the inhabitants of this colony and the officers of His Majesty's force in this colony?' Johnston said.

Bligh simply stared at Johnston, saying nothing.

'Then I will have you put under arrest, by the advice of the citizens of the colony and officers of my Corps. Will you honour the terms of your arrest sir?'

'Major Johnston, I suppose you will take my Secretary away?'

Taken aback at the response Johnston looked from Bligh to Griffin. 'He may remain with you if you wish.' Then Johnston looked around and caught the eye of Nicolas Bayly who was frantically trying to signal the major.

'Mr Bayly?' Johnston said. Bayly raced over and whispered something in Johnston's ear.

'Mr Bayly, perhaps you will be so kind as to ask the inhabitants outside for their opinion on Mr Bligh's request?' Johnston said.

Bayly disappeared for a moment and quickly returned. 'Mr Griffin remaining with Mr Bligh is not approved of.'

Bayly then went up to Johnston and again whispered in the major's ear. 'Lieutenant Minchin, would you and Mr Bayly please find and secure the Governor's papers, the Great Seal of office and any dispatches that may be found. Announce to the people that martial law is declared and that any who aid and abet the Governor will have to defend themselves on criminal charges. Sergeant Major Whittle you may call the companies into formation, and organise sufficient guard details,' Johnston said.

Minchin and Bayly quickly grabbed John Dunn, Bligh's servant, and went upstairs to the governor's office, only to find two of Macarthur's closest allies, Robert Townson and Charles Grimes, the Surveyor General, already trying to force open the locked drawers in Bligh's desk bureau. Grimes swore as he broke the end of a letter opener trying to force a draw open.

Seeing Dunn, Townson stopped his jimmying of the locks. 'Where are the Governor's keys?'

'I don't know where they are at,' Dunn said.

Grimes, still holding the broken letter opener advanced on Dunn. 'The keys, now.'

Dunn stood my mute, turning his face from Grimes and the broken letter opener.

'Right take it downstairs,' Bayly said. He motioned to two soldiers outside the room. The men remained where they stood and looked at Minchin in confusion as to who was giving the orders.

Minchin sighed. 'Take the bloody chest. In fact, clear the room and move it all downstairs to the drawing room.'

Grimes and Townson picked up the desk bureau and started to move it through the door. As they did they jammed the top against the door frame and the whole bureau fell off the desk. Draws burst open and papers scattered everywhere. Grimes swore again and together with Townson and several soldiers managed to pick up the papers and take the two halves of the desk bureau downstairs.

They found the foyer quieter than before, with only a dozen soldiers, Mary Putland, Susan Palmer and Bligh in the room. Major Johnston had left and outside companies of the Corps were marching into formation.

The drums started and the fifes sprung up a tune, 'Britons Weep'. Reversing the journey they had taken only two and a half hours before, the Corps returned down Bridge Street, crossed the Tank Stream bridge and marched back into the barracks having successfully undertaken their coup.

'Bloody hell we did it. We overthrew Bligh,' Smith said to Williams. 'Tell you what Oli boyo, get ready for the biggest party this colony has ever seen.'

Williams smiled a tired smile before a look of concern crossed his face.

'What's the matter, not up for a party. Because that is what is ahead. All those locals who we've saved from tyranny buying us drinks. All those damsels saved from distress. Imagine how popular we'll be.'

'Its not the party that worries me, it's the hangover that follows,' Williams said. Then he bid Smith good night and walked home past the houses already beginning to display pictures of Bligh in chains held by the triumphant Corps.

'What have we just done?' he said to himself. 'What the bloody hell have we done?'

The end

Historical note

The novel begins with the Irish rebellion of March 1804 that ended with the events at Toongabbie. Historical references to the Irish, or Castle Hill rebellion, are inconsistent and in some aspects contradictory. The description of the battle, if it can be called that, has a number of versions all of which have discrepancies from other tellings. In some Major George Johnston is front and centre dealing with the Irish leaders, in others he is beside or leading his troops. What is clear is that a small group of New South Wales Corps soldiers, led by Johnston confronted the Irish rebels at or near Toongabbie and routed those rebels, many of whom then fled, thus breaking the back of the rebellion.

The discrepancies surrounding the events of the Irish rebellion extend to a number of the events, regular practices of life in the colony and actions of individuals described in this book. One of the great surprises in researching this novel was in finding these minor discrepancies along with a few larger points of difference from the history I learnt at school. What began as a work looking into the idea of the roles of Bligh and Macarthur in the Rum Rebellion soon changed significantly to focus on the Corps, which became both a proxy and key player in the conflict between the two men.

For the sake of the narrative where there are discrepancies between sources and accounts relating the same event, or the facts are not clear, I have chosen the version that best supports the book's narrative while trying to stay as true to history as possible.

Beyond that history is my invention and interpretation of events. For example, an American ship called the *Atlas* did dock in Sydney and was refused permission to sell the component of its cargo that was made up of liquor. The events immediately thereafter, where members of the Corps arrange to buy that liquor are my invention.

The most obvious difference from my recollections of our early history was in what role the NSW Corps actually played in the daily life of Sydney. Another was found in the place of convicts in society. Rather than standing over the convicts as they worked, the Corps had very little to do with day to day management of the convict cohort. Instead an entirely separate administration and bureaucracy grew around that convict cohort, led largely by convicts. This separation seemed at odds with my own recollections from learning history at school, but such is the benefit of continued scholarship in relation to our early history. (As well as a comment on the unreliability of my memory!)

To get a better idea of these recent changes in scholarship Grace Karsken's *The Colony* is a wonderful read and I would also recommend Bill Gammage's *The Biggest Estate on Earth* for insight in how the Aboriginal community managed the land. Further information on the Aboriginal people and their place in the emerging colony of Sydney can be found in *Hidden in Plain View*, by Paul Irish and for further reading on conflict between Aboriginal groups and settlers *The Sydney Wars* by Stephen Gapps.

The events leading up to the Rum Rebellion are laid out in detail in HV Evatt's *Rum Rebellion*. What happened after that is told in Stephen Dando-Collins *Captain Bligh's Other Mutiny*. For a more general overview of the role of rum, liquor and alcohol and how they helped shape Sydney's formative years Tom Gilling's *Grog, A Bottled History of Australia's First 30 Year*s is a good read. These are but a few of many histories of early Sydney, white settlement in Australia and the impacts of this settlement on indigenous Australians. The above list is by no means comprehensive, rather a brief potted tour of the range of reference material available.

Measures presented in the book are largely imperial, rather than metric. Where the term rum is used, that can mean red wine, rum or a variety of other spirits, or a mix of any of the above and water. The interchangeability of the term rum as used in the story is consistent with how it was used at the time in Sydney. Where characters read from contemporary sources such as the Gazette newspaper or letters, such as those from Macarthur, quotes used are from the actual sources named. The poems included are my writing (apologies to any real poets out there!).

In terms of language I have tried to keep the narrative in mind, rather than focus overtly on the type of language and forms of expression used in the early 1800s. Readers can gain a flavour of some linguistic construction and use in the excerpts included, particularly those of Macarthur in his letters. In terms of day to day language used by the characters simplicity wins out over more historically accurate language as the simpler construction and phrasing has greater familiarity for modern readers. The use of profanity is based on words that would have been in the language at the time, although some of the utility and use of those swear words is perhaps more contemporary in its employment.

One of the difficulties of writing a narrative that centres on real people is representing their thoughts, feelings and actions. Without first hand sources those thoughts, feelings and motivations for those actions are speculative on the part of the writer, as is the case here. To this end many of the characters, Williams, Smith, Mary Williams, Madame Bridgitte, Henry Adams and Ravi Chandra are fictional. Most of the incidental and peripheral characters are fictional inventions.

Many of those included are based on real people, including Governor's King and Hunter. The Irish rebels named in the narrative, notably William Johnston and Philip Cunningham, and those sentenced to hang, led the rebellion. Those involved in defence of the rebellion included men of the cloth, Marsden, and Dixon. Of the settlers mentioned Thomas Rose, was a member of the 1793 free settlers. The reference to Rose and his marital status is my invention, although some descendants of Thomas Rose will suggest the story is true.

John Macarthur's representation in the story is my invention. I have tried to stay as close to the facts as possible in terms of events surrounding Macarthur. John Macarthur was the first to see and act on the potential for building a sheep industry in Australia. The first fleet brought sheep to Sydney, but when Arthur Phillip left most people saw sheep as a means to a quick dollar. Macarthur changed that and set Australia on a course to live off the sheep's back well into the middle of the 20th century. I have also acknowledged the contribution of Elizabeth Macarthur in establishing the industry. Macarthur spent more than half of the first two decades of the 1800s in England, while Elizabeth was left at home to run the farm, a fact too often overlooked in the Macarthur narrative. The mood swings presented are my invention. There is no direct evidence to support this. What is clear is that Macarthur was involved in a number of feuds, including with Richard Atkins, and spent his final years in seclusion after being certified as insane. None of that should distract from John and Elizabeth Macarthur's important legacy in establishing sheep production and in the early life of Sydney.

Thynne Adlum and John Llewellyn settled in the Hawkesbury and were killed by Aboriginal war parties, as described. Andrew Thompson was a bailiff, and worked for Bligh, but for the purposes of this narrative a role as Chief Constable fits better. Thompson was however sued by Macarthur and would later die in flooding in the Hawkesbury trying to rescue settlers.

Aboriginal warriors and resistance leaders included those mentioned; Branch Jack, Tedbury, Yaragowby, Talboon, Corriangee, Doolboon, Boon-du-dullock, Moonaning, Doongial, Bulldog and Musquito. Any incorrect spelling is mine alone. I have tried not to attribute motivations to their actions in becoming involved in the resistance, although such motives are not hard to discern.

The other indigenous person mentioned is Bungaree, leader of the Aboriginal community in Sydney. One of the continuing issues in early Sydney was how best to 'find a place' for the Aboriginal community, which of course had its land, its 'place', taken by the British upon their arrival. Bungaree was an important figure in efforts by several administrations to 'manage' the indigenous community including moves into potential settlements such as those at Elizabeth Bay and George's Head.

The failure of any policies to create a place for indigenous Australians along with continued dispossession of their land saw intermittent fighting, including that described herein. The skirmish between settlers and Aboriginals in the upper reaches of the Hawkesbury is accurate in that ambushes were set and some settlers were almost lured under cliffs and felled by falling rocks. Similarly conflict on the Cumberland Plain did occur, with the pattern of friendship, conflict and renewal of friendship reoccurring periodically as white settlement expanded into Aboriginal lands.

What Bungaree made of all of this is not clear. Up until some time in the 1820s Bungaree performed the welcome to country to new boats arriving in the harbour and was considered what we would today call a celebrity. He died in 1830 at Garden Island. None of the conflicts, nor recognition of Bungaree helped resolve the issue of Aboriginal dispossession that continues until this day.

The issue of Aboriginal place and dispossession did not seem to affect the rivals in the lead up to the Rum Rebellion. The rival camps, the pro-Macarthur/Corps group, and the pro-Bligh allies, included a number of early settlers and ex-convicts. Working with Macarthur and the Corps were Simeon Lord, Nicholas Bayly, James Badgery and the Blaxland brothers, along with Robert Townson and Charles Grimes. The role of Surgeon John Harris as being a supporter of, but outside the main group of rebel leaders is consistent with several histories. Garnham Blaxcell, Macarthur's partner in ownership of the ship *Parramatta*, was previously Secretary of the Colony under King, but was replaced when Bligh took over. Gentleman John Hoare did escape on the *Parramatta* under the command of Master Glenn.

The ensuing legal cases were presided over by Richard Atkins. In early Sydney magistrates were largely chosen from a small cohort of Corps officers and others with legal training. Provost Marshal Gore and Constable Oakes along with George Crossley were leading figures in the policing of, and application of the law in Sydney, along with Deputy Commissary Fitz. The attempt to prosecute Gore was led by James Underwood. The gaoler Daniel McKay and his partner did agree to work to bring down Gore but failed to follow through in court. The farcical nature of the court cases presented are my invention.

Having failed to win against Bligh in the courts the Corps and Macarthur escalated events dramatically. During the Corps's assault on Government House Mary Putland, John and Susan Palmer and Robert Campbell stood with Gore, alongside Tom Arndell and Reverend Henry Fulton, in attempting to hold off the soldiers. John Dunn and Edmund Griffin also stood with Bligh.

Those Corps men mentioned as being under threat from Bligh and the manoeuvring immediately prior to the rebellion were as it happened. Those officers mentioned, along with the remainder of the Corps men mentioned lived and died in the early days of Sydney. Only Lieutenant Davies, Privates Conner, Newbold and Mulligan are fictional characters. Any actions, thoughts or ideas assigned to the real life officers and soldiers of the Corps are my invention alone.

Events involving the Corp men getting up to mischief are also my invention, including the horse training and race. There are suggestions that horse racing was going ahead in the Hawkesbury region in the early years of the colony.

The events leading up to the Rum Rebellion I have described as accurately as possible within the confines of this narrative, including the manoeuvring of the Bligh and Macarthur camps. I have chosen to omit some court cases for the benefit of the narrative. There has been debate over the years as to whether Bligh or Macarthur should be assigned responsibility as the main cause of the rebellion. Some will argue that Bligh fuelled the rebellion, others that Macarthur was the instigator. Both sides can make strong arguments, however as in most events, there is evidence around motivations and decisions that suggest both Bligh and Macarthur played a part. So too did the NSW Corps.

The reputation of the Corps, like responsibility for the rebellion, is open to debate. There is no doubt that some members of the Corps were prepared to push well beyond the boundaries of both morality and the law. Blatant corruption did occur, as did the use of force by Corps men taking what they wanted, but how entrenched that was in the Corps is not as clear. Whether a handful of the officers and soldiers were responsible or most were engaged in corrupt activities is not entirely obvious. Should this condemn them all? I will leave that decision up to the reader. Suffice to say that for the purposes of narrative what is presented herein is only one reading of the actions of the Corps, and a fictionalised, and rather sympathetic version. The Corps did play an important role in shaping some of the character and growth of early Sydney which is the aspect of their activities this novel tries to capture.

As to the events in the novel, the basic narrative is accurate. There was a rebellion of Irish convicts, the Corps did engage in trading of rum, Aboriginal tribes did unite in a short-lived and tragic war in the Hawkesbury and elsewhere. The leaders of that war were hunted down, just one of a number of dislocations and deaths for Aboriginal tribes in the Sydney region.

John Macarthur imported merino sheep and worked to end Governor King's leadership of the colony. The flooding described at the Hawkesbury occurred, as did the manoeuvring between Bligh and Macarthur and the Corps. Bligh did order houses be pulled down, including that of the the clerk, Mann. During the rebellion Bligh was found under a bed and

Mary Putland almost derailed the vanguard by standing at the gates parasol in hand.

The realities of life for women, simultaneously having greater freedom under the law than they would in England, while also living with the threat of violence and rape, are very much as described. That threat was not a constant, but it did grow in parts of the new colony; those furthest from policing and order being the most dangerous. Relationships were often short-lived, but some women did find lasting partnerships with soldiers or convicts. For those women the importance of a partnership or marriage provided opportunity and helped to create a more welcoming environment, both broadly across Sydney and within homes.

For many convicts their first experiences of Sydney involved living in the house of others, working as servants and the like. The model of family life that many women, and their men, demonstrated helped to move Sydney beyond the crude idea of a penal colony with women as providers of sexual gratification and little more. Over time historical scholarship has come to question many of the myths that formed around the first women convicts, myths based on ideas of what might have happened rather than any actual eyewitness evidence or documentation. For many women, and men, Sydney became a place of opportunity, and this is one of the reasons so many chose to stay on after their sentence ended.

Women played an important role in helping to establish housing for many. Women like Mary Reiby built houses and sold them. Many helped maintain not just the housing, but the sense of community. The role women played was to begin to normalise the idea of relationships, of family and hearth and home. Their role in early Sydney was pivotal to the transformation of the colony from its convict beginnings.

Convicts had a short working day, having most of the afternoon to hire out their services. It was this labour force that helped underpin the development of commerce and accelerate the transformation of Sydney from an agrarian penal colony to a commercial concern. This transition was at the heart of the Rum Rebellion led by Macarthur and the Corps.

The term Rum Rebellion was coined much later in the 19th century as an attempt to warn people of the evils of alcohol. William Bligh, in the immediate aftermath tried to link the rebellion to rum, for the purposes of his defence, but was unsuccessful for no-one at the time believed the rebellion to be about rum. It was not until 1855 when William Howitt, a teetotaller, wrote a history of Australia and referred to the events of 1808 as the rum rebellion, that the term became used. Around this time a movement against alcohol was gaining momentum and Howitt's narrative around the rebellion fit the purposes of those opposed to alcohol. Thus the rebellion became linked to rum. For the first half of the 19th century the actions of Johnston and co were referred to as the Great Rebellion, such was the seismic nature of the events.

Bligh's defence, and Howitt's history helped create a misleading story. This story tied in with the later idea, in part the result of a series of campaigns against alcohol and immorality in the late 19th century, of alcohol as an evil that was widespread in, and led the inhabitants of early Sydney astray. What is fascinating is that the idea of Sydney as a rum-soaked, drunken colony was never really true. Consumption of alcohol on a per capita basis was actually less than in England at the time, and less than in Sydney today. Alcohol at the time was widely used mixed with water to help purify that water, or as an alternative to unsafe water sources, a practice common in many parts of the world until the 20th century.

Rum was also a source of currency, becoming widespread after Arthur Phillip departed as Governor of the colony of Sydney in 1792. The NSW Corps held the lions share of rum and exploited that monopoly. The arrival of a group of entrepreneurs and traders in the early 1800s, men such as Robert Campbell, effectively ended that monopoly. For the purposes of the narrative I have delayed that breakdown of the Corps's monopoly until later.

Ultimately it was the new arrivals that benefitted the most from the rebellion, with men like Campbell thriving under the governorship of Lachlan Macquarie, the man who succeeded Bligh as governor, and did much to find a middle ground between the two sides opposed in the rebellion.

Reflecting on those distant events today is to be reminded that while much has changed some things have not (including the ferocity of, and brutality of politics, both in NSW and federally). There is a great deal of the Australian character that was established in those early days of Sydney: the opportunity to better oneself regardless of background, the value placed on home ownership, love of a drink, larrikin attitudes, equality and distrust of authority to mention a few. The reliance on government support for industry, riding on the sheep's back, the need to trade with the world and the recognition of others from beyond our shores carrying undue weight can also find their beginnings in the earliest days of Sydney.

The narrative presented attempts to illuminate some of that character. In doing so I have chosen to tell a story that has perhaps not gained as prominent a foothold in Australian life as others from the early days of Sydney. Any errors in describing the events, people, places, geography and stories of early Sydney are mine alone.

www.ingramcontent.com/pod-product-compliance
Lightning Source LLC
Chambersburg PA
CBHW070337170726
48291CB00001B/88